Other *Leisure* books by Rick Hautala:
THE MOUNTAIN KING

BEDBUGS

RICK HAUTALA

LEISURE BOOKS NEW YORK CITY

A LEISURE BOOK®

March 2003

Published by

Dorchester Publishing Co., Inc.
276 Fifth Avenue
New York, NY 10001

ISBN 0-8439-5074-9

The name "Leisure Books" and the stylized "L" with design are
trademarks of Dorchester Publishing Co., Inc.

Printed in the United States of America.

Visit us on the web at www.dorchesterpub.com.

To every editor who ever bought a story or novel of mine.
You are the vineyard owners . . .
I am the vineyard worker . . .
and now it is late in the day. . . .

BEDBUGS

CONTENTS

The Back of My Hands

The back of my hands started looking like a man's back when I was—oh, maybe ten or eleven years old.

I remember how fascinated I was by the curling, black hairs I saw sprouting there; how amazed I was when I flexed and unflexed my hands, and watched the twitching blue lines of veins, the knitting needle–thin tendons, and the bony knobs of cartilage and knuckle. Sometimes, I used to constrict the flow of blood to my arms—you know, like a junkie—to make the veins inflate until they fairly bulged through the skin. The bigger they got, the more "manly" I thought my arms and hands looked.

It might seem laughable now, but I still believe hands are a God-given miracle. They let us touch and manipulate the world outside of ourselves. Sure, scientists say that vision is the only sense where the nerve connects directly to the brain, but hands are the only things that let us reach out, to touch and explore the world. They allow us to *feel* love and to *create* what we know and feel, both internally and externally.

1

Rick Hautala

They're our only *real* solid connection to what's "out there."

Our other senses—sight, sound, taste, and smell—can all deceive us. They trick us into thinking we're experiencing something that might not really be there.

But when we touch something, when we hold it in our hands and caress it, we have no doubt whatsoever that it truly exists. When I look at my own hands now, though, I can't help but be filled with revulsion and horror.

Yes, *horror!*

That's probably an overused word these days, but there's no better word for what I feel.

These hands—*my* hands—have done things so terrible, so hideous that I can truly say they are no longer mine.

They've acted as if powered by a will of their own—a will with a dark, twisted purpose. And in the process, they've ended the life of someone—of the one person I've ever really been close to—a life I should have cherished above all others.

Okay, let me start at the beginning.

The easiest part was killing my twin brother, Derrick.

No problem there.

I'm serious.

It certainly wasn't very difficult to orchestrate. You'd think I was a musician, talking like this, but when it actually came time to *do* it, to aim the gun at him and squeeze the trigger, I didn't flinch or have the slightest hesitation.

And I've had no qualms about it afterwards, either.

Why should I?

Derrick had it all. Everything. He was everything I wanted to be.

I know, I know . . . sure, he worked just as hard for it, maybe even harder than I did; but everything came so easily to him, almost as if it fell out of the sky and landed in his lap.

And it never came to me. Certainly not as easily, anyway, and no way near as much.

You see, he was the one who was born with all the talent. I couldn't help but think that because I'd heard it my whole life, growing up. All through high school, Derrick was an honor student—popular, handsome, smart, and talented. He had it all. He graduated at the top of his class from college, too, married a gorgeous and intelligent woman, had a wonderful family—three kids and a beautiful country home about two hours north of Portland.

Far as I could see, he had it all.

And what did *I* have?

Nothing.

Squat.

The leftovers.

Sloppy seconds, if you'll excuse such an inelegant expression.

All my life, I've had to listen to teachers and friends' parents—even our *own* parents—exclaim with surprise that sometimes bordered on absolute shock how Derrick was so amazingly gifted, and that I was so . . . well, that I didn't quite measure up to the standard *he* set.

The worst of it was when people would question, sometimes even to my face, how identical twins could be so . . . so *different*. Oh, we looked enough alike, so anyone who didn't know us well couldn't tell us apart, but it seemed as if all the intelligence, personality, and talent went into his half of the egg, and I was left with. . . .

Well, with sloppy seconds, like I said.

Maybe that really was the case.

I used to wonder about it, mostly late at night as I lay in bed, staring up at the bottom of Derrick's upper bunk. I still lie awake at nights, wondering. Now I have plenty of time to think about things. Back when we were kids, I could hear my brother's deep, rhythmic breathing coming from the top bunk, as if even sleeping was something he simply did better than I ever could.

3

Rick Hautala

* * *

It didn't surprise anyone that Derrick and I both entered the field of art. Ever since we were kids, we'd both shown unusual talent for the visual arts although, as usual, Derrick's paintings and drawings—hell, even his throw-away sketches—always seemed to be several notches better than anything I ever produced.

Not that my stuff was bad, mind you. I do have quite a bit of talent.

Now that I think about it, when I first started drawing was probably when I first really noticed the back of my hands. I remember how I'd spend a lot of the time not even paying attention to whatever it was I was drawing because I would be so fascinated by the interplay of muscle and tendons beneath my skin as I held the pencil or brush in my hands and rolled it back and forth or whatever. Probably the one thing I ever did better than Derrick was anatomy drawing. Especially hands. I seemed to have quite a knack for drawing hands.

So like I said, it didn't surprise anyone when we both went off to college—the same school, of course. We both majored in art, but my grades were never quite up to Derrick's level . . . and neither was my work. He graduated *summa cum laude* while I was simply lucky to graduate with honors.

Following graduation, we both landed jobs within our chosen field. Derrick started right out as a painter—an "artist" with a capital *A*. Within a year or so, he was having one-man shows of his work at galleries in Boston and New York. The "art scene" had apparently already taken notice of him, and his paintings were selling for astronomical amounts. Personally, I thought they weren't worth the price of the canvas they were painted on, but there's no accounting for taste, is there?

And what about me?

I went to work, pasting up ads for a local newspaper, all

4

the while trying to convince myself of the worth of a steady paycheck while I concentrated on my own art during evenings and weekends.

I think—hell, no! I don't have to lie about it anymore, right? I know that's when the full measure of the resentment I felt toward my brother began to blossom.

Until then, that resentment had always been there, festering inside me, maybe even since before we were born; but it had always been—you know, buried deep, like a seed in the soil that was struggling hard to push its way up to the sunlight. It was only after college, once we were out there in the real world, settling into our respective careers and trying to make a living that I finally allowed the seed to break through the surface. Over the next few years, as I watched my brother accumulate success and wealth and fame—everything I wanted and felt I deserved—I watered and nourished that seed of envy and hatred. . . .

Yes, *hatred!*

I cursed the fate that I had been born to, wondering why?—what cruel, uncaring God could do this to me?

Why couldn't I have been given at least *something*—just one single fucking thing more than my brother?

But he had it all, and I had . . . much less.

That's when I started planning to change it all by killing him.

You know, one person I talked to a few days ago, maybe a few weeks ago, now, said that she thought I didn't really *want* to kill Derrick. That what I really wanted to do was kill myself. She said that by identifying so closely with my twin brother, and by envying his success so much, I was turning all my pent-up anger against myself. She used all sorts of fancy psycho-babble terms like "transference" and "guilt projection" and "displacement"—stuff like that, but I'm pretty sure she was wrong.

I *really* wanted to kill *Derrick.*

I *had* to kill him.

The way I saw it, there was no way around it.

5

*   *   *

Getting to do it was much easier than I thought it would be.

Derrick and I live—I should say "lived"—about two hours away from each other. I have a place here in Portland, and he lives up past Fryberg. Driving up there was no problem. Last March, I knew his wife, Alice, had taken the kids to Orlando for the week at Disney World. I figured he'd be at the house alone, no doubt working on some paintings for a show or something. I wasn't expected or anything, but I guess I was lucky that no one saw or recognized my car. Just to be safe, I took back roads. It added a little time to the drive, but then again, what did I care?

Derrick lived in a fairly secluded area—a development on a secluded lake with a lot of fancy-ass houses spaced pretty far apart. He didn't have any security or anything, no bodyguards or electronic gates, so getting into his house was easy.

Hey! Who would want to kill a famous artist, right?

I was right. When I got there, he was home . . . alone.

Before I got out of the car, I pulled on the two pairs of rubber gloves I'd brought. I'd seen something on a cop show once about how a detective lifted a fingerprint even though the burglar or whatever had been wearing rubber gloves. The rubber, you see, was so thin that it still left a faint impression—at least enough to identify the culprit.

I wasn't going to take any chances.

Just shooting him wasn't going to be enough, though. I had to even the score a little bit, too.

But like I said earlier, shooting him didn't bother me any. I just aimed the gun at him, pulled the trigger, and. . . .

Pop.

Of course, before I got to the house, the whole time I was driving, I couldn't stop thinking about *why* I was doing this. I came up with a whole slew of excuses, but I knew they were all bullshit.

The real reason was quite simple.

Even I can see that, now.

He had more talent than I did, and I knew why.

It was all in his hands!

I already told you how I didn't feel anything, not even a tremor of elation when the gun went off, and Derrick was blown back off his feet. He landed on the kitchen floor kind of funny, leaning against the wall with his legs splayed out and bent at the knees. One of his shoes had flipped off. He looked a little like a puppet that's had its strings cut. There was a big splash of blood on the wall behind him, but he was down now, with both hands clamped over the bullet hole in his chest. He was breathing real hard, making this watery, rattling sound in his throat. It sounded something terrible, like he was drowning. After a few seconds, his legs started twitching like he was trying to do a dance or something. It was only when I saw blood leaking out between his fingers that I got a little panicky, thinking that the blood might ruin his hands.

I wasn't worried about any of the neighbors hearing the shot. I'd been to Derrick's house plenty of times before, so I knew what to do next, and I took my time doing it right. There was an ax down in the cellar that Derrick used to split firewood. He never heated the house with wood or anything. Like the rest of his life, having a fire blazing away in the fireplace on a winter evening was just a quaint little "artsy" touch.

All image.

I went back up into the kitchen, made sure he was good and dead, and then chopped off both his hands, halfway between the wrist and elbow. It took me a few whacks on both arms, but I think I could have done them each with one hit if I hadn't been shaking so damned much with excitement.

Yeah, now that I think about it, I guess once he was dead I was pretty excited about it. I'll tell you one thing—I was glad he was dead by then because when I was trying to cut off his arms, I kept missing, and I think that would have really hurt.

I took his severed hands over to the sink and washed the blood off before drying them and putting them into a little plastic trash bag I'd brought along. On the way out, confident there weren't any fingerprints on anything to identify me, I dropped the ax beside Derrick's body. He was staring up at the ceiling with this glassy-eyed stare, looking for all the world like a wax statue.

I wonder what he was looking at. . . .

Anyway, I closed the door behind me, looked around to make sure there wasn't any activity at any of the neighbors' houses, then got into my car and drove away.

I only stopped once on the way home, to get rid of the gun and rubber gloves. What I did was tie the gun up inside one of the gloves, tie the other one around it, and then throw it off the bridge into the river. You know where Route 25 crosses the Ossipee River in Limington? The water runs real fast there and hardly ever freezes.

That was pretty much it until I got home.

I was still a little nervous, I guess, kind of jittery when I got back to my apartment. I knew the cops would be coming around sooner or later to tell me what had happened. They might start asking all sorts of questions. I didn't have a decent alibi, but I figured they weren't going to suspect me much. Hell, Alice and the kids were going to get whatever inheritance was coming, and I'm sure there was plenty of that. I might get a little something, a token, but certainly not enough to make anyone suspicious.

Besides, who'd even think I'd want to kill my twin brother?

All I had to do was act like I was real broken up about it, and I was sure they'd let it slide. And anyway, I already had everything I wanted from Derrick.

I had his hands.

In case the cops came around, I didn't do anything with

the hands, not right away, anyway. I put the trash bag into the freezer under the frozen peas and carrots, and tried to forget about them. Of course, that didn't work because I knew they were there, and I knew sooner or later what I was going to do with them.

As it turned out, the next night after work, I took the plastic bag out of the freezer and defrosted the frozen hands. The skin was as pale as polished white marble. What I did was throw them into a pot of boiling water. You have to understand, I had no idea if what I was planning to do was really going to work. I mean, I figured it would because skin is so tough, but you never know until you try something.

After boiling the hands for a while, I took them out with some tongs, got the sharpest paring knife I could find, and made a nice, deep incision all the way around each wrist, a few inches above the thumb joint, right about where you wear a wristwatch. It took some doing to hold onto the skin because it was so slippery. Pretty tough, too, but once I got a good grip on it with the tongs, the skin peeled right off, turning inside out like I was removing a glove or a dirty sock. Of course, there was no blood involved. I had a little problem with the skin tearing around the fingernails, but nothing serious.

When I was done and turned them back right-side out, I had two pretty close to perfect gloves made out of my brother's hands. I put them down on the counter, and I swear to God I thought they might start moving around on their own or something.

My biggest concern was that they wouldn't fit—that Derrick and I weren't still exactly the same size; but with a little bit of tugging and a few tiny slits here and there to loosen them up, I was able to pull them on over my own hands.

* * *

Man, I'm telling you, I could barely contain my excitement as I raised my new hands up in front of my face and looked at them. I flexed the fingers, thrilled by the taunt pulling of my new skin.

It was exquisite beyond belief!

My hands—Derrick's hands, really—were trembling as I reached out to touch something . . . for the first time . . . with someone else's hands.

I picked up the paring knife I had used to cut and peel the skin. Turning it back and forth, I hardly noticed the light reflecting off the blade because I was so entranced by the way the skin on the back of my hands shifted with every subtle movement.

I can't tell you how excited I was, but I stopped myself because I knew I had other things to take care of, first.

Unrolling my new skin gloves, I carefully laid them aside while I cleaned up. It took a bit of doing, but I scraped most of the flesh off the bone before grinding everything up in the garbage disposal. The bones knocked around some, making quite a racket, but I made sure it all washed down completely. Then I took my new hands—because that's the only way I could think of them—and went into my work room.

I tell you, I was so excited I was dizzy. I felt like I was drunk or tripping or something as I pulled the skin gloves back on over my own hands and wiggled my fingers to make sure everything fit perfectly.

Custom made!

Once I was ready, I picked up a pencil, tacked a clean sheet of drawing paper to the drawing board, and began to draw.

At first I couldn't stop staring at the back of my hands.

Just like when I was a kid, I watched the skin shift and slide across my muscles and tendons as I drew. I was amazed how the skin still felt supple and alive. I could almost feel it bonding with the flesh of my own hands— my less talented hands.

This is it! I told myself—*the moment I've been waiting for my whole life! I'm going to draw what I see inside my own head with someone else's hands!*

But it didn't work out quite as I'd planned.

The sketch I started working on that night still seemed flat and uninspired. The spark wasn't there. I had to remind myself that I was too excited, that I was distracted by watching the way my new hands moved; but deep inside, I started to feel this gnawing worry that I still didn't *have* it. The picture still looked like it was being drawn by . . .

Me.

It'll take time, I told myself, hoping I could calm down enough to concentrate.

That made sense.

Right off the bat, I couldn't expect to be able to feel and touch and control things the way Derrick did. I had to adapt to this new way of feeling and manipulating the world. Everyone's hands are different.

After all, art doesn't happen overnight.

After trying for an hour or so, I carefully peeled the skin gloves off my hands. I wasn't quite sure what to do with them afterwards. I knew if I left them out, they'd rot. I wondered how to go about drying them out, maybe tanning the skin like leather so they would retain their suppleness.

While I was wondering what to do, the phone rang.

It was Alice, calling from Florida. She had just gotten a call from the Maine State Police, informing her that someone had broken into the house and killed Derrick. The gardener had found him that afternoon. I tried my best to sound upset and supportive when she told me she was flying back in the morning. I even told her I'd pick her and the kids up at the airport.

What a guy, huh?

After I got off the phone, I toyed with the idea of wearing Derrick's hands when I picked up Alice and the kids

11

at the airport. I was curious to see if she'd recognize her husband's touch when I hugged her, but I decided that wouldn't be such a good idea. I had no idea what else to do, so I put Derrick's hands back into the freezer for the night so they wouldn't rot.

The next few days were tough if only because I had to act a lot more upset about Derrick's death than I actually was. As expected, the cops came around and asked me all sorts of questions about how Derrick and I got along, about where I was the day he was killed, and was there someone who could corroborate my whereabouts—things like that.

I held up perfectly, I must say.

One time, a couple of days after Derrick died, when I was heading down to the police station to be interviewed, I did wear Derrick's hands. I was a little self-conscious about them, but no one even noticed.

But every night, when I put them on and sat down at the drawing board, I started to get some pretty unusual sensations. My drawings didn't appear to be any better than before, at least not to me, but there was a feeling inside the gloves, inside my own hands when I was wearing the skin that was . . . well, strange.

I had finally come up with a method of preserving the skin. Every night, before I began to draw, I would take fifteen or twenty minutes to rub hand cream into the skin. I didn't scrimp, either. I bought the most expensive kinds of hand cream available, and I spent a lot of time, working it into the thirsty pores. Over the next few days, I learned a lot about emollients and whatever. Night after night, it seemed as though the new skin—my new hands—became increasingly supple and sensitive. Touching things—anything—became a thrill. Vibrant ripples of pure energy tingled from my fingertips, up my arms and neck, all the way to the center of my brain.

Let me tell you, it was exhilarating!

I could barely concentrate on my drawing because I

spent so much time simply *touching* things . . . *feeling* them as if for the first time.

And that's what it was like.

For the first time in my life, I felt like I was *really* feeling things. It was just a matter of time before I could translate what I felt onto canvas and paper. Soon, I would have it all—my brother's talent . . . maybe even the fame and money I deserved even more than he did!

But gradually—and I'm not sure when, maybe a month or so after Derrick died—something happened. It seemed as though my own hands inside the skin of Derrick's hands were changing. At first, all of the sensations were pleasant—warm and moist, comforting, almost as if this new layer was my real skin; but after a couple of nights, the feelings turned more intense. The gentle warmth got steadily hotter until it began to feel like there was a slow-burning fire, smoldering deep beneath my skin. Every time I flexed my hands, watching the veins wiggle beneath the extra layer of skin, I gloried in the way the outermost skin—and I no longer thought of it as Derrick's skin—stretched and pulled.

One night I had been drawing, lost—as always—in watching the way the skin on the back of my hands moved, when suddenly my hands felt like they had burst into flames. At first I tried to ignore the pain and keep drawing. Then I tried to endure it. After a while, though, I couldn't stand it any longer. I put my drawing pencil down and started to roll one of the gloves off, the one on my right hand. Over the past few weeks, the skin had been treated so well that it usually rolled right off. This time, though, when I lifted the top edge, the skin caught. When I tried to pull it down, the skin on my own wrist started to rip.

Let me tell you, I panicked.

It took a great deal of effort to sit back, take a few deep breaths, and then try again. I sure as hell didn't want to damage the hands. Where was I going to get another pair like this? I thought maybe it was just a matter of decay, but when I took the edge of the skin on the other hand and lifted it up, I once again felt my own flesh lift with it.

This can't be happening, I told myself.

Someone—I think it was that lady shrink I talked to a while ago—told me that I was imagining all of this. That Derrick's skin had rotted away by then, and I was pulling at my own flesh. I listened to her, but like all that transference stuff she'd been talking about, I think she was wrong.

I lowered my drawing light and shined it straight down onto my hands, looking closely as I tried several times to peel back the skin. Each time I got the same result. The skin wouldn't roll down. It was fused to my own skin. Hell, I can't deny it; it looked like it had *become* my own skin.

I'm telling you, I was some scared at first, but the more I thought about it, the more I started to accept it.

This ain't so bad, I told myself. *In fact, isn't this exactly what I'd wanted all along?*

Why have hands that I have to put on and off like gloves?

Why not make them permanent?

Didn't I want to feel the way Derrick had felt, and be able to control my pencils and brushes the way Derrick had controlled his?

I had wanted Derrick's hands, had coveted them so much that I was willing to kill him to get them. So what was so wrong if his skin was permanently attached to mine?

We'd been twins in the womb! We shared everything else right down to our chromosomes. Other than the women in our lives, there wasn't anything we *hadn't* shared!

The only problem was, no matter what I did—whether I massaged hand cream into them or held them under a steady flow of cool water or held them inside the freezer— I couldn't make that burning itch go away. It penetrated all the way to my bones, bringing tears to my eyes. I told myself that I'd eventually get used to it, that this was just a stage as Derrick's skin and mine fused, but I didn't sleep much that night.

The pain—oh, the pain!

It was a pure, silver singing inside my hands, and it never let up!

That next morning, a couple of weeks after Derrick's death, I was supposed to be at a memorial service being held in my brother's honor at one of the art galleries in Portland. I forget the name of the gallery, but I'm sure the invitation is still on my desk, back at my apartment. Everyone was going to be there—a lot of important people in the art community as well as Alice and Derrick's kids. I've been trying to feel bad for them, losing their father like that, but pity just doesn't seem to be inside me.

When I got out of bed that morning, hardly having slept a wink, I considered calling the gallery and canceling. I was supposed to say a few words about my brother, but I hoped Andrew—the gallery director—would understand that I was still too shattered and couldn't cope with doing it.

Before I dialed the gallery, though, I started thinking about how suspicious canceling out might look. Sure, the cops had stopped asking me questions, apparently satisfied that I'd had nothing to do with my brother's murder, but I couldn't be sure. They might still *think* I *had* done it, and they might just be waiting for me to slip up so they could nail me.

Maybe they even recognized Derrick's hands!

So I determined, no matter how bad the pain in my hands got, I'd go through with this farce of a memorial service.

The problem was, I had no idea how bad it could get.

Even before I walked into the gallery that morning and saw how many people had gathered to honor my brother, my hands were clammy with sweat and trembling deep inside. I shook hands with as few people as possible, but

15

couldn't help but notice the startled reactions most of them gave me when we clasped hands.

Being one of the guests of honor, as it were, I had to sit in the front row along with Alice and the kids. Every wall in the room was adorned with Derrick's paintings. None of them were really very good, I thought. I would do much better.

Andrew spoke first—a bit too long, I thought—about how he had been one of the first people in the "Art world" to recognize Derrick's extraordinary talent, and how we and all of humanity have suffered a great loss in such a senseless, brutal act of butchery. I could hear people sniffing back their tears, but I hardly paid any attention to them. I couldn't stop looking down at my hands. They felt like they were on fire.

I tried rubbing them, scratching them, folding my arms across my chest and pressing them against my sides— *anything*, but nothing would relieve the pain and burning itch. It got so intense I thought I was going to scream.

I didn't notice when Andrew stopped speaking, but after a moment or two, I noticed that the room had fallen silent . . . a hushed expectancy. I glanced around and realized that everyone was staring at me.

A boiling blush raced up my arms and across my face. My heart was slamming hard inside my chest when I realized that Andrew must have introduced me. I shifted uncomfortably in my seat, preparing to stand, but I wasn't even sure my legs would support me, much less carry me all the way to the podium.

The crowd was utterly still.

A steady, low, throbbing sound filled my ears as I inhaled and held my breath. I took a single step forward. My shoe, scraping across the carpet, made a sound like the rough scratching of sandpaper. Cold sweat broke out on my brow and trickled down the sides of my neck.

I wanted to scream, I tell you, but as I made my way up to the podium, I noticed a glass pitcher and several clean glasses on the small table beside the podium. The pitcher was filled with ice water.

That gave me an idea.

With each halting step forward, the agonizing sensation in my hands grew steadily worse until it became intolerable.

I had no idea what to do with my hands, whether to shove them deep into my jacket pockets so no one could see them, clasp them behind my back, shake them wildly above my head, or claw at them and start screaming.

That's what I wanted to do—scream.

The thought crossed my mind that if I fell completely apart, everyone in the room would think it was simply an outpouring of my grief over the loss of my brother. They would all react respectfully, with sympathy and understanding.

But my throat was closing off. My chest and lungs were so constricted I could hardly breathe, much less scream. I was suddenly afraid that, if I opened my mouth and tried to say a few words—something about my dear, departed brother—deathly cold hands would clasp around my throat and begin to choke me.

I had jotted down a few notes of what I wanted to say, only because I was afraid of what I might say if I started rambling. The problem was, the sheet of paper with my notes on it was in the breast pocket of my jacket, and I didn't dare reach for it. I was suddenly fearful that I would no longer be able to control my hands. The skin—Derrick's skin—had long since dissolved into my own hands, fusing with my hands.

It had become me.

I glanced down at my hands and was suddenly quite convinced that I didn't even recognize them.

They were someone else's hands!

They really were Derrick's hands!

*   *   *

17

I know it isn't possible. You're not the first person to tell me it was all in my mind; but even if it was, it was nonetheless true!

The silence in the room continued to pulsate. When someone toward the back of the room cleared his throat, it sounded like distant cannon shot. Somehow, though, I made it to the podium. Leaning forward and gripping the edge of the podium with both hands, I forced a smile, but I could tell by the way the skin stretched around my mouth that it was more of a grimace. As if moving by its own volition, my right hand reached up and inside my jacket, and clasped the sheet of paper in my pocket. The heat inside my jacket was intolerable, as if I had just reached into a blazing furnace. I almost cried out. Bone-deep tremors shook my body as I unfolded my notes and, without looking at them, spread the page on the podium.

Glancing to my left, I once again saw the pitcher of water. I wanted more than anything to plunge my hands into that icy water to soothe the pain, but I stood there, immobile.

I could tell that the audience was getting restless. It was awkward for them to see me so obviously distraught, but it was just as obvious—to me, at least—that they didn't see the real reason why I was so upset.

I nearly fainted when I lowered my gaze and looked down at my hands, holding the sheet of paper in place. The backs of my hands were discolored a sickly yellow. They were wrinkled like an old man's hands. For a dizzying instant, I felt as though I was looking at my hands through a huge magnifying glass. Every hair, every pore and blemish, every vein and tendon stood out in stark relief. The feeling that these were not my own hands—that they were Derrick's—grew terrifyingly stronger. I thought that—somehow—maybe Derrick was still alive and standing behind me, reaching around and manipulating things for me.

18

I tried to push these thoughts away, cleared my throat. With great effort, I began to speak.

"I want to . . . thank you all for . . . being here today," I said, forcing my grimacing smile to widen.

I locked eyes with Alice, sitting there with her children in the front row. Her expression as she looked at me was soft and sympathetic. I could see that she was on the verge of crying, but she nodded to me, offering her silent support.

The choking sensation in my throat was growing steadily stronger. When I reached up to loosen my collar, I was suddenly fearful that my hands—Derrick's hands—were going to clasp me by the throat and start to squeeze until they choked the life out of me.

I lowered my eyes and shook my head, taking a moment to compose myself. I wiped my forehead with the back of my hand, but it was like striking a match against a sun-baked sidewalk. A line of flames seemed to erupt across my brow.

It was intolerable, I tell you!

I wanted to say something—anything—just a few words about how much I mourned my brother, what a tragic loss his death was to me and his family and friends, but I couldn't focus on the few notes in front of me. All I could think about was the burning pain that was flaming inside my hands and spreading up my arms.

I looked again at the pitcher of water and knew what I had to do. You see, I knew then—or if I had known it before, I finally admitted it to myself then—that these really weren't my hands.

They truly were Derrick's!

His dry, desiccated skin may have rotted away, but some part of my dead brother had fused with me, and this small part of him—the one small part I thought I could possess and control—was *not* under my control.

Maybe I would have been better off if I had killed myself, had strangled myself right there in front of that crowd.

It would have ended it all, and maybe the people there would have thought that I had been unable to contain my grief and had finally snapped.

But that's not what happened.

I didn't plunge my hands into that pitcher of ice water, either.

I had tried that before, and I knew that it wouldn't work.

No, what I did—well, you probably read about it in the papers, but what I did was take the water pitcher and smash it against the side of the podium. I don't remember hearing the sound of breaking glass or feeling the cold dash of water. I sensed some reaction from the crowd, but not much. I was lost inside a cocoon of silence where there was just the raging roar of my breathing and the unbearable burning knowledge that my hands were not my own.

Holding the handle of the shattered pitcher, I turned the jagged edge around and began slashing and sawing at the back of my hands.

"These aren't my hands! These aren't my hands!"

I remember screaming that or something like it, but I was lost in a blind frenzy of panic as I tried to cut and scrape the flesh from the back of my hands. Suddenly, I had the unnerving sensation that I was somehow outside of myself—that I was floating above it all and watching what I was doing as if this were all a movie or a play.

I felt no pain—none whatsoever—but I could see the ragged strips of flesh I was removing from the back of my hands. There was blood everywhere, but no matter how much I tore at the skin on my hands, it didn't stop the burning sensation.

Oh, no.

It continued to spiral up higher and higher until it was all I knew. The mere physical pain of tearing the flesh from my hands was nothing . . . literally, nothing.

From my vantage point, hovering above it all, I watched as I continued to rake the broken glass across the back of my hands, first the left one, then the right. My sheet of notes was splattered with bright red smears, like ruby tear-drops. I almost started laughing when I realized that one splotch of blood—the biggest—looked exactly like the splash of blood on Derrick's kitchen wall, the night I killed him.

Every other sound in the room was muffled, but I sensed a rush of motion as someone—I have no idea who . . . probably Andrew—ran up to me to help . . . to try to stop me.

Then I heard a sizzling, crackling sound, and everything went black.

I woke up sometime later, here in the hospital. I realize now that I must have grabbed onto the microphone and, because I was standing in the puddle of water I had spilled, had gotten one hell of an electric shock.

Not enough to kill me, mind you, and—well, the emergency room doctor said that, thankfully, I hadn't severed any arteries, so I didn't bleed to death.

The most horrible thing about it all, though, was that I didn't get rid of Derrick's skin. It's still here, on the back of my hands.

See?

It's still growing. Maybe you can't see it, but it's inside me now, still growing . . . and look at this. It's spreading out, moving like a fungus up my arm. Pretty soon it's going to cover my whole body!

I swear, it's true.

Look at my hands.

Can't you see?

I still can't control them, either. Even with these bandages on, I've been trying to do a little bit of drawing while I've been here, and you can see that I'm not drawing anything very good . . . certainly not what I want to draw.

Look at these sketches. Every single one of them depicts something from the night I killed my brother.

See here?

This is him lying on the floor, leaning up against the wall. Remember how I said he looked like a puppet whose strings had been cut.

Well, doesn't he?

That's *exactly* what he looked like!

And check this one out.

This is the design the splash of blood made on the wall behind him, after I'd shot him. You'll have to take my word for it, but it's *exactly* like the bloody smear on my sheet of notes.

And look at this one.

See?

It's a close up of Derrick's face, once he was good and dead. He looks really relaxed, doesn't he? It's amazing how much he looks like me. I also did a couple of sketches of what his arms looked like after I'd hacked off his hands, but I had to throw them away. I didn't like the way they were coming out even though I always was pretty good at drawing anatomy, especially hands.

The problem is, you see, I'm not the one who's doing these drawings.

Derrick is.

He's using my eyes and memory to record what happened to him.

His hands are doing all of this!

They betrayed me!

The police never would have even found out that I had killed my brother if his hands hadn't started drawing these pictures.

That's how they finally got me to confess.

They wore me down by telling me that no one except the murderer could have done these sketches, not with such exact detail. They even showed me a couple of photographs taken at the murder scene. I don't know if that was before or after I drew these pictures. They give me drugs and have got me pretty confused here.

And yes, the backs of my hands still hurt like hell. I don't even like looking at them anymore. Sure, they're healing up just fine, but the burning sensation just keeps getting worse, day after day. I tell you, it's driving me insane! Even when the nurse gives me a shot of something, it doesn't really stop the pain. And I know, once these bandages come off, it won't get any better.

Oh, no.

That's why I asked you to come up and see me again today, doctor. I know we talked about all this before, but I'm positive I want you to do it.

Why do you keep saying you won't?

I know you can! You have the equipment here, don't you?

You have to cut *Derrick's* hands off before they do something even more horrible!

Schoolhouse

As soon as he saw the old Pingree School schoolhouse again, Pete Garvey knew that what had been bothering him all along had something to do with it.

No.

It had everything to do with it.

He'd come back home to Hilton, Maine, because his mother was in the hospital, following a major heart attack. Fearful that she might die soon (and at eighty-one years old, that fear seemed entirely reasonable), she had asked her son, Pete, to come home and settle her affairs before she passed on.

Pete had been living in San Diego for the past fifteen years. He made every effort not to come back to Maine more than once every two or three years. For the first time since he had moved away, he finally dared to direct his afternoon walk down Story Street, past the Pingree School—his old grammar school.

Ever since he could remember, he hadn't felt comfortable even going near the old building. Today, he realized he probably should face it and try to figure out why, throughout his entire adult life, he had been bothered by recurring nightmares about the place.

The two-story brick building look innocuous enough. It sat atop a low crested rise with a thick screen of oak and pine trees behind it, like a stage backdrop. Beside the school, at the far end of the wide playing field, was an abandoned playground with a rusted swing set, jungle gym, and weed-choked sandbox. Deep divots beneath each swing and at the bottom of the slide marked the passing of uncountable scuffing feet.

Ever since the town had built the new consolidated grammar school on Tarr's Lane, at the other end of town, the doors to the old Pingree School had been locked. The brick walls were bleached pink by the high summer sun. The pale yellow paint on the windowsills and door frames was cracked and powdery, like crumbling chalk. Several of the second story windows had fist-sized holes in them, where someone had thrown rocks; but even where they weren't broken, the windows seemed somehow spent—lifeless and dull, as though the glass no longer had the ability to reflect daylight. The only bright spots on the building were down around ground-level, where local kids had spray-painted their initials, various obscenities, and the logos of their favorite rock bands.

The August afternoon was heavy with humidity as Pete and Cindy, his wife, started across the well-worn playground, heading toward the gentle slope. Heat waves rippled like water in the air, making the schoolhouse look like a mirage, hovering in the distance.

When they were halfway across the playing field, Pete stumbled and stopped short in his tracks.

His body tensed as he stared up at the building, his jaw muscles clenching and unclenching. His breath came in panting hitches which he knew weren't because of the extra weight of carrying two-year-old Ryan, who was riding high on his back in a *Snugglie*.

26

No, Pete knew all too well that the icy tension winding up inside him was something he had experienced before—dozens, maybe *hundreds* of times in his dreams.

No, not dreams . . . nightmares!

"Shit," Pete whispered, shaking his head. He fought hard against the almost overpowering impression that the building was a dark, swelling wave about to crash over him and sweep him helplessly away.

"Huh? Is something the matter?" Cindy asked, looking at him with one dark eyebrow cocked.

Pete flicked a quick glance at her but immediately let his gaze shift back to the schoolhouse. He swallowed noisily. His right hand felt clammy as he ran it across his forehead, smearing the gathering sweat.

"I—uh . . . No. It's just the. . . ."

His voice faded away to nothing as he shook his head tightly and took a shuddering breath. One side of Cindy's mouth twitched into a crooked half-smile that instantly melted.

"Oh yeah—"

She nodded.

"This is the schoolhouse you're always dreaming about, right?"

She glanced at the building and frowned.

After studying it for a moment, she smiled and said, "You know, in all the times we've come back to Maine, I don't think I've ever even seen this place."

Pete grunted.

"That's because I make it a point never to come this way," he said.

As he spoke, his gaze kept shifting back and forth between his wife and the school building as though searching for something solid for his gaze to anchor onto.

Cindy carefully scanned the front of the building.

As far as she could see, there was nothing imposing or even remotely scary about it. In fact, having been born and raised in San Diego, she found the old schoolhouse to be

27

rather cute, in a quaint, "New Englandy" sort of way.

But she recalled all too well those nights when her husband had awakened her with a strangled shout, and then lay there in bed, his body slick with sweat and trembling as he related to her the most recent variation of his recurring nightmare.

How can something as ordinary as this old building bother him so much? she thought.

"We don't have to walk this way to get back to your mother's house, do we?" she said as she hooked her arm around his elbow. "We can go back the way we came."

"No."

Pete bit down on his lower lip and glanced over his left shoulder.

"It'd be too far to go all the way around Curtis Street. Besides, ole' Ryan here isn't gettin' any lighter. We can just walk past it. No sweat. I mean—shit! What's the big deal?"

"Shit, shit, *shit!*" Ryan piped in as he kicked his feet and leaned forward, wiggling back and forth as he shouted close to his father's ear. "Daddy said *shit!*"

"Oh, yeah?" Cindy said, scowling at her son as she tweaked his nose. "Well you'd just better watch *your* language, mister." She looked at Pete and added, "Doesn't make any difference to me, either way. You're the one who's always talking about how nervous this place makes you feel."

"It's just a stupid dream, for Christ's sake," Pete whispered, more to himself than to her.

Ignoring Ryan's echoing "Christsakes," Pete adjusted the backpack and, taking Cindy's hand, started toward the building.

They angled across the baseball field so they wouldn't have to pass *too* close to the school; but the closer they got, the stronger the image grew in Pete's mind that the dark, looming presence of the schoolhouse was an on-rushing tidal wave. Cold rushes raced through him, making him cringe as he waited for the whole thing to come crashing down on top of him.

"You know what I think?" Cindy said in a low, controlled voice. Pete looked at her, his eyebrows raised questioningly. "I think you should go up to the front door and have a look inside."

"Oh, yeah. Right."

Pete laughed nervously and quickly looked away from her.

"I'm serious," Cindy said, a bit more forcefully. "I've always believed it's what we're afraid of—what we avoid—that's the worst. If we just face down our fears, more often than not we realize just how simple and ridiculous they are."

"More often than not," Pete echoed, horribly aware of the trembling edge in his voice.

He sucked in a deep breath and held it for a second.

"But not always. Look, I just don't like the place, all right? It gives me the creeps. It's that simple."

Pete's grip on her hand was almost painfully tight.

"Sure. Okay. No sweat," Cindy said nonchalantly.

They kept moving toward the schoolhouse; but the closer they got, the slower Pete walked. Craning his neck back, he looked up at the tall, sunlit brick front of the two story building. A light breeze stirred the leaves of the huge maple tree to one side of the school. Shadows danced and rippled like black water across the sidewalk and up onto the cracked and crumbling bricks. A cold clutching gripped his chest, and he felt a powerful impulse to start walking away from there as fast as he could.

But he didn't.

He had to admit that Cindy's advice was probably right.

At the very least, he should take a look inside, if only to prove to himself that there was nothing to be afraid of here. Facing a little apprehension now would certainly be well worth it if he would stop being tormented by those recurring nightmares.

"Yeah, maybe you're right," he said at last. "Maybe I should take a look inside . . . Just a quick peek."

He spoke so softly he wasn't sure if Cindy heard him or not. Turning to her, he said, "Why don't you take Ryan down to the playground for a bit while I take a look around?"

Cindy looked at him and scowled.

"I'll come with you if you want," she said, but Pete shook his head.

"No. This is something I probably ought to face alone. Don'tcha think?"

Cindy shrugged, obviously trying not to make too big a thing of it either way. "Whatever you say."

"I wanna swing, Mommy! I wanna swing," Ryan shouted so close to Pete's ear it hurt. He started bouncing up and down in the backpack, and Pete almost lost his balance.

"Hold on, there, Tiger! Take it easy," Pete said, laughing tightly. "Hang on a minute so Mommy can get you off my back."

"I wanna go *now!* I wanna go *now!*"

"Just a second," Pete said with a trace of desperation creeping into his voice.

His jaw muscles clenched when he glanced up at the school building again. Now that he was actually considering doing something about it, he wanted to move forward in spite of the faint stirrings of apprehension that were tugging him back. His pulse thumped heavily in his ears, echoing like a tin drum, high and fast.

So fast it sounded almost like . . .

—*Running feet*—

The thought slipped into his mind like the burning sting of a razor cut, making him jump.

Pete took a quick breath to strengthen his resolve.

At the very least, he should take a quick peek inside. Better yet, if he could get a door or window open, maybe he should actually go inside . . . take a look around and see what the old place looked like after all these years. That would certainly help him—finally—put to rest all those deep-seated fears he had about this building.

But his mind reeled at the prospect of actually looking into—and maybe even going back inside—the schoolhouse. It would be the first time he'd been in there in. . . . What? More than twenty-five years.

A confused rush of memories filled him with rising apprehension and expectation. He shuddered at the thought, but had to admit that it was exactly what he should do. He had to go inside the old school if only to prove to himself that there was absolutely nothing in there to be afraid of.

—Running feet—

He moved a few steps closer to the school.

The instant he was under the shadow of the huge maple tree, he felt a chill and started shivering uncontrollably. He looked at Cindy as if she was supposed to give him a cue as to what to do next.

After a moment, she smiled and, pointing at the long-unused swingset, said, "We'll be over on the swings."

Finding it nearly impossible to speak, Pete nodded and then turned his back to her and shrugged his shoulders so she could ease Ryan out of the backpack. The instant he was on his feet, Ryan took off down the slope, heading toward the swings. His chubby legs were moving as fast as they could go. Cindy grabbed the cloth backpack from Pete and then, calling Ryan's name, started off after him at a run. She caught up with him after a few paces and held his hand tightly as they walked the rest of the way to the swings. The further they got away from Pete, the fainter Ryan's squeals of delight were as they echoed across the field. Cindy glanced back at him once over her shoulder and waved to him.

"Take your time looking around, honey," she called out, her voice sounding oddly distant. "We'll be fine over here."

"Yeah . . . Sure thing," Pete said weakly, not even sure if she heard him.

He watched them walk out in the white glare of the summer sun. When they were almost to the swings, Ryan broke away from his mother again and raced to the nearest swing. He was scrambling hard to get up onto the seat but couldn't make it until his mom got there and helped him up. She began to push him gently. The heavy, humid air muffled the sounds of Ryan's laughter and the loud complaint of the rusted swing chains.

They were no more than a hundred yards away, but there was a distant, mirage-like quality to the scene that made it look to Pete as though they were no longer quite in this world. He felt like he was watching a movie . . . or seeing them in a dream. He stood in the shadow of the school a moment longer as a cold, lonely anxiety twisted deep inside his gut.

Turning slowly, he looked back up at the school.

It seemed to tower above him, and once again he imagined that the building was about to come crashing down on his head. His leg muscles felt as loose as jelly as he mounted the wide concrete steps to the front door. The feathery flutter in his ears got stronger with every step. He sucked in and held his breath when he stopped within arm's reach of the tarnished brass doorknob and stared at the dull glass windows.

"Jesus Christ!" he whispered.

Feeling oddly dissociated, he watched his trembling hand reach out and grasp the doorknob. The metal was warm to the touch and felt slightly greasy as he squeezed it and gave it a gentle twist.

For a terrifying instant, the doorknob turned, and Pete thought—incredibly—that the door might have been left unlocked; but then the latch fetched up.

Realizing that he'd been holding his breath, he let it out in a long, slow *whoosh* before wiping the sheen of sweat from his forehead with his forearm.

Numbing chills played up and down his back as he leaned closer to the door and peered in through the dirty wire-mesh glass. His breath rebounded into his face from the window, but he barely noticed it as he scanned the dim, empty corridor.

As his eyes tracked up the ancient staircase to the second-floor hallway, he flashed on all those days—so long ago—when he had trod those stairs and that corridor. These memories were mixed with the more recent and, in some ways, more immediate memories of the dreams. . . .

—No, nightmares!

. . . he'd had about this place.

"Jesus Christ," he repeated, shivering so wildly he had to hug himself to make sure he was real.

Reflections from the sunlit street behind him made it difficult for him to see very much in the school, but he could make out a dusty bar of sunlight, angling into the upstairs corridor from an opened classroom door on the left. The light looked almost solid, a sickly brownish-yellow like the sepia tones of an old photograph.

That used to be Mrs. Doyle's fifth-grade classroom, Pete thought with a hollow twisting of nostalgia.

Gussie Doyle. . . . How long ago did she die?

His mind filled with a rush of memories about his fifth-grade teacher—of the time he thought he'd lost his lunch box and had started to cry in front of the whole class, only to find it buried beneath his papers inside his desk; of the time Phil Ricci, one of the school bullies, had beaten him up on the baseball field during recess, right there between second and third base, all because Pete hadn't paid him back the dime he had borrowed for a pack of bubble gum a week ago; of the afternoon when Sally Phillips had heard the town fire horn signal a fire in her neighborhood and, worried that it might be *her* house, had started to cry so hard she peed her pants; of the time Ralph Haley had felt sick to his stomach and, not knowing what else to do, had lifted up his desktop and thrown up into it, all over his books and papers.

Mesmerized by the flood of reminiscences, Pete leaned

forward until his nose was pressed flat against the wire-mesh glass. He couldn't get rid of the sensation that he truly was looking back in time into another dimension.

He glanced down at his watch and saw that it was three-fifteen. Exactly the time when school used to let out.

He tensed, half-expecting to hear the sudden clanging of the school bell and see the rush of students, charging into the hall toward the front door and freedom.

Chilled trickles of sweat ran down his sides from his armpits. Rubbing his hands roughly over his face, he stepped back and cast a nervous glance in the direction Cindy had taken Ryan. The building blocked his view of the playground and cut off all sounds. He could no longer hear the shrill squeal of Ryan's laughter or the squeaking of rusty swing chains. Pete had the impression that he was inside a glass jar, looking out at the world.

"All right . . . all right," he whispered to himself. "You've seen enough." His voice had a harsh quality that grated on his nerves.

Taking hold of the doorknob again, he pulled back on it hard and spun it around. A shocking jolt as bright and hard as a bolt of lightning shot through him when he heard the door latch click. He whimpered softly when he pulled back on the door, and it opened slowly with a low, chattering groan.

"Oh, Jesus! . . . Oh, shit!" Pete whispered, looking around fearfully.

A rush of stale air wafted over him like a dry breeze from inside a tomb. It carried with it a teasing mix of aromas, so subtle yet strong they seemed more like tastes than smells. They stirred Pete's senses and memories—

The warm sting of old varnish that almost burned the back of his tongue . . . the scratchy mustiness of stale air that irritated his eyes and the inside of his nose . . . the smell of ancient floor wax that felt thick and pasty in his throat . . . and—beneath all of that—something else. . . .

Something that had a faint, sickening tinge of decay and

rot. It hit Pete's stomach—hard, like a clenched fist.

For several seconds, he just stood there with the door braced open with his hip. Finally, realizing that someone might drive past and see him breaking into the school, he sucked in a breath of fresh air as if it were his last and stepped into the building. The hydraulic door closer wheezed loudly as it pulled the door shut behind him. The heavy latch clanged with the sharp finality of a jail cell slamming shut. The sound echoed loudly through the deserted corridor.

I can't believe I'm actually doing this! Pete thought as a thrill raced through him.

He moved hesitantly toward the stairway as though hypnotized. Once upon a time, the wooden risers had been painted flat black with black rubber protective edges, but now the tan ovals of bare wood were showing through from wear. Cupped depressions marred each step close to the railing where the heaviest foot traffic had passed over many decades.

As he started up the stairs, Pete automatically reached out for the handrail to steady himself. He was mildly surprised by its smooth, comforting feel that seemed so familiar . . . as if he had touched it every day of his life as recently as yesterday.

He took each step cautiously, one at a time, not at all surprised when the treads creaked loudly underfoot. The slow, groaning sound made him wonder if the stairs were even safe after all these years, but he reminded himself that the school had been used up until only a few years ago. There was nothing to worry about, unless it was getting caught trespassing on public property.

The schoolhouse had trapped the stale summer heat like an oven. Even before he got to the top-floor landing, he was sweating ferociously. In the rectangle of light that fell across the floor, he saw every detail in intensely sharp relief. Every dirt-filled crack between ancient boards, every swirl of wood-grain pattern worn to a dull black gloss with age stood out with near-hallucinatory clarity.

At the top of the stairs, Pete paused to wipe his face on his bare forearm.

The stale air was making his throat feel raw, as if he were running a fever. He looked longingly down the hall to the old porcelain water fountain, which was attached to the wall. He knew there was no chance the water would still be turned on, but just seeing the fountain—the "bubbler," as he and his friends used to call it—made him think of all the times he had asked to be excused from class to get a drink. Beneath the layers of dust and dirt, the dull white gleam of old porcelain showed through the grime like ancient, rotting bone.

One detail which he didn't remember from when he was a student here was the pale brown pine wainscoting that lined both sides of the corridor. The varnish had yellowed with age and was peeling up and laced with cracks like old river ice. Between the parallel joining grooves as well as in the angles where the wall met the floor, there was a thick accumulation of dust and black gunk.

Pete walked over to the door and entered Gussie Doyle's old classroom. He was surprised to see the desks and chairs still there, all lined up in neat, narrow rows as though waiting for another onrush of noisy students. The desks looked much smaller than Pete remembered them. Afternoon sunlight streamed in through the tall windows and glanced like white fire off the dusty aluminum sills. The heat in the room was stifling. Scores of trapped flies and hornets bounced against the grimy glass and tangled themselves in the clots of cobwebs as they sought a way to escape. The sill was littered with the dried husks of those who had failed.

The room looked and felt incredibly ancient, but everything still appeared to be in order. Pete let out a grunt of surprise when he saw what looked like a small, slouch-shouldered person in the coat closet at the back of the room. It took him a heart-stopping moment to realize that it was an old coat someone had left behind. On the teacher's desk was a faded ink blotter, a cobweb-draped cup filled with pens and pencils, and a row of dusty textbooks. Pete had the distinct impression that the closing of the school had caught everyone by surprise. Everything looked like it was just waiting for the new school year to begin.

Closing his eyes for a moment, Pete inhaled deeply, letting the mixture of smells fill his mind with a kaleidoscope of memories. In spite of his gathering nervousness, he felt a deep sense of peace here, too—a quietude that soothed him like he had never been soothed before.

He wondered how he ever could have twisted a place as peaceful and quiet as this, a place so full of warm, nostalgic memories, into such nightmare images.

Maybe, he thought, his nightmares simply originated in a longing he felt for his own lost childhood—a deep, indescribable yearning for those precious times he knew could never be recaptured or relived.

His reverie was suddenly broken when he heard a door slam shut, somewhere out in the corridor.

"Shit," he whispered as the sound echoed and faded away.

Spinning around on one foot, he stared at the door, more than half-expecting to see hump-shouldered, gray-haired Mrs. Doyle standing there and scowling at him as only she could.

His first rational thought was that the custodian might have stopped by to check on the place. Maybe someone had seen him enter the school and had called the police. Or maybe Cindy had come looking for him.

Holding his breath, Pete tip-toed over to the door and looked out into the hall. He was acutely aware that the sunlight coming in through the windows behind his back cast his shadow ahead of him. It would give him away in an instant.

The corridor appeared to be deserted, but Pete froze in place, holding his breath and waiting either to hear the sound repeated, or else the sound of approaching footsteps.

After a while, when he heard nothing else, he exhaled slowly and took a shallow breath.

The stifling air inside the school muffled all sound with such density that it felt as though his ears were packed with cotton. When he caught a quick flutter of motion at the far end of the corridor to his left, he dismissed it as just his eyesight, adjusting to the gloom.

Still, he didn't quite dare move out into the hallway.

Not yet.

He had to be absolutely certain he was alone in here.

What if this is another one of my dreams?

The thought sent a panicky shudder racing through him.

No! he told himself. *This can't possibly be a dream. If it was, then when had it begun?*

Could he still be in bed, back at his mother's house?

Or what if he had dozed off while sitting in his mother's hospital room?

Or maybe the dream had started even further back than that.

Maybe he had never come back east with Cindy and Ryan.

Maybe he was still back home in San Diego, in bed and dreaming *all* of this.

"No," Pete whispered, his voice tight and trembling. "That's simply not possible. This is real. This is happening."

He raised his hands in front of his face and focused on them. The sunlight shining over his shoulder made every hair, every wrinkle and pore in his skin, every vein and tendon in his hand and wrist stand out in sharp relief. He could feel the hot blast of sunlight on his back. The tightness in his chest was getting worse, and the shuddering breaths he was taking did little to relieve his steadily rising panic.

No! he told himself. *You don't get sensations like this in a dream!*

Then, just as he was starting to relax, he heard something else echo in the stairwell at the far end of the corridor. It was low, soft, and sounded like . . .

—someone crying.

The sound reverberated inside the stairwell with a distorted, hollow ring.

Pete's feet dragged like lead weights across the creaking floorboards as he moved slowly out into the corridor, drawn by that teasing, elusive sound.

The soft, muffled cry had sounded more like an animal in pain than a person. Although he didn't want to believe it, he knew that he wasn't imagining it. The sound was coming from the far end of the corridor, probably from somewhere downstairs. His heart was punching hard against his ribs when he realized that it must be coming from down in the boys' basement!

Oh, Jesus! . . . No! . . . Not down there!

A tight, choking sensation gripped his throat as he shuffled slowly past Mrs. Khune's fourth-grade classroom. At the far end of the hall, the large window above the stairwell was filmed with dust and grime, so there wasn't much available light. A soft, sepia glow filled the area.

The closer Pete got to the stairwell, the more it looked to him like a deep, dark pit, much darker and deeper than he remembered it.

All the while, the sound—a faint, sniffing cry—continued to resonate in the corridor, luring him forward like the strong, irresistible pull of the tide.

"This is fucking crazy!" he whispered to himself.

His own voice echoed harshly in the hall, like metal rasping against stone, but that didn't stop him from gripping the handrail at the top of the stairs and starting down.

With each step, the crying seemed to get louder, but Pete also had the odd impression that it was fading away, retreating from him with every step.

No matter how silently he tried to walk, his footsteps thumped heavily on the stairs. Ancient wood creaked beneath his weight, making his ears ring with tension.

There's no way! There can't be anyone down there! he thought.

He desperately wanted to convince himself of that, but then he thought that maybe some kids had been playing in the schoolhouse when he had first entered; maybe one of them, thinking it must have been the police who had come in the front door, had hurt himself trying to get away and hide.

"Hello," Pete called out.

The sudden sound of his own voice startled him.

"Hello down there! . . . Are you—are you all right?"

". . . no. . . ." came the faint reply.

The single word reverberated in the stairwell like the long sound of tearing paper.

Pete stopped short on the landing, halfway down the stairs and turned around, not believing he had really heard a reply. His body was slick with sweat; his breath came in hot, fast gulps. He gripped the railing and leaned forward, peering down into the swelling darkness below. The silence of the schoolhouse was suddenly a palpable, threatening presence, like a beast, long buried and now—after decades—finally stirring.

"Who . . . Where are you?" Pete called out, his own voice catching painfully in his throat.

". . . down here . . ."

"Wha—what are you doing down there?"

". . . down here . . . where he . . . left me. . . ."

A terrible, hot pressure tightened like hands around Pete's throat.

"Who are you?"

". . . don't you . . . remember me . . . Petey? . . ."

Pete opened his mouth and tried to say something, but his throat closed shut with an audible click.

Petey! he thought.

Pete gripped the sides of his head with both hands. No

one except his mother and his two aunts had called him Petey since he was a little kid.

And that voice!

He was positive that he recognized that *voice*, but from where?

It had been years since he'd heard it, but after a heart-stopping moment, from deep in his memory there came a flash of recognition.

That sounded like Ray Makki . . . his best friend—his *best* best friend until sixth grade, when Ray had. . . .

Had what?

Pete frowned as he tried to remember. He hadn't thought about Ray Makki in years. Had Ray moved away from Hilton? Pete wasn't sure. He thought for a moment longer, and then remembered.

No! . . . Ray hadn't moved away!

Murky memories shifted heavily inside his mind, like tired beasts, rolling over in the darkness.

"Why don't you come out so I can see you," Pete called, mildly surprised that his voice worked at all.

". . . I . . . can't. . . ."

Why not? Pete wanted to ask, but he didn't have the strength. There wasn't enough air in his lungs.

Instead, he took a few steps forward, propelled against his will toward the last flight of steps that led down into the dark basement.

Cool air thick with the smells of mold and rot washed up the stairwell into his face, raising goose bumps on his neck and arms. A hot scratching clawed like sickness at the back of his throat.

Why? . . . Why can't you come out where I can see you? he wanted desperately to ask, but he already knew the answer.

The darkness inside his mind shifted, and it assumed a solid, horrible shape.

The answer to his own question hissed in his mind like water splashed onto a hot stove.

Ray Makki can't come out because he's dead! . . . He died back when we were in sixth grade!

The memory left a bitter sting in Pete's mind.

Still moving slowly forward down the stairs, Pete's feet scuffed like sandpaper on the worn steps. He shook his head, fighting hard against the disorienting sensation that this was all a dream. In fact, he found himself hoping—praying that it *was* a dream, but that raised another, more terrifying question.

How long have I been dreaming?

At the bottom of the stairwell, Pete paused for a few seconds, trying to bolster his courage before turning left toward the boys' bathroom. The heavy green-painted door was shut tight, but he could see something outside the door . . . something on the floor—an indistinct blur that glowed a sickly white.

As Pete stared at the vague shape, it shifted subtly toward him, making a faint scraping sound on the cold cement floor.

Pete took a halting step backwards as the figure gradually resolved out of the darkness like a slow-blending special effect in a movie. His breath shot out of him with a short, painful gasp when he recognized eleven-year-old Ray Makki's pale, white face, peering up at him from the darkness of the basement.

This can't be real! . . . This is impossible! . . . He's dead! . . . Ray Makki is dead!

". . . I've . . . been . . . waiting . . . for you . . . Petey . . ."

The apparition's voice resonated with a low warble that didn't quite sound like an eleven-year-old boy.

Pete's legs almost gave out on him. His stomach did a slow, sour flip as he staggered backwards, his hands reaching for support.

Moving like heavy smoke, the apparition shifted and began to rise from the floor, resolving all the more clearly until Pete could see the jagged splash of black that streaked the boy's thin neck like spilled ink.

42

". . . he . . . left me . . . here . . . but you . . . saw him. . . ."

"No! I never did!" Pete stammered. The darkness was pressing in around him. "I . . . I don't know what you're talking about. I didn't see you or anyone! I didn't see *anything!*"

". . . oh, yes you did, Petey . . . and you . . . didn't tell them . . . you didn't tell . . . anyone . . . what the janitor . . . what Mr. Clain . . . did . . . to me. . . ."

"No, I wasn't—I didn't see—this isn't real!" Pete shouted. His voice threatened to break on every syllable. Tears filled his eyes as he raised his clenched fists and pounded them against the sides of his head, but it didn't make the voice or the vision go away.

"I didn't *see* anything! I don't *remember* anything! Please, dear God! Let me wake up! This *has* to be a *dream!*"

". . . no . . . it's not . . . a dream . . . Petey . . . I'm right here . . . I've been . . . waiting here . . . all the time . . . just waiting . . . for you . . . to come back . . . I knew . . . you would . . . eventually . . . I've been waiting . . . a long time . . . a *very* long time. . . ."

Pete took another step back, but his heel hit the bottom step, and he almost fell. He reached out to catch himself on the handrail, but instead his hand curled around something he immediately knew wasn't wood. Looking down, he saw that he was holding onto the bony wrist of an arm that was reaching up out of the darkness for him.

". . . you should have . . . told them . . . about what . . . you saw . . . about the . . . things . . . the terrible things . . . he did . . . to me . . . to you and me . . . before he . . . *killed* me. . . ."

"No! Nothing happened!" Pete blubbered through his tears as he started backing up the stairs. "I don't remember seeing *anything!*"

". . . yes you do . . . and you . . . got away. . . ."

Something snagged Pete's shirt sleeve and pulled. With-

43

out looking, he knew that it was a hand . . . the bone-white hand of his long-dead friend.

Please let this be a dream! Pete pleaded desperately inside his mind. *Please let me wake up now!*

But every sensation, every feeling was much too vivid, too real to be a dream.

Pete pulled back and heard the soft hiss of tearing cloth as his shirt sleeve ripped. Nearly blind with panic, he turned and ran up the stairs, taking them three at a time. He waved his arms wildly, trying to keep his balance, but he slammed into the wall. The impact knocked the wind out of him, but he kept going. Once he reached the landing, he gripped the handrail—sure that it was real wood, now, and not dead bone—and pivoted himself around. Out of the corner of his eye, he caught a rapid shifting of motion at the top of the stairs and lurched to a stop so fast his legs collapsed underneath him, and his shins banged painfully against the steps. Pure, perfect terror gripped his heart when he looked up and saw Mrs. Doyle, standing with her hands planted on her hips as she stared down at him and scowled.

". . . You'd better hurry up, Mister Garvey . . . you'll be late for class . . . as usual. . . ."

Mrs. Doyle folded her arms across her massive bosom, squirting the pale flab of her underarms out from the tight-fitting short sleeves of her faded dress. Her face was expressionless except for her eyes, which blazed like red, angry coals. Her thin, colorless lips looked like an ancient bloodless wound that hadn't healed.

Pete was transfixed by her fiery stare until he sensed a rush of motion behind him. Cold air washed over him like the murky sweep of water. He knew that Ray Makki or whoever or *what*ever was down there in the basement was gathering its strength to come up the stairs after him. He almost fainted, but then a small portion of his brain told him that, if this wasn't a dream, then the apparition at the top of the stairs was just that—

An apparition.

It couldn't stop him.

"I'm comin' right now, Mrs. Doyle," he shouted in a high-pitched, trembling voice.

Clinging to the wall and shying away from her, he darted up the stairs to the second-floor landing. He looked down to the far end of the hallway and could see the door to the outside, glowing with a bright, surreal blaze of afternoon sunlight. The sun-lit, living greens of the maple leaves and their shadows vibrated with an impossible intensity. He started walking toward it, but no matter how much he wanted to break into a run for the door, something weighed him down, pulling him back and slowing his steps to a sludgy, dragging crawl.

He was halfway down the corridor when all of the doors leading into classrooms on both sides of him suddenly opened wide.

From inside each room there came the harsh scraping of chairs and the soft scuff of shoes on old floorboards. Papers and books rustled as desktops creaked open and slammed shut with dull, hollow reverberations.

Muffled voices and faint laughter drifted like heavy currents in the hot air. As Pete moved slowly past the classroom doors, looking in amazement left and right, he saw pale, transparent figures of children, some of whom he recognized, shifting against the deep brown shadows that filled the rooms.

". . . you should have . . . told someone, Petey . . . you shouldn't have . . . left me . . . all alone . . . to die . . . all alone. . . ."

Ray's voice seemed to surround Pete as it echoed with a soft rustle that never quite seemed to stop. It filled Pete's head like a racing, muffled heartbeat that sounded almost like . . .

—*Running feet*—

"Jesus *Christ*, Ray! Honest to *God*, I didn't see *anything!*"

". . . yes . . . you . . . did . . . I . . . saw . . . you . . . there . . . before I died. . . ."

The floorboards creaked horribly under Pete's feet as he kept moving toward the front door, but the corridor seemed to telescope outward, shifting away from him no matter how fast he tried to move. All around him, the schoolhouse was filled with gauzy, fluttering figures and choruses of disembodied voices and echoing laughter.

Then, suddenly, a figure appeared in front of the door that led outside.

The shape was backlit by the harsh glare of sunshine, so Pete couldn't make out the features, but there was something horribly familiar about the silhouette. Slouch-shouldered and crouching, the figure loomed forward and raised its arms like a football player about to tackle an opponent.

". . . come here, Petey . . . you know, I've been waiting for you . . . waiting a long time . . . for you . . . to come back to me. . . ."

Pete stumbled to a halt, suddenly aware that the voices in the classrooms had ceased. He stared, dumb-founded at the figure that was standing between him and the front door. A cold dash of chills ran up his back when he recognized the school janitor, Mr. Clain.

". . . you should have . . . been next . . . to die. . . ." the figure said. ". . . I had you both . . . but you got away . . . from me . . . and I had to . . . kill myself . . . I hanged myself . . . down there . . . before they caught me . . . because of . . . what I'd done . . . to your friend . . . to your . . . *best* friend. . . ."

"Jesus, *no!*" Pete whispered hoarsely. "You aren't real! *None of you are real! You can't be!*"

". . . but I am . . . and it's still . . . not too late! . . . I can still . . . *get* you. . . ."

"Like hell you can!" Pete shouted.

His voice burst like a gunshot from his chest. Tensing every muscle in his body, he lowered his head and started running, charging toward the front door. Wind whistled in his ears, and below that, just at the edge of hearing, he could hear Ray Makki's wailing voice.

"... please ... don't leave me here ... Petey ... don't ... leave ... me ... here ... alone ... again! ..."

—Running feet—

Pete pumped his arms furiously. His sneakers slapped the floor hard as he ran. The dark figure blocking the doorway loomed larger in front of him, swelling and expanding until it blocked out the sunlight entirely. Pete thrust his hands out in front of him, prepared either to wrestle with the apparition or else reach through it and slam the door open. His long, agonized scream was abruptly cut short when he smashed full-force into the wall of wire-reinforced glass.

Cindy was standing on the other side of the door, bending forward as she peered into the school. She let out a high, winding screech and threw herself backwards when she saw Pete running down the hallway toward her.

In a blinding instant, she heard a sickening, wet *thud* as Pete slammed into the door. This was followed by a shattering explosion as broken glass, glittering in the sunlight, sprayed like a fountain of diamonds into the air. A few needle-sharp fragments showered the walkway, but most of them were held back by the wire mesh embedded within the glass. They sliced into Pete's body like hundreds of tiny knife blades. A bright scarlet spray of blood shot out through the shattered glass.

Ryan was playing behind the maple tree. The loud crash drew his attention, but Cindy wheeled around quickly and scooped him into her arms, shielding him with her body so he wouldn't see as his father pushed the door open and staggered out into the afternoon sunshine. Cindy watched, horrified, as Pete took a few staggering steps and then spun around in a lazy half-circle before dropping down dead on the sidewalk.

* * *

The dull brown wash of afternoon sunlight pouring in through the windows seemed to take forever to shift across the floor as Petey drifted down the empty hallway. The floorboards slid like slick oil beneath his feet. He was tense as he waited to hear the harsh clang of the school bell, signaling that—as always—he was late for class.

Glancing over his shoulder, he smiled at his best friend, Ray Makki, who was tagging along a few paces behind him. In a slow, sludgy voice that echoed and never seemed to stop, Petey said, "Come on, Ray! We've gotta hurry up, or Old Lady Doyle will nail our butts."

Ray chuckled softly.

"Heck, Petey, she'll nail our butts no matter what we do."

Ray's dark, dead-looking eyes were like windows that were no longer able to reflect light. His gaze shifted over to Mr. Clain, the janitor, who was standing by one of the open classroom doors. Mr. Clain scowled deeply as he watched the boys approaching. From behind, Ray grabbed Petey's shirt sleeve and gave it a quick tug.

"Hey, come on! Wait up! Don't leave me behind."

Petey drew to a halt. Glancing slowly over his shoulder, he waited until his best friend caught up with him. The corridor glowed with an eerie golden iridescence that made it look like it stretched out forever in both directions.

"Don't worry," Petey said with a soft laugh that echoed hollowly in the hallway. "You know I'll always wait up for you."

"That's 'cause we're best friends, right?"

Petey nodded, his head moving slowly up and down as though on a spring.

Then they started walking again, side by side.

They glided past the motionless janitor and continued on down the hallway to where Mrs. Doyle stood waiting for them in front of her open classroom door. Her flabby arms were folded across her chest. Her pale face was set in a deep scowl as she watched them coldly, shifting her eyes without blinking or moving her head.

Petey stared at her and wondered if he and Ray would ever make it to her classroom on time, but he almost didn't care, now that he and Ray had made it past Mr. Clain. He cringed inside, feeling the cold glare of the janitor's gaze drilling into the back of his head; but when he turned around and looked, the janitor was gone.

"Yeah," Petey said, his voice nothing more than a hollow whisper that rustled like dust in the empty hall.

"We're best friends . . . forever. . . ."

—for Matt Costello

The Voodoo Queen

"Her throat was serpent, but the words she spake
Came, as though bubbling honey, for love's sake...."
—Keats: *Lamia,* 64–65.

Love can change us all, it's true.

You know, there's that old joke about how a woman will try and try to change the man she married, and then complain twenty years later that he's not the man he used to be. An old joke, but true. Love *does* change us all. We all find that out sooner or later. Unfortunately for Dennis Levesque, he found it out a little too late.

It was springtime in Hilton, Maine, a small mill town nestled in the mountains of the central part of the state. Some folks would say that you can't use those two words "springtime" and "Maine" in the same sentence without fear of contradicting yourself, and most years, that's probably true. No matter what the TV weatherman says, there's

51

as good a chance of a blizzard in April as there is in November. Sure, the plow ridges may be gone, the Red Sox may be swinging their bats in Fenway Park, and the dirt roads may turn from ice-glazed skids to mud-slick washboards, but only the swelling buds on the trees and the song of the peepers down in the marsh can convince you that winter might truly be over.

It was a Friday evening, late in April, and a cold wind was blowing down off nearby Watcher's Mountain. In spite of the cold, Dennis Levesque was sitting outside on his porch. He had his feet propped up on the rickety railing, and was drinking a beer as he leaned back in one of the faded lawn chairs. He had left this particular chair out on the porch all winter. The straps were frayed and sagging; they looked like they might not make it through the coming summer, but Dennis was determined to see how long they'd last. The cardboard container that held the three remaining full cans of beer lay on the splintered porch floor, within easy reach. Two empties were crumpled up beside it.

"Returnable cans be damned! Who needs the fucking nickel?" Dennis whispered as he tilted his head back and guzzled from the can he held.

When he patted his shirt pocket, feeling for his cigarette pack, his hand froze in mid-motion. Letting out a sigh that hung like a frosted mist in the night air, his fingers clamped around the small piece of paper and pulled it free. In the dim light from the kitchen window, the piece of paper looked sickly gray; but earlier that day, when Bo Wilson, his foreman at the mill, had handed it to him at the end of his shift, it had been a different color.

Pink.

Bright pink.

A pussy color, Dennis had thought at the time.

"NOTICE OF TERMINATION"

That's all it said at the top, both earlier today and now, as Dennis unfolded the paper and looked at it in the fading light. There were more words in the space below, but they all added up to the same damned thing. He'd been *fired* . . . "down-sized," as Wilson had repeatedly said.

"Bullshit . . . *bull*shit . . . bull-*fucking*-shit!" Dennis sputtered.

His hand crinkled the paper into a tight little ball, which he threw over the porch edge and off into the darkness. He heard it land with a dull *plop* somewhere in the mud slick that passed for his driveway this time of year.

"You say somethin', honey?" Sally, his wife, called out from the kitchen. She had the window open just a crack to let in the fresh, spring breeze.

Dennis twisted around to look at her through the window. She was wearing that same damned baggy gray sweater she had worn all winter, with the sleeves pushed up to her elbows as she stood at the kitchen sink, washing the supper dishes. She was half turned around, and he could see the watermelon-sized swelling of her belly. Her thin, mousy brown hair dangled down over her pasty, pimply forehead. The dim light made her look much older than her twenty-two years.

"Ahh, no. I didn't say *shit*!" Dennis said, scowling as he took another swig of beer. After draining the can, he crumpled it up and dropped it to the floor with the other empties before taking a fourth can from the box. He had popped the top and was just leaning back for a long pull when he heard . . . music.

Jumped-up Jesus H. Christ! he thought, turning again to look into the kitchen.

Has she got that friggin' rock 'n roll station from Auburn on again? Before she knows it, she'll wake up Dennis Jr., and it will be another night of the baby howling and her complaining how she's so big now she can hardly move. And who will get puked and peed on? Why, me, of course.

"Yeah, good ole' Dennis," he whispered, and then spit viciously. "Christ on a cross! I might's well be up all frig-

gin' night, now that I ain't got no goddamned *job* to go
to!"

But as he listened, the music grew steadily louder, and
before long Dennis realized that it wasn't coming from
inside the house; it was coming from Moulton's Field,
across the Androscoggin River. Dennis leaned forward in
his lawn chair and peered out over the porch railing, almost smiling as the music drifted to his ears out of the
darkness.

"What the hell? Why, that's friggin' *calliope* music!"

Through the line of trees along the river's edge, he
could make out a line of headlights, winking and bobbing
as the caravan of trucks and trailers spread out across the
wide, flat field. Taillights flashed, mixing with the glow of
headlights to stain the nearby river with bloody red and
goldenrod-yellow smears. The calliope music didn't sound
like the real thing. It sounded more like a tinny recording,
blaring from a speaker system mounted on one of the
trucks.

"Well I'll be dipped in shit," Dennis said, smiling
broadly for the first time since this afternoon. Turning
toward the open window, he called out, "Hey, Sal! The
friggin' carnival's in town! Come on out here 'n catch a
load of this!"

"Don't yell! You'll wake the baby," Sally said as she
snapped on the porch light and came to the screen door.
She was drying her hands on a greasy dishtowel. The feeble yellow light made her face look like dead meat.

"Look over there!" Dennis said, pointing off into the
darkness. "The damned carnival! Looks like they're settin'
up 'crost the river in Moulton's. You hear anythin' 'bout
it?"

"I dunno—I might've seen a flyer at the grocery store,"
Sally said. Her voice was edged with frustration as she
eased the door open and poked her head out just long
enough to catch a snatch of the music; then she ducked
back inside. "Well, whoop-dee-doo, huh? Is that all you've
got to say? You lose your damned job, and all you can do

is get excited that the damned carnival's in town!"

The screen door snapped shut behind her, cutting off her words with a sharp bang as she went back into the kitchen.

"Well, whoop-dee-*fucking*-doo to you, too—bitch!" Dennis muttered before taking another pull on his beer. Wiping his mouth with the back of his hand, he groaned as he stood up and stretched his arms over his head. He heard something snap in his neck, but it felt good. The music was drifting across the river, rising and falling in volume. Without a word to Sally, Dennis went down the steps and started across the back lawn, lured by the eerie, wavering sound. For a few seconds, he felt like a little boy again—ten years old and free, without a care in the world . . . not the twenty-two-year old, "downsized" mill-working husband and father he really was.

He didn't notice the slight chill in the night air as he crossed the yard and headed into the fringe of woods that lined the river. He moved upstream until he found a good place to stop, then leaned against a thick-boled tree and drank the rest of his beer and watched as the carnival trailers and trucks circled around into position and parked. Dozens of people—dark silhouettes in the night—got out and began to unload. Dust rose from the ground, and over the warbling strains of the calliope music, a chorus of voices shouting commands and directions filled the night with excitement and noise. Even the heavy smell of diesel exhaust wafting across the river thrilled Dennis as he crouched in the darkness and watched.

The trailer parked farthest back, closest to the river, had a huge sign spanning from one end to the other. On it was painted a sensuous-looking black woman, obviously naked except for the huge snake that wrapped around her, strategically covering her breasts and crotch.

LaBELLE—THE VOODOO QUEEN, the sign read.

As Dennis focused on this particular trailer, its windows curiously darkened and devoid of any activity inside, his mind began to race through several fantasies he would indulge in if only the woman inside that trailer was half as beautiful as the one pictured on the sign.

After watching for a while longer, as the roustabouts quickly and skillfully began setting up the carnival tents and booths, Dennis—whose gaze was continually drawn back to the darkened window of LaBelle the Voodoo Queen's trailer—shivered and pushed himself away from the tree. After urinating into the river, he started back home to his pregnant wife and three-year-old child.

Tomorrow, he promised himself, if only for a while, he would forget all about being out of a job, and go to the carnival with or, preferably, without Sally and Dennis Jr.

"Oh, God! This is *horrible!*" Sally said, wrinkling her nose and pulling Dennis Jr.'s Red Sox hat down so it shielded his eyes.

She was pushing the umbrella stroller and walking alongside Dennis as they moved slowly past the lineup inside the FREAK SHOW tent. Each . . . well, "specimen" was the only word she could think of to describe them; "human being" certainly didn't fit—was increasingly disgusting. From TABOO—THE TATTOOED MAN and VINNY—THE PIG BOY they worked their way past TOM, DICK, AND HARRY—THE THREE-HEADED MAN and MATILDA—THE FAT LADY to LUCAN—THE WOLF BOY and TONY—THE SPIDER MAN, a pathetic individual with six—"*COUNT 'EM, BOYS 'N GIRLS—SIX*"—vestigial arms dangling uselessly from his sides.

"I think I'm gonna puke if I don't get out of here soon," Sally said. Her voice had that high-pitched, nasal whine she used whenever she wanted to get her way. She was vigorously rubbing the bulge of her stomach as though fearful that exposure to such horrors could somehow mark her unborn child.

"Aww, com'on," Dennis said, frowning and shaking his

head with disgust. "We paid our friggin' money, so we might's well see the rest of what they got."

"But this is . . . This is *sick!* These things should be . . . be put out of their misery, not paraded around in public like this." Sally covered her mouth with the back of her hand, muffling her voice. "We certainly don't have to stand here and gawk at them!"

"What the hell did you expect? It's a freak show," Dennis said, his voice edged with frustration. "You had your chance to say no outside." He was trying to keep his voice low as he eyed the people around them to make sure no one was listening to their argument.

"I—I didn't know they were going to be real *people*," Sally said. "I thought it'd be like—you know, two-headed cows in a bottle of formaldehyde or something. And I don't think Denny should have to see things like this. God, it'll give him nightmares. It'll give *me* nightmares!"

Dennis waved his hand at her in casual dismissal. "Look, babe—if you don't like it, then you can drag your sorry ass right on out of here. There's no reason you should ruin the fun for me."

"*Fun?* You call this *fun?*"

Dennis stared coldly at his wife; then, unable to stop the words, he poked at her belly and added, "Maybe you saw a little too much of yourself in Matilda the Fat Woman. Is that it?"

Sally's eyes brimmed with tears. "That's not fair," she sputtered. Then, sniffing loudly, she spun the baby stroller around, not even bothering to apologize to the people she bumped into as she made her way back out the front door.

"Good riddance to bad rubbish," Dennis muttered.

Before moving on to the next exhibit, though, he quickly checked his watch. It was a quarter to one—fifteen minutes to go until they started selling tickets for the first show of *LaBELLE—THE VOODOO QUEEN*. He hurried through the rest of the FREAK SHOW, barely noticing the rest of the wonders as his mind filled with anticipation of La-Belle's dance.

In the darkened tent, the music started out low with a slow, sensuous beat. The air was close, heavy with the smell of sweating men, sour beer, damp canvas, and old sawdust chips. Fifteen rows of low, wooden benches were crammed full of men, most of them wearing faded jeans and sweat-stained flannel work shirts. Only at the back of the tent did Dennis spot three or four women—probably college girls from Farmington, there to watch the show on a dare from their boyfriends. The rest of the audience, many of whom Dennis worked with at the mill—until yesterday, anyway—were watching the small stage as the tinny, pseudo-Egyptian music grew steadily louder. A man wearing a frayed tuxedo and top hat, and spinning a white-tipped cane in his right hand, strolled out onto center stage.

"And now, gentlemen . . . di-*rect* from the burning sands of Egypt, to entertain you here today, I present to you— the bea-*uti*-ful . . . the ex-*ot*-ic . . . the e-*rot*-ic . . . *LaBelle*, the Voodoo Queen!"

The audience exploded with wild applause, catcalls, and wolf whistles. No one, apparently, was bothered by the tenuous connection between "Voodoo" and "Egypt" when they saw a long, slender black arm reach out from behind the side curtain and begin to weave up and down like an entranced cobra in time with the music. The music rose louder as a shoulder and then a sleek, well-muscled back slithered into view.

Sitting dead center in the front row, Dennis sat gape-mouthed and staring as LaBelle slinked onto the stage. He had mentally prepared himself for disappointment, but for once, the carnival sign hadn't lied. If anything, it had underplayed the heated eroticism of this woman LaBelle. Dennis shifted uneasily in his seat as he felt himself stiffen.

When she first came out, LaBelle danced with her back

to the audience. The smooth muscles of her arms, legs, and back glided in sinuous curves beneath her oiled, ebony skin. Her ample hips shifted and pumped suggestively to the strains of the music. Over a thin bikini top and bottom made of shimmering purple silk, she wore a flimsy white veil that drifted like smoky mist in time with her swaying body. She moved like a river at night—lazy, curling ripples that flowed and eddied. The whole effect pulled Dennis into a silent, mind-numbed daze.

The audience, meanwhile, was going wild, filling the tent with shrill whistles and hoots. Overweight, unshaven men, who probably had been drinking since early morning, whooped and hollered.

"Come on! Turn around!"

"Take it off, baby! Take it *all* off!"

"Com'on! Let us see your titties!"

Their shouts almost drowned out the music, no matter how loud it was turned up to compensate for the noise.

Ignoring their requests, LaBelle continued her slow dance with her back to the audience, her hips thrusting and gyrating in seductive, sensuous circles as her arms coiled and twined like snakes. As he watched, Dennis found himself wondering what it would be like to feel those arms wrapped around him, to ride those hips, and to feel that body twisting and turning beneath his own thrusting pelvis. His mouth went desert dry when LaBelle reached up behind her back and teasingly pulled off the veil, letting it drift in shimmering slow-motion to the floor.

The audience started shouting all the louder, yelling and whistling with delight, but Dennis just sat there, transfixed. He felt a stirring of disappointment when he began to wonder if this was how it would be for the entire show. LaBelle would maintain her air of mystery by doing her entire dance without once turning to face her audience. He could see the heavy swell of her breasts swaying from side to side as she moved in time with the music, seemingly *creating* the music with every twist and grind of her body.

And then, as the music rose to a crescendo that rattled the cheap speakers, it happened.

With a swirling flourish, LaBelle spun around on one foot.

Dennis almost passed out the instant he saw her face.

Framed in a cascade of frizzy black hair was—not the face of a woman—no, it looked more the face of a cat . . . or a snake! But her sleek forehead, her high, glossy cheekbones, her delicately pointed chin, and her thin, flaring nose and wide lips were nothing but a frame for her eyes.

Her *eyes!*

In the glare of the single spotlight, against the orange backdrop of sunlit canvas, her slitted eyes gleamed with a golden fire as she looked coldly out at her audience.

Dennis couldn't move. He had forgotten how to blink his eyes or take a breath as he gaped at the woman. The noisy audience and the blaring music all seemed to vanish in an instant, and LaBelle was staring at him, dancing for him . . . for him alone. She coiled and uncoiled her arms, her long, delicate fingers waving like slim branches in the wind, reaching . . . beckoning—to him!

She's looking right at me! Dennis's mind screamed. *She wants me!*

He could feel himself almost lifted from his seat as he was drawn into the twin golden pools of her eyes. He barely noticed as LaBelle reached behind her back, unsnapped her costume top, and shrugged it off her shoulders. After swinging it around a few times in the air, she tossed it backstage. Now freed from confinement, her heavy breasts bounced to the rhythm of the music. When Dennis shifted his gaze downward from her eyes, all he could imagine was his own, trembling hands, gently caressing and squeezing those magnificent globes.

As LaBelle continued to twirl and spin on the narrow stage, Dennis was swept away by her motion. Slowly, she peeled away the rest of her costume, sloughing it off like snake skin, but he barely noticed, so lost was he in the whirlpool of her dance and her flashing, golden eyes. When—at last—she slinked off stage stark naked, and the crowd exploded with cheers and whistles, Dennis felt himself only partially pulled back out of the spinning daze he had been in. Another dancer followed, but Dennis, his groin aching as if he hadn't found release in years, got up and stumbled out the nearest exit.

The sudden burst of sunlight and the blaring sounds from other carnival booths and tents was like a cold, hard punch to the gut. Dennis walked on legs as stiff as broomsticks as he made his way over to the kiddie rides, where he had left Sally and Dennis Jr. When he saw his bloated, pimple-faced wife, the last vestiges of the illusion LaBelle had cast disappeared like smoke. It wasn't until later that afternoon, after he and Sally and Dennis Jr. had left the carnival, that Dennis got an idea of what he could do about it all.

Sunday morning dawned bright and cold as Dennis tiptoed to the back door, clutching a battered suitcase in his hand. Every floorboard seemed to creak as loud as a gunshot with each step he took, but he slowly made his way through the kitchen and out the back door without waking either Sally or Dennis Jr. Closing the door quietly yet firmly behind him, he started down the road without a single backward glance.

What the fuck difference does it make? he thought.

He had a wife he didn't love—maybe had never really loved. He had married Sally right out of high school only because he had gotten her knocked up. He had a three-year-old brat who was driving him crazy as it was, and now another one was on the way because Sally said she "forgot" to take her birth control pills. And now, on top of everything else, he didn't even have a lousy job. So there was nothing to keep him here in Hilton. But none of that mattered. If there was even the slimmest chance that he could—somehow—get to spend a night—just *one* night—

with LaBelle, it would be worth leaving all of this behind!

The night before, after Dennis Jr. had been tucked into bed and Sally was dozing in front of some lame-brained show on TV, he had gone down to the river again and watched as the roustabouts dismantled the carnival, packing it up for the trip to the next town. After Sally had gone upstairs to bed, he had quietly packed a few changes of clothes into his old suitcase and hidden it in the downstairs closet.

The morning air was crisp, with just a hint of actual springtime warmth. The woods were damp with dew and filled with birdsong as Dennis made his way quickly down Marsh Street to the bridge that would bring him by the most direct route to Moulton's Field. As beautiful as the morning was, though, it all paled beside the burning memory Dennis had of seeing LaBelle, the Voodoo Queen, dance . . . dance just for him!

He hoped, he prayed that no one from town would see him. It wouldn't take a powder keg mind to figure out what he was doing, walking down the road with a suitcase in hand. In some ways, he felt the same stirrings of freedom and joy he had felt when, as a boy, he had run away from home because of the whopping his father had given him for some long-forgotten offense. But the image that drew him onward now—the sensuous beauty of LaBelle the Voodoo Queen—was something no ten-year-old could even conceive of. He no longer wanted just to watch! No, he wanted to touch. . . . He had to feel LaBelle do her dance all around him!

He made it to Moulton's Field, and it didn't take long to find the trailer of the carnival boss, a man named Josh Logan. After telling Logan how he had lost his job at the mill—and conveniently forgetting to mention the fact that he was leaving a family behind—he had himself a job as a roustabout. The pay was minimum wage, just as he had expected, but he would share a trailer with several other men and be provided with three squares a day. All in all,

Dennis thought, his prospects were looking pretty damned good. He would be able to keep body and soul together . . . hopefully at least until he could see LaBelle again and maybe meet her. After that, he might think about going back home to Sally and his snot-nosed little brat.

Maybe. . . .

By nightfall, the carnival crossed the state line into New Hampshire. Dennis spent most of the night with his new workmates, setting up the carnival in an open field just outside of Franconia. The work was hard—much harder than anything he'd ever done at the mill. Even though the regulars treated him a bit standoffishly, he began to sense a spirit of camaraderie among them, almost like a secret brotherhood, and he felt that—with time—he just might be able to share it.

But none of that really mattered because what he had come for, what filled his mind all night as he worked, was a vision of LaBelle with her long, sleek, black arms wrapped around him, hugging him tightly . . . her legs squeezing his back as he drove himself deeper and deeper into her.

The only disappointment Dennis experienced that first night on the job was that he never caught even a glimpse of LaBelle. Apparently she kept to her trailer when she wasn't performing, and she never came out, even during setup or for the late evening meal. Whenever Dennis got close to her trailer, he would feel a queasy discomfort in his gut as he stared at her closed door, fully expecting to see some man—maybe Josh Logan—step out of her trailer with a self-satisfied grin on his face. What were the chances that a woman like her didn't already have a man in her life, maybe dozens of men?

The few times Dennis even mentioned LaBelle to his co-workers, everyone either would look away as if they hadn't heard him or else cast their eyes to the ground and shake their heads, muttering something under their breaths that Dennis never quite caught.

It was well past midnight when the carnival was finally set up and ready for the crowds the next day. Feeling bone-tired, Dennis was making his way back to his trailer for some much needed rest. Out of a habit he knew he would follow until he at least caught another glimpse of LaBelle, he detoured past her trailer.

As he looked up at the full-length sign depicting her dance, his head felt bubbly and light, but the darkened windows stared back at him like cold, uncaring eyes. He knew he would have to seek out his cot before he collapsed right there on the ground, but he lingered, staring at the closed trailer door and letting his fantasies run wild. He was just turning to leave when he heard a faint *click* and then the high-pitched *squeak* of a door opening.

With his heart throbbing heavily in his chest, Dennis looked up at LaBelle's trailer. He almost convinced himself he was hallucinating when he saw the door slowly swing outward and then stop, less than half-way open. From the darkness within, Dennis thought he saw a soft flutter of motion, black against the darker black of the doorway.

"It's very late," a woman's voice said.

It came to him, soft and husky, from out of the darkness. Like the sound of the opening door, this voice seemed more imagined than real. It floated in the night like a moth fluttering close to his ear—a light, powdery sound.

"I—umm, yeah . . . yeah, it is late," Dennis stammered.

He felt a momentary rush of fear that someone would pass by and see him standing here, talking to an empty trailer doorway.

"You must be tired," the voice said.

Dennis took two or three halting steps forward, his hands jerking uselessly at his sides. "Yeah, I am." He paused, his breath burning in his lungs. "My—umm, my name's Den—"

"I know who you are," the voice said, light and lilting, almost teasing.

And now there was no mistake; the trailer door swung

open a bit more, and Dennis could see a long, sinuous arm reaching out into the night. The arm was dark—darker than the night as the forefinger curled up in a subtle beckoning gesture.

"Uhh—Miss LaBelle—my name's Dennis Levesque. I'm a—"

"And I know *what* you are."

"Well—uhh . . . I was . . . It *is* you, ain't it, Miss LaBelle?" Dennis shifted nervously from one foot to the other, then took a single, halting step closer to the trailer. "I mean—well, you see I don't want to intrude any, but I—"

"Why don't you come inside my trailer and rest?" the voice whispered softly. "I know how tired you must be. But I can make you feel *so* much better."

Dennis's heart was pounding so hard in his chest every pulse squeezed his throat like strong, cold fingers, making him dizzy. He felt a pressure in his groin that started to tingle as he took a few tentative steps closer to the trailer. Finally he was close enough to reach up and actually touch that dark, beckoning hand.

"Please," the wispy voice said, caressing his ears like the delicate hiss of skin against silk. "Please, come inside. You *know* you want to."

Morning sunlight cut through the bedroom curtains and drilled a hole through Dennis's closed eyelids. For an instant, he was confused, wondering where the hell he was; but then, as he rolled his head to one side and glanced around the tiny, cluttered bedroom, it all came back to him in a rush so intense it made an audible *whoosh* in his ears.

His heart constricted when he looked to his left and saw the dark mass of curly hair on the pillow beside him. LaBelle was sleeping peacefully. A faint smile touched the corners of her full lips. The thin sheet covering her did little to hide the rounded contours of her body. He stared at the mounds of her breasts, unable to convince himself that last night he had actually touched them, caressed them, kissed them. Looking at her now, so silent and still, all Dennis could imagine—all he could remember—was how her body had pulsated and throbbed beneath him in the pre-dawn darkness. He smiled with dazed satisfaction as he rolled over and reached for the cigarette pack on the bed stand. Shifting forward, he picked his pants up off the floor and fumbled in the pocket for his lighter. On the small table was the empty bottle of wine they had shared last night after—no, between bouts of lovemaking. He remembered, now, that he had drunk most if not all of it.

"No, no, no," LaBelle said, the suddenness of her voice startling Dennis. Her golden eyes snapped open as she rolled onto her side and, propping herself up on one elbow, waved a long, delicate finger under his nose. The motion made the silky sheet fall away, revealing some of the charms he had enjoyed just a short while ago.

"Don't smoke," she whispered huskily.

"Oh, yeah. Sure. No problem," Dennis stammered.

For a moment, he was unable to stop staring at her breasts. Then, shrugging like a simpleton, he put the cigarette pack and lighter onto the bed stand and lay back down on top of the sheets. He let his hand linger for a moment in the air and then, as if still unable to believe his incredible good fortune, dropped it down to caress the curve of her sleek, black breast. His mind was filled with images of what they had done to and with each other during the night, and he felt another erection growing as he considered that they might start going at it again.

"What's-s-s the—" he started to say, but then he abruptly cut himself off and bolted upright in bed. His body was tingling with tension as his hand drifted up to his mouth. For a panicked instant, he completely forgot what he had been about to say as he flicked his tongue inside his mouth.

Damned if it didn't feel . . . funny, somehow.

Too much work, too much to drink, not enough sleep, and yeah, he thought, *too much screwing!*

Chuckling softly to himself, he pressed his tongue against the insides of his teeth. They felt odd, almost as if they were grooved with numerous tiny ridges.

LaBelle sat up in bed and just stared at him with those slitted, golden eyes of hers. A beam of sunlight caught her eyes at just the right angle, making them sparkle like amber marbles. Her dark skin, in stark contrast with the glaring white of the sheets, made his eyes hurt . . . hurt like hell. His mouth was filled with a sickeningly sour aftertaste, as though he had been on a week-long bender.

"No," he said, forming the word carefully in his mouth. "I was-s-s jus-s-s-st—"

Again, he stopped himself, feeling his eyes widen with a subtle, mounting fear. Almost frantic, he swung his legs out from under the covers.

"Which way to the bathroom?" he asked, fighting like hell to keep his tone of voice casual. The pressure forcing his eyes to remain wide open was almost unbearable. "I jus-s-s-t wanted to s-s-s-ee—"

He lurched suddenly forward and knocked one knee against the bed stand, sending the empty wine bottle and cigarette pack flying as he took a few stumbling steps away from the bed. A jolt of pain from the impact burned up his thigh to his hips. When he glanced down at his injured knee, his breath whistled in his throat with a loud, hissing sound. Covering both legs, from the knees down to his ankles, was a strange brown stuff that looked like . . .

"Oh, Jesus-s-s! *Je-s-s-sus-s-s Chris-s-s-s-t!*"

He reached down with both hands and started rubbing his legs. The skin was dry and scaly. Even as he stood there staring at himself, too stunned to say or do anything, the brown growth shimmered and shifted up over his knees and down his feet until it covered the toes of both feet. An indistinct design of triangles appeared beneath his skin, darkening and more clearly defined with each passing second. A cold prickling sensation raced up Dennis's legs, as if something was burrowing underneath his skin. He imagined dozens—hundreds—of tiny worms, twisting along narrow caverns inside his leg muscles and bones.

From behind him, he heard the bedsprings squeak. Turning, he saw LaBelle, rising slowly from the bed. In slow, liquid motion reminiscent of her erotic dance, she raised her arms and slipped into a thin, nearly transparent nightgown. She stood silently at the foot of the bed and stared silently at him, her golden eyes widening as she watched him staring back at her. Moaning softly, Dennis began to claw frantically at the brown scaly skin as it spread, rippling over his legs.

"What the hell is-s-s this-s-s s-s-shit?" he screamed, clenching both hands into fists and shaking them at her even as he stared, wide-eyed, at her body, made gauzy, like a dream, by the flimsy nightgown.

LaBelle smiled at him, a thin, wicked smile that showed just the edges of her pearly teeth denting her lower lip. The golden gleam in her eyes intensified, becoming brighter than the glare of morning sunlight.

Involuntarily, Dennis clamped his arms flat against his sides. Tearing his gaze away from her, he looked down, watching in mute horror as the thick, brown scales with black and red designs washed like waves up and over his hips, engulfing his arms, stomach, and chest. His legs were suddenly tugged together so violently he almost lost his balance.

"What the fuck's-s-s-s going on?" he rasped, barely able to speak.

The muscles in his neck tingled as the icy sensation of tiny fingers, squeezing tightly, choking him, got steadily stronger. Air came into his lungs in rapid, hissing gulps. He felt his lips peel back like a silent grimace of pain, and when he opened his mouth again to speak, his tongue flashed out and wiggled beneath his nose. In that flickering instant, he had the distinct impression that his tongue appeared to be doubled, as if it were forked!

The scales continued to sweep up over his body. With his legs bonded together, he finally lost his balance and pitched face-first onto the floor beside the bed. Through his blinding panic, he was only distantly aware of the painful impact. Inside his body, he could feel his bones shifting, compressing, crinkling like tissue paper as his muscles and tendons stretched and twisted into new, bizarre shapes. His head was pulled back so, even lying belly-down on the floor, he found that he was looking up at the ceiling. The morning light streaming in through the bedroom window stung his eyes, and all around him—around LaBelle, the bed, the bathroom, everything—he saw bright splinters of luminous light that rippled with subtly shifting rainbow hues. The next time he opened his mouth to speak, the only sound that came out was a deep, rasping *hiss*.

LaBelle stood back with her hands on her hips and watched all of this, smiling thinly as Dennis writhed helplessly on the floor in front of her. Her smile widened as the scales swept up and covered his face and head. Within seconds, his entire body, face and all, was sheathed in glistening scales with a glorious pattern of subtly shifting colors. Without the use of his arms and legs, which were now fused to the sides of his twisting body, he could do nothing but glare up at her with a steady, unblinking stare.

"I told you last night," LaBelle said, her voice teasing and low as she stepped closer to him. "I know *exactly* who you are . . . and I know exactly *what* you are." She chuckled, soft and light. "Why, you're nothing but a . . . a snake in the grass!"

Then she burst into laughter, and Dennis knew that there was a terrified gleam in his eyes that communicated to her that he still heard and understood her. He frantically worked his mouth, but the bone structure of his new body was entirely different. His mouth felt oddly lipless, and without lips, without a human throat, he wasn't able to utter any of the words that cascaded insanely through his mind. Distantly, he heard a loud, hissing sound, and after a moment or two realized that he was the one making that sound.

"Yes, Dennis, you tasted of things last night," LaBelle said softly. "Things that no man . . . no *man* now living has ever tasted. They made you become what you truly were all along."

With a final burst of heartless laughter, she went to the trailer door and flung it open. Leaning out into the brisk, morning air, she cupped her hands to her mouth and called out, "He's ready now. You can come and get him."

The carnival people were happy that afternoon. Mothers, fathers, and children arrived as soon as the gate was open, and they poured hundreds of quarters into the pony and Go-cart rides. The Ferris Wheel and Scrambler hardly stopped all day, and all of the games, events, and food concession stands made more money than they had at the last three stops combined. LaBelle's dance, as always, filled the tent every show with leering, horny men.

In front of the FREAK SHOW tent, the barker repeatedly slapped his cane on the podium, making a loud *cracking* sound as he tempted the crowd with promises of the wonders within. Above him, alongside pictures of TABOO—THE TATTOOED MAN; VINNY—THE PIG BOY; TOM, DICK, AND HARRY—THE THREE-HEADED MAN; LUCAN—THE WOLF BOY; MATILDA—THE FAT LADY; and TONY—THE SPIDER MAN with *"COUNT 'EM, BOY 'N GIRLS— SIX"* ARMS, was a picture of a coiled snake with a human face. In broad, red letters, still gleaming with fresh paint in the early morning sunlight, were the words:

"SEE DENNIS . . . THE SNAKE MAN . . . HE SLITH- ERS AND CRAWLS ON HIS BELLY LIKE A REPTILE!"

—for Dave Hinchberger

Surprise

Your wife Ann found you sometime after midnight, out behind the tool shed. You were sitting with your legs pulled up tightly against your chest. There was an empty whiskey bottle beside you, but you hadn't drunk it all. You must have knocked it over with your knee or something.

Make no mistake; you had been drinking earlier that evening.

Plenty.

It was all part of your Double-A program to help you deal with what was happening in your life.

Double-A . . . *avoidance* and *alcohol*.

A good "solution," if you'll excuse the pun.

But you'd been dealing with a lot of shit that—well, you used to joke with your wife that it would have broken a lesser man by now, and honest to Christ—sometimes you wonder how you hung in there for so long.

In the span of six months—no, actually it was less than six months—you lost your job, your mother died, and the bank, which had been making some not so nice noises before, had begun foreclosure on your house.

You had plenty of life insurance, back from when the money in real estate was good; and quite honestly, you had considered suicide a few times . . . usually at night, when you'd lay there in bed, staring up at the ceiling and wondering where the money was gonna come from for all those bills.

Shit, yes—it would have broken a lesser man, but you religiously practiced your Double-A method, and by Christ, it worked!

Up to a point.

You were getting calls from the bank just about every day, now, asking when you were going to pay up the last six months' mortgage—with interest and late charges—and what you intended to do about your current financial situation. You told that asshole in collections, Karen what's-her-face, that you were doing every goddamned thing you could think of, but *she* should try supporting a family of four on next to nothing.

You had cashed in everything—your retirement account, what was left of your inheritance, and the few valuable antiques you and your wife had acquired over the years. You even sold the collection of Indian head pennies your mother gave you. Day after day, you went through the classifieds until your hands were black with smudged ink, but—well, shit, you don't care what they say about the economy in the rest of the country, up here in Maine there aren't a whole lot of jobs that pay what you need.

And quite a bit of what little money you did have went into your Double-A program.

Why the fuck not?

In your private moments—and you tried like hell not to grind Ann too hard on this—you often wondered why she didn't get the fuck out there and find a job herself. She'd remind you of how she hadn't had a job in better than five years, and the job she used to have at the electronics factory had become computerized, so she would have had to go back to school before she'd be able to jump back into the work force.

What did you expect, anyway, that she'd go out and get a job slinging groceries at the local Shop 'n Save?

Between the two of you, you might have been able to make enough to scrape by a little while longer, but you needed considerably more than a minimum wage paycheck to meet your bills. Besides, who was going to stay home with the kids?

Or were you supposed to put one whole grocery-slinging paycheck toward day care?

But tonight—Christ! You finally reached your limit. You couldn't help it.

What started out as a casual conversation with your wife about your finances set you off, but good. Was it too much of one *A* and not enough of the other? Or maybe there was a third *A* you needed—a little more *ass!* What with all the stress you'd been under, you were staying awake so late at night that you never felt like having sex any more.

But maybe that's *exactly* what you needed.

Beats the shit out of you!

Anyway, you lost it real bad and started yelling at your wife, berating her for all of your problems. Then, when Sally, your six-year-old, wandered into the living room, you started screaming at her to get her butt upstairs to bed.

Damn, you were so mad, you threw the book you were reading against the wall, and it knocked the photograph of your wife's parents' wedding day off the mantel. It hit the floor, smashing the frame and glass to pieces.

That's when Ann lost control.

You had told her that you hadn't even wanted to talk, so it wasn't your fault; but now you'd done something to set her off. Rather than keep the shouting match going, you stormed out into the kitchen, grabbed the nearly full bottle of whiskey from the counter, and walked out the door, making sure to slam it shut hard behind you.

Fuming and sputtering with curses, you went out across the backyard to the tool shed, where you sat down, leaned back against the building, and just stared off at the dark line of trees bordering your property.

God*damn*, you were pissed!

Rage filled you as you spun off the bottle cap and took several long slugs of whiskey. Your heart was punching like a piston against your ribs, and you hoped the booze would help calm you down.

After a while, your breathing slowed, and you felt at least a little bit at peace. Bats or some kind of night birds were darting back and forth across the powdery gray of the star-filled sky. All around you, the night seemed to throb with a weird purplish glow. You focused hard on the solid black line of trees until your vision began to blur. In the tangled lines of branches and leaves, you imagined silhouettes of faces and the cold fire of eyes, staring back at you.

You knew you were losing your mind, but you didn't care.

You were pissed!

Fed up!

So what if you lost your fucking mind. You'd lost everything else, so who gave a shit?

Once or twice you checked your watch, but after a while you lost track of time. You were still fuming with rage. At some point you became aware of a deep, hard throbbing in your neck. At first, you were only mildly worried, but then, as the pain grew steadily stronger and sharper, you started to panic. A cold, deep ache shot down your left arm and up underneath your chin like you'd been cold-cocked a good one.

It didn't take long to figure out what was happening.

You were having a heart attack.

No fucking wonder!

Your breathing came hard and fast, and the icy pain spread like an evil touch throughout your chest and shoulders. You wanted to stand up but were suddenly afraid.

Shit! You didn't want to die, but you didn't even have the strength to call out to Ann for help, either.

You were fucked and you knew it, but suddenly, like a bubble bursting, you no longer cared.

You realized that this was probably what you had been looking for all along—an escape from all your problems; and this way, you didn't even have to commit suicide, so in the end, your wife would be able to collect the life insurance money.

So why not just go with it?

Why not ride it to the end?

You didn't even blink your eyes as you cocked your head back and stared up at the night sky. It was pulsating with dull energy, and seemed at times to shift into two gigantic, dark hands that reached out to grab you. They wrapped around you, and then began to squeeze tighter and tighter.

Go with it!—you kept telling yourself—*Just go with it!*

You thought of a few things you would miss—especially watching the kids grow up—but you knew that the heart attack was too strong and had gone on for far too long. Numbing pain gripped you tighter, like cold, pressing waves.

Go with it! . . . Just go with it!

And then from somewhere deep inside your head, you heard—honest to God, you heard—what sounded like a thick piece of wood, snapping in half. Sound, pain, and light exploded inside you. You vaguely sensed your legs kicking out in front of you as you stiffened and desperately clutched at your chest. Then, in one final, hard convulsion, you pulled your legs back up to your chest and sat there like a fetus, willing the night to take you all the way down.

Only it didn't happen that way.

You were frozen, lost in an impenetrable darkness, but you were still horribly alert and aware of the world around you. The intense pain was still there, too, as strong as ever;

but you were somehow distanced from it, as though it was just the memory of pain. All around you, you could hear the soft sighing of the breeze in the trees, the rasping flutter of unseen wings, the gentle hissing of the lawn, and something else that sounded like someone crying . . . or laughing.

You were convinced that you were dead, and you just sat there, waiting for the darkness to pull you all the way down.

But that didn't happen.

Just at the edge of awareness, you heard something else—the soft thud of approaching footsteps.

Someone was coming!

Was it your wife . . . or someone else?

You struggled to open your eyes.

Or maybe your eyes were already open, and you had blown out something inside your brain and had gone blind.

It didn't matter.

It wasn't simply that you were frozen and couldn't move; you couldn't even *feel* your body. You were nothing more than a tiny spark of awareness, suspended in an endless, black void.

But soon, that void was filled with a shouting voice. Through the confusion, you finally recognized your wife's voice, frantically shouting to someone that she had found you and to call the rescue unit.

You wanted desperately to move, to say something to her, to indicate that it was all right—that you were content to be dead and drifting far, far away. Everything was all right, and maybe everything would be all right for her, now, too. You struggled to open your eyes or your mouth to give her a sign, but you simply couldn't.

Her footsteps thundered like drums in your ears as she came up close to you. Her presence was a pulsating, burning heat that touched your mind as much as your body, and you were instantly aware that she *was* what you needed.

Bedbugs

She was warm, human flesh.

A misery and longing as deep and painful as anything you'd ever experienced before filled you, and the darkness embracing you throbbed with a groundswell rush of deep, blood red. You knew—absolutely—that you were dead, but you also realized that you'd been like this for a long time . . . for a *very* long time.

And you knew what you had to do next to dull that overpowering surge of loneliness welling up inside you.

You couldn't believe how loud your wife screamed when you opened your eyes!

—for Peter Straub

Tunnels

The cop was pretty fast. Ace had to give him credit for that, at least; but a few too many jelly donuts and being at least twice Ace's age was slowing him down.

Ace scurried down the stairs into the subway station, cleared the turnstile with an easy vault that barely broke his stride, and was already weaseling his way through the mass of people waiting for the train on the platform before the cop was even halfway down the stairs. Ace thought he could hear the cop shouting out for him to stop, but that was the last thing he was going to do. He figured he could have been moving even faster if it wasn't for the backpack loaded with cans of spray paint that was weighing him down.

Too bad about Flyboy, though, Ace thought with a slight shiver.

It had been too dark for him to actually see Flyboy hit the pavement, but he'd watched him go over the iron railing backwards, his hands clawing at the air as if he could

79

catch it and hang on. Ace figured it was at least twenty feet down to the street ... probably thirty.

Too bad Flyboy couldn't really fly.

If the fall hadn't killed him, he sure as hell was going to be one racked-up, sorry son-of-a-bitch.

But Ace told himself not to feel *too* bad about it.

Shit happens.

Everything has its risk. Flyboy had been out "bombing" plenty of times before, so he knew the chances he was taking. Either he was dumber than Ace, or else just a little less lucky today.

That's all there was to it.

Panting, but still feeling strong and wired with adrenaline, Ace paused a moment and looked first left, then right.

Fifty-fifty, either way.

Chances were some do-gooder, white-collar asshole was going to tell the cop which way he went, anyway. It all depended on just how seriously this cop wanted to catch his ass. The only thing bugging Ace was that he hadn't had a chance to finish his piece. He and Flyboy had just started spraying the outlines of their logos when the cop saw them and gave chase.

That's when Flyboy slipped and fell.

Jesus, stop thinking about it! Ace told himself.

He licked his thin lips as he looked around. He wasn't familiar with this particular Orange Line station, but— hell, they were all pretty much the same. After one more quick glance over his shoulder to make sure the cop hadn't spotted him yet, he headed off to the left.

Ace felt better as soon as he rounded the corner and was swallowed by the cool, vibrating darkness of the subway tunnel. A chill breeze from a nearby ventilation shaft raised goosebumps on his thin, pale arms. His body was still tingling from the rush of the chase.

Ace was never afraid to be alone in the tunnels. In fact, he liked the way the darkness closed down over him like a lid that shut out the glaring lights, the noise and bustle of the city. He liked the way the *scuff-scuff* sound of the brand-new Reeboks he'd ripped off just last week echoed from the piss-yellow tile walls in the throat of the tunnel. And he liked how he always seemed to be able to hear the faintly echoing *click-click* sound of dripping water somewhere deep inside the darkness. Sometimes he thought it sounded like a huge, dark animal, lapping up water or something.

Within seconds, though, the echoing silence was shattered.

Everything was suddenly drowned out by the bone-deep shudder and rumble of an approaching train.

Feeling more than seeing his way along the edge of the catwalk that ran five or six feet above the tracks, Ace looked up ahead for a service niche in the wall where he could hide. There had to be one close by, but he didn't see it before the train roared around the corner.

A bright light speared the darkness and swept like a searchlight over Ace. He felt like an insect specimen, pinned to the wall as the train came straight at him. The harsh sound of metal grinding against metal was deafening. Ace watched in fascination as the train rushed at him, pulling the darkness along behind it. White sparks snapped and flew like exploding squibs from underneath the wheels.

Spreading his arms out wide, Ace flattened himself against the damp tile wall, but the backpack pushed his stomach out a little too damned close to the train for comfort.

For a single, terrifying instant, he was afraid that the front of the train was going to scrape him up like so much dog shit; but then, with a roaring suction of hot wind and exhaust, the engineer's car took the turn and zipped past him. Ace couldn't help but laugh as he wondered what the engineer might think, seeing him appear so suddenly from out of the darkness.

The passenger cars clattered past, and Ace stared at the dull lemon light inside the train that flickered like an old-time movie through frame after frame of grime-smeared windows. He caught quick, blurred glimpses of the people, either sitting or standing, hanging like apes from the hand grips.

The screeching sound was all-encompassing. The chatter of rails and grinding of steel wheels vibrated the tunnel and shook Ace's body. Just for the pure rush of it, he threw back his head and started screaming as loud as he could, even though he couldn't hear himself. Sweat ran in icy streams from his armpits down the inside of his tee-shirt, tickling him. The dark air was filled with the choking stench of exhaust, the sting of ozone, and other, unnamable things that swirled in a blinding cloud and tugged at Ace like strong, urgent hands that wanted to drag him under the train's wheels. But Ace hung on and kept right on screaming until the train was past him.

Then, his ears still ringing and his body trembling with excitement, he watched as the train's red taillights were swallowed by the darkness. The dull echo of the passing train faded to a low, steady clacking pulse that Ace felt in his blood more than heard.

"Fuckin'-A!" he shouted.

He raked his hair back out of his eyes with his fingers, then took a deep breath of the foul-smelling air, smiling with self-satisfaction. He was confident that no cop was desperate enough—or *stupid* enough—to follow him down here. The only problem he could see was if Flyboy had survived the fall. The stupid asshole would probably be so scared about saving his own ass that he'd give Ace up.

But if the cop *was* desperate enough to come after him— well then, maybe Ace's luck would hold, and the train that had just passed by would clean him out.

That'd serve the asshole right!

But Ace knew he couldn't take a chance that the pea-brained son-of-a-bitch *wasn't* coming for him.

Hell, if Flyboy died from the fall, they might try to pin a murder rap on him. More than likely, though, the cop was just going to wait back at the platform. Maybe he had already called ahead to the next stop to alert the police to keep an eye out for him.

But then again—maybe the asshole would just keep coming down the tunnel after him.

The only thing Ace could do was keep walking—no matter how far it was—to the next stop.

Maybe on the way he'd take a break and smoke some jib.

Maybe he'd throw up a logo, too, just so anyone who came through would know that he'd been here. Once he was sure it was safe, he could catch the train back to Park Street Station and then get the train back to the 'hood.

As he walked along the service walkway, moving with a spider's supple grace, Ace never stopped to wonder if this was ever worth the effort.

Of *course* it was worth it . . . even if Flyboy got his ticket punched, it was worth it!

Ace was one of the best graffiti writers in Boston. Hell, he'd bombed half of Beantown by the time he was sixteen. He'd marked his logo on billboards, city buses, trains, subways, store fronts, rest room stalls, construction sites, sidewalks . . . just about anything in Boston that would hold enamel paint.

And he knew he was good—*fast* and good.

He took pride in his work, and he had the scars to prove it. His arms, legs, face and shoulders were ribboned with thin white lines where razor wire, chain-link fences, broken glass, and pavement had cut him. The six-inch scar on the left side of his head that made his left eye droop down was where a cop had whacked him with his nightstick last summer. Ace called it getting a "wood shampoo."

But he kept bombing because he knew it was worth it.

There weren't many—hell, no! There weren't *any* better graffiti writers in all of Boston!

As Ace walked along, he kept his eye out for a good place to tag. It had to be someplace where the engineer, at least, would see it as he made his turn. Up ahead, where the wall curved gently to the right, looked like a good spot; but before Ace got to it, the tunnel echoed again with the distant squeal of another train. This one was approaching from behind.

The sound of grinding wheels set Ace's teeth on edge. He saw the signal light on the tracks change from red to green. In the dim light, he also saw a wide, dark opening—a service bay—not more than fifty feet ahead. He started running, hoping to make it to cover before the train got to him. He wasn't afraid of falling under the train, but he wasn't too keen on the engineer seeing him, either. If the cop who'd been chasing him had notified the engineers to keep an eye out for him, it'd be just as well if he stayed out of sight.

A dull spot of yellow light swung around the corner behind Ace just as he reached the niche and ducked inside. He couldn't see for shit in the sudden darkness, and he tripped over something and almost fell. He caught his balance and muttered a low curse as he brushed his hands on his pants legs.

"Yeah, well fuck you, too!"

The suddenness of another voice, coming from out of the impenetrable darkness, startled Ace.

For a flickering instant, he thought he might have imagined hearing the voice. His whole body tensed as the sound of the train grew steadily louder, echoing with a strange reverberation in the bend of the tunnel. Clenching both hands into fists, he got ready to fight if this tunnel rat, whoever the hell he was, gave him any shit. Ace wasn't very big for his age, but he was street-tough and wiry. Not many people fucked with him and didn't live to regret it.

The tunnel rang with grinding metal as the train roared by and disappeared down the tracks ahead. Then a deep silence clamped down in the darkness again. Still tense and ready to fight if he had to, Ace started backing toward the opening.

"Sorry, man. I din't know you was down here," he said with only the slightest hint of nervousness in his voice.

"What, you mean you can't see where you're going or something?" the man asked.

This was followed by a low, gravely laugh that ended in a raw fit of coughing.

The voice sounded old and cracked, kind of creepy, coming out of the pitch darkness.

Ace leaned forward, trying to get a glimpse of the guy, but there was nothing there—just thick blackness. He was pretty sure this had to be just some homeless wino, but he didn't like not being able to see him. A vague sense of unreality swept over Ace as he shook his head and tried to convince himself that there really was someone there; but no matter how hard he stared into the well of darkness inside the niche, he couldn't catch even the faintest hint of a shape that might be a person.

"So what the fuck're you doing down, here, anyway?" the voice asked.

The last word reverberated with a dull, steady pulse that hurt Ace's ears more than the sound of a passing train.

"Jus' hangin'. Tha's all," Ace replied, his voice low and tight.

"Doing a bit of writing, too, I suspect. Huh? And maybe running away from the *po*-lice."

The man pronounced the last word the way the brothers say it, heavily accenting the first syllable.

"I ain't running from no one!"

"Is that a fact? Well maybe you think you're some hot-shit because you got away tonight, unlike your friend, huh?"

Ace had no idea how this guy could have any idea what he'd been doing, but he wasn't about to say a word. For all he knew, this might be another cop, setting him up to nail his ass.

Suddenly a soft scratching sound followed by a snapping *crack* filled the darkness as a small flower of orange light cupped inside the man's hands burst through the darkness. A brilliant glow underlit the features of the man's face as he raised a match to the tip of the cigarette in the corner of his mouth and puffed. Ace stared as the light flickered for a few seconds, and the man took a deep drag. With a quick flick of his hand, the match went out, plunging the niche back into impenetrable darkness. A vibrating green and black afterimage of the man's features drifted in front of Ace's vision, no matter where he looked.

"You think you're some hot-shit writer, huh? Or should I say *graffiti* artist." The man chuckled softly. "Is that what you think you are? An *artist?*"

He exhaled noisily, and a funnel-shaped plume of blue smoke appeared like magic from the darkness and blew into Ace's face, stinging his eyes. Ace waved the smoke away with both hands but said nothing. He sure as fuck didn't have to brag to anyone . . . especially not some burn-out tunnel rat.

"Say, why don't you do me a favor," the man said.

His voice sounded mellow enough, like he was going to make a simple request; but there was also a harsh level of command just below the surface that Ace didn't like.

"Look, man, I don't owe you shit, understand? Who the fuck you think you are, anyway?"

Although he couldn't see the man, and he had no idea if he was getting set to jump him or not, Ace bounced up and down on his toes, his fists clenched at his sides and ready to fight.

"Hey, all I'm asking is one tiny favor," the man said, not sounding at all like he was rising to Ace's challenge. "Just do me a quick throw up. Show me your stuff."

"You're fuckin' crazy, man," Ace said as he backed closer to the edge of the walkway. He wanted to turn and leave, but something warned him not to turn his back on this guy. The flesh at the back of Ace's neck began to tingle as though tiny worms were crawling just beneath the surface of his skin.

"If you think you're so damned good, show me what you got," the man said.

"I don't *think*—I fuckin' well *know!* I'm tops in this fuckin' city. D'you know of one block in Boston that I ain't tagged in the last ten years?"

"I'm something of a writer, too, you know," the man said.

He paused and inhaled on the cigarette. The glowing tip illuminated his face with harsh, black lines. When he exhaled, he made a soft, satisfied sound in the back of his throat that might have been laughter.

"Tell you what," the man said. "Give me a can or two, and we'll both do one. Just a quick mark so they'll know we've been here."

"I don't need this shit," Ace said, shaking his head and backing away.

He dropped his right hand to his pants pocket and felt for the bulge of the switchblade he always carried. He was more than willing to cut this mother-fucker if he didn't shut his face.

"Tell you what. Let's call it a little contest," the man said, sounding friendly, almost cheery. He took another drag of the cigarette, then flicked it away with a quick snap of his finger. The glowing tip hissed and spun end over end like a whirling comet inches past Ace's ear before it landed with a dull sputter behind him on the tracks.

"Yeah, 'n what's the prize?" Ace said.

"Show me your best work, and . . . oh, I dunno. Maybe— if it's as good as mine—I'll let you leave here alive."

Ace sniffed with laughter even as cold tension coiled deep in his stomach.

"You don't scare me, mother-fucker," he said, squaring his shoulders and taking a threatening step forward.

"And you don't scare me, either," the man said. "I'm just not sure I like the way you left your buddy back there."

"What—Flyboy?" Ace said. "He's a cold turd. If he can't climb, then he ain't worth the effort it's gonna take to shovel his guts off the street."

"You mean you didn't push him?"

Ace was about to say something, but then stopped himself cold.

How the fuck could this asshole know anything about what had happened up there on the bridge?

Okay, once Ace saw the cop coming, he might have nudged Flyboy a little, but only so he could clear the bridge railing first. He sure as fuck didn't *push* him.

For several seconds, the tunnel was tomb-quiet. Ace couldn't even hear the man breathing. Then he swung the backpack from his shoulder, unzipped the top flap, and grabbed a few cans of paint. Not caring what color they were, he threw them into the darkness, only guessing where the man was. He heard two loud *smacking* sounds as the man caught the cans, then a loud rattling as he started to shake them. The ball bearings inside the paint cans jangled as loud as alarm bells.

"So where do we write?" Ace asked. "I can't see for shit back here."

The tension in his gut was steadily tightening, but Ace chose to ignore it. He knew he was the best. He'd have a whole fucking mural done before this burnout figured out how to pop the lid off the can.

"Why not right outside here on the wall?" the man said.

Ace heard a low, shuffling sound as the man stood up. Then, like a photograph gradually developing, a face resolved out of the darkness mere inches from Ace.

"What the fuck—?" Ace said, taking a quick step back and raising his hands defensively.

He was surprised that the man didn't look anywhere near as old as he had in the glow of the match. Ace guessed the man was in his mid-thirties. His face wasn't lined or wrinkled at all. In fact, his skin glowed with a white smoothness that made Ace think of polished marble. He had a solid build, too—lean and muscular, without an ounce of fat. Ace was damned glad he hadn't tried to fight him. He looked like he could have picked Ace up and broken his back with one hand.

Ace's hand was trembling as he took a can of spray paint, snapped off the cap, and shook it. Side by side, he and the man walked out of the niche and stood on the catwalk by the wide, curving cement wall.

"Wha'do yah want?" Ace asked, trying to control the tremor in his voice.

"Anything at all," the man said, sounding like he was trying hard not to laugh. "Just give me your best shot."

Ace cocked his hip to one side and stared at the grime-stained wall for a moment. He always liked to study the space to see what shape suggested itself. After a moment, he inhaled sharply, stepped close to the wall, and began to spray.

His arm moved in wide, controlled sweeps. The hissing of the spray can was all he heard or *wanted* to hear as he lost himself in his work. The smell of paint fumes tingled his nostrils, making him feel higher than any other drug he'd ever used.

Within seconds, Ace outlined his name in tall, fat-bellied, black letters. He placed the can of black paint down by his feet, grabbed a can of white from his pack, and started filling in and high-lighting the outlines. Ace soon became so involved in his work that he paid not the slightest bit of attention to the man working beside him. He was only vaguely aware of the hissing of the man's spray can and the wide, sweeping movements he was making.

This is too fucking easy, Ace thought.

But all the time he was drawing, he couldn't stop wondering if the man had been joking, or if he had really meant what he'd said about not letting him leave here alive if he didn't like his work.

Ace barely noticed when another train rattled by. After several minutes, he capped the white, picked a can of red paint, and began adding five-pointed sparkles on the tops and sides of each bulging letter. He jumped and actually squealed out loud when the man's voice suddenly broke through the hissing sound of spraying paint.

"Well, I'm about done," he said.

"What the fuck—?"

Ace finished the stroke he was making, then stepped back so he could see what the man had been working on. He gasped with utter amazement.

"No way... No fuckin' way, man!" Ace said, shaking his head in wonder as he stared at the man's artwork.

"You had to have that started before I got here. I jus' din't see it before, is all. No fuckin' way you could've done that so quick."

The man regarded Ace steadily, his eyes gleaming wickedly in the soft glow of light.

"Like I told you," he said in a low and teasing voice. "I used to be something of a writer myself."

"No shit! With work like this... and you know... now that I think about it, I think I seen something like it before."

Ace couldn't disguise the awe he felt as he regarded the man's artwork. He had always prided himself on how easily he could make his letters look three-dimensional, but what this guy had done made everything Ace had ever written look flat and amateurish—nothing more than childish scrawls.

The logo was six feet tall, and more than ten feet wide. Wide, angular black letters were highlighted by pointed streaks of yellow and blue. In the dim lighting of the tunnel, they looked alive with jagged forks of lightning that throbbed with a rich, vibrant life of their own. Ace couldn't quite make out the name the man had written, but he sounded out each letter.

"*L-E-G-I-O-N*. Leg... Leg-ion? 'S that what it says?"

"Legion," the man said. "My name is Legion." And then he shrugged as if it really didn't matter.

What Ace saw—and couldn't help but appreciate—was

the absolute genius of the work. The word seemed to jump right off the wall. Ace thought, if he reached out and touched it, it would feel as hard and dimensional as freshly painted blocks of stone.

"No way, man . . . I don't like this shit." Ace said as he turned to the man. "You're dickin' with me. . . ."

The man smiled at Ace, his flat, white teeth glistening wetly in the semi-darkness.

"So what. . . . What's it mean?" Ace asked tightly.

The man didn't reply. He walked up to his artwork, reached out, and gingerly touched the center of the letter *G*. For a moment, the contact of his fingers with the wet paint made a slight *tick-tick* sound.

Then something strange happened.

Ace knew it had to be a trick of the eye.

Maybe there was a crack in the wall he hadn't noticed before, but—somehow—the man's fingertips disappeared into the design as if he had thrust his hand into a darkened doorway.

A sensation of stark fear slithered up Ace's back as he watched the man lean forward, reaching further into the darkness until his hand disappeared up to the wrist in the solid blackness.

Looking at Ace over his shoulder, the man grinned again, a smile so wide the corners of his mouth almost touched his ears.

"What the fuck're you doin', man?" Ace said. "I don't like people fuckin' with my mind."

Powerful shivers danced up Ace's back and gripped the back of his neck.

"Go ahead," the man said, stepping back and waving toward the artwork. His teeth were gleaming like ancient bone in the moonlight.

"You can touch it, too."

All Ace wanted to do was get the hell out of here, but he felt strangely compelled to touch the artwork, if only to prove to himself that's all it was—just paint on a grimy cement wall. It was an illusion, and nothing more!

But no matter how long he stared at them, the black letters seemed to extend backwards into thick, impenetrable darkness.

Ace tried to control his trembling hand as he raised it and reached out to the wall. A numbing chill zipped up his arm to his neck when he touched the painted surface, and then his fingers disappeared into the blackness.

"What the fuck—?" he muttered, vaguely aware that the man beside him was snickering softly.

Ace leaned forward, reaching further into the darkness and waiting for his hand to hit solid wall; but his wrist, then his forearm disappeared so completely it looked like his arm had been cut off just below the elbow.

In Ace's peripheral vision, the jagged yellow and blue streaks surrounding each letter slithered on the wall, crackling and shifting like pale, electric fire. Ace told himself that this had to be an optical illusion, but his body felt suddenly charged. Every nerve and muscle twitched and vibrated with a deep, humming energy.

"This is . . . this is *totally* fucked, man," Ace sputtered.

He tried to laugh when he leaned back to pull his hand away, but a numbing coldness gripped him and held him there. In the first, sudden flash of panic, he thought he could feel a cold, scaly hand from inside the wall, gripping him firmly by the wrist.

"What the fuck, man?" Ace's voice had a high, baby-sounding pitch.

"Well—you know what they say. Sometimes the artist has to *become* the art." The man's voice sounded muffled and hollow, like far-off thunder.

Frantic with fear, Ace struggled to pull away from the wall, but an irresistible force was pulling him closer and closer to it. His new Reeboks squeaked loudly on the slick cement floor as he braced himself and yanked backwards as hard as he could, but the dense, churning blackness was getting inexorably closer. Its coldness spread up Ace's arm and through his body like a wash of ice water.

"Come on, man!" Ace said, his voice breaking on every syllable. "Whatever the fuck you're doin'? Make it stop! Please! Make it stop!"

"I'm afraid it's too late for that," the man said. "Maybe it wasn't such a good idea for you to reach into it."

Ace's legs pumped furiously as he tried to get a solid enough footing to thrust himself away from the wall, but he could feel himself being absorbed by the darkness. His arm had disappeared all the way up to the shoulder, now. He tried to look away, but his face was being pulled closer . . . closer to the vibrating blackness.

When it was less than an inch away, Ace sagged forward, suddenly drained of all strength. The bones in his hands felt like they were being crushed to a pulpy mush. Wave after freezing wave of pain shot through him.

"Shit, man! . . . Please! . . . Help me! . . . You gotta . . . help me!"

Hot tears gushed from Ace's eyes and flowed down his face, but the man did nothing.

"Help you? You mean, the way you helped Flyboy?" he said.

"It was an accident!" Ace wailed. "I didn't push him! Jesus Christ, man!"

The man sniffed with laughter.

"No. I'm sorry," he said. "I'm afraid you're not talking to *him*. I'm the other one."

"What do you mean, the other one?" Ace sputtered. "Jesus, man!"

The darkness was opening like jaws inches from Ace's face, churning with a cold, raw energy, that sapped what little strength Ace had left. The stench of raw, rotten flesh filled Ace's nostrils the instant he was pulled into the surrounding darkness. He wanted to scream, but his voice choked off. He felt himself dissolving . . . spreading out . . . lost in the utter, impenetrable darkness that now engulfed him.

He had no idea which way to turn.

It wasn't long before the only sound he could hear—other than his own labored breathing—was the faint *click-click* sound of dripping water.

But it wasn't dripping water.

It was something else.

It was the sound of an animal . . . huge and unseen . . . somewhere deep in the darkness . . . lapping up . . . something. . . .

". . . From a Stone"

BILL STONE
"Especially when it's dark, so dark I don't even know if my eyes are opened or closed, I can hear him walking around upstairs. Pacing back and forth. The floorboards creaking and snapping as nails pull in the old wood with long, rusty-throated groans.

"Or maybe that's me groaning.

"I'm not sure anymore.

"I don't know where I am, and I've lost all sense of time.

"I feel so weak, and being tied down like this to the table or workbench or whatever the hell this is—is so goddamned uncomfortable, I can't really sleep. I just doze off and on since I got here . . . since he brought me here.

"When was that? Could have been two days ago or two weeks ago. Christ if I know!

"Feeling as miserable as I do, and being so scared, how could I know how long it's been?

"Even during the daytime, not much light gets down

95

here. So instead of sleeping, I just keep slipping in and out of consciousness.

"And that's just what he wants, the lousy bastard! He wants to wear me down . . . drain me . . . reduce me until there's nothing left.

"But—Jesus! He sure is taking his sweet time about it!

"I don't know why he doesn't just kill me and get it over with. Why keep feeding me? And why keep that damned needle stuck in my arm?

"No, I can't get it out.

"Jesus, don't you think I've tried?

"It's taped down nice and tight. I can't wiggle or shake it loose. It's in there, solid!

"I think it's an IV. He wants to keep me alive, even if I don't eat. I think I remember seeing in this guy's file that he used to work at a hospital, as a nurse or a physician's assistant or something.

"No wonder he knows how to hook up an IV.

"But—shit! Especially when it's dark, if it isn't his god-damned pacing upstairs that keeps me awake, or how much my back and legs hurt, it's that goddamned sound of drip-ping liquid.

"Drip . . . drip . . . drip . . .

"It's going to drive me crazy, I tell you! Like Chinese water torture.

"I have no idea where it's coming from. Sometimes it sounds real close to my ears, almost like it's inside my head . . . at other times, it's real faint and far-away sounding, like he's got a leak in a water pipe somewhere in the house.

"But—Jesus! I wish it would stop!

"I know I'll never get out of here. Not alive, anyway.

"He's got me tied down damned good. I can't work my-self free. I've been trying. And even if I could, he comes down here regularly and tightens the straps that are bind-ing me.

"Hour by hour, minute by minute, I feel weaker and weaker. . . .

"I'm slowly fading away.

"I know I'm gonna die.

"I wish that's what I could do. Just close my eyes and fade away.

"But every time I do that, he seems to sense it or something, and he comes down and wakes me up. Then he forces me to eat or drink something. Usually half of it ends up dribbling down my chin, so I'll bet that's why he has the IV hooked up.

"After I finish eating, he goes back upstairs and starts pacing again.

"Back and forth. . . . Back and forth. . . .

"Doesn't this guy have a job or something he's got to go to?

"Doesn't he ever leave the fucking house?"

—ANDY CAMPBELL

"I know they're gonna find me eventually. . . .

"Find him.

"There's no way around it. The cops have already been by the house a couple of times, asking questions and sniffing around.

"I'm pretty sure it was Stone's appointment book that tipped them off to me.

"Damn!

"I thought I'd covered every base!

"I should've swiped it off his desk the last time I was in his office.

"My name must've been in his appointment book, so as soon as the jerk turns up missing, the cops check his calendar and interview everyone he saw over the last couple days or weeks.

"So I know they'll be back.

"No doubt about it.

"That detective—what's his name? Logan? Yeah, Henry Logan. The whole time he was talking to me yesterday, he was eye-balling me like he already knew that I'd done it.

"And his partner. . . . Damn! I can't remember his name!

"Fuck it. What's it matter? His partner was a god-damned dim-bulb, anyway. He just stood there, listening and nodding his head like a fucking puppet while Logan did all the talking.

"Don't the cops call it 'Mutt 'n Jeff-ing' someone?

"So—anyway, I know . . . sooner or later, Logan will be back.

"I just hope it isn't before . . . you know, before I get what I want out of Mister William J. Stone.

"Mister IRS auditor!

"After that, I don't give a rat's ass what happens to me."

—HENRY LOGAN

"Look, it's like this, okay? After you've been on this job long enough, you get so's you have a sixth sense. Cops call it their "blue sense." We know whether or not someone's lying.

"Now take that guy, Campbell . . . Andrew Campbell.

"Sure as shit, he's lying through his fuckin' teeth. He knows exactly what happened to that guy Stone. He just ain't talking about it.

"Not yet, anyways. But he will.

"I'll wear the little cocksucker down, don't you worry 'bout that! I got a nose for this shit, you see?

" 'Course, I can't say as I exactly feel sorry 'bout what happened to this guy Stone. Sure, he wasn't responsible for my problems with the IRS, but he works for them, don't he?

"Well then—in my book, that's good enough. After what those cocksuckers did to me last spring! Hell, I lost my house and family, and almost lost my shield because of it.

"But don't you worry. I never let personal problems interfere with my job.

"No-sir-ee.

"Dead or alive, I'm gonna find this fella, Stone, and I'll bet the first six inches of my dick it was that asshole Campbell that offed him!"

—BILL STONE

"I don't know how long I can last . . . not like this. . . .

"There's no point, anyway.

"I want to die! I pray to God to die!

"I can't live like this, and I know he's never gonna let me go. . . . Not after some of the things he let slip the last time he was down here.

"How long ago was that?

"An hour?

"A day?

"What's it matter?

"I don't care anymore, anyway . . . except for Maureen . . . I care about Maureen and the baby.

"Oh, Jesus. . . . The baby!

"I know Maureen must be going crazy, wondering where I am. She's gotta think I'm dead by now because I must've been missing at least a couple of days, if not longer.

"But she's not going as crazy as I am.

"It's that sound . . . that dripping sound. It never stops. I hear it all the time, when I'm awake, when I'm asleep, and when I'm somewhere in between.

"Drip . . . drip . . . drip . . . until it sounds like thunder in my head.

"It just keeps getting louder and louder, and now I'm starting to hallucinate. I keep seeing . . . someone . . . a dark figure, standing in the corner . . . over by the door. . . .

"Sometimes, when I'm really out of it, I imagine that it's Death, come to take me.

"But then I realize that it must be that bastard Campbell! He was down here gloating again last night.

"Last night, or was it this morning?

"I don't know. I can't remember.

"But he knows I can't last much longer—that I'm going to die soon.

"That's exactly what I want, too . . . for it to be over.

"But it's almost like he wants to keep me alive, like he wants me half-way between being awake and asleep . . .

"Between being alive and . . .

" . . . dead. . . .

"Oh, God! Please! I want to die!"

—HENRY LOGAN

"Campbell knew I was coming back. The little cocksucker was waiting for me at the front door.

"He thought he was ready for me, but I could see it in his eyes. He's scared shitless. He couldn't hide it for long.

"First off, he wouldn't let me into the house, saying how I couldn't come in unless I had a search warrant and all that bullshit he must've learned from watching cop shows on TV.

"I told him, if he didn't let me in now, it'd be a matter of a couple of hours, tops, before I'd be back with a fucking search warrant and a warrant for his arrest. I told him—for now, anyway—all I want was talk.

" 'So why won't you let me in just to talk?' I ask him. 'It ain't like you're hiding anything, is it?'

" 'No, I'm not hiding anything,' he says, and then—by Jesus—he lets me in, and it doesn't take more than a couple of minutes—fifteen, tops—to break him down.

"I start by asking questions, all the while pacing back and forth in the kitchen and making like I didn't believe a fucking word he's saying.

"He was some nervous, lemme tell yah.

"It was cold as a fucking barn in his house, but his face was beaded with sweat. He looked like he'd been drinking, too, but I didn't see any empties around.

"Actually, I felt kinda sorry for the poor bastard. Fifteen

minutes later, he breaks down and confesses that he's got William Stone tied up in his basement.

" 'Tied up?' I says. This genuinely caught me off-guard.

"I would have bet my left nut he'd already whacked Stone and dumped his body somewheres, maybe out at the town dump or something.

"I can't exactly say as I'd blame him, if that's what he'd done, either. He got to telling me how the IRS had screwed him over big time. He broke down, sobbing like a little girl. That pissed me off, but—I have to tell yah this, I kinda felt sorry for the guy.

"Anyways, I read him his rights—did it all according to the book—but before I cuffed him and radioed for backup, I asked if he'd take me down into the cellar so's I could check on Mr. Stone. Make sure he's still alive and all.

"Campbell—let me tell you!—he was shaking something awful when he snapped on the cellar light and we started down the stairs.

"I wasn't taking any chances, though. I never do, so I drew my service revolver and let him lead the way.

—BILL STONE

"The sounds of footsteps seemed to come from far, far away. I'd been concentrating on the fast, steady *drip-drip-drip* sound, and then it started to change.

"I wasn't sure when it happened . . . but I heard voices. . . . Two people, talking upstairs.

"I was so far gone, I couldn't tell what they were saying or anything. It was like my ears were packed with cotton. Their voices sounded like bees, buzzing in a hive.

"But I snapped back to consciousness when the light came on, and I heard them—two of them—coming down the stairs.

"I knew they'd found me!

"I was saved!

"Everything was going to be all right! I could go back home to my wife and baby!

"My eyes kept trying to close as I stared at the diffuse light coming in under the closed door. It was terribly painful to look at.

"I took a breath and tried to speak—tried to call out for help, but I couldn't get enough air into my lungs. The only sound I could make was a low, watery rattle in my chest and throat that hurt my head.

"I was getting dizzy, struggling hard to keep my eyes open . . . to stay conscious.

"The door cracked open. First Campbell, then some other man came into the room. I could tell right away that this other man was a cop.

"I tried to say something, but a loud, roaring sound filled my head. The room swelled with darkness that crashed all around me.

"I must've passed out.

"Everything seemed like a dream when, sometime later, I regained consciousness and realized what they were doing. . . ."

—ANDY CAMPBELL

"I won't lie to you. I was scared out of my mind when I saw that detective at the door again. I even pissed my pants a little, but not enough to show, I don't think.

"The cop and I talked some. I don't know what did it, but something he said got to me, and I broke down and confessed.

"No, I know exactly what it was.

"It wasn't anything he said. It was because I couldn't take the pressure anymore!

"Sure. That's what it was.

"I'd been planning this for so long I was kind of freaking out that I'd actually done it.

"I remember that afternoon two weeks ago, in Stone's office. We'd met many times since last spring. I'd been trying to convince him that there was no way—no way in Hell I could come up with the money he said I still owed the IRS After my wife took me to the cleaners—and stuck me with all the bills for her charge card—I had nothing left to live on.

"But Stone—that miserable motherfucker!—wouldn't listen to me, no matter what I said.

"I remember saying something to him then—something that later got me to thinking. I told him that he 'couldn't get blood from a stone.' That's an old expression my mother used to use.

"And that's when I got the idea to do what I'd done.

"Stone was going to pay because *I* was going to get blood from a stone . . . drop . . . by drop . . . by drop."

—HENRY LOGAN

"Once we got down into the cellar, I couldn't believe what I was seeing, lemme tell you! Being a detective for the last twenty-three years in a fair to middlin'-sized city like Portland, Maine, I've seen more than my share of weird shit, okay? But I ain't never seen anything like this!

"This Campbell fella has Stone all trussed up like a baked pig or a Thanksgiving turkey, for Christ's sake. He has him strapped to a big, oak door that's propped up on two old saw horses over against the cellar wall.

"Stone's face was fucking white as a sheet. My first thought was that he's already dead, but then I hear him sigh and see his eyelids flutter.

"But it was the medical equipment that got my attention.

"Campbell has this guy hooked up to what at first looks like an IV. I can see a big red splotch of blood on the bandage where it's taped to his forearm. The plastic tube leading from his arm is filled with thick, red liquid—

"Blood.

"The other end of the tube is hanging over the side of the table above a large metal wash bucket. I can see that the bucket's practically filled with blood that's dried black and has crusted over.

"The smell in the room was something awful. Stone had

obviously pissed and crapped himself, but there was also this sour, metallic stench of the coagulating blood that he's got collected in the bucket.

"Moving over toward the table, I inspected the hookup Campbell had made.

"It was pretty ingenious, I have to give him that.

"Up near Stone's wrist, there's a little plastic valve with a spigot attached. My guess is the tube underneath the bloody bandage has a fairly wide needle in it that goes directly into the artery in Stone's arm. By opening and closing the valve, Campbell can adjust the flow of blood from Stone's arm. He's probably giving him anti-coagulants to keep the blood flowing because that's what he's doing . . . he's slowly draining the blood out of him.

" 'You are one sick motherfucker, you know that?' I said, turning to Campbell.

"He's cowering by the door, still looking like he could be dangerous. Or maybe he was thinking of boltin'. I figured he's too scared to try anything.

" 'But you . . . you have to understand,' Campbell says to me, stammering in a high, wavering voice.

"He suddenly drops forward to his knees and, clasping his hands together like a little choirboy confessing to the priest that he's been playing with himself, closes his eyes so tightly tears squeeze out and run down his face.

" 'He was fucking me over! . . . Royally! . . . He ruined my life . . . and I was gonna lose my house . . . maybe even go to jail because he was squeezing me. . . . He was busting my balls for the back taxes I owed.'

"I looked at Campbell, disgusted by what I was seeing— a grown man, breaking down and crying like a little baby.

"But beneath that, I could also see that dealing with this IRS guy was what did it to him. I could see it, because, like I said, a while back, I had my own run-in with the IRS, and they never showed a drop of mercy toward me, either.

"I waved my revolver at Campbell, signaling for him to get up and stop his blubbering.

"Trying to look past my disgust, I says to him, 'The problem we have here is, you have really fucked it up.'

"Campbell lets out another cry and drops his head. Now he looks like a condemned prisoner on the scaffold, waiting for the executioner to chop his fucking head off.

"But then I start laughing, and before I know it, I can't stop laughing.

" 'Come on. Come on. Get up,' I say between fits of laughter.

"I had to yell to get Campbell's attention, and when I did, I saw Stone's body twitch. His eyelids slid open, and he's looking at me with a glazed, distant look in his eyes. A single teardrop runs from the corner of his eye, down his cheek, and into his ear.

"I turned away from Stone and concentrated on Campbell, who was shakily rising to his feet as I waved for him to come over to the makeshift table.

" 'Look here,' I say. 'See this?'

"I point with my revolver at the plastic valve that controls the flow of blood from Stone's arm.

"Absolutely numb with fear and shaking terribly, Campbell frowns and then slowly nods.

"He's trying to understand. He opens his mouth and tries to say something, but the only sound that comes out is a little girlish squeak.

" 'Well. . . .' I say. 'I'm no doctor, but I'd say you have the valve open a little too much. If you *really* want him to linger, you have to close the valve a little more. Like this.'

"I holster my revolver, grip the spigot, and adjust the flow so there's only the tiniest trickle of blood sliding down the inside of the plastic tubing. We wait until we hear it plop in the bucket on the floor.

"Standing back, I fold my arms across my chest and nod with satisfaction.

" 'There,' I say. 'That ought to just about do it. Don't you think?'

"I look at Stone and see his eyelids flutter. If it was at all possible, he looks even paler than before. I could tell he didn't have the strength to resist or even to cry out, but the way I figure it, with a little more care, me and Campbell can keep him like this for at least another couple of days . . . maybe even a week or two."

—for Joe Lansdale

Crying Wolf

-1-

The summer sun had started to fade, stretching long, blue shadows across the lawn. Billy Lewis was sitting on the front steps of his house, staring earnestly at Sarah Cummings, who was straddling her bicycle and leaning over her handlebars on the walkway in front of him. Billy was eleven years old, so there was nothing provocative about Sarah's stance; it just made him feel a bit uncomfortable.

"You're just like that kid in the story who was always crying wolf, you know that?" Sarah said. "I'll bet this is just another one of your stupid stories." She huffed and blew her breath up over her face, making her bangs jostle.

"It ain't," Billy said. "You gotta believe me. I saw lights up there in the Laymon house for the past three nights in a row. Honest to God!"

Against her will, Sarah shivered. Although she couldn't see the Laymon house from Billy's front yard, she knew all about the decrepit old place. Built at the end of the dirt road that wound through the woods and past the swamp behind Billy's house, the house looked at least a hundred years old. No one had lived in it for . . . well, at least as long as Sarah could remember. The few times she had asked her mother about it, her mother had simply commanded her to stay out of the place. "It's dangerous," she had said, her voice edged with exasperation. "You never know when a floor or something will give way and cave in on you. Just stay out of there!"

Warnings like that from just about every parent in Hilton, Maine, hadn't stopped just about every kid in town from entering the Laymon house at least once in their life. Most of them made their entries during the day, usually with several friends for mutual support; and just about all of them came away disappointed. There was no dust-covered furniture, no heavy curtains that shifted eerily in the wind, no ghostly shapes in the dark corners. It was just an empty house with faded, peeling wallpaper and exposed lath where the plaster walls had crumbled away. The windows had practically no glass left in them, and the rocks that had done the damage were scattered over the floor like boulders in a New England field. Oh, yeah—sure there were probably rats in the walls, and there certainly was a terrible smell wafting up from down in the dank cellar; but that was to be expected.

The Laymon house was nothing but an old, abandoned house—scary and spooky only to overactive imaginations, and certainly not haunted—not *really*!

Over the years, a few kids *had* dared to enter the house at night. More often than not it was part of some silly initiation rite for some gang or other. No one, to Sarah's knowledge, had ever spent an entire night there, but then again, she was only twelve years old. She had heard stories from her older sister, and had no intention of going there—even on a sunny day like this!

"Well, I think you're just trying to scare me," Sarah said. "This is just like the time you had me and everyone else convinced there was a ghost out at Cedar Pond Cemetery. A bunch of us went out there, and you had rigged up a sheet with a flashlight under it, hanging from a tree."

"That was just a Halloween trick—a little early," Billy said, glancing down at the ground. Still sitting, he leaned forward, his elbows on his knees.

"And how about the time you got my brother, Johnny, and Curt all convinced there was a werewolf in the woods behind the Canal Street school? Remember that?"

Billy shrugged coyly, focusing more intently on the ground.

"You convinced a whole bunch of guys to stay out in the woods all night looking for it, and what did you get? Johnny came home with a cold that almost turned into pneumonia. And he got grounded for two weeks after he got better 'cause he lied to my folks about sleeping out in your backyard that night."

"Well . . ." Billy said, almost whining. "There was something out there in the woods. I heard it—and both Johnny and Curt heard it, too!"

"And I'll just bet you're making this one up, too," Sarah said sharply. Her grip on her handlebars tightened, and she cast a fearful look behind her. "And even if there *is* someone out there, how come you're so sure it's that killer that escaped from Thomaston?"

"It's *gotta* be him," Billy said, his eyes wide and glistening. "If any of the guys were staying out there, don't you think we would've heard about it?"

"Then how come you haven't told Johnny and Curt about it?" Sarah asked pointedly. "*They're* your best friends."

"They wouldn't believe me," Billy said. " 'Specially not after the werewolf thing."

"But you expect *me* to believe you?"

Billy shrugged and said nothing.

"Well . . ." Sarah said. "I don't!" She shifted her foot on the bicycle pedal, making ready to ride away.

"Wait!" Billy barked, so suddenly Sarah let out a surprised squeal.

"What is it?" she asked, exasperated.

"Look, how often do I ask a favor from you?" Billy said.

Sarah shrugged, thinking that more often than not Billy, like her brother Johnny, made it a point of honor to ignore her—and irritate the shit out of her when possible.

"You've gotta believe me, Sarah. I'm positive that killer's out there, and I—"

"Then why don't you just go to the police and tell them instead of me?" Sarah asked. She kept gnawing at her lower lip, and Billy took this as a sign that he was getting to her.

"Because they'd believe me even less than you do," Billy said. "I want to go out there tonight and peek in the cellar windows. Just to make sure. But I need someone else there to see, too, so they can back me up when I go to the cops."

Sarah shook her head and scratched the side of her neck. She could still feel the sprinkling of goosebumps that had arisen when Billy had first mentioned the Laymon house. Another, deeper shiver ran up her back now as she stared blankly at the long shadows on the ground.

"Make a unanimous phone call to the police, then," she said.

"You mean anonymous."

"Whatever!" Sarah's frustration was rising higher as she see-sawed between skepticism and belief.

"You ain't chicken-shit, are you?" Billy asked.

Sarah was about to say that she *was* chicken-shit, and she didn't care if Billy or Johnny or anyone else knew it; but something made her hold her tongue. She just stared at Billy.

"I figure," Billy went on, "if we keep this just between you and me, then we're gonna be the town heroes for helping catch this guy. I'll bet we even get our picture in the newspaper—maybe even get on TV—and meet the governor and stuff!"

"Who'd *want* to meet the governor?" Sarah asked.

Bedbugs

She knew Billy was throwing this stuff out just to tempt her. He was laying down a line of honey to draw her in; and she knew she should follow through on her first impulse—tell Billy to take a hike to the moon before she biked away. She should forget all about him and his harebrained story about an escaped murderer living out at the Laymon house. Why would a convicted killer go there in the first place? How would he even have known about it? This was just another case of Billy trying to sucker people in with another one of his wild stories.

But, just like her dad was always telling her, there's always another side to everything. Granted, the escaped killer might not be living out there . . . there might not be *anyone* out there; but what if there was? If there *was*, then, like Billy said, she would be a hero. And if nothing else, *that* would certainly slap Johnny into place, the fact that she was counted in, and he wasn't.

"So . . . uh, what are you gonna do?" Sarah asked. She swung off her bike, laid it gently down on the ground, and came over to sit on the steps beside Billy.

"Can you get out tonight and meet me behind my house around . . . say, eleven o'clock?" Billy asked. His voice had a conspiratorial hush, and she didn't like the way he wouldn't look her straight in the eyes.

Gnawing at her lip again, Sarah nodded. "It might take some doing, but I think I can manage it."

"Good," Billy said. "Wear dark clothes, and bring a flashlight. And make sure no one sees you leave!"

-2-

The night was filled with the chirping sound of crickets. Overhead, stars sprinkled the sky like powder. A crescent moon rode low in the east.

The ground beneath Sarah's feet was lost in darkness as she cut across the neighbors' yards between her house and Billy's. She didn't dare chance walking down the road where a neighbor driving by or glancing out a window might see her. She was wearing a thin jacket against the chill, and, in her hand, she gripped a flashlight she had taken from the glove compartment of her father's truck. Summertall grass whisked at her legs, soaking her cuffs with dew and sending a thin chill up to her knees.

All of the lights were off at Billy's house as she approached it from the side. A faint current of fear raced through her as she looked at the silent, dark house. Her parents had stayed up a little later than usual, and she knew she was at least fifteen minutes late.

. . . What if Billy had given up on her coming and had already gone back to bed?

. . . Or what if he decided to go out to the Laymon house alone?

. . . Or—most likely, she thought—what if he was off hiding somewhere in the trees behind the house, just waiting to give her a scare, pretending he was the escaped convict?

"Psst! Hey, Billy!" she whispered, looking back and forth along the length of the dark house. "You out here?"

The sound of the crickets went on undisturbed. From where she stood, she knew, if she turned around and looked, she might be able to see the Laymon house through the trees. If she turned around, she thought, maybe she *would* see a light in the cellar window.

But as much as she wanted to look, she just couldn't bring herself to do it. If this *was* one of Billy's half-assed jokes, he might already be up there at the old house, shining a light in the window to lure her. And now that she thought about it, maybe her rotten little brother Johnny was in on this, too. Come to think of it, he had gone off to bed tonight without too much complaint; none of his usual fussing about wanting to stay up to watch Leno or Letterman.

"Damn you, Billy! Where the hell are you?" she muttered, stamping her foot angrily on the ground.

"Huh? What's the matter?"

Coming so suddenly out of the darkness, his voice sounded less than an inch from her ear. Stifling a scream, Sarah wheeled around just as Billy walked toward her from around the side of the house.

"You scared the crap out of me!" Sarah said, her voice ragged from her repressed shout.

"Keep it down," Billy whispered, signaling her with a wave of his hand and then pointing upward. "My parents' bedroom window is right there."

Without another word, Billy turned and started walking across the backyard, keeping to the shadows of the trees cast by the thin moonlight. Within seconds he was lost from sight; but before following him, Sarah had to stand there a while longer, waiting for her heart to stop racing.

"You coming or not?" Billy whispered from the shadows. She could hear him but not see him.

For an instant, Sarah considered saying, *No, I'm not coming! This whole thing is ridiculous!*

Any way she looked at it, she was foolish to be following Billy to the Laymon house—or *anywhere*—at night. If the killer really was there, then they would both be in serious trouble. If he wasn't there . . . well, just to deny Billy the satisfaction of scaring her, she was determined to steel her nerves against the inevitable surprise he probably had planned for her. Knowing Billy and his practical jokes, he probably had one heck of a surprise planned for her. Finally deciding that she had come too far now to turn back, she took off in the direction Billy had taken across the yard and through the stand of trees that skirted the dirt road leading up to the Laymon house.

In the dark, she tripped and stumbled in Billy's wake as they felt more than they saw their way through the woods. Wind rustled the leaves overhead, the sound—as much as Sarah tried to resist the idea—reminding her of dry, hard bones clicking together.

"Did you see the light out there again tonight?" she

asked at one point when he stooped to let her catch up with him.

In the dark, she saw him nod. "Yeah, just before I snuck out of the house I saw it blink on and off a couple of times. Sorta like he was signaling someone or something." He peered through the darkness to where he could see the looming black bulk of the house through the night-dark puffs of foliage. The abandoned house was no more than a dark smudge against the black stain of the night.

"You're just trying to scare me, that's all," Sarah said, angry at herself for letting her teeth chatter as she said it.

"We'll see. We'll see," Billy replied. "Come on. I figure we can swing around and come up on the back of the house. That'll probably be the safest, and we can avoid the swampy ground."

They fought their way through a thicket of briars that bordered the swamp. Both of them got their feet wet, and their sneakers made soft, sucking sounds as they left the cover of the trees and crept, shoulder to shoulder, up the grass-choked slope behind the Laymon house.

Sarah's heartbeat sounded all the louder in her ears and she couldn't repress a shiver as they crouched at the crest of the hill and stared at the deserted house. She had never been this close to it, looming up against the night sky. The peaked roof glinted like metal in the moonlight, and the blank, glassless windows gaped like yawning mouths. Everything about the house was silent, dark, and dead. Her conviction that Billy was setting her up grew all the stronger.

"I figure we can try the cellar window nearest us," Billy whispered as he pointed toward the foundation steeped in shadow. "I think it was that one where I saw the light."

"Don't you know?"

Billy grunted. "It's hard to tell. All we gotta do is check."

"I don't think I want to go any closer," Sarah whispered. It surprised her that, although she usually didn't even like

Billy, she found a strong measure of reassurance just being close to him. "There's noth—"

Before she could finish, as if on cue, a light came on, illuminating the cellar window from the inside. A distorted rectangle of sickly yellow light spilled out onto the ground, showing in sharp detail the tangle of grass and weeds that grew there. The window was skimmed too thickly with dirt for either Billy or Sarah to see inside clearly.

"We've *got* to get closer," Billy whispered harshly, sounding almost desperate. He shifted forward, preparing to scramble the rest of the way to the house, but he was checked by Sarah's hand tugging at his sleeve.

"You don't have to," she said, keeping her voice low, forcing herself not to let it quaver. "I know *exactly* what you're up to!" Turning toward the house, she rose to her feet and, cupping her hands to her mouth, shouted, "Okay, Johnny—and Curt, too, no doubt! You can come out now! Game's over!"

Suddenly, from behind, something hit her in the back of her knees. Her legs gave out, and she twisted as she went down, crumpling to the ground. Billy's weight came down hard on her stomach and chest. The air was forced out of her lungs in a single burning gasp. She wanted to scream and shout, but all she could manage was a breathless moan.

"What . . . are you crazy?" Billy hissed, his mouth close to her ear.

Sarah struggled to get out from under him, but he worked his arms and legs to keep her pinned flat to the ground.

"You—just—get—off—me—right—now!" she sputtered. Try as she might, she couldn't dislodge him by wiggling.

"You'd just better hope to Christ he didn't hear you," Billy said. He had his head cocked up and was anxiously scanning the house. The dull glow from the window washed over his face, giving it a ghostly cast.

"You didn't fool me for a minute," Sarah managed to say now that Billy had shifted his weight a little, and she was able to draw a breath. "I know darn well that my brother's in there, shining that light just so you can try to scare me. Well, Billy Lewis—it just won't work this time!"

"Ahh, but I think it *will* work," a man's voice said, coming to her like a boom of thunder from the surrounding darkness. Sarah had no idea of the direction. "I think you will be scared . . . a whole lot!"

Still unable to see, Sarah listened as steady footsteps approached them from the side of the house. When she looked up, she saw the huge bulk of a man towering above her. He was almost featureless, no more than an inky silhouette against the starry sky as he stood there with his hands on his hips, looking down at her.

"I want to thank you for bringing her to me, Billy-boy," the man said, followed by a hollow laugh. "Now, be a good boy 'n help me get her into the cellar. That way, you'll get to see what I like to do with people like her."

-3-

Sarah couldn't believe any of this was happening, but it was real; she knew that when she felt the man's strong hands slide under her and heave her up onto his shoulder as if she were a sack of grain. Her throat closed off; nothing more than a feeble squeak would come out as he carried her around to the back of the house. With each step, his shoulder bumped into her like a soft fist in the stomach, taking her breath away. Pinpricks of light spun like comets in front of her eyes. The night song of crickets roared like the ocean in her ears.

Before heading down the cellar stairs, the man paused and turned to look back at Billy. "So, Billy-boy, this is your lucky night tonight, huh?" he said. Down inside the cellar, Sarah could see the faint light of a single candle washing the floor and walls like a coat of cheap paint.

Billy said nothing; he simply followed when the man started down into the dank cellar.

A choking, musty smell tinged with something else, possibly the smell of sewage, nearly gagged Sarah as her mind, like a transmission that had lost all of its teeth, kept whining, louder and louder. No matter how fast it revved, it just wouldn't catch and hold onto anything.

Who is this man? And what is he doing? she wondered frantically. If the point was to scare me—all right, he and Billy have done it. The joke's over and done! They'll be letting me go home now, I'll bet. But then why is he taking me down into the cellar.

These and other questions roared through her mind like a funnel of wind. There were no answers, but Sarah knew it was going beyond a joke; she knew she was in serious trouble when the man unslung her from his shoulder and dropped her roughly to the floor. She hit hard; a jolt of pain as bright as lightning ran up her spine. Her chest ached, and she still couldn't get enough air into her lungs to scream as she watched the man stand back from her, fold his arms across his chest, and smile menacingly. The faint sounds of other footsteps on the cellar steps made her look around, but her heart sank when she saw Billy.

"Just what—are you trying—trying to do?" Sarah said between gasps. Her question was directed not at the man but to Billy, who was lurking in the dark corner by the cellar door. It was the man, however, who answered her.

"We're not *trying* to do anything, missy," he said. His voice was low, booming like a cannon in the distance. "We've already done it, haven't we, Billy-boy? You see, Billy-boy, here, has been helping me out the last few days . . . ever since I blew into town after breaking out."

"You mean. . . ."

Knowing what the rest of her question was, the man chuckled and nodded. "You must've read about me in the paper, or maybe seen me on the TV."

Sarah's eyes felt as though they were bulging six inches

out of her face as she stared up at Billy. He was still cringing in the shadowed corner. The feeble light of the candle
made his shadow dance and weave. She couldn't begin to
accept that Billy had set her up for something like this,
and her blood ran cold when she began to imagine what
might happen next.

"You didn't happen to bring that food you promised,
did you, Billy-boy?" the man asked. He never once took
his eyes off Sarah as he spoke.

"No, I . . . uh, I couldn't bring it when I was coming out
with her," he replied, his voice sounding thin and weak. "I
mean, she would've suspected something was up."

"I been gettin' kinda hungry, Billy-boy," the man replied. He shot Billy a quick, angry glance, then turned back
to Sarah, who was pressing herself back against the stone
wall.

"Then again," the man went on, "I always was a business
before pleasure kind of guy." With that, he reached behind
his back and quickly snapped his hand out in front of him.
Held tightly in his right hand was a thick-bladed knife, at
least six inches long. The blade glinted wickedly in the
candlelight as the man turned it back and forth admiringly.

"You . . . ? What are . . . you?" Sarah sputtered. Her
mind was nothing more than a black blur as she stared,
horrified, at the gleaming knife.

This is going too far! her mind screamed. *This man isn't
kidding! This isn't just some practical joke. He means it!*

"Billy . . . ?" she said, no more than a whimper.

"Billy-boy ain't gonna help you, little girl," the man said.
He took one slow step toward her, the knife weaving in
front of him in a lazy figure-eight. "Oh, no! Billy-boy's the
one who brought you up to me. He's the one who said he
wouldn't mind if I carved you up. Ain't that right, Billy-
boy?"

Wide-eyed and trembling, Billy nodded in agreement.

"You see, little girl?" the man said. "Billy-boy found me

living out here, 'n—well, my first recourse was to waste him. I couldn't very well have him blabbing about the escaped convict living up here in this deserted house, now, could I? But before I gutted him, we started talking; 'n before long, he and I had worked out a little deal. Ain't that so, Billy-boy? He'd bring me food so I could hole up here until I figured where to go next, but what was in it for ole' Billy-boy, here? Then, just yesterday, we struck on our little deal."

"I can't believe you're doing this to me!" Sarah yelled at Billy. Hot tears stung her eyes, but she forced herself not to cry. Her chest still felt like it was bound with steel bands, but the horror of her situation now fueled her anger.

"Oh, Billy-boy ain't gonna do a thing . . .'cept watch," the man said, taking another step closer. "When we got to talking about what I was put in jail for, he told me he'd just like to see what it looks like when someone dies. You see—that was our deal. He'd bring someone out here, and I'd put on a little show for him. Right, Billy-boy?"

Before Billy could respond, the man laughed a deep, watery laugh and came closer to Sarah, leaning down so the knife blade was level with her face, no more than three inches away.

Sarah's hands and feet scrambled wildly on the floor, but the solid granite blocks prevented any further retreat. It took several seconds for her brain to register that her right hand was wrist deep in some gritty-feeling stuff, either sand or crumbled mortar; but once she realized it, she acted quickly. Grabbing as big a handful as she could, she screamed and flung it straight into the man's face.

In the split second the man staggered back in surprise, bellowing his rage as he tried to clean his eyes, Sarah coiled her legs and jumped to her feet. She was running full speed for the cellar stairs when she heard the man shout behind her. It sounded like he was right behind her, inches away.

"Stop her! Goddamn yah! Stop her!"

In a blur, Sarah saw Billy jump out to intercept her. She felt his hand snag the loose flap of her jacket. With a shriek, she turned and swung out, hard, at his hand, but he held on tightly as she lurched forward, dragging him toward the cellar stairway.

"Don't let her get away, you son-of-a-bitch!" the man yelled.

Sarah could hear him stumbling toward her, and all she could think about was that gleaming knife blade slicing cleanly through her throat. Panic whined in her ears like a power drill and fueled her efforts to get away. She was just starting to think all was lost, she wasn't going to make it, when she heard the harsh whisper of tearing cloth. The backward pulling pressure on her jacket suddenly released, and she stumbled forward. Her shins slammed into the bottom step, but she quickly regained her balance and leaped up the stairs and out into the night. Not waiting to see how close her pursuers were, she clenched her fists into tight balls and ran straight down the dirt road toward home, screaming as loud as she could.

-4-

"You let her get away, Billy-boy!" the man snarled as he watched Sarah disappear up the stairs and into the night. His eyes were still stinging from the grit she had thrown at him, and he repeatedly wiped at them with his shirt sleeve. He moved over to where Billy was standing by the cellar wall.

"I . . . I'm sorry," Billy said, helplessly dangling in one hand the piece he had torn from Sarah's jacket.

"Do you realize how much of a problem this is going to cause me?"

Billy wasn't able to keep eye contact with the man, so he looked down at his scuffed, dew-soaked sneakers. "I really am sorry," he muttered. "She was moving too fast."

The man walked over to the cellar doorway. With a sudden sinking feeling in his gut, Billy realized that he had positioned himself between him and the stairs.

"This blows it all for me as far as *I* can see, Billy-boy," the man hissed. "We had a nice set-up here, and now, sure as shit, she's gonna have the cops down on this place in a matter of minutes."

Billy took a shuddering breath, wishing he could edge his way over to the doorway that led to freedom.

"I'm sorry I didn't get that food to you," Billy said. His voice was so tightly constricted, he sounded more like a girl.

"Ohh, I wouldn't worry 'bout that," the man said.

Billy couldn't help but notice that the man hadn't put his knife away. Shouldn't he start gathering his few things so he can make good his escape before the police show up? he wondered.

"I'm just sorry you didn't get to see what you came for," the man said. He shook his head sadly. The anger had left his voice; his words now were as smooth as honey. Coming up close to Billy, he placed his hand gently, almost lovingly on Billy's shoulder. Then the fingertips started to dig into his shoulder . . . at first, just enough to hurt, then unrelentingly.

" 'Course, we can take care of that before I have to take off, now can't we, Billy-boy?"

With that, he snagged Billy by the wrist and roughly jerked him around so his arm was pinned up between his shoulder blades. A jolt of pain ran up to the base of Billy's skull, but that was nothing compared to the fear that suddenly surged through his body when he fully realized what was about to happen.

"Now, I know you could see this a damn-site better if we had a mirror or something," the man whispered. His breath was hot on the back of Billy's neck. From the corner of his eyes, Billy saw the six-inch blade come from around in front of him.

"But we'll just have to make do, won't we? Now, lookey

here, Billy-boy," the man hissed. "This is what you came for . . . this is what it looks like."

With a quick, tearing slice, the blade tore through Billy's shirt and drove into his stomach. Surprisingly, Billy felt no pain at first, just numbed shock as he watched the man's clenched fist push the knife against the rubbery resistance of his stomach muscles. Blood gushed out of the wound and over the man's hand, and then—at last—Billy's brain registered the pain, silver splinters that exploded through his body.

When Billy's legs started to tremble and give way beneath him, the man jerked him roughly back up. The knife was buried to the hilt in Billy's stomach as the man tugged on it, opening the wound even wider. Guts spilled onto the cellar floor, uncoiling like heavy, wet ropes.

"Now don't go passin' out on me, Billy-boy," the man rasped close to his ear. "I don't have much time, and you've *gotta* see what you came here to see."

—for Dick Laymon

The Sources of the Nile

"Why are you tormenting me like this?" Marianne Wilcox asked. I looked at her, cringing beside me in the soft darkness of my car, her pale, blue eyes illuminated by the faint glow of a distant streetlight. I couldn't deny the almost overpowering swell of emotion I felt for her at that moment. I wanted to take her right then—that instant! I knew that much, but I couldn't—not yet . . . no, not quite yet. . . .

"Look, I don't like having to be the one to break it to you like this," I replied. "Honest! I mean—Christ, I just met you for the first time—what? Last week. At the Henderson's party. You hardly even know me, and I'd understand if you didn't trust me. But sooner or later, you would have learned the truth."

"Maybe I . . . maybe I didn't *want* to learn the truth. Not really," she said. Her chest hitched. Her eyes glistened as tears formed, threatening to spill. "Maybe I just wanted a— wanted a. . . . Oh, Christ! I don't know what I wanted!"

She beat her small fists on the padded dashboard once,

then heaved a deep sigh. Blinking her eyes rapidly, she turned away from me and looked out the side window. We were parked at the far end of the parking lot at the Holiday Inn in Portland, Maine, back where the streetlights didn't reach so we wouldn't be noticed. Minutes ago, we had watched Ronald Wilcox—Marianne's husband—walk into the motel arm in arm with another woman. This wasn't the first time—nor was it the first "other" woman.

"Look, I'm just telling you this because—well, I've known your husband for quite some time—through mutual friends, you know—and frankly, I like you."

I was struggling hard to keep my voice as soft and sympathetic as possible. Women fall apart when you talk to them like that.

"Something like this hurts me too, you know? But after meeting you, I felt a—I don't know, an obligation, I guess, to let you know that your husband was having an affair." I nodded toward the motel entrance. "Now you've seen that for yourself. As painful as it is, you asked me to bring you here. I . . . I didn't want to do this to you."

"I—I know that," she said, glancing at me for a moment.

My heart started beating faster when I saw tears filling her eyes. They would spill any second now. A cold, tight tingling filled my belly, and I can't deny that my erection hardened as I shifted closer to her and placed one hand gently on her shoulder.

"I don't like seeing you upset like this," I said. "I'm not enjoying this at all, but you have to remember that *I'm* not the one who hurt you. It's him—" I jacked my thumb toward the motel entrance. After a moment of silence, I leaned forward and withdrew a manila envelope from underneath the car seat. "If you'd like, I could show you those photographs I—"

"*No!*"

Her lower lip trembled as she looked at me. Her eyes were two luminous, watery globes. Just seeing the wash of tears building up in her eyes twisted my heart.

I tried to push aside the feelings I had. I wanted to ignore the powerful urge to take her in my arms and caress her. But I couldn't deny that there was an element of spite in what I was doing. I wanted her to see *everything!* I wanted her to *imagine* it all. And if she couldn't imagine it, then I was ready to *show* it to her—every instance, every second of her husband's infidelity. I wanted to—I *needed* to push her until she broke because after she broke—ahh, sweetness!—after she broke, she would be mine!

"No . . . I don't . . . don't need to see your—your fucking photographs." Her voice was tight, constricted. "I don't want them!"

"No. Of course not," I whispered, tossing the envelope onto the dashboard and inching closer to her. "I understand completely."

My heart throbbed painfully in my throat when I saw a single, crystal tear spill from the corner of her eye and run down her cheek. It slid in a slow, sinuous, glimmering line that paused for a tantalizing moment on the edge of her chin and then, pushed by the gathering flood of more tears, ran down her neck and inside her coat collar.

Gone. . . .

Lost . . . !

"Please . . . please don't cry," I whispered, knowing that it was a lie as I brought my face closer to hers, feeling the heat of my breath rebound from her smooth, white skin. My gaze was fastened on the flow of tears as they coursed from her eyes, streaking in silvery lines down both sides of her face. Her shoulders hunched inward as if she wanted to collapse, to disappear inside herself.

"But I . . . I—"

Her voice choked off as she stared at me, her glazed eyes wide—two lustrous blue orbs swimming in the pristine, salty wash of tears. My hand trembled as I traced the tracks of her tears from her chin up to her cheek. Heated rushes of emotion filled me when I raised my moistened finger up to the light and studied the teardrop suspended

125

from the tip. It shimmered like a diamond in the darkness. Slowly, savoring every delicious instant, I brought it to my lips. The taste was sweet, salty. The instant I swallowed it, I knew that I loved her as deeply as I have ever loved any woman.

"I—I wish I could have spared you all of this pain," I whispered heatedly as I lowered my face and kissed her lightly on the cheek. The briny taste of her tears exploded in my mouth. The effect was as overpowering as a narcotic. I could no longer hold back. Like a snake, my tongue darted between my lips and, flickering, trembling, caressed her skin. I grew dizzy, intoxicated by the hot, sweet taste of her.

She moaned softly, barely at the edge of hearing. My arm went around her, pulling her closer—comforting, reassuring, like a good friend.

"Go on," I whispered. "If you have to cry, let it out. Let it all out."

I could barely hear my own voice above the roaring rush in my ears as my face brushed against hers. Ever so lightly, my tongue worked its way up from her chin, over the soft contours of her cheek until—at last—I reached her eyes. My hand grasped the back of her head and turned her to face me. I pulled her tightly against my greedy, eager mouth. Moving my head from side to side, I kissed and lapped her lower eyelids, savoring the salty explosions of taste on my tongue. With slow, sensuous flicks, I licked the bulging circles of her closed eyes.

"No . . . please!" she whispered, squirming on the seat. "Not now . . . not here!"

But I knew she didn't mean it. Her body was molded against me like a tight-fitting glove. The passion consuming me filled her, too. I could feel it thrumming through her body like an electric current. Her hands worked around behind my back, clutching, clinging desperately to my coat. She shook with repressed sobs as I moved back and forth, kissing the corners of each eye. While I was busy drinking the flood of tears from one eye, my hand wiped the other until it was slick with moisture. Then I slipped my fingers into my mouth and sucked them clean, not wanting to miss a single, delicious drop.

"Please. . . ." she moaned, and I knew what she was asking for now. This wasn't denial. It was passion, raw and desperate.

Puckering my lips, I feverishly kissed first one eye, then the other. She gasped for breath as the tears streamed down her face, but my lips were there, eager to savor every pearly drop. Oceans of passions raged in my head. My heart pounded heavily in my chest as I pressed myself against her, crushing her back against the seat of my car. The world outside disappeared in my blind, swirling passion. For a flashing instant, I knew she sensed danger, but it was already too late. I possessed the source of her tears, the twin rivers that fed the raging of my desire.

"White Nile"—I said before kissing her left eye—"and Blue Nile," before I kissed the other. Then I clamped my mouth over her right eye and, pressing my tongue hard against her eyelid, began to suck—at first gently, then more insistently. I'm sure she thought, at first, anyway, that I was lost in sexual desire. But I knew she would never truly understand.

None of them ever did.

I applied more pressure, sucking harder and harder until her eyeball began to bulge against her closed lid.

Then she began to struggle, making soft, whimpering sounds, but here in the shadowed corner of the parking lot, I knew no one was going to notice us. As my sucking grew stronger, more insistent, she screamed, sharp and shrill. I covered her mouth with one hand and pulled her back, staring into her eyes, glistening and wide with fear.

"Please . . . don't," she said, her voice no more than a wet rasp. Her throat was raw from the tortured emotions and the tears she had already shed . . . tears I had so hungrily tasted. Her fists beat helplessly against my back as I leaned forward and began to suck all the harder. Her resistance was futile. She was mine now. I had her!

Her low, bubbling scream continued to rise, stifled by my hand. I was afraid I would have to kill her before I could finish. It usually happened that way, no matter how hard I try to keep them quiet. Marianne thrashed with frantic resistance, but I wouldn't stop—I *couldn't* stop. I had to have her! I had to lay claim to the source of my passion! I was only dimly aware of her long, agonized screech as my cheeks, working like strong bellows, pulled harder and harder until—at last—something warm, round, and jellied popped into my mouth. I nibbled on it until I felt the resilient tube of her optic nerve between my teeth and then bit down hard, severing it. A warm, salty gush of tears and blood—an exquisite combination—flooded my throat. I moaned softly with satisfaction, dizzy with ecstasy as I reached down to the car floor for the jar I kept under the seat for nights such as this. I found it and spun open the top, and then spit her eyeball into it. Then I went back to draining the empty socket dry of tears and blood. Precious drops dribbled from the corners of my mouth, but I eagerly wiped them up with my fingertips.

"I . . . love . . . you," I gasped.

With one hand still covering her mouth, I sat back and wiped my chin on the back of my wrist. Then, moaning softly, I shifted over to her left eye and clamped the suction of my mouth over it. She struggled again, harder now, writhing and screaming in pain and terror; but my weight held her fast as I dragged the tip of my tongue hard against her closed eyelid, lapping up more of her tears.

Finally, unable to hold back any longer, I sucked her other eyeball out of its socket and spit it into the jar. For long, dizzying minutes, I sat there, pressing her down against the seat while my tongue tenderly probed both empty holes for the last traces of her tears. After a while, her body shivered and then lay still as her heart quietly slowed ... slowed ... and then stopped. My rapid-fire pulse eventually lessened, as well.

But all of this happened nearly four weeks ago, and I can feel it coming on me again. I have to go out again tonight. That urge, that demanding, thirsty need is raging strong inside me, like the irresistible pull of the ocean's salty tide.

—for J. N. Williamson

Silver Rings

Her hands felt small and cold in mine as we walked the rain-slick streets of Quebec City that night. We were going back to her apartment, and I remember thinking as we walked along about the time when I was a young boy, and I had caught a barn swallow in the hayloft of my Uncle Walt's barn. Trying desperately to escape, the bird had fluttered frantically against the dusty, cobweb-draped window. The instant I closed my hands around it, its fragility had terrified me. Yes, terrified. Small and warm, it lay trembling in my cupped hands, its heart beating so fast I couldn't possibly count the rate. I was afraid that even the slightest bit of pressure would crush the life out of it.

But her hands had none of the heat and pulsing life of that small bird. Her hands were cold, and she shivered as she leaned hard against me and gripped my hand almost desperately with both of hers. She laced her fingers between mine and cupped my hand just as I had once cupped that terrified bird.

I also remember the cold sting of the silver rings she

wore. Four on each hand. I'll never forget that she wore so many silver rings. It's significant, I think.

We followed a winding pathway through back alleys and along uneven cobblestone streets that seemed strangely deserted. The bright lights of downtown Quebec City fell behind us, looking oddly distant, like the dim memory of another city, another world. The night's chilled dampness drifted in off the St. Lawrence River and closed around us, seeming to bond us, making my flesh hers, and hers mine.

You have to understand one thing right from the start. That's what I had been looking for all evening. Someone who wanted to bond her flesh to mine, so to speak, to "make the beast with two backs," as Shakespeare so elegantly phrased it. It was Spring Break, and rather than spend two straight days driving from Maine to Fort Lauderdale, a few friends and I had decided to head up to Quebec for a week of hell-raising. I'd left my buddies back at some strip joint and had ended up—I'm not even sure how—in a small cafe. That's where I met her. I can't recall that the place even had a name. I didn't notice a sign outside, either when I was going in or, later, when we walked out together.

She spoke very little English. She never even told me her name. But I remember that her voice had an oddly accented lilt to it. When I try to recall it now, though, I can only approximate it in my memory. It remains tantalizingly distant, but the teasing memory of it fills me with a deep, nameless yearning. Even when she spoke French, her words sounded strangely accented, as though she were speaking a form of French from a different part of the country or from a different era.

But it wasn't just her touch or the sound of her voice that enchanted me. It was her eyes. Moist and dark, they glistened in the candlelight like rain-slick streets shimmering with silver rivers of shifting light and darkness. They were eyes you could get lost in. Eyes that I *did* get lost in even though I kept reminding myself not to feel too much.

Bedbugs

I certainly wasn't looking to fall in love that night.

Far from it.

I was looking for one thing and, although we never mentioned it directly, I assumed that she knew exactly what I wanted, and that she was looking for the same thing that night.

We first touched hands there at the table in the cafe. I commented on her silver rings and then boldly reached across the table to grasp her hands and inspect them. Her fingers were long and slim, delicately tapered like white church candles. I won't say that the first touch was electric. It was somehow more than that. Deeper. Stronger. It was like taking tentative hold of a high-powered electric cable and knowing that a charge of electricity strong enough to kill you in an instant was rippling dangerously just below the surface. Even then, in the cafe, I noticed that her hands were cold, but I could also sense some indescribable power in them.

Turning her hands over in mine, I made a show of studying each of her rings although, in fact, none of them were anything more than plain, ordinary silver bands. But they flashed in the orange glow of candlelight, reflecting bright spikes of light that dazzled my eyes. I jokingly asked if the ring on her left ring finger was her wedding band. I wasn't sure if she even understood me until she replied in mixed English and French that they were *all* wedding bands, and that if she accumulated many more husbands, she would soon be wearing silver rings on her toes. I'm fairly certain that the word she used meant *husbands*. My French wasn't even as good as her English. She might have meant *lovers*.

Of course, that's what I wanted to be—her lover, at least for the night. One of the friends I was with had taught me what he said was the only sentence in French I needed to know: *Voulez vous coucher avec moi?* But that night in the cafe, I never had to say it. Simply touching her hands, I experienced a level of unspoken communication unlike

133

anything I had ever experienced before or after. I was certain that she felt it, too.

After sharing a bottle of red wine, I paid the tab, and we got up to go. As we walked toward the door, I remember how the other patrons of the cafe—mostly scruffy, elderly men gathered in small groups around dark tables—watched us, shifting their eyes and hardly moving their heads. I could feel their envy and their barely disguised desire, wishing they were young enough and handsome enough to be walking out of there that night with someone like her. I experienced a thrill of pride and grew almost dizzy with elation as we stepped outside into the rain. The cafe door swung softly shut behind us.

She directed me along dark, narrow streets. By the time we found where she lived, I was disoriented enough to have no idea what part of the city we were in. Smiling and squeezing my hand tightly, and still leaning her head against my shoulder, she directed me up the narrow, darkened stairway to the second-floor landing. After fishing a key from her purse, she unlocked the door and opened it to allow me to enter the apartment first.

Her place was small and dark, but what I could see of it in the dim light looked quaint, charming in an old-fashioned way. I remember, as soon as I entered, that I was almost overwhelmed by a curious aroma. It was an exotic mixture of scented wax candles, cloves and other spices, and something else . . . something much more elusive that stirred memories buried deep within me.

I stood there in the doorway, waiting for her to turn on a light. Without a word, she walked into the kitchen. Suddenly a sputtering tongue of flame flared out of the darkness as she struck a wooden match and touched it to the wick of a candle on the small kitchen table. The blossoming orange glow filled the small apartment like a sliver of sunrise.

She indicated for me to sit down at the table. Still without speaking, she took down from the cupboard a bottle of red wine and two crystal cut glasses. I remember noticing how the wine looked thick, almost black in the candlelight as she poured it. Taking my glass, I held it aloft, waited a moment, and then said, "To the night's beauty," as we clinked glasses and then drank.

She smiled before she sipped her wine although I wasn't entirely sure that she understood what I had said.

Taking the candle from the kitchen table in one hand and my hand in the other, she led me into the living room. Distorted shadows shifted at odd angles across the walls as she placed the candle on the coffee table. Side by side, pressing close, we sat down on the couch, our knees brushing against each other as we drank and talked. The wine went to my head quickly. I can remember little of our conversation in broken English and halting French, but I was caught up simply listening to the gentle lilt of her voice. The living room window overlooking the city. The dark slash of the St. Lawrence beyond was dimpled with rain that refracted and distorted the candlelight into dizzying patterns.

She smiled and laughed at our attempts to communicate. For some reason, her laughter—light and airy—reminded me again of the barn swallow I had caught so long ago when I was a boy. I wanted to tell her about this but didn't know enough French to explain the significance, if there was any. I'm not sure I know the significance even now, much less then.

Before long, though, we had no need of talk. She laughed at something I said in French and then reached out to touch my face. Her hand was warm now as she caressed my cheek and then ran her fingertips lightly down my neck and inside the collar of my shirt. We embraced and kissed tenderly. There was none of the passionate, almost desperate groping I usually felt when I'm with women. When she took my hand and led me into her bedroom, I remember wondering if it was a cultural thing—that French girls knew more subtle ways of making

135

love—or if it was something else . . . something deeper.

The wine was still buzzing in my brain, whispering like a soft breeze blowing through a field and pressing down the grass like a huge, invisible hand. Her touch and the feel of her skin against mine sent thrilling shivers of ecstasy through me. Lulled by the soft patter of rain on the window, we folded together and were transported to places that I, at least, had never been to before.

I awoke to see the dawn streaking the sky with pale fingers of gray clouds. It was Sunday morning. The rain had passed, and I could sense, even without going outside, the bracing freshness of the day. I rolled over in bed to look at her, to admire her beauty, to kiss and touch her again, but was surprised to see that she was not there. Thinking that she might have gotten up early, possibly to go to church, I swung out of bed. Wrapping the bed sheet around me like a toga, I walked into the kitchen.

"Hello . . . *Bon jour*," I called out softly, but there was no reply.

I realized that I was alone in the apartment. I had no idea why she had left or where she might have gone. Even if she had left me a note on the table, which she hadn't, it no doubt would have been in French, and I wouldn't have understood it.

Shivering, I went back to the bedroom and hurriedly dressed. Then I walked back into the kitchen and sat down at the kitchen table, absorbing the subtle, quiet atmosphere. For several minutes, as the apartment steadily brightened with strengthening daylight, I wondered what to do next. I was hungry, and I considered helping myself to the contents of her refrigerator. Maybe I'd even prepare breakfast for both of us in case she returned soon. But I gave up that idea because it struck me as something a crass American might do, and I wanted to preserve the other-worldly delicacy of her place.

After a while, I got up and walked into the living room, looked around, then sat down on the couch. A small clock on a table by the window filled the room with a faint *tick-ticking*. In the gray light of dawn, the apartment looked much older than it had appeared by candlelight the night before. I sniffed the air but could catch no lingering trace of the spicy, scented aromas of last night. All I could smell was an antique mustiness that reminded me of how my grandmother's house used to smell. I noticed a thin patina of dust coating everything like gray shadows. The candle she had lit the night before was still on the coffee table. It had burned out, but even the glass candle holder and the waterfall of melted wax appeared to be coated with a fine layer of dust.

I sat there on the couch and watched as the sun rose over the shimmering river, all the while wondering when she would return and if I should sit here and wait for her. I was fairly certain that my friends wouldn't be worried about me. They would no doubt assume that I had "gotten lucky" and would show up back at the hotel sometime before noon, which was when we planned to head back to the States.

I waited in silence for more than an hour, listening to the steadily ticking clock measure out the time. Finally, feeling increasingly impatient and worried about my friends who would be departing today, I left. I considered leaving a note with my name, address, and phone number in the States, but then thought better of it. After making sure that her place was in order, I carefully locked the door behind me and descended the narrow stairs to the street below.

I wandered aimlessly around the sleepily stirring streets for more than two hours before I finally found a landmark I recognized. The air was filled with the pealing of church bells and the distant sound of passing traffic. I got back to the hotel sometime around ten o'clock.

I say I got back to the hotel, but already I was feeling as though a part of me wasn't there. I felt as though I—or at least some small but vital part of me—was still back at her apartment, wrapped in a bed sheet and sitting on the couch in the dusty, pre-dawn silence, waiting for her to return.

I never even knew her name.

It was Sunday morning, and my friends wanted to get back to the Orono campus before evening so we wouldn't be too burned out when classes resumed on Monday morning, but I told my friends that I didn't want to leave yet. Since it was my car we had come in, they couldn't very well argue the point. When they asked why I didn't want to leave yet, I didn't answer them.

How could I?

What would I say?

They tried to guess, and before long they started teasing me about having fallen in love. I denied it, of course, and as God is my witness, it was true, I *wasn't* in love . . . at least, not the kind of love I had experienced up to that point in my life.

It was something else.

Something deeper.

Something more involving and more consuming and, I knew even then, more dangerous. After lunch, I told my friends that I was going out for a walk. They wanted to come along with me, but I refused, saying simply that I had to meet someone. When they asked when would I be back, I didn't reply.

In the harsh glare of the midday sun, the streets didn't look at all like they had the night before. I walked around in circles, looking for some familiar landmark, but the rain-swept streets we had walked last night now seemed like an illusion, the faintest memory of a dream that was rapidly dissolving into airy nothingness.

Somehow—miraculously—toward evening I found the cafe. Just as I remembered, there was no sign above the door, but I knew I'd found the right place. I entered the shallow darkness of the room, pausing a moment to let my eyes adjust before seating myself at one of the tables. A few patrons sat in silence at nearby tables. I couldn't help but cringe when I sensed them watching me askance with slitted eyes.

The waitress came over and took my order for a cup of tea. I hadn't eaten anything all day, but the hollow feeling of hunger in my stomach was somehow pleasurable. I sat in silence, staring across the room to the table where, just last night, she and I had sat and talked. But the table, even the cafe itself, seemed altered, somehow. It appeared to be much smaller and danker than I remembered. The only words that come close to expressing how I felt was that everything seemed somehow more *solid*, more *real* than it had the night before.

I shivered, and when the waitress arrived with my tea, I merely nodded my thanks before taking a sip. The warmth did nothing to dispel the aching feelings I had of loss and loneliness, of being caught up in something that I couldn't understand, that I wasn't capable of understanding. I drank my tea in silence. When I was finished, I considered paying my tab and leaving, but I had noticed one particular group of men seated at a table in the far corner. I was positive that they were the same patrons who had been there last night, so I got up and walked over to them.

All of them regarded me with thinly veiled mistrust when I smiled and said, "*Bon jour*." It was obvious that they had already pegged me as an American, and it was just as obvious that they didn't like me simply on principle.

But I had to try, so in English that was sprinkled with the smattering of French I remembered from high school, I asked if any of them knew the girl with silver rings. I didn't know the French word for *rings*, but I kept making a motion, circling one of my fingers with another.

I was positive that they understood me, but none of them said anything except for what I knew was French for *Sorry, but I don't speak English*.

"The girl," I kept saying impatiently. "*La femme* with

rings . . . with silver rings," and I circled my finger again and again.

They all smiled tightly and shook their heads, grunting as they glanced at each other.

"I was here with her . . . Last night . . . I know some of you saw me with her."

I was starting to get mad and couldn't help but let it show, but they continued simply to stare at me and mumble to each other while shaking their heads. Finally, one of them nodded and said *oui*. He made it clear that he recognized me and had seen me here the night before; but when I pressed him, asking if he knew where I could find *la femme*, he merely shook his head sadly and said something that ended with the word *solo*.

"What do you mean, *solo*?" I practically shouted. "I wasn't here alone! Yes, I came here alone, but I left with her. I left with *la femme* with silver rings. Last night. Around midnight. I know you saw me! All of you saw me! So please—tell me. Who is she? Where can I find her?"

They exchanged meaningful glances again and shook their heads as though confused. Several of them shifted their glazes away from me, apparently not wanting to look at me except from the corners of their eyes.

"I wasn't here alone! I went home with her! With the girl—the *femme* with the silver rings!"

It was useless.

They either didn't understand me or chose not to understand me. Finally, in frustration, I turned away. I paid my tab and walked out into the purple evening. I considered trying to retrace our steps from last night and find her apartment again, but I knew that I couldn't. I had no idea even in which direction to start. I began to wonder if she hadn't purposely doubled back a few times and taken me in a roundabout way to her place in order to confuse me.

What I couldn't figure out was, why?

She had wanted me. Perhaps not as much as I had

wanted her, but she had been willing, and she had made passionate yet tender love to me in the warm and inviting darkness of her bedroom. I could still feel the cool sting of her silver rings on my naked back as we made love.

This all happened more than twenty years ago. I'm married, now, and have a nice home, a job I can tolerate, a wife I love, and three terrific children. Still, though, once or twice a year, I drive up to Quebec. Alone. I walk the streets after dark, and I'm particularly happy if it starts to rain like it did that night so long ago. But I can no longer even find the old cafe without a sign. I watch the rivers of light reflecting off the rain-slick streets, and my mind fills with the memory of how her hands had felt as they held mine. And I often think about that barn swallow I had caught and held when I was a boy.

I can almost accept the idea that the men in the cafe may have been right—that I never left with her that night. It happened so long ago, I have myself more than half-convinced that it might never have happened, that I never met her, that I never went with her to her room, that it had all been a dream, and that she was nothing more than a figment of my imagination . . . or maybe something else. . . .

But there are some things I do know.

I know that she still holds something of mine in her hands. I can feel the cold sting of her silver rings as she cradles my heart like a small, trembling bird in her cupped hands. And I know that, even now, with the slightest bit of pressure, she could still my heart's warm, steady beating. I also know that, someday, she will quiet my heart, and maybe then I will see her again.

—for C. R.

Colt .24

-1-

Diary entry one: approximately 10:00 A.M. on Valentine's Day—How ironic.

If you've ever spent any time in academic circles, you've no doubt heard the expression "Publish or perish." Simply put, it means that if you want to keep your teaching position, at least at any decent college or university, you've got to publish occasionally in academic journals. I suppose this is to prove that you've been doing important research, but it also contributes to the prestige of your school.

My experience, at least in the English Department here at the University of Southern Maine, is that the more obscure and unread the periodical, the more prestige is involved. I mean, if you don't write novels or stories that pretend to "art"—well, then, you can kiss your chances for tenure good-bye.

Bob Howard, a good friend of mine here, did just that. He wrote and sold dozens of stories and two novels; but because his work was viewed by the tenure committee as "commercial" fiction, he didn't keep his job. After he was denied tenure a few years back, he and I used to joke over drinks about how he had published and perished!

I have reason to be cynical. The doctor who talked with me last night might have some fancier, more clinical terms for it, but I'm tempted to translate his conclusions about me to something a little simpler: let's try—*crazy as a shithouse rat!*

That's crazy, all right.

But keep reading.

I'm putting all of this down as fast as I can because I know I don't have much time. I'm fighting the English teacher in me who wants to go back and revise, hone this sucker until it's perfect, but if I'm right . . . Oh, Jesus! If I'm right! . . .

Okay, I'll try to start at the start. Oops. Got a little redundant there. Sorry. Anyway, as I've always told my students, every story has a beginning, a middle, and an end. Life, I've found, unfortunately doesn't always play out that way. Oh, sure—the beginning's at birth and the end's at death—it's filling up the middle part that can be such a bitch!

I don't know if this whole damned thing started when I first saw Rose McAllister . . . ah, Rosie! She was sitting in the front row on the first day of my 8:00 A.M. *Introduction to English Literature* class last fall. It might have been then that everything started, but I've got to be honest here. I mean, at this point, it may not matter at all . . . or it may be *all* that matters. I think I'll be dead . . . and *really* in Hell within . . . possibly less than four hours.

One thing I do know is, when I first saw Rosie, I didn't think, right off the bat—*Goddamn! I want to have an affair with her!*

That sounds so delicate—"have an affair." I wanted to, sure; but that was after a while, once I got to know her. Once we started, though, we slept together whenever we could . . . which wasn't often, you see, because of Sally, my wife. Ah, my dear, departed wife!

I guess if I were really looking for the beginning to this whole damned mess, I'd have to say it was when we started our study of Marlowe's *Doctor Faustus*. You know—your classic "deal with the Devil" story. I didn't mention too much of this to the police shrink because—well, if you tell someone like that that you struck a deal with the Devil, that you sold him your soul—yes, I signed the agreement with my own blood—you've got to expect him to send you up to the rubber room on P-6. If I'm wrong about all of this, I don't want to spend the rest of my life writing letters home with a Crayola.

Wait a minute—I'm getting ahead of myself, but as I said, I don't have much time left . . . at least I don't think so.

Okay, so sometime around the middle of the semester, Rosie and I began to "sleep together." Another delicate expression because we did very little *sleeping*. We got whatever we could, whenever we could—in my office, usually, or—once or twice—in a motel room, once in my car in the faculty parking lot outside Bailey Hall. Whenever and wherever!

The first mistake we made was being seen at *The Roma*, a fancy restaurant in Portland. Hank and Mary Crenshaw saw us. *The Roma!* As an English teacher, I can appreciate the irony of that, too. Sally and I celebrated our wedding anniversary there every year. Being seen there on a Friday night, with a college sophomore ("young enough to be your daughter," Sally took no end of pleasure repeating), by your wife's close (not *best*, but *close*) friend is downright stupid. I still cringe whenever I imagine the glee there must have been in Mary's voice when she told Sally.

Hell, I'll admit it. Why not? I *never* liked Mary, and I know she never liked me. Hank—he was all right, but I always made a point of telling Sally that Mary was *her* friend, not *mine*.

So, Sally found out.

Okay, so plenty of married men (and women) get caught cheating. Sometimes the couple can cope and work it out. Sometimes, they can't. We couldn't. I should say, Sally couldn't. She set her lawyer—good ole' Walter Altschuler—on me faster than a greyhound on a rabbit. That guy would've had my gonads if they hadn't been attached. You must have heard the joke about the lawyer and the shark . . . well, never mind for now.

But I'm not the kind of guy who takes this kind of stuff—from anyone! And, in an ironic sort of way, I guess I'm getting paid back for that, too. Bottom line? If someone sics a lawyer on me, I'm gonna bite back!

Now here's where it starts getting a little weird.

If I told the police shrink all of this, he'd bounce me up to P-6 for sure. I mentioned that we'd been reading *Faustus* in class, and that's when I decided to do a bit of . . . let's call it *research*. I dug through the library and found what was supposedly a magician's handbook. Not sleight of hand kind of stuff. I mean what's called a *grimoire*. And I decided to try my hand at necromancy.

Look, I'm not crazy. I went into it more than half-skeptical. And I want to state for the record here that I . . .

-2-

Diary entry two: two hours later. Time's running out, for sure!

Sorry for the interruption. I'm back now after wasting two hours with the police shrink again. He ran me over the story again, but I held up pretty well, I think. At least I didn't tell him what I'm going to write about now. But like I said earlier, I want to have this all recorded so if I'm right . . . Oh, Jesus. . . . If I'm right. . . .

Where was I? Oh, yeah—necromancy . . . a deal with the Devil. Yes—yes—yes! A deal that was signed in blood!

The library on the Gorham campus had an ancient *gri-*

moire. Well, actually it was a facsimile of one, published a few years ago by the University of Nebraska Press. It's amazing what gets published these days. I wonder if the person who edited the text got tenure. I can't recall his name just now. Anyway, I looked up the spell for summoning the Devil and . . . now I know you're going to think I'm crazy, but you have to believe me on this; I did it!

I actually summoned the Devil!

Go ahead. Laugh. What does it matter? I'll be dead—and in Hell—soon enough!

I have a key to Bailey Hall, so I came back to my office late one night—sometime after eleven o'clock, so I could be ready by midnight. After making sure my office door was locked, I set to work. Pushing back the cheap rug I had by my desk (to keep the rollers of my chair from squeaking), I drew a pentagram on the floor using a black Magic Marker. I placed a black candle—boy, were *they* hard to find!—at each of the five points of the star and lit them. Then, taking the black leather-bound book, I began to recite the Latin incantations backwards.

Actually, I was surprised that it worked. My Latin was so rusty, I was afraid I'd mispronounce something and end up summoning a talking toadstool or something.

But it worked—it *actually* worked! In a puff of sulfurous fumes, "Old Scratch" himself appeared.

Looking around, he said dryly, "Well, at least you're not another damned politician!" Then, getting right down to business, he said, "Okay, what do you want in exchange for your soul?"

With his golden, cat-slit eyes burning into me, I had the feeling that he already knew—more clearly than I did at the moment. Anyway, I told him. I said that I wanted an absolutely foolproof way of killing my wife and not getting caught. I told him I was willing to sign over my soul to him—*yes! Dear God! In blood!*—if I could just get rid of Sally and be absolutely certain that I wouldn't get caught.

I'm writing this, you must have realized by now, in a jail cell. I'm the prime suspect for my wife's murder, but I haven't been charged with anything—not yet, anyway. I have a perfect alibi, you see, and there are these other problems, too. If you read the *Portland Press Herald* tomorrow, you'll find out whether or not I got away with it.

What the Devil did was hand me a revolver. He called it a Colt .24—a "specially modified" Colt .45—and a box of nice, shiny, brass-jacketed bullets. He told me all I had to do, after I signed the agreement, of course, was load the gun and aim it at Sally—he suggested I sneak home sometime before lunch someday—pull the trigger, throw the gun away, and make sure I went to work as usual the next day. If I did exactly what he said, he guaranteed that I'd go free.

Sounded okay to me. At this point, I was well past analyzing the situation rationally. I'd been under a lot of pressure, you understand. My wife's lawyer had stuck the end nozzle of his vacuum cleaner into my wallet and was sucking up the bucks. I'd been without sleep for nearly two days and nights running—I was getting so worked up about Sally.

And the capper was Rosie. As soon as she found out that Sally knew about us, she cooled off. Cooled off? Hell— she froze! Maybe—I hate to think it!—but maybe it was just the chance of getting caught that had added to her excitement, her sense of adventure, her passion. Once we got caught, the thrill was gone for her. Could she really have been that shallow? I can't help but think so.

I wasn't completely convinced this whole business with the Devil had really worked, because . . . well, I must've fallen asleep after he pricked my finger so I could sign the contract in blood, gave me the gun, and disappeared. I woke up, stiff-necked and hurting all over, flat on my back on my office floor, mere minutes before my eight o'clock class. The candles had burned down and extinguished themselves, but in the pale wash of morning light, I could see the pentagram on the floor, so I knew I hadn't dreamed everything. Also, I had the gun . . . a Colt .24!

I'd been asleep—I don't know how long. Not more than four hours, I guessed. I remembered that I had started the summoning right at midnight, like I was supposed to, but I had no idea how long it took. At least for me, old Satan didn't waste any time with dizzying visions of power and glory, or processions of spirits. Nothing, really—just a straightforward business transaction. Thinking about it later, it could just as easily have been Old Man Olsen, the night janitor in Bailey Hall.

But like I said, I did have the gun, and—damned if I didn't decide then and there that I'd use it. I had my two morning classes first, but right after them, I planned to go straight home, point the gun at Sally, and pull the trigger—even if, then and there, it blew her through the picture window. I'd reached my limit, which, I'd like to think, is considerably beyond what most men can stand.

So I did it.

After my second class—between classes I had time to drag the rug back and gulp down some coffee and an Egg McMuffin—I took off for home. As luck would have it, Sally was—Damn! Here they come again!

-3-

Diary entry three: more than an hour wasted—not much time left!

This time the police came in again, not the doctor. Talk about being confused! I know they want to charge me with the shooting, but my alibi is rock solid, and the funniest thing about it all is, they can't get my gun to fire. So they asked me some more about my relationship with Sally, using the excuse that maybe it'll give them a lead on who else might have wanted to kill her. They said I might be released soon.

Hah!

As if that's going to make a difference!

Where was I . . . Oh, yeah—Sally was home, and her lawyer, old Walter-baby, was there with her. I sort of wondered why he was there at my house. Maybe nosing around gave him better ideas how to skin me alive. Or maybe getting into Sally's pants was part of his fee. You know what they say about lawyers. . . . But I couldn't afford to leave a witness, so whatever he was doing there, that was just his tough luck. One more lawyer in Hell wasn't going to make a difference, anyway.

I walked in from the kitchen and nodded a greeting to the two of them, sitting there on the couch. I mumbled something about having forgotten some test papers as I put my briefcase down on the telephone table, opened it, and took out the gun. Shielding it from their sight with the opened top of the briefcase, I brought the gun up, took careful aim at Walter, and squeezed the trigger. Not once—not twice—three times! Good number, three. A literature professor knows all about the significance of the number three.

But nothing happened!

Although I'd been careful to slip a bullet into each chamber before I left the office, there was no sound, no kick in my hand. There wasn't even much of a *click*. The only thing I could think was that maybe the Colt .24 wouldn't work for someone who wasn't part of the deal, so I pointed it at Sally and fired off three more shots . . . with the same result.

Nothing.

I do remember—or thinking I remember—smelling a faint aroma of spent gunpowder, but I chalked that up to wishful thinking.

Sally and Walter never even noticed what I was doing. They just kept right on talking, ignoring me as I gawked at them; so I slipped the gun back into my briefcase, shut it, and went up to the bedroom, shuffling around a bit up there while I tried to figure out what to do. I'd been packing my things to move out, but Sally—against old Walter-baby's advice, I might add—had said it was all right for me to stay in the house until the apartment I'd rented in Gorham opened up the first of the month. Thanks, Sal. As it turned out, that was the last favor she ever did for me—except a day later, when she dropped dead!

So anyway, I came back downstairs, got my briefcase, and headed back to campus with Sally and Walter still sitting on the couch just as alive as they could be. I was feeling like I'd been ripped off, set up or something by the Devil. As far as I was concerned, his Colt .24 was a dud.

Back at my office, about two o'clock, I checked the Colt. I was surprised as all hell to see six spent shells in the chamber—no bullets, just empty shells. I wondered if I could have been so dumb as to load the gun with empty bullets. I didn't think so—I'd used the ones the Devil had given me. I shook the empties out into my hand and then tossed them into the trash. Then I slipped six fresh ones from the Devil's box into the chamber. I was getting a bit scared that maybe I had hallucinated the whole thing, but that still didn't explain where I had gotten the Colt.

I'm sure by then I wasn't thinking too clearly, lack of sleep and tension and all, so I decided to test the gun right there in my office. I sighted along the barrel at one of the pictures on my wall—one of my favorites, actually: a silk-screened advertisement for the Dartmouth Christmas Revels—and gently squeezed the trigger.

Nothing happened.

Turning quickly, I aimed at my doctoral dissertation on the top shelf of my bookcase. Now *there* was something else to hate! I pulled the trigger a second time.

Nothing.

Again, aiming at the pencil sharpener beside the door, I squeezed the trigger.

Nada!

Pointing at the wall, I snapped off three more shots, and still nothing happened. I caught the same faint, tingling aroma of gun smoke I'd smelled back at the house, but I guessed it had to be my imagination. But you should *never* guess when you're dealing with the Devil . . . not once you've signed your soul over to him.

Again, though—and this time it struck me as *really* weird—when I opened the chamber, all six bullets were spent. Maybe they were dummies or something, I thought—not really made of lead . . . or maybe *I* was the dummy being led!

I picked up the box of shells, now missing twelve bullets, and after inspecting them very carefully—they sure as hell seemed real enough to me—I reloaded, placed the gun on my desk, and tipped my chair back to think about all of this.

I'd been had, I knew that much!

Rage and stark fear tossed around inside me. I had signed my soul over to the Devil for *what?* For a revolver that didn't even work!

Anyway, like I hinted at, the next day, by noon, Sally was dead.

A neighbor of ours, Mrs. Benton, said she heard three gunshots from our house. Afraid there was a robbery or something going on, she stayed in her house and, clutching her living room curtains to hide herself, peeked out at our house while she called the Gorham police. They came right away and found Sally dead of three gunshot wounds to the head. I've heard it wasn't a very pretty sight.

I, of course, didn't know this at the time. I was just returning to my office on the Gorham campus after conducting my graduate seminar on Elizabethan Drama in Portland. I hadn't gone home the night before and had slept—again—on my office floor, so I wasn't in the best of moods.

I spent the next hour or so at my desk, working through a stack of papers and pondering everything that had happened lately when there came a hard knocking at my door.

Almost without thinking, I scooped the Colt into my

desk drawer but—foolishly—didn't slide the drawer completely shut before I answered the door. Two uniformed police officers entered, politely shook my hand, and then informed me that my wife had been murdered . . . shot to death with a Colt .45.

I fell apart, wondering which I felt more intensely—shock or relief. *I* hadn't been able to do it, but *someone* had! The policemen waited patiently for me to gain control of myself, then explained that they wanted to know where I had been in the past three hours. Apparently Mrs. Benton had seen fit to fill them in on our domestic problems. They also asked if I owned a Colt .45.

If this whole story has a tragic mistake—for me, at least—it was not following the Devil's advice precisely to the letter. That's how he gets you, you know. I should have realized that. I'd read enough plays and stories about him. He had told me that if I aimed the gun at Sally, pulled the trigger, and then threw the gun away, I'd never get caught.

But there was the gun! Right there in my desk drawer! I hadn't thrown the damned thing away!

If you had asked me then, I suppose I would have said the gun was worthless. What difference would it make if I kept it or tossed it? That wasn't the gun that had killed Sally. I had to accept that I hadn't summoned the Devil that night. I had fallen asleep and, worn out by exhaustion and stress, I'd had a vivid nightmare. I hadn't really summoned the Devil. Stuff like that just didn't happen!

I gave the cops my alibi, and it was solid. When the shots rang out, I was in class on the Portland campus, lecturing on Shakespeare's use of horse imagery in *Richard II*, more than twenty miles from my house. You can't go against the testimony of a roomful of graduate students.

About then, one of the policemen came around behind the desk and noticed the Colt in the desk drawer. Eyeing me suspiciously, he asked if he could take a look at the gun. Sure, I said. There was no denying now that I owned a gun like the one used to kill my wife. After he inspected it for a moment, he put it back on my desk.

"Look," I said, a bit nervously as I hefted the gun. "This sucker doesn't even work. It's a model or something." I opened the chamber, showed them that the gun was loaded, clicked it shut, and then with a flourish, pressed the barrel to my temple.

"See?" I said, and before either of them could react, I pulled the trigger three times in quick succession. "Nothing happens. It's a fake."

They were unnerved by this display, but it seemed to satisfy them. After thanking me for my cooperation, they left, saying that they'd wait in the hallway until I felt ready to come with them to the morgue to make a positive identification of my wife.

But they had no more than swung the office door shut behind them when shots rang out in my office! I was just turning to pick up my coat when the center of the Dartmouth Christmas Revels poster blew away. I turned and stared, horrified, as the top row of books on my bookcase suddenly jumped. I saw a large, black, smoking hole in the spine of my dissertation. Then the pencil sharpener by the door exploded into a twisted mess of metal. Three more shots removed pieces of wallboard and wood from my office wall.

With the sound of the six shots still ringing in my ears, I saw the two policemen burst back into the room, their revolvers drawn and ready.

"I thought that gun didn't work!" one of them shouted as he stood braced in the doorway, his revolver aiming right at me. His expression shifted to one of confusion when he saw that the Colt wasn't in my hand. It was lying on the desk, exactly where I had put it before they left.

"Man, I don't know what the hell's going on here," the other cop said, "but you'd better come down to the station until we can check out the ballistics to make sure."

I was in a state of near shock. I'm positive my face had turned chalk white; I could feel an icy numbness, rushing across my cheeks and down the back of my neck as a terrible realization began to sink in.

It had been almost—no! It had been *exactly* twenty-four hours ago that I had aimed and shot the Colt in my office!

Six times!

And nothing had happened . . . until now!

And this bit about the ballistics test had cracked my nerve. I mean, at this point I was already convinced that it hadn't been coincidence. The shots I had banged off twenty-four hours earlier must have been what did in Sally. I knew, if the cops checked it out, the ballistics would be a match.

And what about good ole' Walter Altschuler? Was he dead, too? With a sickening rush, I remembered what the Devil had said the night he gave me this gun . . . He said it was a Colt *.24!* A special, modified Colt .45!

I tried to force myself to remain calm, but damn my soul to hell! I had pointed the gun to my head as a *beau geste* and pulled the trigger three times! I remembered—now—that when I had done that, I had smelled a trace of spent gunpowder . . . as I had yesterday morning at my house when I had targeted Sally and Walter, and then again in my office.

Just then Joan Oliver, the department secretary, poked her head into my office—cautiously, I might add—to inform the policemen that they had a phone call. I started to lose it, knowing exactly what it would be. I lost control entirely when, seconds later, one of them came back and informed me that Walter Altschuler, my wife's attorney, had been found shot to death in his car in the Casco Bank parking lot in downtown Portland. He had three .45 caliber bullet wounds in his head.

I'd been had!

I'd signed the damned contract—in blood! I had the damned gun. It had worked! And the Devil had cheated me but good in the bargain.

So while I've been sitting here in the jail cell, after coming to my senses this morning, I asked for some paper and a pen. If I'm wrong, I don't want to tell my story and be committed to the psycho ward. I still might be able to get away with this.

But if I'm right . . . if I'm right, it's been just about twenty-four hours, and I want to have all of this written down to leave a permanent record before those bullets from Hell blow my hea—

—for Charles Waugh
Marty Greenberg
and Isaac Asimov

Bird in the House

Ohh, it's so nice of you to bring me lunch today. You can probably imagine how trying the last few weeks have been. Terrible, simply terrible! But I thank the Good Lord, our troubles are finally over. That is, I suppose, except for my own. But I have to tell you, I was more than willing to risk what I did. And I—I'm prepared to suffer the consequences, you can be sure of that.

Yes, I'd like some iced tea. It looks like you brewed it just this morning. Why, it's the perfect thing to go with a tuna fish sandwich, don't you think? Mmmm, that looks good. Thank you very much.

Now, where was I? How shall I begin?

I suppose you'll want me to tell you everything. How it all came about. Fine. I can do that. I just need a moment to compose myself.

There. . . . Well. . . . As you can probably imagine, losing my only daughter the way I did was horrible, absolutely horrible!

I—I'm sorry. . . . I still—It pains me so to speak of it.

Oh, no . . . no. I've been holding up quite well, thank you. I think I'd do even better if Elizabeth would come to visit me. But I have to be strong, just as I have to talk about it all to someone. I suppose it's the only way I'll ever truly begin to put it all behind me. Don't you agree?

Then again, sometimes I wonder if I ever will be able to forget what happened. The loss of a child . . . your own child is—is. . . . Well, the good Lord knows, no parent should ever survive their own children. It's not the natural order of things. The fact that Nancy was the only child Edward—God rest his soul—and I ever had only makes it all the more painful, all the more bitter.

But as you know, I still have my granddaughter, Elizabeth, thank the Good Lord. Whenever I think about my little granddaughter's face, I recall how it reflects her mother's beauty so much. I know that my daughter's earthly beauty will live on in her daughter. Elizabeth is my treasure now.

Oh, no—no! She's staying with friends until I get better. I don't think her father will want her to move in with him. He's too busy now with his own life. Got a whole new family out there in California. No, she'll stay close to me as long as there's breath left in this body, I'll see to that.

Oh, how nice. Sweet-and-sour pickles. Could you please open the jar for me? You can see that I wouldn't be able to do it. God, you'd think they'd make these jars so someone my age could open them, wouldn't you? Umm, thank you.

Now, where was I? Oh, yes, I was going to tell you how it all started. I remember that it was the third day of June. I wrote it down on my calendar because I knew, even at the time, that it was a significant day. Nancy and I had just finished washing the supper dishes when we heard Elizabeth start screaming in the living room. We rushed in and saw immediately what the problem was.

A tiny sparrow had gotten into the house somehow. The poor, frightened creature was fluttering frantically around the room, beating itself against the picture window. Just a pitiful sight!

Yes, I'm afraid Nancy might have hurt one of its wings when she caught it and threw it out the front door.

If only I had been quick enough to catch it, then perhaps things would have happened in a more natural way, the way they're supposed to happen, with me dying before my only child. But I'm not nearly as spry as I used to be.

No . . . no—I'll be fine. Just give me a minute.

There, that's better. Now, what was I saying? Oh, yes—about the bird in the house. Well, from that day on, I lived in constant dread for my Nancy. A bird in the house is always an omen of imminent death, don't you know. My mother told me that years ago, and I have yet to see or hear of an instance where it didn't prove true.

Unfortunately, this turned out to be no exception because, well, less than a week later, my dear daughter Nancy died . . . of a cerebral hemorrhage, the doctor told me, from banging her head when she fell down the stairs.

Just think of it!

A young, healthy woman . . . taken away just like that!

Look at that. An old lady like me, and I can't even snap my fingers.

Surely, the Good Lord works in mysterious ways, but I knew from that very day when we caught that bird in our house, one of us was living on borrowed time here on earth. Because Nancy had been the one to catch the poor creature, I naturally assumed it was she. What I didn't realize was how much jeopardy it would also present to Elizabeth. I thank the Good Lord that I did what I did to protect her.

The days immediately before and following my daughter's funeral were horrible, absolutely horrible! I had a lot of friends who helped me through that difficult time. I certainly wouldn't have made it without them. As it was, I was almost too preoccupied with my own grief to realize the serious danger Elizabeth was in.

I think it was—well, it must have been her curiosity that got the better of her. What youngster isn't curious, right? You see, just as my mother taught me, and my grandmother before taught her, I did all of the appropriate things around the house during the days right after Nancy died. I made sure they carried her out of the house headfirst. I kept the cat outside for a week. I covered all the mirrors with white cloth and turned all the paintings toward the wall. I even placed the kitchen chair Nancy used to sit in upside down so her spirit wouldn't appear in its accustomed place. I did everything that is appropriate.

But you know how it is. Leave it to the young ones who haven't got a lick of the respect they should have in the face of Death to be curious. And just like they say about curiosity and the cat, Elizabeth's curiosity almost killed her.

Oh, dear! Now look. You've spilled my iced tea. Be a dear and wipe that up with a napkin, will you?

There. Oh, thank you for pouring me some more. Now where was I?

Oh, yes—I was telling you about the mirror, wasn't I? You see, I remember that day as clearly as I remember the day that poor bird flew into our living room. I was in the front hallway, standing up on a chair to drape a piece of white cloth over the mirror when Elizabeth came in and asked me what I was doing.

"Well," says I, "You can see that I'm covering the mirror."

She then asked me why and, realizing that she might not be aware of the proper things to do in a situation such as this, I explained it to her. Of course, being only nine years old, I'm sure she didn't fully understand; but I told her how mirrors aren't what they appear to be. I explained how what people call their "reflection" is, in fact, something much more than that. It's actually the physical embodiment of your eternal soul.

Bedbugs

You don't believe me? Well, you certainly don't sleep in a room with a mirror in it, do you?

My goodness, you do? Aren't you afraid that your soul, drifting around while you're asleep, will be trapped inside the glass?

Well, in any event, I explained to my granddaughter the dangers of looking into a mirror in a house where someone has recently passed on. I know I certainly would never chance it. I didn't look into one for at least two weeks after Edward died. My hair must have been a fright. I suppose I looked as terrible then as I must look now.

Oh, thank you. You're too kind.

But no—I'd never dared to look into a mirror in a house where somebody has died recently. Why, I'd be terrified of who I might see, standing there, looking over my left shoulder!

And so, you see, I explained to Elizabeth the dangers of catching even a glimpse of the soul of the departed, which could be trapped in the glass and—well, as I said, what child isn't curious, hmm? I'm sure she took the very next opportunity when I wasn't looking to uncover the glass and look into it.

Why?

Well, I suspect because she probably wanted to see if her mother was in there, don't you?

This was the day after her mother died, for Lord's sake! You can imagine how distraught my granddaughter was at the time. We both were! Even now, I hear that she spends most of her time in her bedroom, not seeing or talking to anybody.

Of course, wounds like this take time to heal . . . if they ever do. The Good Lord knows I still miss my Edward. Why, sometimes late at night, even here, I could swear he's lying there beside me in bed. Sometimes, you know, I can even hear him *breathing!*

So I suppose it's understandable that Elizabeth would

want to look into the mirror, if only to see if what I said could possibly be true.

How did I find out about it?

Oh, that was simple. That very next afternoon, the day before the funeral, as I was walking through the entryway to go upstairs to change, I noticed that the white cloth I had used to cover the mirror had fallen to the floor. When I bent down to pick it up, I—well, I happened to see something.

No, not on the floor. . . .

In the mirror!

Bright afternoon sunlight was pouring in through the front door window; but in the mirror, I saw a dark blot, as if the sun had disappeared, and a hazy shadow was being cast across the floor.

Heavens, yes, I was *terrified!*

I turned and looked at the door but saw nothing there at all. Just God's pure sunlight streaming through the window and reflecting off the wooden floor. But when I looked into the mirror again, I saw that the shadow had thickened. It had taken on depth. I swear to you, it was so *real* looking . . . as if a huge puddle of black ink had splashed across the wooden floor. And even as I stared at it in the mirror, I saw it deepen and spread until it covered nearly the whole front entryway. And then I—saw. . . .

I saw. . . .

No, no—I'll be all right. Just give me a sip of my tea.

There, that's much better.

No, I'm fine. I honestly feel as though I have to talk to someone about it. You're so kind to sit here and listen to me. I know that I can trust you to understand.

So anyway, I just stood there, staring as the stain rippled across the floor, and then it began to take on a distinctive shape.

It didn't take me long to realize what I was looking at.

It was the silhouettes of two people.

Not one. Two!

And I knew in an instant who those two people were!

Yes, you're absolutely right! They were the shadows of my daughter, Nancy, and her daughter, Elizabeth. They were invisible except for their shadows, standing side by side in the entryway. I watched, absolutely terrified, unable even to breathe as their shadow hands slowly rose and extended toward each other.

My gracious, yes! I nearly fainted! They were just about to touch, to clasp hands when I—well, it wasn't me. It was the Good Lord who gave me the strength to act. I was barely aware of what I was doing as I clenched my fist and smashed the mirror.

"No!" I screamed. "You can't have her! She's mine now!"

Glass exploded everywhere, and my hand—well, you can see the bandages. My hand was cut quite severely.

No, thank Heavens, the artery wasn't cut. The doctor here tells me that the stitches will simply dissolve, and he'll take the bandages off in a few weeks.

Well, yes—of course it's a bit difficult to do anything. But let me finish telling you what happened.

The instant I broke the mirror and screamed, I heard another scream that truly frightened me. It was as if . . . as if someone in the house was dying. To tell you the truth, it sounded like the echo of the scream Nancy had made when she fell down the stairs and banged her head so hard on the floor.

It was terrible! Frightened me half to death. I was absolutely terrified about what I had done—about the consequences of breaking a mirror—when I looked around and saw Elizabeth. She was in the living room, sitting up on the couch and staring at me, her eyes wide open. Her face was ghostly pale.

"Gramma," she said, her voice high-pitched, almost a wailing sound. "What on earth—? Look! You're hurt! Your hand is bleeding!"

I was numbed to the pain, probably close to being in

shock. It felt almost as if I wasn't even inside my own body as I looked down at the large drops of blood that were falling to the floor and splashing onto the shattered glass around my feet.

"Are you all right, dear?" I asked her.

Even at the time, I remember thinking how odd and shaky my voice must sound.

"Of course I'm all right," Elizabeth replied.

I remember how badly her voice trembled, too.

"I was just taking a nap here on the couch," she said.

Poor thing. She wasn't even the slightest bit aware of the mortal danger from which I had just rescued her. I went quickly over to her and hugged her to me, unmindful of the blood dripping all over my carpet and couch.

Yes, I'm afraid the stains didn't wash out entirely, but I didn't care. I hugged my granddaughter to my breast and kissed her, too frightened to let myself believe that she was truly all right. At the time, I was too choked up with emotion to tell her what I had just done to save her life.

Oh, yes, absolutely! You bet your lucky stars I believe I saved Elizabeth's life that day! If I had waited even a few more seconds before smashing that mirror, her mother would have taken her by the hand and brought her soul to Heaven with her that very day. I would be alone now . . . all alone.

What? Oh, no. I'm not worried about that. My Heavens, no. I'm nearly eighty years old. I probably won't even live long enough to get my full seven years of bad luck for breaking the mirror. Besides, the Good Lord knows I've certainly had my share of bad luck already!

So all in all, it's been a few weeks since I arrived here, and, as I told you, I guess I'm getting by. I'm sure that, with time, Elizabeth will get over the worst of her grief, too. But you know, I just wish you people would let her come up here to visit me. I get *so* lonely sometimes, and you must understand that I wouldn't be dangerous to her. Oh, no . . . not to her!

Bedbugs

Oops! My goodness, you certainly are clumsy today. Look, you've knocked over the saltshaker.

What was your name again? Benjamin?

You seem so young to be working in a place like this. Be a darling, will you Benjamin? I can't reach that spilled salt with this straitjacket pinning my arms down.

You know, it never hurts to be too careful. Would you take a pinch of that salt and throw it over my left shoulder?

That's a nice boy.

—for Peter Crowther

Cousins' Curse

The castle was isolated from the rest of the world for at least six months out of the year, sometimes as long as eight months. In the winter, heavy snows sealed off the narrow mountain passes. In the spring, the roads either washed out or turned into knee-deep quagmires of mud from the runoff of melting snow and ice. Although in autumn the mountains looked their most beautiful, very few people ventured into them for fear of being caught in an early blizzard. In the nearby villages and farmhouses, however, other, darker reasons to avoid the castle were also whispered about. Only in the summertime did visitors of any sort arrive at the castle, and over the years—especially following the death of the mistress of the castle—the number of visitors each year could most often be tallied on one hand.

But every summer, for at least a month at a time, the three sisters—Mara, Ester, and Philipa—always came to visit. They arrived late in June or early July to escape the heat and crowded streets of Buchresti. Sometimes their father would stay with them at the castle for as long as a week, visiting with his brother-in-law and drinking with him late into the night. But for the last several years, particularly following the death of his sister, he would depart within a day or two, leaving his daughters behind.

For the first nine or ten years of his life, the young boy who lived in the castle had thoroughly relished these visits with his cousins. It was a special treat for him to have anyone to play with, even if they were girls and several years older than he. There were a few peasant boys his own age in the nearby village, but their parents would never even consider allowing their sons to play with the boy who lived in the castle. The boy wasn't sure why. His father told him that it was the peasants' natural disinclination to associate with their betters; but on one or two occasions while in town, the boy had overheard some of the strange and disturbing comments about the castle, his home, and his family.

As he entered his teen years, however, he became increasingly uncomfortable even being near his cousins. They, too, were growing up, maturing, and he couldn't help but notice the dramatic changes in their figures—the swelling of their breasts, the gradual rounding of their hips, the delicate curves of their legs and arms and necks. Oddly disturbing feelings stirred within him, making his interest wane in such childish games as "hind-'n-seek" and "one-legged beggar." He felt increasingly uncomfortable being around the cousins because so many times he'd catch himself staring at them and having secret thoughts and urges that he didn't entirely understand.

On several occasions, the boy tried to talk to his father about his concerns, but his father was a distant man, and he kept such odd hours, rising after sunset and going to bed just as dawn was breaking, that at night, when he would have an opportunity to ask about such things, the boy lost whatever courage he had built up during the day. Embarrassed and ashamed of the things he thought and felt whenever he saw or, sometimes, even thought about his cousins, he kept everything to himself, bottled up tightly inside himself, like fermenting wine. But it was a wine that was spoiling, rather than mellowing properly as it aged.

One hot July night in his fourteenth year, the boy found it particularly difficult to sleep. The sounds of crickets and night birds in the forest and field kept him awake long past midnight. Not even the slightest stirring of air moved through his opened window. The high whine of a mosquito tormented him, making him swat blindly in the darkness and curse in a childish way. He watched the slow progression of moon-cast shadows swing across the stone window casement, and he measured the passing of time with his slow, even breaths.

At some point—he wasn't sure when—he became aware of another sound intruding upon the night. It flitted lightly, like the soft whisper of silk in the darkness. Once he was aware of it, he realized that he was hearing the soft, high twitter of a woman's laughter.

His mother had died more than ten years ago, and the few female servants employed in the castle had all gone back to their homes in the village for the night, leaving as they always did well before dark. So the boy immediately deduced that the sound must have been made by one of his cousins. Thinking about the girls instantly caused a cold, hard knot to tighten in his stomach, and his male member began to stiffen. Before long, it was as hard as a rail spike. Confused and concerned by this new, tingling sensation in his groin, which he found had been occurring more and more frequently lately, he slipped one hand up underneath his sleeping gown and grasped himself, squeezing hard, hoping that the pressure would make the throbbing ache go away.

But it didn't.

It only got worse.

His ears were ringing as he arched his head forward and listened for the ripple of feminine laughter to come once again. Almost as if it had a will of its own, his hand started moving up and down in tight, choking strokes. A quivering, gushing rush, like hot pins-and-needles, filled his lower belly. His head was swimming as badly as the time two summers ago, when his father had allowed him to drink a full measure of red wine. Finally, unable to stand the pulsating sensation any longer, the boy swung his legs off the bed, stood up, and began pacing back and forth across the cool stone floor of his bedchamber. His thin nightgown whisked at his ankles like a winding sheet.

Then the high laughter came again, like birdsong, fluttering in short, sporadic bursts. It pierced his ears and drove into his brain like a javelin. The sound teased and tempted him, exciting him so much the stiffness in his groin ached even more painfully . . . yet also pleasurably.

Sucking in a deep breath and holding it, the boy tiptoed to the door of his bedchamber, swung it open, and stepped out into the pressing darkness of the corridor. In spite of the hot night air, a shiver tickled between his shoulder blades. Without a candle or torch to light his way, he was momentarily lost, but soon enough his feet, as though moving of their own volition, directed him down to the far end of the corridor toward the chamber door behind which he knew his cousins slept.

But they weren't sleeping now.

When he was halfway to their door, he heard a hissing rustle of sheets and bedclothes . . . then the fluttering ripple of laughter came again, followed by a deeper groaning that almost sounded like one of the cousins was in pain. The boy wondered if one of them had eaten green apples and was suffering from a stomachache.

His bare feet scuffed the stone floor like tiny whispers as he made his way to their chamber door. The darkness of the corridor enfolded him like soft arms, giving him a measure of security as he leaned forward and gently pressed his ear to the door, trying to determine what was going on inside that room. No words had been spoken—

none that he heard, anyway—but the laughter and low-throated groaning sound continued, rising louder now, like a gathering storm wind.

Somehow, miraculously, the boy kept himself from crying out when the door, apparently unlatched, swung open from the pressure of him leaning against it. Like a dagger blade glowing in the fire of the forge, a sliver of light lanced out at him, slicing his left eye. He jerked back, afraid that the subtle shifting of the door might have alerted his cousins to his presence, but the laughter and the other sounds continued to rise unabated. Sweat stood out like morning dew on the boy's forehead. His throat was raw with tension as he took a gentle breath and held it, still fearful of being discovered, yet consumed with curiosity to see what was going on inside that room.

After the span of several pounding heartbeats, after his eyesight had adjusted to the narrow beam of light, he dared at last to bring his eye back to the slitted opening of the door. A single candle burned on the bedstand, washing the room with a dull orange glow. At first, all the boy saw was the corner of the large bed that his cousins had shared during their stay at the castle since they were little girls. He placed his fingertips against the rough wooden door and pushed it ever so lightly, opening it just enough so he was able to see a bit farther into the room.

The sight made his heart stop cold, like a dead thing in the center of his chest. His male member throbbed even more painfully, raising its head like a proud warrior and thrusting against the restraints of his nightgown. One hand shifted down to his crotch and tightly grasped the bulge.

Two of the cousins—Philipa and Ester—were lying on the bed outside of the sheets. Both of them were stark naked. The third cousin, Mara, was naked except for a sash of white cloth that was wrapped around her waist and draped down to mid-thigh. The three girls had their arms and legs wrapped around each other in a most curious position, and all of them were moving in slow, undulating rhythms like a single beast with three heads and six arms and six legs, all intertwined. Their soft, white skin glowed like snow on a mountaintop at dawn as hands and mouths kneaded and kissed and caressed thighs, breasts, shoulders, and necks. Soft bursts of laughter rang out like the silver-clean babble of a fast-running brook.

Heated blood rushed to the boy's head, nearly making him swoon. Once again, his hand reached up underneath his nightgown. He grasped himself firmly and began to rub up and down, keeping time with the twisting undulations of the young girls. The boy had a vague sense that this was a new and interesting game his cousins were playing, and he knew instinctually that it was a game he could play, too. He had seen the animals in the barn mating. For now, though, he felt safer hiding in the darkness and just watching.

With a high trill of laughter, Philipa tugged at the white cloth wrapped around Mara's waist.

"Come on, darling," she said in a playful, teasing voice. "Don't be so shy. You must let your sisters see *your* jewel, too."

In an instant, Ester also grabbed at the white cloth and tugged at it, all the while laughing. "Yes . . . please, Mara," she said with a trilling lilt to her voice. "Please let us play with your toy, too."

"No! Not tonight!" Mara cried out, twisting away from her sisters' embraces and sitting up in bed. Her facial expression looked shocked, but her voice had an excited edge to it as well, and the boy sensed that she didn't mean at all what she was saying. He watched in rapt fascination as the white cloth was pulled away and, with a gentle push, Philipa forced Mara back onto the bed. All three of them were laughing now as each of the two girls took Mara by the ankles and spread her legs open wide.

The boy felt equally and violently repulsed and intrigued by what he saw. A wide swatch of fresh blood smeared the inside of Mara's thighs, glistening a dark, oily red inside the thin wisps of hair between Mara's legs. He watched in amazement, unable even to take a breath as Philipa and Ester both leaned forward and began to kiss and lick the blood from the insides of their sister's alabaster thighs. He was motionless except for his hand, which continued to pump vigorously up and down beneath his nightgown. When his groin flooded with a hot, tingling rush, he was suddenly fearful that if he continued to rub himself in this manner, something horrible might happen. Perhaps blood, like the blood flowing from Mara's private parts, would spurt from his male member.

But he couldn't stop himself, and he couldn't tear his eyes away from the entwined bodies of the girls and the scarlet smears of fresh blood that shimmered against Mara's pearly skin.

How alluring!

How exquisite!

How exciting!

Suddenly the boy's awareness was swept away by a dizzying rush as something hot, wet, and sticky shot out from inside his cupped hand. The feeling was so intense he almost fainted. Moaning softly, he leaned forward to catch his balance and inadvertently banged his head against the partially opened door. He was reeling with such an intense, almost giddy sensation of release and surprise that he experienced only a vague sense of alarm when he heard all three of his cousins squeal in surprise. He distantly sensed that they had all turned and were staring at him, lurking in the doorway, but he couldn't tear his horrified gaze away from the streaks of blood that smeared Philipa's and Ester's mouths and chins.

"Well now, sisters," Philipa said in a low, throaty growl. She lapped the blood on her lips with a quick flick of her tongue. "We seem to have ourselves a little audience tonight."

"Yes, a little mouse has crawled out of the walls to watch us play," said Ester laughingly.

The boy could hardly stand up, much less move. He looked numbly down at his hand, which was still reaching up underneath his nightgown. The white cloth was saturated with a thick, clammy fluid, which, he saw to his relief, at least was not blood.

He looked back at his cousins and watched in silent, motionless horror as Philipa, stark naked, rose from the bed. She raised her arms, extending them toward him as she moved quickly to the door and pulled it all the way open so fast that the boy staggered into the room.

Startled, he blinked his eyes like a mole that had been caught in the midday sun. His brain seemed to have shut off as he allowed Philipa to grasp him by the hand and lead him over to the bed. His legs moved stiffly, like stilts. He cried out softly when she pushed him roughly forward, but the sound was lost beneath another chorus of laughter from the girls as he flopped face-first onto the bed, landing between Ester and Mara. In the next instant, Philipa rolled him onto his back and leaped on top of him and he was suddenly lost in a maelstrom of white softness—of sheets and pillows and skin—as hands tugged at his nightgown, pinched his cheeks, and clawed at his neck, chest, and stomach . . . and lower.

Within seconds, his nightgown was ripped to tatters, and his slim, slightly muscled body was exposed to the probing touches of their cool fingertips and hot tongues.

"I say he has to pay," one of the cousins said teasingly. "He has to pay a penalty for spying on us."

"Yes, oh, yes!" said another voice excitedly.

"Oh, indeed he does," said a third, more commanding voice. "He must pay a very *severe* penalty!"

The boy was lost in such confusion that he could no longer distinguish the girls' voices. They all blended into a chorus of shrill, birdlike laughter, and their words were almost lost beneath the roaring sound that filled his ears like a thundering cataract.

"But what price shall we demand?" asked one.

"Oh, that's easy," said another voice. "Just like when we were young, and he insisted that we play his foolish little boy's games, perhaps now we should force him to play *our* game."

"Yes, yes! Cousin Vlad has to play our game, too!"

"No! I don't like that idea," one of them said in a sharp, commanding voice.

Through the swirl of confusion, the boy thought he recognized Mara's voice.

"I—I'm still embarrassed that he saw me like . . . like this, suffering as I am under the 'woman's curse.'"

"Oh, my dear Mara, it's no curse."

"No, not at all! Why, it's a *blessing*!"

"And if he's so interested in watching us play, perhaps, just like when we were children, he still wants to play with us."

"Yes, perhaps we should invite him to share in your 'blessing,' Mara dearest, and let him drink from your darling little fountain, too."

The boy was lost in a dizzying spiral of confusion as hands and knees prodded at him, turning him over and over in the soft twining of whispering bed sheets. The moist cushions of lips and breasts pressed and rubbed against his face, his stomach, his back, his groin. As flexing fingers grabbed his male member, he felt it begin to stiffen again, pulsating with a strange, urgent heat. Then someone took him by the back of the head and pushed his face down against the soft, yielding flesh of Mara's belly. His nose was squashed flat, making it difficult for him to breathe as the other two girls forced his head down . . . down. Not quite against his will, the boy found himself kissing a wet line along the pale skin of Mara's leg until he was lapping at the sweet saltiness in the hinge of her thighs. A damp, musky aroma tinged with the coppery sting of fresh blood filled his mouth and nostrils, making his head spin.

His male member was now as stiff as a tree branch as he pressed his face into the downy cleft between Mara's legs. He cried out a muffled protest when one of the cousins grabbed his maleness and, pulling on it hard, cried out, "Oh, but, sisters, he's not made the way we are. Perhaps this will get in the way of all of our fun!"

"Yes, what shall we do about it?"

"*I* know what to do," Mara cried out, her voice warbling with barely restrained passion.

She suddenly shifted around, pushing the boy's head violently away from her bloody crotch. Then she rolled him over onto his back and straddled him. She moved her face forward as if she were about to kiss him, but her soft lips only brushed lightly over his blood-smeared mouth before pressing against his thin neck. Her lingering kiss burned the skin below his left ear as the heated moistness of her tongue lapped the artery that throbbed heavily in his neck. The boy was swept up in such a terrifying euphoria of seduction that he thrashed his head from side to side, completely abandoned to the sensations of fiery pleasure. Then Mara's lips began to track down, her heated tongue flicking across his chest and stomach until, at last, her mouth came to rest on his throbbing member. Moaning softly, she licked him several times, then opened her mouth wide to engulf him and started sucking on him.

At first she sucked gently, the way a newborn calf will suckle, but then she took his shaft deep into her throat. Her teeth began to nibble on him, hard enough to be hurtful, but even that pain was exquisite, unlike anything he had ever experienced before.

The boy was nearly delirious with ecstasy, tossing his head back and forth and moaning deep in his throat. But Mara's gentle ministrations were interrupted by a cold, sharp sting, like the delicate cut of a razor-edged dagger as her teeth sliced into the base of his member. He was too lost in the mind-numbing swirl of pleasure to care or worry about what she might be doing to him.

"No, Mara! Don't!" one of the girls suddenly shouted.

The boy detected the fine edge of panic in her voice,

and he sensed a flurry of activity as the violent sucking and nibbling abruptly broke off. As he struggled to sit up in bed, his vision slowly cleared. He let out a high-pitched squeal of fright when he saw Mara crouching on the edge of the bed, glaring at him like a cornered, feral animal. Her eyes were wide and wild, glistening with raging blood-lust. Her lips were peeled back, exposing two sharp, curved canine teeth that stuck out like a wolf's fangs. A bright trickle of blood—his blood—ran from her lower lip, which was trembling with eager anticipation.

Mara stuck out the tip of her tongue and circled her lips, smearing the blood. Nearly numb with terror, the boy reached down to his crotch and felt the slick flow of blood on his skin.

"Please, Mara! You can't do that!" Ester yelled.

"It's not time yet!" shrieked Philipa. "He's not ready to become *completely* ours!"

"No, not yet!"

The bite on the boy's groin throbbed painfully with burning surges as a hot trickle of blood ran down between his legs and soaked into the sheets. He was nearly blinded by the whirlwind raging inside his head as he felt hands reach out and roughly push and pull him from the softness of his cousins' bed. He teetered on the edge of the mattress for an instant, and then fell. He twisted around, trying to break his fall before landing, but he hit hard and lay there stunned for a moment, facedown on the cold, stone floor.

Then, as he scrambled to his feet, a bundle of shredded clothing shot from out of nowhere and hit him like a solidly placed punch in the back of the head. He heard a deep sobbing sound and was surprised to realize that it was coming from him.

"Go!"

"Get out of here!"

"Leave us!"

"Leave us *now*!"

Shivering and naked, and stinging with embarrassment

and pain, the boy covered his wounded crotch with the remnants of his torn nightshirt and started backing away from the bed. He felt blindly behind himself with one hand until he came to the door. Then, whimpering softly, he turned and ran out into the corridor, swinging one hand wildly at the enfolding darkness, as if he could somehow tear it aside.

Miraculously, he found his way back to his own bedroom door and, sobbing wildly, burst into the room. Trembling and weak with humiliation and exhaustion, he fumbled to light the candle on his night stand. The sudden glow of yellow light hurt his eyes, but he leaned forward and stared in stark horror at his face, reflected in the polished metal mirror above his dresser.

He was horrified by what he saw, yet also strangely thrilled at the sight of the clotted blood that smeared his chin and lips. The stain looked like a fiery, dark beard. Tears streamed from his eyes, blurring his vision as he leaned over the washbasin and splashed cold water onto his face. All the while, his thin shoulders shook with unrepressed sobs.

With water streaming down his face like the sweat of passion, he straightened up and finally dared to look once again into the mirror. From deep inside his chest, there sounded a low, strangled cry as he studied his face. In the flickering glow of the single candle, his reflected features seemed oddly distorted, and for a dizzying instant, he had the sensation of standing outside of himself. In the dull oval mirror, he saw—not his own boyish face, but the face of a man not much older than his father. The man stared blankly back at him from the mirror, his unblinking eyes two black, swelling pools. Long, curved canine teeth pressed down against his lower lip, and when his reflection smiled, an ink-dark wash of blood trickled from the corner of his mouth and down his chin, staining his bare chest.

For uncountable heartbeats, the boy stood there staring, fixated by his own hypnotic stare. He wanted to cry out, but the instant his lips parted, another, stronger gush of blood flowed in twin dark streams from his mouth. A hot, tingling rush of elation warred with the cold surges of repulsion that swept through him. He was ashamed and thrilled by what he had done and by what his cousins had made him do! Against his conscious will, his member began to stiffen again, and he closed his eyes in pleasure as he began to caress himself lightly.

Uttering a low cry, he suddenly shook his head and tore his gaze away from the face reflected in the mirror and looked down at his bleeding crotch. Still trembling, he scooped up a handful of water and carefully dribbled it over his wound. Then he took a clean cloth and daubed gently at the tooth marks on the flesh at the base of his member. Tiny, ruby beads of blood rose from the wound. The pain burned strongly, pulsing through him in knife-sharp rushes. He couldn't deny or pretend not to know what Mara had been about to do to him. The thought nauseated him, but what sickened and thrilled him even more on a deep level was the certainty that, were she here right now, in his bedroom with him, he would lie back and willingly allow her do whatever she wanted to do to him, if only for the blinding instant of pure pleasure that pain would give him.

Once the bleeding stopped, he pulled on a clean night-gown, blew out the candle, and threw himself onto his own bed, curling up into a tight ball beneath the covers. As the glow of moonlight slid silently across his floor, he lay there, clutching his bed covers close to his chin, and shaking and sweating as though wracked by fever.

He sought escape from his pain and panic and confusion in sleep, but sleep didn't come for many hours, not until the first faint traces of morning light edged the eastern sky with gray.

And even after he had finally drifted off into a fitful sleep, he was haunted by distorted dreams of the exquisite pleasure and torment that his cousins might have given

him and his own uncontrollable urge to taste once again the intoxicating coppery sting of blood as it coursed over his lips and down his throat.
—for Alice Alfonsi

Speedbump

I can't go swimmin' any more, 'n all because Phil had to go and kill our son-of-a-bitch of a boss, Lester Croix. I suppose it was bound to happen, but . . . I dunno. I think Phil coulda done a better job of it. Lucky thing for Phil, though, I work with him and was the first one to notice Lester's body—his hand, anyway. That way, just as a favor to Phil, I could clean things up to make sure no one else ever found out 'bout what he done.

You prob'bly remember—it was bitchly hot for quite a stretch back there last August. What with tar bubblin' up out of the road, 'n gardens 'n yards dryin' up like tinder 'n all, I guess we shoulda expected somethin' bad to happen to that "son-of-a-bitchin'-whore." That's what me 'n Phil—'n just about everyone else in the trailer park—called Lester. Hell, he even had that nickname back before he got the job as head of maintenance in our park. Pine Haven Trailer Park. Quaint soundin' name, though, ain't it?

Anyway, I was sayin' 'bout Lester. You see, he truly was one mean son-of-a-bitch. From what I heard, he was mar-

181

ried once, but you can imagine that didn't last too long. He lived alone out there in a beat-to-shit trailer up back, in what we call the "old part" of the park. It was the first part, built back in the fifties, long b'fore Pine Haven was as big as it is now. You know, though—now that I think 'bout it, it's kinda funny . . . ironical, I guess you'd have to say, that Lester's trailer bordered on the back of the Hilton town cemetery.

None of us could believe it when Harrimon—he's the owner of Pine Haven. He don't live here, though. I guess he thinks he's just a bit too fancy to live in a place like this. Anyway, I was sayin' how none of us could believe it when Harrimon gave Lester the job instead of Phil. Just about everyone in the park—everyone who cared, at least—was surprised as shit. Phil'd been workin' park mainte-nance since . . . Oh, Christ! I'd say since '77, maybe '78. Lester hadn't even moved here when Phil started workin' the roads, cuttin' lawns 'n such, so we considered it down-right wrong that he got the job instead of Phil.

I knew there'd be trouble sooner or later, but I told Phil more times than I care to count that he should watch what he said or he'd end up losin' his job. I'd tell him maybe Lester would up 'n move back to Florida where, so I'd heard, he had a kid. I can't imagine Lester havin' a kid, but anyway—now that I think about it—maybe, plain 'n simple, Lester was askin' for it. He was always bossy as hell with both me 'n Phil, 'n only a damned suicidal fool is gonna schedule anyone to repave roads in the middle of an August heat wave.

But that's what Lester did, the son-of-a-bitch! He had me 'n Phil out there from dawn 'till dusk, pourin' 'n rollin' asphalt. Hot as fuckin' all Hell, lemme tell you! But that weren't so bad. What made me just 'bout shit my britches was when he told us to make all of them speedbumps throughout the trailer park. Key-rist!

I don't wanna bore you with ancient history here, but speedbumps have been one of them topics that generated a lot of heat with the residents of Pine Haven over the years. Not many folks was in favor of havin' 'em, but I guess enough parents with little kids pushed for 'em 'cause they figured it'd make people slow down enough so's if one of their brats was run over, he'd just be hurt, not killed. They put enough pressure on Harrimon, so he told Lester to get the job done. But it was Lester who got me 'n Phil out there, bustin' our humps in the peak of that heat wave.

I s'poze, in general, speedbumps is a good enough idea, but both me 'n Phil complained some loud when Lester showed us that he wanted one of them damned things just about every thirty feet throughout the park.

"Folks ain't gonna like that," I remember sayin' to Lester more than once. Sometimes I'd say it just 'cause I didn't want Phil to start in. Once he got goin' on speedbumps, it was just a matter of time b'fore he started upbraidin' Lester for workin' us so hard 'n for takin' his job away from him 'n such.

"Folks don't have to like 'em," Lester had replied, just about as often as I said what I said. "They just have to slow down for 'em."

"Yeah, well . . . we'll see about that!" was Phil's one 'n only comment. I have to chuckle, now that I think about what happened later.

Like I was sayin' before, though, it was a good thing for Phil that I was the first to find out he'd killed Lester. I found Lester . . . his hand, anyways—oh, must've been six, maybe seven months after we finished the roadwork. As much as everyone in the park bitched about them speedbumps bein' every Christly thirty feet, we made 'em just like we was told to. Nice 'n round so as, if you didn't come to a complete stop before goin' over 'em, you'd bottom out for sure and scrape the shit outta your muffler. Ruin your shocks, too. 'Course, there was always them folks who didn't give a rat's ass 'bout their mufflers or shocks, 'n they'd roar on over 'em, makin' sure to squeal their tires on our fresh-done asphalt. That must've been what wore the tar away eventually so's one mornin', must've been in late April, maybe early May the next year, I noticed Lester's hand, lookin' like a flattened leaf or somethin', stickin' up out of the speedbump we'd made right there at the park entrance. I just about shit myself, lemme tell you!

At first, I couldn't hardly believe what I was seein'. I mean, I thought it must've been a handprint or somethin' one of the kids left in the hot tar—you know, like we used to do, puttin' our names and footprints in fresh cement. 'Course, that mornin' when I first noticed that hand there in the road, I had no way of knowin' or suspectin' it was Lester's. Not until I got out 'n inspected it closely—then I knew it was him. The first thing I did was go right to Phil 'n ask him if he'd killed Lester and planted his body under one of them speedbumps.

You gotta understand, now, that Lester'd been missing for—well, hell—now that I think about it, it was just 'bout since me 'n Phil finished up that roadwork back last August. There'd been police 'n detectives 'n all sorts of reporters and such looking for him, but everyone came up dry. I guess after a while they just sorta gave up. It wasn't like Lester was the president or somethin'. So after a few months, once winter had come down hard on us, pretty much everyone forgot all about Lester. Most folks figured he must've lit out for Florida or some damn thing. 'Course, there was that talk about him shacking up with Sally Hampstead in Bangor, but I paid no never mind to it. None of my damned business in the first place.

So anyway, back to that mornin' when I found Lester's hand stuck there in the surface of the road. I got out of my car 'n checked it out good. That's when I noticed the ring on the third finger. It sure as shit was the same cheap, green stone that Lester always wore on his left hand. I remember it 'cause it put a fair to middlin' sized gash along my left cheek the night me 'n Lester had a bit of a fracas down to Randy's bar, in Old Town. Still got that scar, too.

See? But that's got nothin' to do with what I'm talkin' 'bout here.

I went right over to Phil's trailer 'n rousted him outta bed. His wife didn't take too kindly to that, but—Christ on a cross!—I'd just found Lester's hand, 'n I was pretty sure the rest of him was under that mound of tar, too. 'Fore long, I was damned well positive Phil had planted him there.

But you know—I was kinda surprised . . . hurt, too, that Phil wouldn't talk to me 'bout what he'd done. Wouldn't even admit to it. Even to me! Hell, we'd been best friends for as long as I could remember. In truth, I moved out to Pine Haven 'cause me 'n Phil were such good friends. That was 'bout a year after my wife left me. She ran off or some damned thing. Fuck, all I know is, I never saw her again. So it bothered me that Phil wouldn't let me in on what he'd done. I mean, Christ! I'd been the one who complained to Harrimon 'bout him not givin' the maintenance boss job to Phil. 'N it was me who told Harrimon all about what a son-of-a-bitch Lester truly was. I even started a partition or whatever the Christ you call them things to get Lester out 'n put Phil in.

But you know, after I told Phil that I'd found out what he'd done, he started actin' real funny toward me 'bout the whole thing. Got real quiet, you know? Skittish, like he was thinkin' he couldn't trust me or somethin'. Finally, figurin' just to calm him down, I told him I wasn't 'bout to breathe a word of this to anyone, 'n I expected that he wouldn't, neither. When I left his trailer, I went straight out to the maintenance shed, got the truck, 'n drove into town for a fresh load of asphalt from Bishop's Pavin'. Then I high-tailed it straight back to the park 'n neatened up that speedbump, makin damned sure I laid on that new coat of tar nice 'n thick. Then I rolled it down good 'n hard so's Lester wouldn't be pokin' out no more.

It was the least I could do for my buddy.

But then that night, 'n for the next coupla days, I started

thinkin', 'n I didn't like what I was thinkin' 'cause I started wonderin' if maybe there was somethin' more I could do for Phil. Maybe there was more I should do for him. I dunno. I prob'bly should've gone over 'n talked to him some more, gotten him to admit—at least to me—what he done. Or maybe I should've—you know—arranged for him to see someone like . . . maybe a shrink or priest or someone else he could talk to 'n not worry about bein' turned in to the cops.

What bothered me the most, though, was that the longer I thought about the whole thing, the more I became really worried for Phil. Christ on a cross! He was my best friend, 'n rightly or wrongly, he'd killed a guy! If he ever got found out . . . Shee-it! I don't know as I could handle that.

What I decided to do wasn't easy, but after a coupla weeks, once summer was in full swing 'n we'd broken ground for the swimmin' pool for the trailer park, I finally made up my mind. I had to do ab-so-fuckin'-lutely *everything* I could to protect my buddy Phil, 'n make sure he didn't get found out. So late one day, when it was just him 'n me workin' on the concrete floor of the swimmin' pool down in the deep end where it slopes down the most, I smashed Phil's head in with my shovel. He died real quick. Just dropped without a sound. I like to think he never felt a thing—just *BANGO*, 'n the lights was out for him. It took me almost until dark to finish smoothin' that last layer of cement over where I buried him in the bottom of the swimmin' pool. Once the cement was dry, 'n it got a good coupla coats of paint, 'n the pool was filled with water, nobody'd ever know Phil was down there . . . 'cept me, of course.

So now do you see why I can't go swimmin'?

I know you've told me a bunch of times that there's no swimmin' pool here in the hospital. 'N even if there was, it wouldn't be the same pool as the one back to the trailer park where I buried Phil. But my mind's been workin'

Bedbugs

kinda overtime on this one, 'n I just can't stop thinkin' that the very first time I took a dive into that pool—or any pool—I'd see Phil's pale face, lookin' up at me through the green-painted bottom. His skin'd be all wrinkly 'n such, and his left eye'd be bulgin' out of the socket like it was after I hit him. Much worse than Lester's face was after Phil nailed him with that sledge hammer. 'Least ways, that's how I think Phil did it. Have'ta ask him, I guess.

But you were tellin' me yesterday 'bout them fears called phobias, right, Doc? 'N I've been thinkin' 'bout them. Maybe that's what's wrong with me—maybe I got *hydro*-phobia, you know? Fear of water. I dunno . . . You're the shrink here; you tell me.

—for Roman Ranieri

Rubies and Pearls

At first there was pain . . . an incredible, searing pain that made every nerve in his body burn like an overheating wire. Then, with an audible *snap*, as if a cheap electrical fuse had blown inside his head, the pain stopped, and he was instantly, miraculously transported beyond the pain . . . or above it . . . floating like a rain-laden cloud, drifting through the cold, black void of the night sky.

But even then he suspected that the void was internal, deep inside his own mind.

What the shit? . . . Am I dying?

The thought was sharp and clear, but, curiously, it held no terror for him. His name was Alex St. Pierre, but throughout the state of Maine and the rest of the country, he was better known as the "Stillwater Slasher." He had seen plenty of death in his thirty-eight years. Hell, nearly twenty times, now, he had stared death straight in the eyes, watching with a dizzying mixture of glee and curiosity as, one by one, his victims—all eighteen of them—died slowly in his arms, their lifeblood seeping from the long, curved slash he had carved into their throats, running from ear to ear like a horrible grin.

He had watched, fascinated, as the blood, looking like small, rounded rubies, had beaded up all along the gaping edge of the cut, and then—all eighteen times—he had drawn his knife along the slit a second time, running the blade in deeper so the blood would gush down the young woman's throat until it looked like she was wearing a scarlet turtleneck sweater.

And then, once she was lying still, maybe not quite dead yet, but certainly beyond all resistance, the glow of life dimming in her eyes, he would unbuckle his belt, drop his pants to his ankles, and, kneeling beside her, masturbate onto the dying woman's blood-smeared throat.

"Rubies," he would always whisper tenderly, like a lover to all eighteen of them. "The drops of your blood . . . are a necklace . . . of rubies."

Then, just as he reached his climax, his mind spinning with ecstasy, all eighteen times he would lean close to the woman's senseless ear and, gasping and panting with exhilaration, whisper, "And my cum . . . is a necklace . . . of pearls."

Later, after he regained his strength, he would clean himself up and take the body down to the Stillwater River, where he'd dump it in, not caring if it sank or floated down to the Penobscot and then made it all the way to the ocean.

But after nearly four years, in which he averaged four victims a year, one for each season, the police had finally caught up with him, and for the past two months, he had been a prisoner in the Maine State Prison, awaiting trail. He was in prison, working out in the exercise yard, when a blood vessel in his brain popped, and they had to rush him under heavy guard to the emergency room at Mid-Coast Medical.

He had only a vague recollection of the timeless ambulance ride to the hospital. Once or twice he wished he could have mustered enough strength to put up a fight, maybe use this situation to try to make a break, but he knew there were at least three armed guards in the ambulance along with the medical team. Besides, he was strapped securely to the stretcher.

Nearly every sound he heard, even the caterwauling wail of the siren, seemed muffled with distance, as though his head was packed with cotton.

Only one sound had any clarity.

That was the heavy thumping deep inside his head. He hadn't realized it was his own pulse until it started to flutter and slow, keeping a herky-jerky pattern. Then, from far off in the distance, he heard a wild commotion of disembodied voices shouting frantically back and forth. He sensed a flurry of activity around him and felt his limp body being jostled about, but it didn't affect him.

Nothing affected him.

He felt curiously detached from everything when he opened his eyes and found that he was looking down from the ceiling as a platoon of doctors and nurses worked on the motionless figure lying on the operating table.

After a timeless beat, he realized that he was looking down at his own lifeless body.

Well son of a bitch! . . . I must be dead! he thought, but surprisingly, the thought still held no terror for him.

In life, he had known death as a friend, almost as intimately as a lover. He had seen death drop like a shimmering gauze curtain over the eyes of eighteen young women and countless cats and dogs that he had tortured and then killed when he was younger. He had seen death extinguish the glow of life, making the facial expression of each woman go suddenly slack and frozen, casting their skin with a weird, gray pallor, their eyes focused *so* far away. He had studied it, trying to understand it, to experience it, but until now, he had never truly tasted death's sharp sting.

And the surprise was, there wasn't any sting.

There had been no panic, no pain, no struggle whatsoever.

That surprised him because he was positive he had seen extreme pain and agony and fear in the eyes of all eighteen of his victims. He had been thrilled as he watched each of them try so frantically to cling onto life, but it had slipped away like fine sand, sifting between their fingers.

So why did he feel none of that now?

There was only a curious, almost giddy sensation of flying, of floating high above the pain and agony of what he thought death should be.

For another timeless beat, he hovered above the scene in the operating room, watching as the medical team fought hard to save him. His mind was clear and focused, honed as razor-sharp as it had been on those eighteen glorious nights when he had taken his victims. He could see everything the medical team was doing to save him and hear everything anyone said. He noticed funny little details, like what color shoes they were wearing and on which wrist they wore their watches.

But he found that he didn't care.

He almost laughed at their pathetic efforts to revive him. It was funny because he didn't need them ... he didn't *want* them to succeed.

No, this was just fine with him.

One way or another, he had escaped.

Finally, however, he became aware of a subtle shifting behind him. Although it took no physical effort on his part, and he had no sense of motion, he turned his head and saw a bright tunnel receding into the distance like a long, luminous telescope. The tunnel was filled with a soft glow of lemon light that drew him toward it like comforting, beckoning arms.

Didn't I hear something about death being like this on Geraldo *or something just a little while ago?* he thought. *But— hey, I thought that was all bullshit!*

He was filled now with a curious flutter of excitement

and expectation as, floating weightlessly, he was drawn inexorably toward the inward spiraling tunnel of light. At the far end, the light seemed to brighten, shifting subtly from yellow to a pure, white radiance. He didn't even consider resisting the euphoric rush as he drifted like a wind-blown dandelion puff along the softly pulsating walls of the light-filled tunnel. And then, up ahead, he could dimly make out the hazy silhouettes of people who appeared to be moving toward him, blowing and shifting like drifting snow. As they drew closer to him, and his vision cleared, he saw that their arms were uplifted as though in greeting.

Son of a bitch!

This is just like what those nut cases on Geraldo *said it would be like!*

He remembered how all of the people on the show that day who claimed to have died and then come back described the overpowering sensation of warmth and well-being, of flying, and of seeing friends and relatives who had died before coming to greet them.

Swept along through the tunnel, he heard the soft whispering rush of wind in his ears. A gradually strengthening blast of embracing heat washed over him. With the bright, pulsating light behind them, the figures were still indistinguishable, but he smiled to himself as he watched them draw closer, their arms held out to him in greeting.

And then, just as suddenly as the realization that he had died had hit him, everything changed. The yellow light quickly blended to a hurtful, stinging red pulse that throbbed like a frantic, racing heartbeat. Hard, grinding thunder rumbled all around him, deafening, and the tunnel seemed to collapse inward on him, squeezing him. With their arms raised high over their heads, the figures swept toward him, and in a moment of blinding intensity, he saw and counted eighteen of them.

Jesus God! No!

Something punched hard against the inside of his chest as he glanced from one blank face to another. Cold, unblinking eyes stared at him, glowing horribly as they bored into him with the acid of their eternal hatred. Their thin hands were hooked into claws that twitched and trembled as they swung at him, slicing the air with shrill, whistling hisses. Dangling around each woman's throat, glowing dully in the eerie light, was a large necklace of alternating rubies and pearls. The gems swung back and forth with the women's motions, making harsh grating noises that sounded like a dreamer grinding his teeth in his sleep.

Panic as deep and cold and stinging as the cut of a razor blade sliced through Alex as he stared at the eighteen women. Their eyes were glazed with death as they stared straight back at him. He withered beneath their steady gaze as they formed a circle around him and clawed at him. The steadily narrowing tunnel was filled with the sound of their high, squealing laughter.

No! . . . Oh, Jesus!. . . . Please! No!

He thrashed and twisted about, trying to avoid their icy touches, but every time their hands passed through him, he experienced a sting of numbing, sharp pain.

In the back of his mind, he realized that he didn't have a body anymore, but this pain was worse. Every nerve, every fiber of his being vibrated with unbearable agony. The women's howling screams rebounded inside the tunnel, wavering with maddening intensity. For a timeless instant, he imagined that he was nothing more than a thick column of heavy, black smoke that was being ripped apart by fierce, cold winds.

But then, with a sudden burst of energy, he somehow managed to propel himself away from the women. His mind echoed with their high, receding laughter and his own agonized wail as he fell, spiraling around and around in a fast-turning, backward spin. Impenetrable darkness and icy terror embraced him as he struggled futilely to stop the headlong, dizzying rush.

And then—abruptly—it was over.

With a roaring intake of breath, he opened his eyes and

looked up at the glaring light suspended above the operating table. Through his watery vision, he saw the knot of figures huddled around him. For a flashing, panicky instant, he thought they were still the eighteen women, but then he recognized the pairs of concerned eyes peering at him over the edges of green surgical masks.

"Oh, Christ! Oh, *Christ!* I . . . I'm not dead," he said, his voice nothing more than a trembling gasp.

"No, sir, you're not," said a stern voice that resonated all too close to his ear, all too real. "But for a minute there, we thought we'd lost you."

"Wish we had," whispered a faint, feminine voice.

"Please," Alex said with a dry gasp. "Please don't let me die!"

His hands felt like they were being controlled by someone else as he reached up and fumbled to grab onto something—an arm, he thought—and squeezed tightly.

"Please! Oh, Jesus, *please!* You can't let me die! I *saw* them . . . I saw them, and they . . . they're *waiting* for me over there!"

"Huh? Who's waiting for you.

"Jesus Christ! *They* are! They *all* are!"

A numbing torrent of chills washed through him like a flood of ice water. He found it almost impossible to breathe because of the compression in his chest.

"They're waiting for me . . . on the other side . . . and they're all wearing their necklaces of rubies and pearls!"

A Little Bit of Divine Justice

It all happened so fast, David Bensen might have sworn it hadn't happened at all . . . except for the soft *thump* that shook the front of his car and jolted the steering wheel in his hands. The windshield wipers were having a hell of a time keeping up with the snow, which was falling so fast now it was nothing more than long, yellow streaks in the glare of his headlights. Several times, he had rolled his window down, reached out, and given the wiper blade on his side a quick snap to knock off the ice buildup. And every time when he swore softly to himself, each curse word was a frosted puff-ball in the cold air that sucked into his warm car.

It was very late—well past midnight—and David had just enough clear-thinking mind left to know that he probably shouldn't be driving in this storm. What had started as a few beers in celebration of his promotion at Unum had escalated through the evening up to quite a few beers . . . and, finally, it had gone to too damned many!

What kind of friends, he wondered, *would let a friend drive all the way back to Standish on a night like this?*

He chuckled softly to himself as he used the back of his gloved hand to clear away the glazing of frost on the inside of the windshield. Tom—or maybe Blaine—what the fuck ... *someone* should have asked him to sleep it off at their house. He could have called Gail and told her that he was delayed because of the storm. Shit, one missed birthday wasn't going to be the end of the world, was it?

But no.

The ever-faithful husband that he was, he was risking his life to drive the twenty-three miles from South Portland to his home. Twenty-three point seven miles, to be exact. Lord knew he had calculated that distance enough times to make him puke!

Blizzard be damned! he thought, glancing at the speedometer even though its dull green-lit numerals turned into needles that jabbed his eyes. He couldn't look at it for long. The numbers on the speedometer would start to swim as through he was looking at them through the bottom of a bottle of Jim Beam. *Jim Beam ... high beam ...* after a while, it all started to blur.

It happened just as he was crossing the Running Hill Road bridge near the Westbrook town line. He sensed more than saw the iron bridge span overhead—heavy and black. Both to his left and right was an impenetrable wall of swirling gray as dense as soot. He had to take it on faith that somewhere below on either side was the frozen Stroudwater River. The person—he had looked large, darting out of the storm like that—was suddenly, simply ... *there* ... right in front of him, appearing like an apparition.

David's first reaction was to hit the brakes, but as soon as he felt the ass-end of the car start to shoosh around, he took his foot off the brake pedal, trusting that he was going slow enough so the man would see the headlights and get the fuck out of the way.

But—*damn it!*—he didn't!

Either he truly never saw what hit him, or else he tried to get out of the car's path and failed.

Or maybe, David thought, *maybe, if he was nuts enough to be out walking in a storm like this in the first place, maybe he wanted to get hit.*

It didn't matter how David looked at it. Within a fraction of a second, before he could even blink, the man was there. The soft *thump* shook the steering wheel, and then he was . . . gone . . . like a puff of smoke, or a sudden, dark mirage that was quickly swallowed by the solid wall of gray.

There was such a sense of unreality to it all that David wasn't even sure it had really happened as he gently pumped the brakes and played the steering wheel loosely in his hands to avoid going into a skid. He strained his eyes, looking into the rearview mirror, more than half-expecting to see a dark shape sprawled on the road behind him; but in the hazy red glow of the taillights, the road looked clear, except for the twin tire tracks he'd just made.

"Son-of-a-bitch!" David muttered as the car went into a sickening slow slide and then came to a stop. He slammed the shift into park and, resting his arm on the back of the seat, turned around to look. Through the shifting curtain of snow, the girders of the bridge overhead looked like a gigantic spider web. Low-throated wind howled around the car, the only sound other than the steady *slap-slap-crunch* of the wiper blades on the icy windshield.

"Hmm . . . nothing there," David whispered. His brain was still swimming with booze. He sighed heavily and ran the back of his glove over his forehead, surprised by the slick, sweaty feel.

Why the hell was he sweating?

If there had been someone there . . . but no—the longer he looked back along the desolate stretch of bridge, the more convinced he became that there *couldn't* have been anyone there. He had imagined seeing that person . . . And even if he hadn't . . .

"Well, only an idiot would be out on a night like this," David whispered as he groggily shook his head. "One less pimple on the ass of this poor planet." He chuckled softly at his alcohol-honed wit.

But what if he *had* knocked someone off the bridge?

Craning to see over the side, David guessed there had to be at least a couple of feet of snow down there— probably more in the hollow. If anyone fell down there, he'd probably land neck-deep in a cushion of snow. Probably right now, he was looking up at the underside of the bridge and wondering how the hell he got down there so fast. In a minute or two, after he got his bearings, he'd climb back up the embankment and continue on his way to . . . wherever he was walking on a night like this.

Whatever!

David figured it wasn't his problem this jerk got in front of him. He should have seen the headlights coming and gotten the Christ out of the way!

But as drunk as he was, David knew he should at least get out and take a look. If the guy did need help, he should do whatever he could.

Pulling his gloves up tightly over his wrists, David opened the car door. Leaving the car running to keep it warm, he braced himself and stepped out into the howling storm. Stinging pellets of snow hit his face like bullets. The frigid wind buffeted him like unseen punches. Even in the short time since he'd left The Bull's Eye, the weather had worsened. David tucked his neck deeply into his coat collar. Feeling like a silly-ass turtle, he trudged back along the swerving tracks his car had made in the snow, all the while wondering, if the good citizens of Westbrook paid their taxes, where the hell were the snowplows and sanders?

As soon as he stepped beneath the bridge girders,

though, his give-a-shit attitude wavered. Something much colder than the wind, more biting than the snow blowing into his face tugged at him. He jerked to a stop, his eyes opening wide as he looked all around, trying to locate what could possibly have been making him feel so . . . so damned jumpy.

The storm was howling. Wind-driven snow hissed along the road. High overhead in the racing, twisting clouds, lost to sight, deeper voices moaned, sounding like people . . . dozens of people, moaning in agony.

It didn't take long for the cold to bite through David's thin jacket, which he had bought more for style than protection from the weather. His eyes were watering from the cold, and his teeth were chattering as he took two—three—four tentative steps onto the bridge.

As much as he tried to push it aside, he couldn't deny the tension that was building up inside him. With each step he took—slow and trudging through the knee-deep snow—his nervousness jacked up another notch. David grew fearful that his rising panic was like an electrical charge generated, somehow, by the storm that would be transformed by the iron structure of the bridge. Any second now, if he wasn't careful, the charge would arc out and ground out through him.

As his fear increased steadily, David faltered and stopped. He cast a fearful look over his shoulder at his car. It seemed strangely diminished as it sat there, its taillights glowing like baleful eyes in the wind-swept snow. The tornado-shaped cloud of exhaust swirling up into the night was quickly whisked away by the strong wind.

What David wanted to do—right now!—was get back into his car, slam it into gear, and drive the hell away from this bridge. Get home before Gail got too worried . . . or too pissed because he'd gone out drinking on her birthday.

Fuck it! Let the poor bastard fend for himself!

He might have gone over the bridge railing even if David hadn't driven by just then . . . or maybe he *wanted* to go over! Maybe he wanted to die!

But in his heart, David knew that he had to check it out. If someone was down there needing help, maybe stuck hip-deep in the snow, and he just walked away . . . well, he knew he'd never be able to live with himself. Maybe, David thought, he would even go the extra distance and offer the poor bastard a ride home, just to assuage his guilty conscience.

He wasn't ready for what he saw when he reached the side of the bridge and looked down. There were marks in the snow, all right. Definite evidence that someone had been walking by here recently. The man's dragging footprints marred the otherwise unbroken snow. And there, not six feet from where David stood, the tracks led right up to the edge of the bridge to one place where the accumulated snow on the railing had been knocked clean off. David held his breath as he leaned over the railing and peered down into the darkness below. He was expecting to see someone looking up at him, his arms held out in silent supplication.

But that's not what David saw.

He felt a sudden blast of horror as his eyes were drawn to the jagged, black hole in the snow that covered the frozen river. Below the hissing whistle of the storm, he could hear the throaty gurgle of running water.

"Aww, Christ! Aww, Jesus, you poor bastard!" David mumbled as he stared down at the black water lapping up onto the snow. Cold terror and a hollow sadness filled him as he imagined what it must have felt like to see headlights suddenly appear from out of the night, and then to feel the rock-hard impact and to find yourself falling backwards . . . backwards and down into the darkness.

What thoughts would have filled that person's mind, David wondered, when he hit the ice, then felt it crack open beneath his weight as the frigid water reached up, quickly soaked through his clothes, and then dragged him down with cold, leaden hands?

"Jesus Christ!" David shouted as the impact of the sudden realization hit him.

"I just killed a man!"

He took a lurching step back from the railing. His hands ached as he clenched them into fists and pressed them hard against his head.

"I can't believe it! I just *killed* someone!"

His words were whisked away on the storm, disappearing like the slow, rolling echo of thunder.

Frantic with fear, David whimpered softly as he scanned the road in both directions. At least right now, there were no other cars in sight. Although he knew—all too well—how suddenly one can come up on you from out of the storm, at least for right now, he was safe—no one had seen what had happened.

"Okay! . . . All right!" David muttered as he stared down at the gaping hole in the river ice. "I'm sorry about this, you poor bastard, but there was nothing I could do about it, all right? I didn't see you . . . not until it was too late. And now there sure as shit ain't *nothing* I can do for you!"

The tension churning inside him suddenly unleashed. Spinning on his heel, David started running back to his car. His feet skidded on the slick road, and the deep snow tripped him up, pulling him back as he staggered forward. The only thought in his mind was—he had to get the hell away from the bridge.

Let the poor bastard be!

He was dead and gone!

It made no sense to ruin his own life just because of a simple, stupid accident. There was nothing he could have done . . . especially on a night like this!

It could have happened to anybody!

But it happened to me!

He tried to run fast, but the harder he pushed, the more the snow seemed to drag him back. He knew it had to be an illusion from the falling snow, but it looked as though the road was pitching crazily down at a sharp angle, and that his car was gently, silently slipping away from him. The bridge appeared to telescope outward, expanding to compensate double for every trudging step he took. Sudden powerful gusts of wind whistled in the iron girders overhead, making the whole bridge vibrate and hum. Again, David was convinced that the bridge was thrumming with a steadily building electrical charge.

Can there be lightning in a blizzard? he wondered.

All he could picture was a forked bolt of blue light, ripping down from the storm clouds and striking the bridge, instantly frying him. He could almost feel the black hole in the ice below the bridge, and in his terror-filled imagination, that hole was growing steadily larger, spreading out below him and creating a hungry vortex that would eagerly suck him down . . . down into a long, spiraling fall that would end the instant he plunged into the freezing, black water.

But then—suddenly—he realized he was getting closer to his car. It seemed to leap out at him just as he tripped and fell, pitching forward as though a rug had been pulled out from under his feet. David slammed onto the back of the car with enough impact to knock the breath out of him. He was dimly aware that he must have left a dent in the trunk, but he didn't pause to look as he scrambled to open the driver's door and jump inside the car.

Once he was safely behind the wheel, he just sat there, dazed and panting heavily as he tried to stop imagining the hole in the river ice growing and pulsating as it seeped out of the storm . . . coming toward him. He wrenched the gear shift into drive and stepped down hard on the gas.

The tires whined as they spun in the deep snow, searching for traction on the asphalt below. The car started moving forward with infuriating slowness. David's breath felt like fire in his chest as he hunched over the steering wheel and jockeyed it back and forth, trying to make the car move faster. The rear end of the car kept swinging around toward the front, but he adjusted for it, turning into the skids and telling himself that the last thing he needed was to be stranded out here on a night like this . . . especially with a man he had just killed less than a hundred yards down the road.

The tires found the road, and the car gradually gained speed. Soon enough, David was heading toward home, driving a bit faster than he knew he should, given the terrible driving conditions. Any alcohol fumes lingering in his brain had been burned off in his raging panic to get away from that bridge and that jagged black hole in the river ice. Before long, once his hammering pulse began to slow, his mind felt as crystal sharp as ever, and he tried to sort out what had happened.

What he needed to do first, he told himself, was just get the hell home—sit down with a whiskey, maybe a double, give Gail the birthday present he'd gotten for her, and then, after giving his wife a birthday screw, go to sleep and forget all about what had happened.

That's all he could do!

He sure as hell couldn't help that poor bastard down there on the bottom of the Stroudwater River!

David's hands clenched the steering wheel so tightly they began to ache. In his mind, he could imagine—much too vividly—the man as he drifted down to the muddy riverbed where his coat, made heavy by the water, held him as solidly as a coat of cement. David tried—and failed—not to imagine the man's hollow, glazed eyes . . . dead eyes, staring up at the shimmering, receding glow of the surface. The only comforting thought about any of this was that the cold water probably had killed the man long before he knew what was happening—

. . . *probably!*

The road unwound slowly as David drove through the swirling snow. The wind whistling around the car was masked by the raging noise inside David's mind—

Rick Hautala

I killed a man!
I fucking just killed a man!

He had to accept that. He knew at least that much. More than likely, once he got home, he probably wouldn't even mention it to Gail.

Why should he?

It made no sense to get her all worked up about it. If, sometime in the spring, the poor bastard's bones washed up somewhere downstream, then maybe he'd find out who the jerk had been. After all, what the hell was he doing out this late, walking alone in a blizzard? In all likelihood, unless the man's mysterious disappearance made the newspapers, David figured it was all over and done with . . . history, locked beneath the river ice.

David was having enough of a problem focusing on the narrow spread of his headlights as they sliced through the raging snow. The wiper blades kept icing up, and he noticed, with a touch of irony, how killing a man hadn't changed everything. His face was slick with sweat, and his heavy breathing made the defroster work overtime. But try as he might, he couldn't stop thinking about that hole back there in the river beneath the bridge. Staring straight ahead, trying to stay on the road, he couldn't shake the gnawing sensation that he was driving down a long, black tunnel.

. . . Like that black hole in the ice, he thought, shivering wildly.

. . . Like that long, black ribbon of river, sliding silently beneath the thin crust of ice. . . .

. . . Like the dark, narrow passage between life and death.

The snow-laden trees lining both sides of the road leaned inward, threatening to fall down and crush David's car as he skidded and swerved his way through the stormy night. The car's engine whined loudly as the tires spun, nearly useless in the deep snow. The storm swallowed his headlights and distorted his view of the road so badly he doubted at times that he was even driving on the road. For all he knew, he could be carving an entirely new path across the fields and through the woods.

Only a few houses lined the roadside. When he passed them, seeing the warm glow of living room lights spilling out onto the snow-covered front yards made David think it might be a good idea to drive up to one of those houses, ask to use the phone, call the police, and report what had happened. That was the honest thing to do, he knew; but then again—thinking honestly—what the Christ good would it do?

The man was dead . . . drowned like a rat.

If the cops got involved, and if they gave him a breath test, he'd come out point 3 or higher, for sure. He'd get nailed for "operating under the influence" and maybe vehicular homicide. What good would that do either him or that poor bastard back there?

Why ruin his life just because some asshole was out walking in a Goddamned blizzard after midnight?

As the road unscrolled in front of his headlights, David had to resist the illusion that he was actually stationary, and that the road was sliding past him. He had no sense of motion. The steering wheel played loosely in his hands, but more often than not, the car's motion seemed not to respond to anything he did. The night pressed in close, buffeting the car as it whistled and howled like a dark beast, intent on pulling him out into itself.

Although it didn't feel like it, David knew that he was driving much slower than he usually did. He realized that, in a storm, time and distance had a funny way of distorting. After a while, though, when he still hadn't come up to the turn onto Route 22, he started to panic.

Was the junction still somewhere up ahead, or had he missed it in the dark somehow?

Could he be lost somewhere in Scarborough? He could see nothing but snow-covered woods and the occasional house outside his window, so for all he knew, he could be in God-forsaken Aroostock County!

After another few curves in the road, when he still hadn't come up on anything familiar, he told himself that he would turn around in the next driveway he saw and start heading back. The night closed down around him like a curtain. Snow streaked at him like tracer bullets, creating the dizzying impression that the entire world was slipping past him. His mind began to spin, and he got so lost in his slow-rising panic and the curious feeling that he wasn't even moving that he almost forgot he was driving. He kept shaking his head and yanking his awareness back onto the road before he found himself nose-deep in a snow bank on the side of the road.

With a sudden drop in his stomach, he realized that it had been—what? Maybe two or three miles since he had last seen a house. Now, he knew damned well that there were houses all along Running Hill Road. The urban sprawl of the Maine Mall and its associated business parks had turned this once gentle, rolling farmland into prime real estate. He should have been able to see the inviting glow of light in at least one window. The snow wasn't coming down that thick! But strain as he might to see in either direction, the road was nothing but solid black bleeding into the thin gray of diffused light from his headlights.

"Where in the name of Christ *am* I?" he muttered, fighting back a cold rush of panic. He realized that he was breathing heavily and eased back into the car seat, forcing himself to relax. There was no use getting all stressed out about this. He was letting himself get too carried away. For all he knew, he may even have hallucinated that guy back there on the bridge. He'd had too much to drink; even though he would have sworn he was fit enough to drive, maybe the alcohol was still playing tricks on his mind.

There had to be a rational explanation for everything, right? And just as soon as he got home and had a drink to brace himself, he'd try to rationalize all of this. Right now, all he needed to do was figure out where the fuck he was. Hunching over the steering wheel, he silently prayed for a sign, for just one thing he might recognize, one tiny landmark so he would know he was still on the right road. It was impossible that he could have gotten lost on a road he covered to and from work pretty near every day of his life.

Up ahead, David saw where the road veered to the right. As he eased on the gas for the turn, thinking this was it—he would see the stop sign he was looking for—his stomach suddenly dropped. His fingers clutched the steering wheel, and a chill sharper than the storm winds swirled inside him.

Ahead of him was the Running Hill Road bridge!

"What in the name of—?" David sputtered.

His foot pumped the brake, and the wheels locked, but the car didn't slow down as it skidded down the hill toward the iron girders of the bridge.

This is impossible! he thought, even though he had the testimony of his own eyes. How could he have gone around in a complete circle to end up here? He would have had to drive past the Maine Mall again! There was no way he'd done that! This had to be some other bridge. That's what it was. He was on the wrong road and had found a different bridge that simply *looked* like the Running Hill Road bridge.

But as his car slid to a stop, belly-deep in the snow in front of the bridge, David looked around and saw that he was wrong.

This most definitely was the bridge he had just crossed over . . . what? No more than an hour ago? The same bridge where he had run into that man and knocked him over the railing and into the river.

With a sudden, sickening rush, David could feel the dark, ugly presence of the hole in the river ice below him. He could feel it, swelling and spreading, reaching up toward him out of the storm like hungry hands, trying to catch him and drag him down.

A scream began to build inside David's chest as he sat there for a moment, his car idling as the blizzard screamed all around him. Carefully, now, he stepped down on the gas and started slowly across the bridge. His breath was burning, raw in his throat, and his eyes felt like they had been glued open as he scanned the section of the railing where the snow had been knocked off. He was just starting to accelerate to get the hell out of there when a flicker of motion off to his left drew his attention. For a moment, the storm darkened and congealed; then, swooping at him from overhead, the dark shape of a man came flying out of the raging snow straight at the car.

A scream burst from David when the man landed with a *thud* on the hood of the car. The sudden impact sent a jolt of pain up David's arms all the way to his teeth. He jerked the steering wheel hard to the left, all the while staring straight ahead in utter disbelief.

The man didn't bounce off the front of the car like he had the first time. Looking like a dark, awkward crab, he clung to the hood. David's eyes widened with terror when the man slowly raised his head and smiled at him. Thick, black muck oozed from between his teeth, and heavy strands of slime hung from his face and shoulders. The man's eyes swelled with rage as he opened his mouth wide, and a torrent of dark water shot out at the windshield.

David cried out and reflexively raised his arm to shield himself as the water splattered against the glass. For an instant, the wipers stopped their steady sweep. As soon as they swept the water away, David saw that this was no illusion—the man was still clinging to the front of the car. His face was underlit from the reflected light of the headlights as he leaned back and opened his mouth in silent, horrible laughter.

"Get the fuck away from me!" David shrieked as he quickly spun the steering wheel back and forth, trying desperately to dislodge the man. With his pulse firing like a machine

gun, he watched the man lean forward and begin climbing up the hood toward the windshield. In desperation, David stepped down hard on the accelerator. The tires caught on the pavement beneath the snow, and the car leaped forward. In the frozen glare of the headlights, past the looming bulk of the man, David saw the bridge railing—and the small area where the snow had been cleared off—directly in front of him.

He fought frantically to turn the car, but no matter how hard he pulled on the steering wheel, he couldn't change direction. In flickering slow motion, the car careened toward the side of the bridge. David could feel the jagged, black hole in the river ice below the bridge. It was pulling him forward like the inexorable suck of a vacuum.

"Leave me the Christ alone!" David shouted as the man, scrambling forward, brought his face up close to the windshield—so close the wiper blade whisked less than an inch from his nose. The man's face was pale and crusted with frozen, black ooze from the river bottom as he watched David with glazed, unblinking eyes. A smile twisted his mouth into a horrible rictus.

"Please. . . ." David said, pleading, but then his voice warbled rapidly up the scale until it was nothing but an ear-piercing screech. The car shuddered with another, heavier impact, and then it tore through the railing and shot out into the night. Metal scraping against metal sent sparks flying like fireflies into the storm as the car shot out into the darkness and then plummeted downward. It hit the river ice nose-first, leveled out for a single, sickening instant, and then began to sink. Frigid water seeped into the car, curling its icy fingers around David's legs, then up to his waist, his chest, and finally over his face. He struggled to get the door open, but before long, his hands and arms were numb, useless. The last sound he made as the water closed around him like a black shroud was a strangled, bubbly gasp.

"Holy shit! Did you see that?" Benny Larsen shouted, even though he knew he was alone, and whoever was in that car certainly couldn't hear him . . . not anymore, anyway. He ran through the knee-deep snow to the bridge railing and looked down at the bubbling, black hole in the river ice. Waves sloshed out of the hole, but the splashing sound they made was lost beneath the high roaring sound of the blizzard.

Benny's car had died about a mile back on Spring Street. He knew there was a service station back by the Maine Turnpike entrance, and he had set that as his goal to get the help he needed. If the gas station was closed because of the storm, he could at least ask for help at the Turnpike toll booth . . . unless the Turnpike had been closed because of the storm, too. If that was the case, then he didn't know what he'd do.

Benny was still trembling from the sudden appearance of the car from out of the blinding snow just as he was starting across the bridge. One second, the car hadn't been there . . . the next, it was practically on top of him.

His hands were clenched into tight fists as he cautiously approached the ragged gap in the bridge railing and looked down at the roof of the car, floating in the river. All around the car, thick, black water bubbled up like stew in a cauldron. The crackle and snap of hot metal being instantly cooled filled the night. Benny hunched up his shoulders and sucked in a deep breath as he watched the car sink out of sight.

"Fuckin'-a!" he muttered as he leaned forward, looking down, and vigorously rubbed his arms.

He knew he should be brave about this. He should strip off his coat and dive right into that freezing water—swim down there and try to save the poor bastard in that car. He probably hadn't drowned yet, and every second he delayed increased the odds that he wouldn't make it.

"Jesus Christ!" Benny whispered as he contemplated how deathly cold that water would be. "No fucking way!"

If the poor bastard wasn't dead yet, Benny knew he soon would be. If he jumped into that water now, all he'd accomplish would be his own death. No sense ending up a dead hero, that's for sure. As he watched the black water settle down, he convinced himself that whoever had been driving that car had probably been drunk and should have known better than to try to drive in a blizzard like this in the first place. But whatever he had been, he was *dead* drunk now! Benny smiled at his own sick humor.

Turning quickly away from the railing, he snuggled deeper into his coat and started walking again. He was up from Connecticut to visit his sister, so he wasn't entirely familiar with these roads, but he guessed it was no more than a mile or two back to the Turnpike. Of course, walking in a storm like this made every hundred yards feel like a mile. If nothing else, he figured he should find a phone booth and call his sister, Gail, and let her know that his car had broken down, and that he wasn't going to be able to surprise her for her birthday as he had hoped.

On and on, Benny trudged through the raging storm, convinced that at the next bend in the road, just over the next snow-swept hill, he'd see the distant glow of the gas station lights. After walking much further than he thought he would have to, he saw the dark girders of another bridge up ahead. As he drew nearer, he frowned, unable to recall crossing two bridges on his way out. He wondered if he had taken a wrong turn somewhere back on the road.

What if he was lost?

Cursing softly under his breath, he started across the second bridge, being careful to keep well to the side in case a snow plow came by. He had to fight the eerie feeling that this was the same bridge he had crossed earlier—what? Maybe thirty minutes ago? The same bridge some crazy-ass, drunk driver had careened off.

He jerked to a stop when, through the curtain of snow,

he saw up ahead the large, gaping hole in the twisted metal railing.

Without warning, two glaring yellow headlights suddenly blossomed out of the night. Benny's throat vibrated with a wild scream as the car slammed into him, and he bounced high into the air. As he ricocheted off the car's windshield, one of his last thoughts was that he felt like a springtime bug, ricocheting off the car as he flew through the air.

Distantly, he felt his legs bang against the railing, knocking it clear of snow, but he missed in his desperate grab to catch onto something to stop his fall. With his arms waving wildly above his head, and a shrill scream muffled by the stormy night, he plunged down . . . down and through the thin river ice and then sank slowly to the thick, black mud below.

Karen's Eyes

-1-

"My bedroom door has eyes in it," Sarah said.

Her breath rebounded warmly into her face from the telephone mouthpiece, but that didn't stop the shiver that ran up her back.

"Yeah—I'm sure," Tom replied at the other end of the line. He was finding it difficult to keep the snicker out of his voice. "And I suppose the walls have ears, too. Better be careful! They can hear everything we're saying!"

A flash of anger, hot and red, made Sarah's vision go unfocused for an instant, but then a voice whispered in the back of her mind . . .

—If you can't trust Tom, who can you trust?

"No, Tom, I'm serious!" she said, without trying to mask the whining sound in her voice. "I can see . . . eyes! In the wood!"

Tom cleared his throat before speaking.

"Look, uhh, Sarah—I've been bustin' my ass studying for this chemistry prelim, and if I—"

"They're right there . . . on my closet door," Sarah whispered. "Right in the middle—near the top."

Tom let out an exasperated sigh.

"In case you don't remember, I've had the pleasure of spending a night or two in your bedroom, and I don't remember any. . . . Well, let's just say that I had more interesting things to look at than your closet door, all right? I thought you had a poster or something on it, anyway."

"Are you going to help me or not?" Sarah said, her voice cracking as it slid up the scale.

"Help you what? You're getting yourself all worked up about . . . about nothing! You've got some cheap wood door that's full of knots. That's all it is, you know? You're just . . . creating some kind of illusion from the grain in the wood or something."

"I want you to come over! Right now!"

Karen heard Tom sigh again, heavily. While she waited for him to answer, she glanced out the bedroom window. Snow had been falling steadily for the past four hours. Her view of the streetlight on the corner of College Ave. and Main Street was blurred by the thick flakes. The eerie nimbus of blue light hung suspended in the night like an exploded star.

"Do you—ah, realize how bad the driving is right now?" Tom asked. His voice betrayed his concern that Sarah might have been drinking too much or maybe had taken some kind of drug that was flipping her out.

"I don't care how late it is!" Sarah wailed. "Do you realize how scared I am?"

"So just put something over it so you won't have to look at it," Tom said coolly. "After my test tomorrow morning, I'll swing by and take a—"

"Haven't you been listening to me? I can see *eyes*—someone's *eyes*. I—I tried to cover them up, but I don't dare to get near them. And don't tell me to turn off the light. Even with it off, I can see them. They just kinda float there in the dark. Oh, God, Tom, I'm really scared!"

"Well, then . . . I dunno."

Tom heaved another deep sigh.

"Can't you just leave your bedroom? Sleep on the couch or something?"

He knew better than to suggest that she sleep on her roommate Karen's bed.

"Yeah, but—" Sarah's voice cracked, and when she continued, her voice was even higher, tighter, bordering on hysteria now. "I—I'm starting to see eyes everywhere I look! And just now, I . . . thought I saw a *face*, grinning at me from the door."

"Are you on anything?" Tom said.

After a long, awkward silence, Sarah replied, but she didn't sound at all like herself when she did; her voice was high and warbling, like a little girl's.

"No, I'm not on anything! Are you going to come over or not?"

"Do you know what'll happen to me if I flunk this chemistry exam tomorrow?" Tom asked sharply. "Even my father's pull won't keep me in school after that! The roads are probably slick as shit, too, and in case you haven't noticed, it's after one o'clock in the morning. I have—Fuck! Less than eight hours to study for this test."

"And *I* can't stop seeing those eyes!"

"Look, Sarah," Tom said, lowering his voice and fighting to keep it steady. "I mean—after what happened to Karen a couple of weeks ago, I can understand if you're still a little bit nervous. I'm still pretty freaked out by the whole thing, too, you know."

"*Nervous?*" Sarah shouted. "Is that what you think it is? I'm *nervous?*"

"Well . . . what else do you think it might be? You're probably just letting your imagination get carried away."

Tom regretted saying it as soon as the words were out of his mouth. In fact, he regretted this entire phone call.

217

He wasn't even close to prepared for the chemistry test in the morning, and now, with his last minute cram session interrupted, there was no way he was going to pass the test.

"Look, umm, Sarah—I'm sorry I said that, okay?" He tried to keep his voice as calm and restrained as possible. "The doctor gave you something—right? Some tranquilizers to help you calm down."

Sarah merely grunted a reply.

"So why don't you just take one of them, and tomorrow morning, right after the test, I'll—"

"I already took some," Sarah said in a voice that sounded tired and strained. "I've got every light in the apartment on, and I can *still* see them! Everywhere I look, there are eyes! Right there in the middle of my closet door, on my bedroom door! *Everywhere!* And they're all looking right at me!"

A cold hollow pit opened up in the middle of Tom's stomach. He hadn't missed Sarah's use of the word *some*. She hadn't said, she took *one* already. She had said she had taken *some* already!

Oh, Christ! Oh, shit! he thought as the chill spread throughout his body, making his shoulders shake. *Especially after what happened to Karen. . . .*

"You know you're just imagining all of this, don't you?" he said, trying one last time to bring Sarah back to a rational level. He looked down at his right hand, surprised to see that he was gripping his car keys. He couldn't believe that he was actually contemplating going out on a night like this. Hell! Just because they had slept together once or twice, it wasn't like they were lovers or anything.

"I'm *not* imagining this!" Sarah wailed.

Her voice blended into shrill laughter that cut through Tom like a buzz saw.

"I'm not imagining *any* of it! I'm sitting here on my bed, looking straight at my closet door, and I can see someone's eyes staring back at me." She took a sharp, rasping breath. "And do you want to know what?"

Tom licked his lips and, against his will, said, "Yeah . . . what?"

"They look *exactly* like Karen's eyes!"

-2-

The snow stung the back of Tom's neck as he stood outside the door of Sarah's apartment building. His forefinger was numb from pressing the door buzzer so many times, but above the whistling shriek of the blizzard, he couldn't even tell if the buzzer was working. Finally, out of desperation, he started pounding on the metal door.

"Hey, Sarah! Open up! It's me! Tom!"

His voice sounded frail, almost non-existent against the howl of the storm. Each hammer-fisted blow on the door rumbled like a bass drum.

Tom couldn't push aside his rising panic when Sarah still didn't come to the door. Fear and worry, more chilling than any Maine Nor'easter, churned in his gut as he stared in frustration at the darkened door.

Was she asleep, completely oblivious to him knocking on the door?

Or, as much as he tried to push such thoughts aside, had something happened?

Could she have been so upset that she could have done something like what Karen had done?

"Please, God, no!" he whispered as he leaned his face close to the cold door, fighting to push back his rising panic. "*Sarah!*'" he screamed suddenly as he gripped the doorknob and gave it a violent shake. "*Come on, Sarah! Open the goddamned door!*"

When this produced no result, he backed away from the door, wondering what the hell to do next. His shoulders and hands ached from his efforts, and his breathing came it sharp, burning gulps.

Was Sarah playing some cruel practical joke on him? he wondered.

Maybe even now, she was crouching by one of her darkened windows, looking out at him, and snickering behind her hand.

Or had she . . . had she done what her roommate, Karen, had done?

Behind him, the storm swept the length of the street, hissing as it smoothed over the plow ridge he had smashed through to get his car into the apartment parking lot. He could see his car was already skimmed with an inch or more fresh snow that crackled as it melted and then turned to ice on his heated windshield. The snow-hooded headlights had a sad, almost frowning look as they peered at him over the ridge of snow.

For several minutes, Tom just stood there, shivering and wondering what the hell to do. The frigid night air burned into his lungs and made his eyes sting.

Maybe he should try to break into the apartment. He certainly couldn't break through the door, but he might be able to jimmy open a window. He scanned the side of the building, feeling his fear and frustration growing steadily.

Or maybe he should roust the apartment complex manager out of bed. So what if it was two o'clock in the morning. If anything had happened to Sarah. . . .

Then again, the sensible thing to do might be simply to go back to his apartment and do what he could to prepare for the chemistry exam. In all likelihood, Sarah had taken his advice. She had calmed herself down, maybe with a cup of herbal tea, and then gone to sleep, leaving him out here in the cold, feeling like a total idiot.

"Come on, Sarah!" he said, so softly he could barely hear himself above the whistle of the storm. He brought his face up close to the front door and whispered, "I guess I'll be heading home now. If you need me, give me a—"

His voice broke off, and he staggered back down the

stairs, fighting to keep his balance. The last step tripped him, and he went sprawling backwards into the snow. Horrified, he stared up at the apartment door, convinced that he had seen . . . something on the door.

No! he told himself—not on the door.

In the door!

For a flickering second, just as he had brought his face up close to the cold metal, he was positive he had seen a pair of eyes wink open and look at him.

"Jesus H. Christ!" he muttered as he stood up and furiously brushed the snow off his butt. The steady blast of wind sent hard pellets of snow into his face. "I imagined that!" he muttered, shaking his head with astonishment. "I had to imagine that!"

Craning his neck forward, he stared through the hazy curtain of snow between him and the door, and finally saw the small, black circle of the security peep hole.

"Ahh—that's all it was," he said aloud, to bolster his courage.

But he couldn't shake the unnerving sensation that was growing steadily stronger in his gut. The image of Marley's ghost appearing to Scrooge as a door knocker rose darkly in his mind, tickling him with spikes of fear.

"Now she's got me all worked up," he said, trying to reassure himself with the sound of his own voice. "She's got me seeing things."

But what about Sarah? he wondered.

Why hasn't she answered the door?

Even if the door buzzer isn't working, she must have heard all the commotion he was making.

What if she had taken too many of those tranquilizers, and she was out cold . . . or maybe worse!

Maybe she was in a coma . . . or dead. . . .

—Like Karen!

Okay. So lots of college students decide that school or life or romance or whatever is too tough for them, and they decide to drop out. It's just that not many students decide to drop out as permanently as Karen did when she discovered that her roommate had been sleeping with her boyfriend. And not many students have to find their roommate sitting splay-legged on the floor with her brains splashed all over the living room wall from a self-inflicted gunshot, the way Sarah found Karen. And what about the guilt either Sarah or Tom still felt—and would always feel? Well, Tom figured that was just something they would both have to deal with on their own!

But what if, now, *Sarah* has done something . . . ?

A brilliant bolt of fear lanced through Tom. Taking the steps two at a time, he ran back up to the door and slammed his gloved fist against the metal as hard as he could. Pain spiked up his elbow to his shoulder, but he continued to rain heavy blows against the door. He was in such a frenzy that he hardly noticed it when the doorknob clicked, and the door started to swing inward.

"Oh, shit! Oh shit!" he muttered when he realized that the dark opening in front of him was gradually widening. Sucking in a sharp breath, he reached into the dark room and fumbled until he found the light switch. When he clicked it on, the sudden blast of light stung his eyes like a splash of salt water. Just then a fitful gust of wind seemed almost to push him into the entryway. His feet clumped heavily on the floor, knocking snow onto the rug where it began to melt.

"Hello . . ." he called out tentatively, craning his neck forward. "Sarah . . . ? It's me, Tom."

Only the entryway light—the one he had switched on—was on. In the back of his mind, he could still hear Sarah's high-pitched voice repeating. . . .

"—*I've got every light in the apartment on.* . . ."

"Big deal! So she's turned them off and gone to bed," Tom told himself as he stood shivering in the entryway.

He knew what he should do is tiptoe out of here, go back to his apartment, get some sleep before the test, and forget all about what he had been thinking *might* have happened. He had enough problems of his own.

But he couldn't do that, so, slipping off his gloves and unmindful of the mess the melting snow from his boots made on the floor, he made his way down the hallway toward Sarah's bedroom. Even without turning on any more lights, he could see that her door was closed. Staring at the flat wooden door, he couldn't help but wonder if, even now, hidden by the darkness, eyes were forming in the pattern of the wood and were watching him with a cold, steady, unblinking stare.

He hesitated in the hallway, wanting more than anything in the world just to turn around and leave, but he couldn't bring himself to do that until he checked Sarah's bedroom and made sure she was safe, asleep in bed before he left.

Stepping up to the closed door, he felt his hand trembling as he reached for the doorknob and turned it slowly. The worn brass sent a chill up his wrist. Then the latch clicked, and the door swung inward.

The snow-hazed light from the streetlight outside Sarah's window did little to cut the darkness, but Tom could see that there was no one in Sarah's bed. His hand found the wall switch and clicked it on. Rumpled sheets and twisted blankets were thrown about onto the floor. There was a depression in the middle of the bed, as though someone had been lying down recently, but Sarah was gone. Tom's body tensed as he stepped cautiously into the room and looked around.

Okay, he told himself. So Sarah wasn't here.

Maybe after he had made it clear that he wasn't coming over, she had phoned some other friend and gone over there for the night.

If she was as freaked out as she had sounded over the phone, he couldn't very well expect her to spend the night alone in the apartment, could he?

But if she had left, why hadn't he seen her footprints in the snow by the door?

"Hey, Sarah?" he called out.

His nostrils flared as he walked over toward the bed, sniffing the stale air. There was an odd aroma in the room that he couldn't quite identify. It had almost a metallic tinge to it. Bending over the bed, he ran his hand over the sheets, trying to feel any trace of residual body heat.

Nothing.

The bed was cold.

Tom straightened up, thoroughly confused. Sarah had called him less than an hour ago, and she had said she was sitting on her bed. Wouldn't the sheets still be warm?

And what was that smell?

As he stood there, staring blankly at Sarah's empty bed, another sensation intruded upon him. The hairs on the nape of his neck began to stir, and he had the undeniable sensation that *someone* was behind him, watching him.

A cold, sour knot tightened in his stomach. He started turning around, trying like hell to convince himself that it was Sarah, just returning from the bathroom and wondering who the hell this was in her bedroom, leaning over her bed.

"Hey, Sarah. I decided that I'd—"

His throat closed off, holding back the shout of surprise when he saw two glowing eyes staring at him from the closet door. His heart gave a quick, cold thump in his chest as he watched the eyes, hovering in the darkness.

"Jesus H.—" Tom muttered.

He took an involuntary step backwards and knocked into the night stand. Something fell to the floor and shattered.

He tried furiously to convince himself that this was just an illusion produced by the streetlight outside the window—the same trick of light that had fooled Sarah into thinking she was seeing eyes on the door.

Maybe it was just a shadow cast from the dirty window or something, but whatever it was, he didn't dare take his eyes off it.

—*That's all it is—a shadow . . . an illusion!*

With effort, he calmed himself and studied the two circles that peered at him from inside the woodgrain pattern.

Yes, if he let his imagination stretch just a bit further, he could see where someone might find the suggestion of a face surrounding those cold, unblinking eyes. He could almost see a nose forming between the eyes, and just below that, there was a faint wisp of a mouth.

But that's all it is, he told himself, just an illusion produced by the grain of the wood.

Keeping his eyes on the closet door, and taking short steps so he wouldn't trip on anything, Tom made his way slowly over to it, being careful not to look away even for a second. He figured the image would disappear the closer he got, but even when he was within arm's reach of the door, the illusion of eyes staring at him remained.

Slowly, he raised his hand, intending to touch the back of the door, but when his fingers were inches from the wood, the image of the face suddenly intensified.

Startled, Tom quickly withdrew his hand, and even as he did, the features of the face seemed for just an instant to solidify and become three-dimensional, bulging out of the wood at him.

In a flash, he realized that the face he was looking at did in fact look like *Karen's* face. And the eyes staring at him with a frozen, unblinking rage were *Karen's* eyes!

With a strangled cry in his throat, Tom turned and started to run; but before he could take more than two or three steps, a black curtain came down over his mind, and he dropped to the floor, unconscious.

-3-

Consciousness returned with an audible, gray rush.

Tom jolted up off the floor and, for a confused moment, stood there, staring numbly around Sarah's apartment. Pale morning light filtered through the grimy window as the last vestiges of the storm sputtered thick flakes of snow from the rushing gray clouds.

Tom's gaze immediately flashed to the closet door where he expected to see those eyes—*Karen's eyes*—still staring unblinkingly at him. He was even mentally prepared to see the facial features more clearly defined in the clear morning light . . . maybe even projecting three-dimensionally out of the wood like they seemed to last night, so he felt an immense measure of relief when he saw nothing more than the swirling woodgrain pattern of the door.

Nothing else!

No eyes!

No face!

Nothing at all!

"For Christ's fucking sake!" Tom mumbled as he rubbed his face with the flats of his hands. He flushed with embarrassment for having . . . what?

Had he actually passed out from fright?

Had Sarah's frantic phone call gotten him so worked up that he had actually fainted?

A quick glance at his wristwatch showed him that it was almost six o'clock in the morning. He groaned aloud, thinking that the chemistry exam was less than three hours away. He was going to flunk out, so he might just as well go back to his apartment and start packing as he worked up some excuses for his father.

But as he walked out into the hallway, he realized that Sarah still wasn't home—not unless she was asleep on the living room couch, oblivious to everything that had happened.

"Sarah?" he called out, craning his neck as he looked down the hallway first toward the living room, then toward the bathroom. The bathroom door was closed, but he thought he heard a noise from down there. Suddenly, he sniffed loudly as his nose caught a whiff of that strange aroma he had noticed when he had first entered the apartment last night. It was sharper, now; a stringent, metallic odor. He started down the hallway toward the bathroom.

226

Black fear coiled in his stomach as the sound he had noticed got steadily louder. It was definitely coming from the bathroom—a deep-throated *glug-glug* sound.

"Are you in there Sarah?" he whispered as he approached the closed door.

Fighting back the fear that the woodgrain on this door would suddenly resolve into a pair of unblinking eyes, he rapped on the wood twice, then twisted the doorknob and pushed the door open.

When he saw Sarah, sitting in the bathtub, her head thrown back, her mouth gaping open, and her eyes wide and staring sightlessly at the ceiling, every muscle in his body instantly unraveled. He fell to the floor on his knees and vomited into his lap. He was unable to take his eyes away from the pale, slender, naked arm that was hanging over the edge of the tub, its fingers dangling in a thick puddle of crusted blood.

Then he started to scream.

-4-

"I'm all right, Dad. . . . Honest, I am."

Tom spoke softly as he stared straight into his father's eyes through the bars of the jail's holding cell.

Tom's father, Dwight, shook his head with disgust. Unable to maintain eye contact with his son, he stared down at the tips of his shoes. One foot was tap-tapping on the cold cement floor. The floor was painted the same dull green as the walls. The color reminded Dwight of the bottom of a long-unkept swimming pool.

"Well, I told you over the phone, and I'll tell you again, you don't have to worry about a thing, son," Dwight said. "My lawyer's taking care of your release. We'll have you out of here before noon. As for that chemistry exam you missed this morning as a result of this—" He wrinkled his nose. "—this unfortunate incident. Well, I'm sure we can arrange for you to take it at another time."

"Sure, Dad," Tom said softly.

"I think it's an outrage that they arrested you in the first place!" his father went on. To think that they'd even *consider* the possibility of murder in what was so—so obviously a case of suicide!"

"I'm all right, Dad," Tom repeated, as if that was the only thought in his mind. Any concerns he had—even for his own situation—were erased by the stark horror of finding Sarah dead in the bathtub.

—Just like she found Karen, he thought over and over.

"You know," his father continued, not even listening to Tom, "it's these damned small-time campus cops. Their idea of police work is checking student I.D.s at the pub and ticketing cars without campus parking stickers. When they come up against anything real, they can't begin to cope with it."

"It's no problem," Tom said weakly.

He shifted on the edge of his cot and glanced at the wall beside him. He was thinking that it hadn't been necessary for his father to drive all the way up to Orono just to straighten out—what was the phrase he had used?—this "slight misunderstanding."

Sarah's dead, and he sees it only as an *inconvenience!*

Tom supposed it made sense that the police would at least suspect him of murder. When they arrived, alerted by a neighbor who heard him screaming and sobbing, they had found him, sitting beside the bathtub with Sarah's head cradled in his arms, rocking back and forth.

Clumps of dried blood had smeared all over his hands and face. Even after he was cleared of any criminal charges, he was sure there would be weeks, possibly months of questioning.

"Well, there's no reason for you to be here in the first place," Dwight said, scowling. "And once we have this cleared up, maybe I'll consider filing some charges of my own."

Tom looked away from his father, cocking his head at

an awkward angle. His throat was raw from all the screaming he had done, and his eyes were still stinging and brimming with tears as he stared at the institutional green painted walls.

"I can't even begin to tell you how upset your mother is by all of this, either."

His father's voice took on an irritating drone as Tom stared intently at the prison cell wall, no longer even registering what he was saying.

At first he thought what he was seeing was an illusion, merely two lumps in the concrete wall which, once painted, had bubbled up and now cast a shadow from the overhead lights that made them *look* like a pair of eyes. But as Tom shifted on his cot and stared intently at them, they became more clearly defined.

A trace of a smile flickered across his lips, unnoticed by his father.

"At first, I thought it best not to even mention any of this to your mother," his father said. "You know how upset she gets. But then I realized that there was no way we could keep it out of the newspapers. Sooner or later, she'd find out."

"Tell Mom that I—" Tom started to say, but then he fell silent as he stared into the steady, unblinking gaze of the eyes that were forming on the wall.

He recognized them.

Karen's eyes!

"I'll tell her this will all be over, soon!" his father said firmly. "That's what I'll tell her."

"Sure . . ." Tom said, his voice no more than a whisper. "It will all be over soon."

On the prison wall, Karen's eyes continued to resolve, taking on depth and detail.

Tom could see, now, the faint trace of a mouth below them that was smiling coldly at him. Then, ever so slowly, the left eyelid lowered and winked at him. He understood what he would have to do as soon as he had the opportunity.

Master Tape

Abigail was feeling nervous, and she was very tired.

For the last three nights, she'd been awake for most of the night . . . ever since she received that "official" letter from Louie Phillips.

Louie the Scumbag, as she always thought of him. As if "Scumbag" were his God-given last name. Not far from the truth. Talking to Louie over the phone was always bad enough, but on this January morning, Abigail had to go up to the office and deal with him, face-to-face.

That was never easy.

The office of Caribou Ranch Records was a small corner room that looked out over Congress Street from the third floor of the Canal Building. It was sparsely furnished with a battered desk, a rusted file cabinet, a beat-up couch, a couple of chairs, and a storage case behind the desk that was covered with several tape and CD players. The instant Abigail entered, she thought that the room was much too cold.

Cold as a witch's tit, she thought, and had to bite down on her lower lip to stifle a ripple of nervous laughter.

231

Shivering, she sat down in the chair in front of Louie's desk but had to look away from him when he leaned across his desk and smiled widely at her.

She couldn't *stand* to see him smile like that. She'd always thought his teeth looked too large for his face.

All the better to bite your ass with, my dear, she thought bitterly, thinking that it was the perfect look for a slime-ball record producer like Louie.

Lacing her fingers tightly together in her lap, Abigail glanced out one of the office windows where thick wedges of ice, stained brown by the city air, clung like ruined spider webs to the corners of the panes. Off in the distance, she could hear the warbling wail of a police car or ambulance going by.

Yeah, and they'll be calling for an ambulance for you soon, Mister Scumbag, if I have my way.

It took a great deal of determination and effort, but Abigail turned and looked at Louie.

"So . . . you *do* have the master tape with you, I assume," Louie said.

His voice slid up the scale, dragging out the last word as if it were something that tasted irresistibly delicious. He ended with a not-so-subtle *I've got you by the 'short-'n-curlies,' honey, and you know it!* grin.

Once again—as she always did whenever she had to deal with Louie face-to-face—Abigail thought about how big his teeth were. They looked like tiny dinner plates . . . or little white shovels that could just chomp and *chomp* and *CHOMP!*

Just like what you're doing to my music career, she thought, and the bitterness of the thought was a palpable taste on the back of her tongue.

As much as it hurt to do so, she sighed and nodded. She patted the large gray tape case that rested on her lap.

"You know," she said, her voice almost breaking before she sucked in a quick sip of air. "You . . . don't have any right to . . . to *do* this . . . to *force* me to turn the tape over to you."

As often as she had rehearsed that particular line on her way over to Louie's office, it came out halting and unconvincing, even to her own ears. A scumbag like Louie, who was used to screwing people to the wall on a daily basis, surely wasn't going to be intimidated by the likes of her.

"Oh, is that so?" Louie said, leering all the more at her. His wide, flat teeth gleamed like shiny porcelain in the diffused light of his office.

"Well, then, I suggest you take another look at your contract, sweetie. I paid for the studio time, and that tape belongs to me!"

Abigail cringed away from the vulpine look in his eyes. She wanted to, but didn't dare, to tell him that, while the master tape might belong to him legally, every damned song on it was hers, and hers alone!

Louie smiled, his lips parting even wider to expose both top and bottom rows of his teeth all the way to the pale, pink gum lines.

"And you signed that contract, baby. Nobody *made* you sign it. You *wanted* the record deal, so you damned well better learn to *live* with it."

Squinting slightly, Louie sniffed laughter through his nose. A foamy bubble of saliva formed in the corner of his mouth, but he wiped it away without a thought.

"Otherwise," Louie went on, still smirking at her, "I'd just have to have my shark call your shark. We could thrash the whole thing out in court, if that's what you'd like."

Squeezing and wringing her hands together, Abigail looked down at the tape case in her lap and slowly shook her head.

"No?" Louie said with a hearty laugh. "Did you shake your head *no?* Well, I didn't think you'd want to go that way because—frankly—you and I both know that you don't have the . . . shall we say the 'necessary resources' to go that route with me. Do you?"

Lacing his hands behind his head and looking self-satisfied, Louie leaned back in his worn leather chair, making it creak beneath his shifting weight. It sounded like a rusty nail being slowly pulled from a piece of wood, and set Abigail's teeth on edge. Louie's smile widened all the more, and Abigail couldn't help but wonder if his mouth could possibly stretch any wider.

Maybe it will spread all the way around to the back of his neck, and his fucking head will pop off! she thought; but instead of seeing the humor in that thought, it filled her with a grim sense of satisfaction and expectation.

"So-o-o-o," Louie said after a lengthening moment, letting the word drag out slowly. "Are you going to give it to me or not?"

Abigail grasped the cloth handle of the tape case tightly and cleared her throat.

Catching her hesitation, Louie arched one eyebrow, leaned forward even more, and said, "Yes, my dear . . . ? You have something more to say . . . ?"

Abigail could see how much he was enjoying this, and she hated him all the more for it. Biting her lower lip, she nodded her head curtly.

"Yeah . . . well . . . I should . . . probably tell you that I . . . I worked on it—on the album—a . . . a little more."

"You *what?*"

Bright purple lines of broken blood vessels spread like a ladder of flame across Louie's cheeks. "I hope to hell you don't think *I'm* paying for any more studio time!" Louie snarled. "I'm telling you right now, sweetheart, if you screwed with this—"

"Oh, no . . . no. It's still the same record," Abigail said, fighting hard to keep her voice steady. "Every song's exactly the way it was. I just . . . redid a bit of the vocals, is all. I . . . I wasn't satisfied with them."

"Whaddayah mean, you weren't *satisfied?*" Louie bellowed.

The color rose higher in his face, and all Abigail could

do was hope that he'd bust a blood vessel and drop dead on the spot. No loss there.

"Well *I* was satisfied with it the way it was!" he shouted. "And as far as I'm concerned, that's all that counts!"

Clenching his fists, he suddenly leaned forward across the expanse of his desk toward her. Raising one hand, he shook a chubby forefinger under her nose.

"And I swear to Christ, if you screwed with that material, I—I'll sue your lily-white ass from here to Fiji!"

"They're my songs," Abigail said, surprised that she could speak at all. Her hands were shaking and slick with sweat as she gripped the sides of the cloth tape case.

"That very well may be," Louie said with a snarl, "but it's *my* record, and it's going to be put out on *my* label, and I have the performance copyright on the material, so only *I* have final approval! If you don't believe me, just read clause eight in your contract."

"I didn't mess with it. Honest," Abigail said, trembling inside. "Go ahead. Listen to it for yourself."

With a quick nod of her head, she indicated the array of tape decks and speakers on the shelf between the windows behind Louie.

"I just over-dubbed a second vocal track on the first song to . . . to punch it up . . . to give it a bit more depth."

The tape case felt like it was made of lead as she held it out to him. Louie snatched it from her so fast her finger got caught on one of the metal clasps and broke a nail. Wincing, she looked down at her finger and smiled thinly when she saw the dark red bead of blood well up from her cuticle.

Louie didn't seem to notice or care. He was too busy opening the case and taking out the master-ready tape. His face was still flushed with anger, and his fat hands were shaking uncontrollably as he turned around and threaded the leader tape through the machine's tape head.

With barely a glance over his shoulder at her, he said, "I promise you, baby-cakes, if you've altered this tape in any way, I'm gonna sue your ass for *all* the studio and promotion costs plus all my expenses!"

Abigail's breath was caught like a burning cinder in her chest. Unable to speak, she simply nodded at him and stared past him at the tape deck.

Still growling under his breath, Louie jammed down the *play* button.

The tape began to roll.

After several seconds, an opening guitar riff filled the office, drowning out everything else, even the high, rapid flutter of Abigail's heartbeat in her ears. A faint smile touched the corners of her mouth as she waited in anticipation, but she said nothing as she tried to settle back in her chair and listen.

After the opening bar, the drums and bass kicked in; then, after another measure, her voice swelled up until it reached full volume in a sustained wail that sent a shiver racing up her back.

Damn, that's good, she thought.

Louie glanced at her and scowled. His jaw was set with grim determination, and his upper teeth were exposed, making him look like the flesh-eating jackal he was. Abigail's recorded voice began to sing the first verse of "After the Rush."

"Hmm . . . sounds okay to me," Louie said after a few seconds of listening.

Abigail could barely hear him above the sound of her music, but then, as her voice spiraled into the bridge, another voice, so faint it almost wasn't there, came through the speakers.

Louie's expression dropped, and his face went suddenly pale.

"What the hell—?" he said. "That wasn't there before. Who the fuck is that singing with you?"

He stripped his lips back, and his wide teeth flashed like fangs as he glared at her.

Abigail forced a smile as she focused on the second

voice. It was almost—but not quite—buried beneath the mix. Like a tantalizing wave of the hand seen dimly through a thick mist, the second voice wavered up and down with an odd echoing effect as it gathered strength.

"That's the second vocal track I told you I added," she said, struggling hard to remain calm and not start laughing out loud.

"But that . . . that doesn't even sound like you!"

Louie's face was flushed beet red, and he looked like his head was about to explode.

"That's a . . . a goddamned *man* singing! And it sounds like you're playing his vocal track backwards! What the fuck are you trying to pull here?"

Abigail tried to ignore him as she bounced her head in time, grooving with the music. The two voices were matched so closely they quickly dominated the sound of the instruments. Like dancers . . . like lovers, the voices twined in and around each other, weaving up and down.

Abigail closed her eyes and, for a moment, imagined that the voices were two fast-growing strands of columbine that were so entangled they were becoming indistinguishable. When she opened her eyes again, she couldn't tear her gaze away from Louie's expression of pure, blind anger.

"This isn't . . . *No!* This is absolutely *not* acceptable!" he shouted, shaking his clenched fists at the machine.

Before he could continue, he paused and, wincing slightly, raised one hand to his mouth. A look of perplexity, then of utter shock filled his eyes when he took his hand away from his lips and saw a pink smear of blood on his thumb and forefinger. His frown deepened as he skinned his lips back and grasped one of his front teeth and started to wiggle it back and forth.

"Jesus Christ," he whispered, shaking his head in confusion.

Abigail could barely hear him above the steady wash of music, but she had a pretty good idea what he was saying. Her own smile widened all the more as the voice she had recorded backwards continued to weave in and out with her own voice.

"So who the hell is this singing with you?" Louie asked, shouting to be heard over the music. His eyebrows lowered like storm clouds.

Abigail wanted to laugh out loud when she saw the thin trickle of blood that ran like a scarlet ribbon from one corner of his mouth. At first Louie seemed not to notice it, but then unconsciously he wiped his chin with the back of his hand and froze when he glanced down and saw the dark red slash of blood across his wrist.

"What the—?"

Reaching up with one hand, he felt around inside his mouth. Then he grabbed his front tooth again and started to wiggle it back and forth, hard. Beads of sweat glistened like dew on his forehead.

Abigail almost squealed with joy when she saw his front tooth shift back and forth like an ancient, teetering tombstone. Then, with a sudden snap that seemed almost as loud as a gun shot, Louie's hand pulled away. His eyes widened with genuine shock—maybe even terror—as he stared at the bloody stump of tooth he was holding between his thumb and forefinger.

At first he seemed too stunned to notice the pain; but after a moment—as Abigail's voice and that other voice continued to wail away in the background—his eyes clouded over. He cleared his throat with a deep, watery rattle, then leaned forward and spit a clotted glob of blood into the cup of his hand.

Abigail held her breath.

It's working! she thought.

Before he could find a tissue or something to wipe his hands on, the trickle of blood issuing from Louie's mouth suddenly gushed, running so fast it dripped in a steady stream from his chin onto his chest and lap. His eyes were frantic with fear as he started to rise from his chair, then sat down heavily and stared vacantly at Abigail.

When he opened his mouth again and tried to speak, several more teeth shot out in a bloody spray and hit the top of his desk, rattling on the wood like a dozen lead pellets.

Abigail didn't say a word as she rose slowly from her chair. All the while her eyes were locked onto Louie, who now slumped forward onto his desk and reached out to her with one trembling hand. The other hand clasped the worn arm of his chair, but it couldn't support him. Moaning softly, he lurched forward and then slid slowly to the floor.

Abigail smiled, thinking how much he looked like a melting candle. Moving with a quick dance-like skip, she came around the side of the desk and looked down at him on the floor. His white button-down dress shirt and tie were now saturated with a spreading bib of blood. His shirt clung to his heaving chest as he looked up at her and panted heavily.

Like a mad dog in August, she thought but still didn't quite dare to say to him. *And that's just what you are, Louie. Nothing but a cheating, scumbag, rabid dog!*

Louie's eyes rolled wildly in his head as he looked up at her and pleaded wordlessly for help. With a thick, bubbly groan, he thrashed from side to side and hit his head hard against one of the chair legs. Tears were streaming down his face, mingling with his blood as he tried once again to speak, but his words were choked off as more teeth fell from his gaping mouth onto the floor. Abigail almost couldn't see them inside the thick wash of blood and mucous that was flowing from his mouth and nostrils.

Abigail's smile widened even more when she glanced over at the still-running tape deck. The music and voices—especially the male voice that she had recorded backwards—were subtly but steadily gaining strength, shifting into a low, sonorous chant that soon overwhelmed the steady musical backbeat. The backwards words were unintelligible, but they throbbed with an undeniable power.

Abigail felt a twinge of pain in her own jaw and knew that she had to get out of the office soon.

After one last glance at Louie on the floor, she was satisfied that he didn't have the strength to get up and turn off the tape machine.

That was good.

The music would keep playing while she got away, and he lay there, drowning in his own foul blood.

It's really working! she thought excitedly.

Before she turned to leave, she knelt down beside Louie and, leaning close to his ear so even through his panic and pain he would hear her, she said, "Oh, by the way—you wanted to know who that is singing with me. . . ."

Louie's eyes were glazed milky white with pain. His face was pale as old bone, and his body had started to twitch as though a powerful electrical current was passing through him. He looked so far gone that he wasn't even on the planet anymore, but Abigail almost didn't care whether or not he could hear or understand her.

It didn't matter.

It was the effect, the power of the music—*her* music that counted.

"You remember that you wrote me a letter threatening to sue me if I didn't deliver a *master*-ready tape of my new album, right?"

She had been smiling for so long, now, that her cheeks were beginning to hurt. She had to massage her jaw before she could continue speaking.

"Well, that's who's singing with me."

The male voice now dominated the music, chanting in low, somber, almost inhuman tones that reached down into her heart and deep into her soul. . . .

"Like the old ads say, that's my master's voice."

—for the members of "Dead Eyes Emerson"

Breakfast at Earl's

The only time Earl's Cafe was filled with customers by four A.M. was in November, during hunting season. Normally, Earl didn't even open his doors until five-thirty in the morning, when folks heading in to work at the National Paper Products mill stopped by for coffee, donuts, and gossip. Once hunting season started, though, Earl would put on his traditional hunters' breakfast menu every Saturday morning, and just about every hunting man in Hilton, Maine, would show up.

The place always seemed unnaturally bright that early in the morning, what with the fluorescent lights on and it still being dark outside. At least thirty men, all dressed in hunter's blaze orange, crowded around the counter and stuffed themselves into booths as they fueled up for a day in the woods. Earl himself was one of the customers every morning throughout hunting season because, like just about every other man in town, he wanted to be out there in the woods. For the duration of the season, he turned complete operation of the Cafe over to his one and only full-time employee, Gary Clark, who kept the Cafe going with the help of a part-time waitress or two and Sam Curry, the dishwasher. Gary didn't seem to mind running the place alone all that much because he had never hunted a day in his life, and he swore time and time again that he never would.

Mixing with the strong aromas of fresh-brewed coffee, frying eggs and bacon, and the body sweat of men who had been in the woods for days on end without coming near soap and water, was the thick, almost cloying smell of Earl's famous hunters' stew. In truth, Earl had nothing to do with the stew that had made his pre-dawn hunters' breakfast so special. Gary had first concocted it some five or six years back, when he first came to work for Earl after being laid off at the N.P.P. mill. Earl probably never would have even hired Gary except that was the same year Gary's brother Albert died. Being second cousins, he figured Gary was pretty shook up, losing both his brother and his job about the same time. Any doubts he might have had about Gary's abilities disappeared after Earl saw how much his customers went for the stew. It had a hefty broth and was loaded with chunks of potato, carrots, celery, onions, and meat seasoned to perfection. Anyone who tried it raved about it, swearing it was the only thing to eat before a day in the woods. It stuck to your ribs all day, as they say, and most of Earl's customers swore that it carried them most of the way to supper time.

On this particular Saturday morning, the second weekend of hunting season, talk at Earl's Cafe was a bit on the gloomy side. Roy Coleman had been missing since late yesterday afternoon.

"I'm telling yah," Pete, Roy's son, said as he sat hunched over his bowl of stew at the counter and looked from face to face. "It just ain't like my pa not to show up. He's hurt bad or . . ." He wasn't able to finish the thought, but he didn't have to.

Herb Logan and Frank Harris, who had started out the

day before with Roy but had split up sometime around noon, seemed most inclined to agree with Pete. Like every man in the Cafe that morning, they had known Roy all their lives. They knew damned well that Roy wasn't the kind of man who'd get himself lost. No-siree! Roy Coleman knew the woods around Hilton like most folks know their own backyards.

"You wanna know what I think?" Ollie Johnson piped in, as if someone had asked his opinion. "I think you're getting your undies in a bundle about nothin'." He had his face down and was busily sopping up runny egg yolk with a piece of toast. "Your ole' man was prob'ly too deep in the woods when dark came, 'n he jus' hunkered down for the night. He'll more'n likely show up sometime today."

"I reckon Ollie's right 'bout that," Herb said, looking intently at Pete. "Your pa's too damned smart to get hisself lost."

"Gotta be smart if he didn't stick with you this year, Herb," Dennis LeCroix said with a snorting laugh. "Christ, you make enough noise in the brush to alert every friggin' deer in the county. When was the last time you bagged a buck, anyways? Couldn't've been this century."

Herb glanced down at his bowl of stew and muttered, "It ain't killin' the deer that I like. I jus' 'preciate the opportunity to get out into the woods 'n enjoy nature."

"I suppose that's why you don't go down to Florida with your wife every winter, huh?" Dennis said. " 'N I 'spoze that's why you spent so goddamned much on that new 30-30."

"Well," Herb drawled, casting a long look at Gary, who was ladling stew into a couple of bowls. " 'Least ways I bother to get out there . . . unlike some folks 'round here."

Gary's ears flushed red. He knew the comment was directed at him, but he finished filling the two bowls and carried them over to the two men at the end of the counter before meeting Herb's gaze.

"Get off the man's case, will yah, Herb?" Earl snapped.

"I just . . . never had much of a mind to go hunting, is all," Gary said, wiping his hands on his greasy apron. Several men at the counter snickered.

"Probably watched *Bambi* too many times when he was a kid 'n didn't like the idea of Bambi's mother ending up as venison steaks," Frank Harris said with a wide, buck-toothed smirk.

The Cafe filled with a brief gale of laughter. Gary's flush deepened as he looked squarely at Frank and Herb. In a low, even voice, he leaned across the counter and said, "No—it ain't that at all. I just don't cotton to the idea of killin' deer." He paused, apparently considering his words carefully, then added, " 'N I don't need to carry around a big rifle and shoot defenseless animals to prove I'm a man, neither."

He was about to say more but then caught the withering glance from Earl that told him to shut his mouth and not insult good paying customers. He turned back to the stew pot and began stirring it, trying hard to control his anger.

"Come on, lay off him, Frank," Johnny Kaufman said sharply. He was one of the two men eating stew at the end of the counter. "I don't expect I'd be all that keen on hunting either if what happened to his brother happened to mine."

Everyone in the Cafe grunted and nodded thoughtfully, some with downcast eyes.

"Yeah," Herb said, "it's been—what? Six years now since your brother got lost and died out in the woods. Ain't that right?"

Gary glanced over his shoulder at Herb and nodded tightly. "Yup. Six years almost to the day."

"And weren't that a bitch, how nobody found him 'till next spring when those Boy Scouts stumbled over him—or at least what was left of him."

"Christ, Herb! Knock it off, will yah?" Earl said sharply.

Herb turned and looked at Earl, bristling for an argument, but then he shrugged and innocently said, "Hey, man, I'm just sayin' what every damned one of us already knows. It was mighty peculiar how someone like Al could get hisself lost and then die of exposure."

"If you recall," Gary said, turning to face Herb, "we had a bitch of an early snowstorm the afternoon Al didn't show up at home. No one was gonna find him down there in that stream bed, buried under a foot of snow." Then, looking at Johnny, he added, "And what happened to Al ain't got nothin' to do with my not hunting. I just plain don't like it. Period!"

"Oooww," Herb said. He snorted and wiped his nose, leaving a shiny trail of snot on the back of his hand. "Well, someone found him, and you know as well as I do that when they did, his bones were stripped clean."

"—By scavengers," Gary said.

Herb snorted again and said, "Well, that ain't what I heard. My cousin works for the state, and he said the coroner's report mentioned there was evidence your brother's bones had been scraped, and maybe not by some animal's teeth, neither. That they might've been scraped by a knife."

"Bullshit!" Earl snarled. "You been listenin' to the wrong people." Then, to Gary, he added, "Don't listen to that asshole."

"Hey, I just know what I heard," Herb said, and with that he turned back to his breakfast.

"Yo! Gary! How 'bout another round over here?" someone shouted from the table over in the far corner. Gary nodded and called back, "Be right with yah." Taking a tray to carry the empty bowls back, he walked slowly over to the table, making a point of locking eyes with Herb as he went around the edge of the counter.

Herb tracked him with slitted eyes, then took a slurping sip of coffee and cleared his throat before speaking. "Well, you know, now that I think 'bout it, don't you all think it's rather peculiar how Al and Roy ain't been the only fellas to get lost out huntin'?"

245

Just about every eye in the restaurant turned on him, and he blushed under the attention.

"Well, I mean it seems 's though every year someone from 'round here goes missing or gets shot or some damned deal. Why, just last year it was Ruben Matthews, 'n the year before that, Pat Riccoli, that guy up from Pennsylvania."

"That's right," Frank piped in, "And the year before that, that fella from Mast-a-two-shits was found. Looked like he'd been chewed bad by some wild dog or something."

"You know what I think?" Gary said as he made his way back over to the stove. "I think you're both full of shit. I think you been breathin' them fumes in the paper mill too damned long, and your brain's gone all mushy."

"Fuck you," Herb snarled, but now that he'd been interrupted, he let what he'd been talking about drop.

"Yeah, well I still say—" Frank began as he spooned a mouthful of stew into his mouth. Before he could continue, his teeth made a loud cracking sound. His eyes widened with shock as he worked his jaw back and forth. "What the fuck—?" he sputtered as broth dribbled through his beard and down his chin.

Herb was the first to burst out laughing when Frank hawked noisily and then spat a tooth out onto the counter. It lay there, the enamel glistening like a shiny pearl on the pale green linoleum.

"Maybe you oughta think 'bout switchin' to Poly-Grip," Herb said, chuckling.

"Jesus H. Key-rist, Frank!" Earl snarled. "People have to eat off this counter!"

"I broke my fucking tooth!" Frank yelled as he pressed his hand against his jaw and started massaging the cheek. A few of the hunters closest to him regarded him and the small pearly knob that lay on the counter in a puddle of stew. Frank's cheek bulged as he ran his tongue around inside his mouth, taking a quick tally. Then he reached over the counter, snagged Gary by the shoulder, and spun him around.

"What the fuck is this?" he shouted, pointing at the tooth on the counter.

Gary shrugged, a thin trace of a smile flicking across his mouth. "Looks to me like you lost a tooth. I knew you was getting soft in the head. Must be from hangin' around with Herb."

"I broke my fuckin' tooth on something in your god-damned stew!" Frank yelled, his face flushing bright red. His hand shook as he pointed angrily at Gary. " 'N you're gonna pay for this!" He opened his mouth and began running his forefinger around inside. After a few seconds, his face clouded with confusion, and he muttered again, "What the fuck?"

Earl reached in front of Frank after grabbing a napkin from the dispenser and quickly mopped up the smear of stew. Frank snatched up the loose tooth before Earl could get it.

"I'll be a son-of-a-bitch," Frank said, staring earnestly at the tooth. Turning to Herb, he stretched his mouth open wide with both hands and in a distorted voice asked, "Can you see which one's missing?"

Wrinkling his nose, Herb peered into Frank's mouth, then shook his head and said, "Nope. Everything looks fine to me. But I ain't no friggin' dentist."

"I'll be a son-of-a-bitch," Frank said as he probed deeper into his mouth with one hand. "I can't feel a damned thing missing."

Suddenly he stiffened and, shifting his gaze to Gary, regarded him with a hard, cold stare. Gary met him with clear-eyed detachment.

"What the fuck'd you put in this stew, anyway?" Frank said angrily.

Gary shrugged again. Wiping his forehead with the back of his hand, he said, "Jus' some broth, meat 'n vegetables—carrots and potatoes, mostly."

"So how the fuck do you explain *this*?" Frank said, holding the broken tooth out for Gary's inspection. "If it didn't come outta my mouth—"

"What the hell're you talking about, Frank?" Earl said, his voice lowered with sternness. "I just saw you spit the damned thing onto my clean counter!"

"I don't mean that!" Frank shouted. "I mean this isn't my goddamned tooth! What the fuck is someone's tooth doing in my bowl of stew?"

"For Christ's sake, that ain't no tooth," Gary said as he flipped an order of eggs onto a plate and placed four slices of toast and three strips of bacon beside them. "It's just a chip of bone that must've been in with the meat I used. I just dumped in a whole batch of it straight out of the package. Must be something that got in at the processing plant."

"Bullshit!" Frank bellowed. "This sure as shit looks like a tooth to me!"

"Well—it beats the shit out of me," Gary said casually as he slid the plate of eggs over to Lloyd. "Hey—you want some sausage with that?"

Lloyd shook his head as he cut into the eggs with the edge of his fork. "Thanks, no. Teeth or no teeth in it, I wanna save some room for at least one bowl of that stew 'fore I head out." He glanced at the restaurant front window, hoping to see the first traces of morning light that would mean they could all head out into the woods, but the sky was still slate black.

"You gonna sit here all day staring at that hunk of bone, or do you want me to throw it away for yah?" Gary asked, walking over toward Frank with his hand extended.

"I dunno," Frank said, narrowly eyeing the chip of bone. "I just might want to take it over to the Board of Health and let 'em see what kind of shit's in the food you serve here."

"Now wait a minute, there," Earl said. "You don't want to be doing that. I got enough trouble with them guys tellin' me how to run my business as it is." He held his hand out, palm up, and with a quick flick of his fingers, indicated that he wanted Frank to give him the piece of bone. When he did, Earl bunched it up inside a napkin and handed it to Gary, who casually hook-shot it into the trash can by the door leading into the kitchen.

"So anyway," Pete Coleman said in the momentary silence that followed. "Are any of you guys gonna help me look for my pa today or not?"

For several seconds, the only sound in the Cafe was that of the stew bubbling in the pot on the stove. Finally, Earl cleared his throat and said, "You know, Pete, I tend to agree with Ollie, here. I'd wager a week's income, such as it is, that your pa shows up 'fore evenin'."

"Prob'ly with a seven-point buck slung across his back, too," Ollie added.

Pete looked from Earl to Ollie, trying to find reassurance in their faces, but a cold, dark gnawing, like hunger in the pit of his stomach, was telling him that sure as the sun was less than half an hour from rising in the East, his pa was dead somewhere out there in the woods. Looking glum, he took a piece of roll, ran it around inside his bowl, sopping up the last traces of stew, then popped it into his mouth.

"And anyways, we're all gonna be traipsing our sorry asses through the woods all day," Johnny Kaufman said, his voice muffled by a mouthful of stew. "If something's happened to your pa—which I don't think did, but *if* something did, then one of us is bound to find him. No sense getting the Forest Service guys involved 'till we know for sure something's happened. When was the last time you fellas seen him, anyway?"

The question was directed at Herb and Frank, who glanced at each other for a moment before Herb said, "Well, we split up when we was west of Watcher's Mountain. Roy said he was gonna try to strike a trail down to a ravine near the base. Frank 'n me went over to the fire road 'n headed toward the river."

Frank nodded and then, glancing at the window, said, "Almost daylight." Through the window, they could see the first gray streaks of dawn in the eastern sky.

Johnny waved his hand to get Gary's attention. "Hey! How 'bout another bowl 'fore we leave?"

Gary came over to the counter, took the bowl from Johnny, placed it on the work bench, and then, tipping the pot to one side, scooped up a ladleful and poured it into Johnny's bowl. As soon as he handed it back to Johnny, three other men signaled that they, too, were ready for seconds. Earl let out a low sigh, grateful that Frank's discovery of a tooth or piece of bone or whatever that thing was wasn't going to ruin the morning's business.

While some men finished up their meals, others paid their bills and headed out to their trucks and Jeeps to drive out to their jump-off points. The Cafe filled with the loud clatter of silverware and plates as Gary scraped the dishes clean and stacked them up for the dishwasher, who wasn't due in until seven o'clock. He had about half of the counter cleared and was wiping it with a damp cloth when Johnny Kaufman suddenly shouted and dropped his spoon to the floor. The loud clatter drew the attention of everyone in the Cafe.

"Well I'll be a goddamned son-of-a-bitch!" Johnny shouted.

"What—? You got a piece of bone, too?" Frank asked, scowling.

Johnny was staring down into his bowl with a thoroughly confused expression on his face. After a moment, as several men edged closer to him to see what the problem was, Johnny reached gingerly into the bowl and, hooking his index finger, held up a stew-smeared ring. "Looks like I hit the jackpot today, huh?" he said, glancing around at the curious faces surrounding him.

Gary glanced casually over his shoulder. His expression

didn't waver a bit when he saw that Johnny was holding a ring up to the light and was turning it around, inspecting it. The square red stone gleamed dully beneath the grainy brown smear of stew on it.

"Hey! That looks like my ring," Gary said. His voice was low and even, perfectly controlled. "I lost it this morning. It must've fallen into the pot when I was making the stew." He shook his head from side to side. "Damn! I've got to be more careful."

"No fuckin' way!" someone shouted.

Everyone turned to see Pete Coleman, staring at the ring with an expression of stark horror on his face.

"I'd recognize that ring anywhere! That's my pa's ring!"

Gary stiffened as he glanced from Pete to the ring and back to Pete again. Then, clearing his throat, he nodded and said, "Oh—yeah, yeah. Sure. My mistake. Mine didn't have a red stone in it."

"What the hell's going on here?" Earl said, glaring angrily at Gary. "First Frank coughs up a piece of bone, and now this!"

Gary shrugged. All of the hunters pressed close to the counter and watched as Johnny took a napkin and carefully wiped the ring clean before handing it over to Pete. Not a man in the room could describe the expression on Pete's face as he turned the ring over and over in his hand, staring at it in disbelief. His face paled, and a distant, almost vacant glaze filled his eyes as if he was staring straight into the face of his dead father. His hands were shaking as he scanned the faces surrounding him. His lips trembled. He tried to say something, but the only noise that escaped his throat was a feeble little squeak that sounded like a mouse that had been stepped on.

"Hey, you know what it is?" Gary said, snapping his fingers in the air. "Your pa was in here for breakfast yesterday morning, right? I'll bet what happened was his ring fell off and landed in the stew pot. I keep it right here under the counter when I ain't usin' it. I probably never even noticed it was there when I started making the stew last night."

"Yeah—sure," Earl said, nodding his head eagerly. "That's gotta be what happened."

"Tell you what," Gary said, focusing his eyes on the Cafe's front window, filled now with a wash of gray morning light. "The sun'll be up soon. Why don't you head on out and start lookin' for your pa. I'm sure everyone who's out today will keep an eye peeled for him, too. Right fellas?"

Everyone in the Cafe responded with loud affirmations.

" 'N I agree with what Ollie said," Gary went on. "I'll bet you a free breakfast tomorrow mornin' that your pa shows up here later today, fit as a fiddle." He held his hand out to Pete and continued, "Why don't you leave his ring here with me, 'n I'll give it to him if I see him before you do."

Pete hesitated a moment, then, his hand still shaking, he placed the ring in the flat of Gary's outstretched hand. Neither he nor anyone else in the restaurant noticed how quickly Gary clenched his hand over the ring; and no one saw the look of immense satisfaction that washed over Gary's face as he watched the hunters, their bellies filled with a hearty breakfast of hunters' stew, pay their tabs, file out the door, get into their trucks and Jeeps, and head out to the woods for another day of hunting. And not one of them suspected that they had already consumed Gary's quota of game for the season.

—for Stanley Wiater

Closing the Doors

I'd thought for days—maybe weeks—that someone was following me, but I didn't realize until that last night in Paris how much I was haunting myself.

That's why I've come back to the States. Back to the New Mexico desert. Back to where it all began all those years ago. To sort it all out if I can. To see if I can find that man, find that dead Indian I saw out here when I was a kid.

Maybe he has the answers I'm looking for.

I'm keeping this journal to help me remember and to help me work it all through. There have been too many times when things I've written in songs and poems have come too close to the truth.

Much too close.

Sometimes, I think I have no control over my life— never have . . . ever since when I was a boy, and that dying Indian's soul entered my body, replacing . . . whatever was there originally—the *real* me. It's as if I write about these things first, then I have to live them. Now that he's left me, I don't know who I am.

But it's all there in the songs and poems. Listen to "Hyacinth House" on *L.A. Woman*. I give it all away—everything that happened in the apartment that hot July night in Paris.

In 1971, Pam and I had gone to Paris to get away from it all, y'know? The media circus that was all part of being a rock 'n' roll star—the "Lizard King." Shit! I was burned out, and we both needed a break. To tell you the truth, we were seriously trying to patch things up between us, to make it good again. Problem was, when Pam wanted to make it better, I didn't. When I did; she didn't.

The *yin* and the *yang* of it all.

Maybe that's why we were so compatible in our incompatibility.

Of course, since coming to the desert, I can see now with a newfound clarity that I never had before that I was the one who needed the break.

Oh, sure—Pam had her share of problems. No doubt about it. But I can't help but think, even now, that I was the source of all of her problems. Maybe I'm making myself too important in her life.

Maybe not.

But yeah, the drinking and drugs had gotten out of hand. Way out of hand!

And the writing?

Shit! The writing wasn't coming at all. No poetry! No songs! Nothing!

I was looking for inspiration—or escape—in a bottle. Even then, part of me was warning me that I was overdoing it. I've read some of the things written about me since—that I had a death wish—that I was sick of my celebrity and wanted to die because I'd gotten everything I was after and found that it was all hollow—that I no longer wanted to be a rock star, just a "serious" poet.

Some of that may be true.

You certainly don't make a lunch of a few Bloody Marys and a bottle of scotch unless you're running away from *something*.

I see now, though, that I was also running *to* something. Maybe I needed one last hit of LSD that night in Paris to make it all clear to me. Maybe that's when the Indian's spirit left me so I could find out exactly who I used to be.

Who is this person inside me—this child who never got the chance to grow up?

That Friday night, July 2, I'd gone out to the movies—alone—to see *Pursued*, starring Robert Mitchum.

Pretty fuckin' apt title, now that I think about it.

Pam was off somewhere with those friends of hers, no doubt looking for something to shoot into her arm. I'd been drinking most of the day, so I was in no condition to care where she went. After the movie, I wandered down to the *Rock 'n Roll Circus* to check out what was happening.

Can't remember much about what I did there.

No idea who was playing that night.

The only clear memory I have was feeling like someone was watching me. I'd been feeling like that for days . . . weeks, thinking I was being followed. I kept looking around, trying to see who it was, but I could never catch even a glimpse of him . . . not until I got back to the flat that night.

Shit like that happened a lot back then. People would recognize me and follow me around. The new album had been released in April and had done pretty good. It had some great reviews, some of our best, and the first single had a good run in the top ten. The rest of the band was excited about what we were going to do next, but I wasn't ready to come back to the States.

Not yet.

I had to die first.

But shit, I should have been thrilled to have someone recognize me, what with all the weight I'd put on over the past few months. I've lost most of that weight now, and I feel a hell of a lot better.

One thing I do remember clearly from that night was scoring a hit of acid while I was there. I must have scored a bit of heroin then, too. I think maybe Peter might have given it to me. I took the acid first, and before long, the music, the people, and the night were all blending together into a riot of sounds and colors.

Like a vision of Hell.

Something straight out of a Bosch painting.

After tripping my brains out for an hour or so, I snorted the heroin to help bring me down. Never could stand to take a needle. Then, sometime around midnight, I guess, some friends piled me into a cab and sent me back to the flat.

Pam was there when I finally made it up the stairs. She was sitting cross-legged on the bed, nodding out but looking like she wasn't feeling any pain.

I was.

My head felt like it was encased in cement. The slightest sound was magnified so loud it hurt my ears. I thought I must be going crazy and vowed to stop taking acid. It wasn't doing me any good anymore, anyway. The world seemed so far away, like I was looking through a foot-thick plate-glass window. I thought maybe I'd fallen through some kind of hole in reality. Maybe—I remember thinking and laughing about it—I've finally broken on through to the other side.

I went over to Pam, and before I knew what was happening, we were naked and fucking our brains out on the bed. Time and reality lost all meaning. They always did whenever Pam and I connected. That didn't happen often enough. Too bad for both of us we didn't realize until too late that it was us, not the drugs, that made us feel that way.

When we were finished—who knows when?—Pam

started drifting off to sleep with a contented smile on her face.

God, it breaks my heart to think of how seldom I saw her smile like that! I was still feeling like shit, so I told her I was going to take a bath, thinking that would help bring me all the way down. I ran the water—hot—and eased on down into the tub, feeling every pore in my body open up to the gentle, lapping water.

I was floating in space, dreaming . . . watching the muffled explosions of color behind my eyelids. I have no idea how long I lay there with my head back and my arms resting on the sides of the tub. I might have been there for hours . . . or days, for all I know. It was still dark outside, and the water had turned ice cold when I opened my eyes and saw myself standing there at the foot of the tub.

For a moment, I thought I was looking at my own reflection in the mirror that hung on the bathroom wall. Then I realized that whoever this was—me or someone else—he was wearing a white button-down shirt, tan chinos, and a pair of beat-to-shit Frye boots just like I had been wearing earlier that evening. I was confused as hell, thinking for a moment that maybe I hadn't yet undressed and gotten into the tub.

"Hey, what the fuck're you doing here?" I asked.

A small voice in the back of my head was telling me that this wasn't really me; it was just someone who *looked* like me. I didn't have enough energy to get nervous or to wonder how the fuck he'd gotten into the flat.

He smiled and said nothing as he stared down at me, lying there in the tub. The acid was still worming its way through my brain, so I was having one hell of a time trying to figure out which was the real me—the one in the tub or the one standing there beside the bidet.

"Are . . . you . . . me?" I asked, faintly surprised that his lips didn't move when I spoke.

He nodded his head slowly and answered, "I *want* to be."

"You're the one who's been following me around, right?"

Again, he nodded.

"I want to be you," he said, running his fingers through the tangle of his long, dark hair.

I know now that there's a term for something like this. *Schizophrenic dissociation.* This guy might not have really looked like me, but the LSD was twisting reality into all sorts of new shapes. I finally understood that I wasn't really talking to myself there in the bathroom. This guy—I never asked his name—was my ultimate fan. For all I know, he might have even had plastic surgery to alter his face to look as much like mine as possible. He had long, curly hair like mine; he was dressed like me; and he acted like me—even to the point of embracing my supposed death wish. I sensed that in him right away: that he had come here either to kill me or to die.

I don't know what possessed me, but I nodded toward the bedroom door and said, "Pam's in there. If I'm going to die, go in there first and say good-bye to her for me."

He looked at me, momentarily confused. Then his smile widened and he said, "Do you mean, make love to her?"

I rolled my head lazily back and forth, and answered, "Naw! Just fuck her!"

I laid back in the bathtub and listened while he went into the bedroom. I heard him take off his clothes, rouse Pam, and then—for several minutes—all I heard was the squeaking of bedsprings and soft moaning. When he was finished, he came back into the bathroom, his naked body—thinner and stronger-looking than mine—glistening with sweat.

"Here," I said, standing up and stepping out of the bathtub to make room for him. "Why don't you get in?"

Without a word, he walked over to the tub, stepped into the icy water, and lay down.

Naked and dripping water from my face and hair, I leaned over him and stared long and hard at his face, unable to rid myself of the impression that I was gazing at myself in a mirror. His dark eyes were large, glistening as he looked up at me.

"Relax, now," I said, caressing the back of his head. "Close your eyes and relax . . . I'm going to die now."

He heaved a heavy sigh, then closed his eyes and slumped back against the tub edge. When I saw that he was completely relaxed, I went over to the sink and took a fresh razor blade from the cabinet. Moving back to the bathtub, I handed him the blade and said, "If you hold your wrist under water, it won't sting as much."

He did just as he was told.

Gripping the blade between his thumb and forefinger, he carefully, almost lovingly ran the sharp edge from the heel of his thumb up the inside of his arm. The skin split open like a lizard shedding its skin. His blood spurted into the water in bright red strands that twisted like windblown hair before diffusing and turning the water pink. All the while he looked at me, and I saw myself—felt myself dimming as his energy and life flowed from his opened arm into the cold water.

I caressed his head again, combing back his long, damp hair with my fingertips as I watched him. I saw the very instant when the dark, moist light left his eyes and changed to a glazed, empty stare.

"Good-bye, Jim," I whispered, leaning forward and kissing him gently on the forehead.

A soft, angelic smile curled the corners of his mouth.

I hurriedly dried off and got dressed. Making sure I had plenty of cash in my wallet, I left the flat in the pre-dawn stillness. At the time, I didn't know that I would never see Pam again. That certainly wasn't part of my plan, but I knew that I couldn't have trusted her with my secret. I hoped she'd be strong enough to ride out the emotional storm before I finally dared to come back to her.

As it turned out, she wasn't strong enough. The heroin had gotten too firm a grip on her.

The general press reported my death somewhat accurately, stating that I had died of heart failure. What do they think's going to happen if you slit your wrist? Of course your heart is going to stop. Perhaps the French doctor who so hastily signed my death certificate and sealed the coffin simply wanted to avoid the scandal of a famous rock star committing suicide in Paris.

There have been other things written about me since that night—that I died of a heroin overdose or a punctured lung from that fall I took out of a hotel window. There's been some speculation that I overdosed in the rest room of a nightclub and was dragged back to the flat and placed in the tub to look like I'd died of heart failure. And there were always rumors that I had committed suicide in a variety of ways for a variety of reasons. A few investigative reporters have raised concerns that Pam was the only person to identify my body before I was buried in *Pere Lachaise* cemetery, that neither Bill nor anyone else examined the body, that the doctor's signature on the death certificate might have been forged, and that no autopsy or exhumation was ever conducted.

Some of these stories come close to the truth, but none of them hit the truth. When do they ever?

But what about Pam?

I often wonder about her.

I know she took it real hard, thinking that I was dead, but I wonder if she knew or suspected what had really happened. Was she so far gone with grief, or so fucked up on drugs that she actually thought that guy in the bathtub was me? Or did she go along with it, covering up the truth and trusting that I'd eventually come back to her. Or maybe she figured I'd done what I did to get away from her.

Most people believe that I'm dead, and I'm willing to leave it at that. The man who took my place in the bathtub that night certainly didn't seem to mind playing out the final act for me. Sometime, late at night, the memory of his voice as he died soothes me.

"... *I want to be you!* ..."

There is liberation in death!

But now, for the past few weeks as I've been driving through the desert in New Mexico, searching for that dying Indian I passed by so many years ago, I can hear other voices talking to me, calling to me ... voices inside my head, telling me to ... to—

—This final journal entry, which ends in mid-sentence, was found in 1976 in an abandoned rental car several miles south of Albuquerque, New Mexico.

—for Jim

Worst Fears

Laura Griffin, who is my absolute closest friend, says to me, "Do you realize what you sound like?"

I hardly notice the dampness of the wooden bench we're sitting on outside The Book Shelf on Exchange Street. It's a gorgeous late September afternoon. A rain shower passed through an hour or so ago and is moving off to the East and out to sea. The setting sun is shining at a sharp angle from underneath the retreating edge of the cloud bank. Seagulls circle high in the sky, bright white W-shaped dots against the gray, swift-moving clouds. Twisting wisps of steam rise like phantoms from the rapidly cooling street and sidewalk.

It's getting late, and shops are closing, so the street isn't nearly as busy as it was during the day. Still, a few people stream silently past us—one or two couples, a few moms with babies in strollers, groups of teenagers and college kids, and some professional people out running last minute errands before heading home from work. As warm as the autumn day is, though, it can't come close to stopping the shiver I feel deep inside me.

"Yeah," I reply after swallowing hard. "I know *exactly* what I must sound like, but I—"

My voice cuts off with a sharp *click*.

I want to say more.

I want to tell Laura what I'm *really* thinking, but I know that I have to ease into it. More than any other of my friends, Laura knows perfectly well what I've been going through ever since my—well, ever since what happened to my husband, Jimmy.

"Did you ever go talk to that therapist I told you about?" Laura asks.

I shake my head *no* and say, "I didn't think she could really help . . . not the way I want help, anyway."

Laura's brow creases with concern. I know from more than fifteen years of friendship that her concern is genuine. Her dark eyes glisten like wet marbles in the gathering twilight. A maple tree arches over the bench where we're sitting. Shimmering drops of water dangle like tiny jewels from the tips of each flame-edged leaf. The air has a clean, fresh-washed smell to it.

Laura looks to me like she's about to cry, but I can see that she's holding back her tears, trying not to cry so she can help me.

I feel nervous. My stomach feels like it's filled with a thick, cold jelly. I want to reach out and hug her, if only for the solid warmth of a human touch, but I hold myself back. Even sitting right here beside me, she seems so far away. I can't bring myself to touch her, no matter how much I want to.

I need to say what I have to say first.

"I—I know it sounds crazy, like a . . . like it's from a nightmare or something, but I swear to God it really happened."

Laura's concerned frown deepens. She runs her teeth across her lower lip, sawing back and forth as she considers what I've said so far and what she should say to me.

It's almost like I can read her mind and can tell what she's thinking.

She's thinking that my situation is much more serious than she thought or than I can recognize. She's thinking that, maybe, I might even need to be hospitalized or something.

"Tell me *exactly* what happened," Laura says mildly. "Don't leave *anything* out."

I hesitate, trying to gain at least a small measure of composure. Usually, I can stay pretty much in control of things, but after everything that's happened lately, I'm not so sure anymore.

I blink my eyes rapidly to fight back the warm gush of tears I feel and tilt my head back and look up at the top stories of the brick and granite buildings across the street. In the slanting orange sunlight, every detail is dusted with powdery light and stands out in painfully sharp detail. The buildings look almost ethereal against the backdrop of the dark, rain-laden clouds. I can easily imagine that they're not real . . . that they're just projections against the rapidly darkening sky.

I look around, tracking one of the cars as it creeps past us down the street. Its tires make a sound on the wet pavement that reminds me of a nest of hissing snakes. No matter where I look, everything seems to be lost in a dim, dreamy haze.

"It seems so long ago, but it was . . . just last weekend— last Friday night," I begin, almost choking. I don't like the way my voice sounds so tentative, as if someone else is speaking through me.

"We were—I was—Jimmy and I went out to eat . . . at *Costello's*. It always been one of our favorite places."

Laura crosses her right leg over her left and shifts an inch or two closer to me. I think she's thinking that I'm going to fall apart completely real soon, now, and that she has to be ready to grab me, hug me, and tell me that it's all right, that I can cry all I want to as long as I need to.

"We were sitting downstairs, over in the far corner. I was trying hard to pay attention to Jimmy, to what he was saying, but I couldn't stop staring at this man who was sitting at a table diagonally across the room from us. He was far enough away so I could only catch a glimpse of him every now and then. Jimmy was going on and on about how his boss at the station was driving him crazy, but I'd heard it all before, plenty of times, so I guess I just sort of tuned him out. I thought that—"

A sudden wave of emotion grabs hold of me, and my voice falters.

Looking fearfully over my shoulder, I glance up the street in the direction of *Costello's* restaurant. Its arched wooden doorway looks dark and foreboding. I can't see any lights on inside, which creates the impression that the restaurant has been closed for a very long time. People passing by on the street seem to sense this, too, and they hurry their steps until they are past it.

I look back at Laura, but it's hard to see her clearly in the gathering gloom. Tears are welling up, warm in my eyes, making the lights shatter into bright spikes.

"So he caught you looking at another man and maybe got a little mad—is that it?" Laura offers. "Did you guys have an argument?"

Biting down on my lower lip, I shake my head and barely whisper the word, "No."

Finally, after I catch my breath, I continue.

"It wasn't that at all. Jimmy had already said several times that he thought I looked really distracted, and that he was worried about me. He mentioned more than once that he thought I looked pale, kind of sickly. I finally couldn't stand it any longer and told him what was bothering me—that I thought I recognized the man who was sitting across the room from us, but that I couldn't for the life of me remember from where. It was bugging the shit out of me."

"Did you eventually figure out who he was?" Laura asks.

I nod, but even the slightest motion sends a ripple of shivers up my back.

I look around at the people passing by on the street. I can't rid myself of the impression that they all look so . . . unreal. I'm convinced that I can see right through some of them, and that their shadows are somehow more real than they are. A city bus roars by in a blast of diesel exhaust. The sound of its engine seems to come at me from all sides, filling the air like the long, rolling concussion of thunder.

"What happened next?" Laura asks.

Her voice sounds so loud and vibrant and close to me that it pulls me back. I shake my head. Closing my eyes, I rub them hard enough to make bright, jagged patterns of light shift across my vision.

"I . . . I saw someone else," I reply, even though it takes almost all the air out of me.

Suddenly fearful, I open my eyes and look at Laura again if just to convince myself that she's really there. I am unable to speak for several seconds, but Laura doesn't push or prod me. She just sits there, looking back at me with all the patience and understanding in the world.

"A woman walked in with a man," I finally say.

My voice almost breaks, and when I lick my lips, they feel as dry and rough as sandpaper.

"They looked like they were in their late twenties, maybe early thirties. Both of them were nicely dressed. Healthy-looking people. Jimmy kept right on talking, not even noticing that I was tracking them as the hostess led them over to a booth near us. When they sat down, the woman was facing me. Sitting in the darkened corner, I felt almost invisible, so I could take the time to study her face."

"And that's when you recognized her?" Laura asks, obviously already knowing the answer.

"Yeah," I say.

The word sounds like nothing more than a dry gulp.

"I was *positive* I knew her, but—just like the man sitting across the room—I couldn't remember where I'd seen her before."

Feeling desperate and alone, I want to reach out and grab Laura's hands, but I hold myself back.

"Honest to God, Laura," I say, and my voice is trembling terribly now. "It was the weirdest sensation I've ever had in my life—like a feeling of . . . of *déjà vu* that wouldn't stop. I felt sort of like I was experiencing someone else's memories or something. It was weird."

I sigh so heavily that it hurts my chest. The sun has set by now, and the shadows are deepening around us. Even the autumn-colored leaves on the trees look like ink spots.

"I . . . I just don't know what's happening to me."

Laura re-crosses her legs and leans forward, planting her elbow on her thigh and covering her mouth with her left hand. She stares intently at me for such a long time that I start to feel uncomfortable. I don't like the way her gaze makes me feel as though she can see right through me.

I suddenly feel a powerful impulse to get up and just run away—from Laura, from everything. I find myself wishing that I could dissolve, just disappear into the rush of activity around us, but everything seems so far away . . . so distant, like I'm watching life through a thick plate-glass window.

Besides, I know that Laura won't let me run away.

She's always been the kind of friend who doesn't let me get away with anything. And she's always been there whenever I've needed her.

"So then what?" she says in a voice as airy and light as a spring breeze.

It sounds to me almost like we're talking in a vacuum. All the other city sounds around us seem strangely muffled and distant compared to the closeness of her voice. When a car passes by, less than ten feet from the bench where we're sitting, I almost can't hear the soft whisper of its tires on the wet pavement.

"It . . . it wasn't until Mr. Nolan came into the room that I finally realized what was going on," I say.

Laura shakes her head, her liquid brown eyes clouding with confusion.

"I don't know who Mr. Nolan is," she says mildly, but her voice is also strong enough to urge me on.

"He was my high school English teacher during my senior year at Gorham High School."

Laura nods, her whole demeanor saying—*yes . . . and?*

I find it difficult to breathe. The blood in my veins feels like it's turning to ice. Every nerve in my body is numb, like I have pins and needles all over.

"But you see—" I finally manage to say. "Mr. Nolan is . . . dead."

I can hardly hear myself speak, and it's dark enough now so I'm having trouble seeing Laura's face clearly, but I can tell by her reaction that she heard me. When she looks at me and silently mouths the word *dead*, I nod, my head sagging like a marionette whose strings have been cut.

"He died of liver cancer more than twenty years ago, a year after I graduated from high school."

The worried expression on Laura's face cuts me deeply. I can see the concern she feels for me, but I can also tell that she's realizing just how bad off I really am. I know that she's thinking what happened last week has totally unhinged me.

I want desperately to tell her that this isn't what's happening. Even considering the circumstances, I still feel pretty stable, but I can tell, no matter what I say, that she won't believe me.

If our situations were reversed, I wonder if *I* would believe *her*.

"You're sure it was him?" Laura says edgily. She's no longer able to disguise what she's really thinking behind a low, calming voice. "It wasn't just someone who looked a lot like him?"

I bite my lower lip and shake my head firmly, blinking

my eyes rapidly to force back the tears. A thick, salty taste fills the back of my throat, almost choking me.

"No, I know it was him. Without a doubt. I'd recognize him *anywhere*."

I look around, suddenly afraid that I must be shouting and drawing attention to us, but the passersby seem not even to see or notice me.

"And then," I say, "when I looked back at the woman who had walked in earlier, I realized that I knew her, too. She was Gail Grover, my roommate from college, freshman year. But you see—I read in the alumni magazine maybe four or five years ago that Gail Grover had died in a car accident out in California."

Laura has nothing to say. She just sits there, looking at me with total patience and understanding, but I know that she's thinking I definitely will have to be hospitalized if I keep talking like this.

"And the other man—the one sitting across the room—I finally realized that he was Frank Sheldon, a longtime friend of my father's."

"And he had died, too, I suppose," Laura says.

I hear something crackle in my neck when I nod.

"Yeah. He used to fly small engine planes and take aerial photographs of people's houses, then go door to door trying to sell the pictures to the homeowners. He took me up in his plane a few times when I was a little girl. I remember being really scared. I was maybe ten or eleven years old when his plane crashed somewhere in New Hampshire."

Laura lets her breath out in a slow sigh. She uncrosses her legs, folds her arms across her chest, and leans back against the slats of the wooden bench and just stares straight ahead, acting as if I'm not even there. Before long, I can't take it any longer, so I say to her, "And there were more."

Laura looks at me with a faint, distant light in her eyes. She looks dreamy and far away in the deep twilight. The streetlights have come on, and some of the shop windows glow with soft, buttery light. The maple tree we're sitting under throws a long, angular shadow across the sidewalk and up the wall of the store across the street from us. Somewhere in the distance, I can hear the high, winding wail of a siren. It sounds like someone crying out in pain.

"There were other people in the restaurant—lots of them, and all of them were people I had known before and who had died."

Laura's expression doesn't alter in the slightest. She just sits there and stares at me, but for some reason I can no longer tell what she's thinking. I have no idea if she believes me or if she thinks I'm lying to her. In some ways, I decide, it doesn't matter because at least I'm finally talking to someone about it!

"I saw my cousin—Rachel Adams. She died many years ago, when she was fourteen. She drowned swimming in the Royal River out behind her house. And my Aunt Lydia was there, and all four of my grandmothers and grandfathers, and Mrs. McMillan—Edna McMillan, the old lady who used to live next door to us when we lived out on Files Road."

The whole time I'm talking, Laura just stares straight ahead, but I can tell that she's still listening to me. The muscles in her jaw rapidly tense and untense. I can see and almost hear the rapid throbbing of her pulse in her neck. She takes several shallow breaths as though trying to calm herself.

"It sounds like an absolute nightmare," she finally says, still not turning to look at me.

"It was!" I shout, and this time I notice that a middle-aged man wearing a three-piece suit who's walking by turns and looks at me like I'm a crazy person. He gestures and starts to say something, then, still looking mystified, shakes his head and continues on his way. His footsteps echo hollowly in the darkness.

"It was like. . . . like having to face all of your worst fears all at once," I say in a low, trembling voice. "I had no idea what was going on, but finally I couldn't stand it any longer, so I got up and ran out of there. Jimmy called after me, and I stopped and looked back at him to see him scrambling to get up from the table to come after me, but I was out the door and on the street before he could catch me."

"And did he catch up with you?" Laura asks.

I lower and shake my head sadly.

"No. The heavy wooden door slammed shut behind me, but he never came outside. The night was cold and dreary. The street was slick with rain, but I ran as fast as I could down the street. I was terrified that all those *dead* people had left the restaurant and were coming after me."

Laura sighs and clicks her tongue as she shakes her head. I can see tears streaming down her face. They glisten against her pale cheeks, looking like quicksilver. She swallows with difficulty and then turns to me.

"So what happened after that?" she asks.

I open my mouth, but before I can say anything, I realize that I don't remember what happened next. Whatever it was, it feels like the memory of a dream that's rapidly fading away, like fine beach sand, sifting through my fingers.

"I . . . I don't know," I finally say.

Huge chunks of my memory seem to be missing, like the faint tracing of words that have been written on a chalkboard and then erased.

"I remember running down the street, heading this way, toward Exchange Street. I was thinking that I'd parked my car around here somewhere. I remember seeing the city lights reflected in the rain on the street and sidewalks, ribbons of bright, shifting color. I remember hearing the clicking sound my shoes made on the asphalt. The sound echoed like gunshots from the buildings on both sides of the street. I wasn't paying attention when I crossed the street, and a passing car almost hit me. The driver blasted his horn at me, but I didn't care. I just kept running. And after that, I . . . I—"

I shake my head again and sigh.

The soft, steady rush of wind still smells fresh with rain. It whisks my voice away like smoke.

"—I can't remember where I went or what I did after that."

"Try . . . try to remember," Laura urges.

The mild tone in her voice has returned, and it soothes me, at least a little. When I look at her again, I see the warm glow of friendship and love and trust in her eyes, and I think—for just an instant—that everything might still be all right, as long as I have a friend as faithful and loyal as Laura.

"The next thing I remember is . . . being back at my house. It was dark, and I'm pretty sure it was still raining, although my hair wasn't wet and there was no other evidence that I had been outside. No wet raincoat. No puddles on the floor or anything. It was only after I got home that I realized—like I was remembering it—that Jimmy was—"

My voice chokes off again, but Laura completes the sentence for me.

"*Dead,*" she says. "You remembered that Jimmy was dead."

For a shattering instant, I have the unnerving impression that my voice is coming from Laura. I'm terribly aware of the darkening street around us, of the shops and passing cars, of the people drifting by in gauzy slow motion, but they all appear to be impossibly distant. They're no more . . . or less . . . substantial than the memory I have of all those dead people in the restaurant.

"Yeah," I say. "I remembered that Jimmy was in a . . . a car accident and that he was. . . ."

I can't finish the sentence because I still can't bring myself to say the word *dead.*

Saying it would mean that I accepted it.

Then I hear Laura whisper softly, so close to me.

"Good Lord," she says. "I wish there was something I could say or do to help you."

She sighs again and shakes her head from side to side. I hear the soft whisking sound of her long, brown hair, brushing against her shoulders. Tears are streaming like tiny rivers from her eyes, but—surprisingly—I don't cry.

I *can't* cry!

I think I must have used up all of my tears over the last few days just getting through Jimmy's funeral. That must be it.

"So what you're telling me," Laura says, "is that you think, even when you were sitting there in the restaurant with Jimmy, that he was already—"

This time, even Laura can't say the word that echoes hollowly inside my brain.

I close my eyes and shiver the whole length of my body as I nod and whisper, "Yes."

The rushing sound of the busy street around me warbles and fades away even further, and I am swept up by an incredible sinking sensation of being alone. . . .

Utterly alone.

For a timeless instant I keep my eyes tightly closed. I feel lost in a dark, directionless void that seems to want to absorb me, but I struggle to focus on the tiny, flickering spark of my own identity.

When I speak again, my eyes are still closed, and I hear my own voice booming inside my head like the rumbling roll of kettle drums but I know it barely makes a sound in the real world.

"I don't know what to think anymore," I say.

I can't help but notice how different my own voice sounds when I listen to it with my eyes closed.

"I'm absolutely *positive* that what happened in the restaurant really did happen, Laura. I'm positive that I saw all those dead people there. I *know* I did. I even saw *Jimmy*! And I know what you're thinking. You're thinking that it has to have been a dream or something, a . . . a hallucination."

I squeeze my eyes shut even tighter until the shifting patterns of light behind my eyelids intensify. Jagged lines of light and darkness spiral inward like razor-lined whirlpools, sucking me in.

"You're the only person I've ever mentioned this to," I say, feeling the heavy vibration of each word in my throat.

"I can't explain what happened. I have no *idea* what it was or what it could mean, but I do know that . . . somehow . . . Jimmy was reaching out to me. He was trying to . . . contact me . . . to comfort me . . . like you're doing now."

My hand is trembling as I reach out, feeling for Laura's hand to grasp and hold. The emotions swelling up inside me are almost too much to bear. I feel as though I can't breathe, that a huge iron band has been wrapped around my chest and is steadily squeezing . . . squeezing. . . .

"*Laura!*" I call out.

My voice is a long, wavering moan that reminds me of a soft gust of wind in a lonely, deserted alley.

A thin sliver of panic stabs me when I open my eyes and look around. For a terrifying moment, I can't see anything except the dark street and faint hints of darker motion shifting all around me.

"Don't worry. I'm right here beside you."

Laura's voice sounds impossibly far away.

No matter how desperately I reach for her hand, I can't touch it.

"*Laura! . . . Where are you?*" I cry.

As my vision adjusts, I stare into the dense darkness of night that has descended around me. A thrill of fear races through me when I see that the bench beside me is empty.

A faint puff of warmth, like someone's breath, blows gently into my ear, but it doesn't come close to stopping the terrible shiver of fear and loneliness that trembles inside of me.

I look around at the city street and see that it is empty, too.

Deserted.

The sun has long since dropped below the western horizon, but its light still edges the underside of the clouds to the west with a baleful red glow. Ink-deep shadows reach out like grasping hands from across the street and between the buildings.

I realize that I am surrounded by dense silence, and that I am alone . . . absolutely alone. . . .

—for Charlie Grant
and Wendy Webb

Winter Queen

BANGOR DAILY NEWS Wednesday, January 17.

MUSICIAN'S JET MISSING AND FEARED DOWNED.

Bangor, Maine (UPI)—Aviation officials in Bangor confirmed this morning that rock musician Alex VanLowe was one of six passengers on board a flight that is reported missing and presumed to have crashed.

Although there has been no official confirmation that the jet has been lost, air traffic controllers at Bangor International Airport state that at 11:34 P.M. EST., the pilot, Michael DeSalvo, reported navigational problems and requested an emergency landing at Bangor International. After giving the pilot approval, the tower lost contact with the jet.

The flight originated in Quebec, Canada, and was heading to Portland, Maine, when it flew into a severe blizzard which for the last twelve hours has been ravaging the entire Northeast.

Rescue and search efforts will not be initiated until the storm diminishes, which is expected late tonight or early tomorrow morning.

Around the world, rock 'n' roll fans are anxiously following this story to hear if popular music has suffered yet another casualty, cut off in his prime. VanLowe, the lead singer for the rock group *Phobia*, was scheduled to perform at the Civic Center in Portland, Maine, tonight.

*   *   *

CLICK

The batteries in the Sony still seem to have some life, so I'll make a tape of everything that's happened—you know, in case I don't . . . well, I don't want to consider any of that right now, but it . . . *Jesus!* It sure don't look good.

It's so fucking cold!

I'm freezing my ass off!

I've gotta remember to keep an eye on the tape. Being cold like this will probably make it brittle, but it's relatively warm here inside the jet—what's left of the jet, anyway. At least we're out of the wind. I should be able to keep recording—at least until the batteries run out. Don't know if there are any spares around. I'll have to check later.

I have no idea if it's day or night right now. My watch says it's quarter past six, but who the fuck knows?

Jesus, listen to that wind!

I knew we were in trouble long before Mike came on the intercom and told us all to buckle up, but after that, everything happened so fast, I'm not really sure I can keep it straight. I know I heard the jet engines start to whine real high, and the jet definitely felt like it was dropping. I could feel the pressure in my ears. At some point I heard something hit against the outside of the jet—the side opposite from where me and Jodie were sitting. It sounded like we'd been hit by a boulder or a cannon ball or something, and then there was this big grinding sound of metal ripping, and glass breaking. And then. . . .

I don't know.

I must've hit my head or something and blacked out. I have no idea how long. I'm lucky I haven't frozen to death already!

I'm sure, once they find the wreckage, there are ways of determining exactly what went wrong with the plane. Whenever there's a news report about a plane going down, they always talk about trying to find the "black box."

I suppose this piece of junk must've had one of them, too, huh?

The only concern I have right now is, when . . . when will they find us and that little black box?

As far as I can tell, everyone on board is dead except me and Jodie. Jeff and Johnny sure as hell aren't moving. Why me and Jodie didn't die is beyond me. Must've been just plain dumb luck—where we were sitting or something. We're doing the best we can, I guess. I was bleeding pretty bad from the cut on my head, but other than that and some pulled muscles in my neck and back, I guess I'm okay.

Jodie, though—God, she's a fucking basket case!

I can't really tell how bad off she is 'cause every time I even try to get close to her, she starts screaming and pushing me away like she's fucking out of her mind!

I keep telling her that she ain't got a prayer of making it if she loses it like this, but as far as I can see, she's way off the deep end.

'Least she's sleeping right now.

I covered her up with whatever coats and blankets I could find by feeling around in the dark. The only way I know she's still alive is, every now and then, she starts whimpering and groaning in her sleep.

Shit, I wish I had a flashlight or something, but I can't even start looking around until this storm's over, and it gets light.

Jesus, listen to that wind howl!

Sounds like a goddamned pack of wolves. Every now and then something bangs against the side of the plane. Probably a branch, or maybe some piece that was knocked loose from the plane. It's fucking weird how it sounds like there's someone outside, knocking on the plane. . . .

Trying to get in.

No!

I've gotta stop thinking like that!

I know I shouldn't say this, but Jodie's not going to be any help in this situation. I wish to hell Mike and Denny hadn't been killed. They were both up front in the cockpit, so they hit the ground first and hardest. As soon as I could move, I crawled up there and saw all I needed to see. But shit! They were the technical people. They probably would've been able to rig up something with the radio or something so we could get help out here. I don't know jack-shit about how to do something like that.

And I don't even have a fucking clue where we are. Then again, it's not as if they'll be sending out any search parties until the storm's over.

And I don't know if I'll be able to hang on till then.

That's the biggie, as far as I can see.

No one knows where the hell I am.

For all I know, they might not even realize I'm missing yet.

Food's going to be another problem. I found a couple of prepackaged meals, TV dinners, in the kitchen area, but they're frozen solid, just like everything else. I can't start a fire—not with the wind and snow blowing like it is, and the microwave oven sure as shit ain't gonna work without power. I would guess there's an emergency backup system, but damned if I know where it is!

Christ, I'm hungry.

I . . . I guess I'll try to get some sleep now, but . . . Oh, Jesus!

CLICK

*   *   *

Eyes that glowed with a deep, vibrant green stared from the surrounding darkness of the forest at the hull of the jet. Thin, panting streamers of frosted breath were quickly whipped away by the swirling winds. The wolf watched, waiting with the coiled patience of the wild. It could smell the warmth of living, human flesh that was inside the metal hull, and the smell filled it with a savage urge to rip open the human's belly and for the first time in its life, feast upon steaming human entrails—the true meal of its kind.

But as the creature crouched in the whistling storm and watched, another figure, smaller and more graceful, its dark fur highlighted with a pattern of white swirls, moved silently out of the deepest shadows and came to stop at the beast's side.

You know you can't do it, she said.

The communication happened without sound, even without eye contact—a mind-link between the two creatures.

But can't you smell it, can't you?

Of course I can smell it, and it fills me with disgust.

Not me. Just inhale! . . . Deeply! . . . Let yourself feel what it stirs deep inside you. You can't tell me that it doesn't excite you! Have you ever tasted human flesh?

No! the she-wolf said, her body stiffening as she snarled aloud and glared at the wolf beside her.

You know the Decree, she said, *and you must obey it. Come with me now. The Pack is waiting to hunt.*

*   *   *

CLICK

Seven-forty-five. Morning. Must be Thursday, the eighteenth.

I spent last night shivering my ass off underneath a pile of coats and clothes that had once belonged to good friends of mine.

Very good friends.

Even Johnny, the fucking asshole. I'm even sorry he's dead. But they're *all* dead, and there's nothing I can do about it. It isn't my fault that they're dead. I have to keep telling myself that.

It isn't my fault!

I didn't sleep very much—if at all. I just lay there, watching until—eventually—a thin, gray wash of daylight brightened the porthole windows of the jet.

By the sounds of things, the storm's pretty much over, but last night . . . man, the things I heard. I—I don't even want to *think* about it!

My first impulse was to wake up Jodie, but I decided to let her sleep. She isn't going to be any help to me, anyway. I've got to check out this situation. See what's up.

CLICK

Nine-eighteen. Same day. The eighteenth.

Well, the first thing I did was go back into the cockpit. I didn't want to, but I figured any emergency stuff would be up there. The place was a mess—stuff strewn all over the place, but I found a medicine chest, a flashlight, and a flare gun. There are only six flares, so I'll have to use them wisely. I figure I'll wait until it's dark before shooting off the first one. I also found Mike's butane lighter in his jacket pocket—Jesus, it was tough, just bringing myself to touch him, but I got it, so at least I'll be able to get a fire going later . . . after I dig out of here. Probably a good thing he never listened to me when I was hounding him about quitting smoking.

Jesus, I wish I could forget what I saw in there!

The front of the jet must've hit into the trees head on. I saw . . . Jesus! The blood was . . .

No!

I'm not going to talk about it, or even think about it! Let them rest in peace, for Christ's sake!

Bedbugs

CLICK

Ten-fifteen.

It's taken me the better part of half an hour to get the side door open. Snow's drifted up pretty much over the hull, and I had to dig my way out like some goddamned animal. Mostly, though, I'm just really tired from not sleeping well. Don't know what the temperature is, but it feels like fucking fifty below.

CLICK

One-thirty-five. Still the eighteenth.

The sun's out, and it actually feels relatively warm. I even worked up a bit of a sweat, collecting a bunch of dry wood for a fire. I'm not used to working hard like this.

I got a fire going just outside the jet by the opened door. Hopefully the smoke won't drift in and fill up the cabin. Kinda funny, but I started the fire with the first thing I found—the lyric sheet I was working out a new song on when we went down.

The working title?

"Gonna Be a Big One."

Jesus, I guess to fuck it *was!*

Jodie's been awake for a while, but she isn't moving much. From the smell of it, I'd say she must've crapped herself during the night.

Can't say as I blame her.

I tried cooking up some of those frozen dinners from the kitchenette, but they ended up pretty much black. I gave the best one to Jodie—chicken and rice, I think the package said, but she didn't touch it . . . Didn't even look at it.

I ate what I could of mine and threw the rest outside. As soon as I did, some crows swooped down out of the pine trees and finished it off. Those are some big damned birds. I never realized how big they are till I saw 'em up close. But nothing goes to waste out here, I guess. I wonder . . . if Jodie and I die, will the crows fly down and eat us . . . ?

No, damnit!

I can't think like that!

I gotta stay focused and—and positive.

Next time, I'll try to cook the meals more slowly. I don't want to waste what little we've got here. There's only three more of those dinners. As long as we stay warm and have something to eat, I figure we can stay alive and it's just a matter of time before they find us, isn't it?

Well, isn't it?

CLICK

*   *   *

"It's been almost twenty-four hours since the private plane carrying rock star Alex VanLowe disappeared somewhere between Quebec and Portland. Fans of the missing singer are maintaining a candlelight vigil here outside the Portland Civic Center where he was supposed to perform tonight.

"There's been little word from the Aviation Administration as to how search and rescue operations are going, but with each passing hour, as these candles burn in the blustery gusts of winter, hope, too, seems to be fading.

"We're going to switch back to the studio where David Gurney, lead guitarist for *Phobia*, is standing by for an interview.

"This is NewsCenter 13's Doug Moody, reporting to you live from in front of the Civic Center in downtown Portland.

"Back to you, Elizabeth."

*   *   *

CLICK

Eleven o'clock. Second night. Almost Friday the nineteenth.

I guess I should have collected more firewood. This stuff's really dry and is burning up faster than I expected. I suppose I could use a branch for a torch and go off into the woods and look for some more, but I . . . I don't know.

As soon as it gets dark, the forest starts to seem really . . . I don't know . . . really weird, man. I don't want to say it, but it's kinda scary, like maybe it's haunted out here.

The wind's died down, and it doesn't seem as cold, but still, far off in the distance, I can hear this—I don't know what it is. It's like this howling. I suppose there are wolves or coyotes or wild dogs or something out here. Must be.

Shit, I hope they want to avoid me just as much as I want to avoid them.

Jodie's no better off than she was. All day, she just sat there in the back of the wreckage, staring off into space. I don't think she even knows where she is or what's happened. I moved all the bodies outside. Four of them. Mike, Denny, Jeff, and Johnny. I figured it'd be better if we didn't have to look at them. Especially when we're trying to sleep. Jodie still hasn't eaten anything. I can't even get her to drink water from the snow I've melted. I just don't see how she's going to make it if she doesn't eat and drink.

I tried my hand at cooking again and got a half-decent meal this time. It's kind of funny, I guess, to think if this had been room service, I would have thrown the tray on the floor and ripped the bellhop who'd brought it a new asshole. I didn't cook one for Jodie this time. I figured, if she isn't going to eat anything, I might as well save what's left for me later.

Earlier today, I inspected the damage to the plane. A tree sheared the left wing clean off when we were coming down. I think I remember feeling the plane kind of spin around just before we hit. After we were on the ground, the plane skidded a few hundred feet under the trees. I can't see very far in any direction. There's just pine trees all around me. So I don't think anybody's gonna be able to see us from up in the air. Not too easily, anyway.

Just after the sun set, I shot off two of the flares, but other than the stars, I haven't seen or heard a goddamned thing. An awful lot of stars up there, though. I've never seen so many. It kinda makes you realize how insignificant we all are, really.

God, it's so lonely and quiet out here. I'm gonna lose my mind if I have to stay here much longer. So alone. It's hard to imagine there's anyone alive anywhere on earth. It's like being crash-landed on another planet.

Well, I guess I should try to get some sleep. I'm gonna need all my strength in the morning.

CLICK

*   *   *

The flickering firelight stung the wolf's light-sensitive eyes as he crawled slowly forward toward the wreckage. His chest dragged in the snow, leaving a deep furrow. The scent of dead meat was heavy in the night air, in spite of the cold wind that was blowing down from the north.

Prey was always hard to find this time of year when the snowfall was as heavy as it had been this winter. A cold, deep hunger growled in the creature's belly. It had been three nights since he had last eaten, ever since the last Turning, when the moon was full. The smell of human flesh—even the rancid stench of the four dead humans that had been lined up outside the plane—was irresistible and drew the creature forward.

A low whimper escaped the wolf's throat when he reached the bodies and stood up to paw and sniff at the frozen corpses.

The creature was no scavenger.

He was a proud predator used to the speed and exhilaration of the hunt. He didn't eat *carrion!*

But this was no ordinary carrion.

This was flesh!

286

Human flesh!

The creature licked at the hot saliva dripping from his jaws as he took hold of one of the dead man's legs and pulled back, hoping to drag the carcass off into the woods where he would—finally—be able to indulge his burning desire to taste human flesh.

But the wolf had dragged the body no more than ten feet when a commanding female voice spoke inside his head.

How dare you violate the Decree?

The creature whined pitifully as he released the man's leg, letting it drop stiffly to the ground. The stinging taste of anticipation turned sour in the wolf's mouth as he turned and looked at the she-wolf, standing at the edge of the forest. Reflecting the dying firelight, her eyes glowed a terrible, vibrant green.

But this one is already dead. The Decree was made to stop the killing of humans, not the eating of them. What harm is there in eating what is already dead?

In answer, the she-wolf snarled.

You bring shame to our Tribe. Already your breath reeks of the stench of rotting meat. Have you no pride? Perhaps you wish to change Tribes and become a Red Talon.

The wolf shifted his gaze back to the human corpse, licked his chops, then, lowering his head, looked back at the she-wolf.

Come now, said the she-wolf. *The moon is past full. Come and hunt with the Pack.*

With that, she turned and ran off into the night-stained forest.

The young male wolf had no choice. His desire to taste human flesh became a hard, sour burning in the pit of his stomach, but he knew that he couldn't defy her. Not tonight, anyway, so he turned and followed her and the rest of the Pack into the forest.

They hunted all that night but found nothing, not even a squirrel or raccoon. As gray shafts of morning light streaked the eastern sky, they made their way back to their Den.

As they slept, their bellies growled and churned with tight knots of hunger; but for the male wolf who, if only for a moment, had held the frozen flesh of a human in its mouth, the pain was deeper and much worse.

*   *   *

CLICK

Six-thirty in the morning. Second day, so I'm guessing it's Friday, January nineteenth. Yeah, it's gotta be that. Funny, though, how time seems to stretch out and not make much sense out here.

As if something like time really matters!

Our way of keeping track of time probably doesn't mean a goddamned thing out here. I can feel that there's a sense of a natural rhythm, a way things move here in the forest that has absolutely nothing to do with us humans and our machines.

Anyway, I have to record what happened last night before I forget it or convince myself I was only dreaming.

It was late. I guess I must've drifted off to sleep, but I'm not really sure. I don't feel all that rested. Anyway, the sounds of something moving around outside the plane woke me up. I could hear whatever it was pawing around, the snow crunching under its weight. As much as I wanted to, I didn't dare go out and take a look around. Maybe if I had a gun, I would've gone outside, but I stayed inside the plane more than half-expecting whatever it was to charge in and attack me.

As soon as the sun was up, I went outside and saw what had happened.

Something—a very large and powerful *something*, judging by the tracks in the snow—had dug up Jeff's body and tried to drag it off into the woods. It was probably one of those wolves or coyotes I heard the first night. Jeff's pant legs were all ripped up, and I could see some pretty deep teeth marks on his legs. It was weird how there wasn't any blood, though, and it. . . .

No. I can't think like that!

I've got to handle this.

The first thing I have to do is something to stop whatever's out here from getting at the bodies.

These are my friends, for Christ's sake! I can't let them just . . . just. . . .

CLICK

*   *   *

"Authorities at the Civil Air Patrol and the State Forestry Services told News Center Six today that they are expanding their search for rock star Alex VanLowe's missing jet to include large portions of western Maine and the White Mountains of New Hampshire.

"Plummeting temperatures and another blizzard that is moving into the area tomorrow are narrowing hopes that any of the passengers could have survived the crash.

"At the Portland Civic Center, a few dozen die-hard fans are still maintaining an around-the-clock candlelight vigil in hopes of hearing news that their rock idol is alive and safe. And while it may be too early to give up all hope, time does seem to be running out.

"In other news today. In Lewiston, the trial was begun for Marilyn Larabee, the woman who's been accused of keeping her baby daughter locked up in a. . . ."

*   *   *

CLICK

Three-forty-five in the afternoon. Same day. The nineteenth, yeah, the nineteenth.

I'm exhausted after spending most of the day piling snow up over the . . . the bodies of my dead friends.

The best thing I could find for a shovel was one of the lunch trays that I broke off the back of one of the chairs in the plane. I piled the snow up as high as I could and then smoothed it all over, flattening it as much as I could. I don't think whatever was out here last night will know anything's under there.

I hope not, anyway.

Food's my only real problem now.

There's nothing left of those crappy TV dinners. I finished the last one earlier today, and already my stomach is feeling hollow. There's not much to those meals in the first place.

I try not to think too much about what I'm gonna do next, but I have no idea what.

I can't just wait here and starve to death!

Then—*Jesus!* I start thinking about that soccer team that crashed in the Andes or something, and in order to survive, some of them ate the flesh of the ones that had died in the crash.

Is that what I'm going to be driven to?

God, just the idea of it makes me nauseous!

I could *never* do that!

I'd rather *die!*

I'm not a fucking cannibal!

The only change in Jodie is for the worse. She might just as well be dead, too, as far as I can see. She just sits there, staring up at the ceiling and groaning as she rocks back and forth. If I had the balls to do it, I'd kill her myself just to put her out of her goddamned misery.

Yeah, that's it.

And then I'd *eat* her.

Christ, I can't believe I just said that!

Sorry. I shouldn't be laughing about it, but it *is* kind of funny how I—I just pictured me as sort of like a character in one of those cartoons—you know, the ones where there's a stranded miner or something who's looking across a bare table at his partner and seeing him as a stuffed, steaming turkey on a platter.

But no!

Not Jodie!

Hell, she's too skinny, anyway. Wouldn't be good eating. Too bony. God, I can't believe I'm talking like this. I must really be losing it.

It's got to be exhaustion, that's all.

Exhaustion and hunger.

How long has it been, now?

Two or three days?

I'm not even sure. But—Christ—what does it matter? It feels like weeks!

You'd think I could last a little longer than this, wouldn't you?

But the cold!

It's *so* fucking cold!

No matter how much firewood I collect or how high I build the fire, I just can't get warm enough. The fire's blazing away now. Just listen to it crackle. And then, when I think how I wasted most of the day, and all that energy covering up those bodies with snow when I could have been collecting more firewood. Maybe enough to make a big enough blaze so someone would see it.

No, I know what I should have done. I should have cut off some of the best chunks of meat off those guys and fried it up. Lord knows Johnny's ass is big enough.

Jesus! Stop thinking like that!

And now night's coming.

As soon as it starts getting dark, the wind starts to howl and moan. Sometimes, I swear to God it sounds like there's someone moving around out there in the woods. Sometimes there are sounds like someone dying.

Hey, maybe that's it.

Maybe it's me.

Now there's a thought!

What if I go out there and find someone facedown in the snow. After I cut off a big chunk of meat to cook up, I roll him over and see that it's *me!*

No, no, I gotta keep it together better than this if I'm

gonna make it out of here alive. I ain't doing this for Jodie anymore. Hell, I don't know if she's still alive or not.

Who the fuck cares?

I'm gonna try to sleep now, and if I die in my sleep, who the fuck cares?

Huh?

I asked you . . . Who the fuck cares?

CLICK

* * *

The firelight pushed back the darkness, making dense shadows waver and dance across the orange-tinged snow. Dry knots in the wood heated up and exploded, sending sizzling showers of sparks corkscrewing up into the sky where they dissolved against the stars.

At the edge of the forest, five pairs of eyes glowed green in the night. Five pairs of not-human eyes, but one pair was narrowed to mere slits of evil and hunger as they stared at the wreckage of the plane.

I still have the right to disagree with the Council, do I not? the young male wolf said.

There was a brief silence, filled only with the low hissing of the wind in the trees, the distant crackle of the fire, and the soft thump of snow, falling from heavy-laden branches.

At last the she-wolf spoke.

Yes, you have the right to disagree with Council, but you do not have the right to act contrary to a decision handed down by them. And you can never defy the Decree and remain within our Tribe. However, if you choose to become a Silent Strider . . .

No. I never said I wanted to do that!

The one pair of green eyes stared at the female and narrowed all the more with a deep, burning hatred.

But what if the Council is wrong? What if their decision is foolish?

The she-wolf turned and glared at the young male wolf, making him cringe.

The Council thinks it will not prove so, the she-wolf replied coolly.

But the Council does not know everything. Perhaps the Council should reconsider. Saving the life of this human could prove harmful to the Tribe. We have worked for generations to keep this forest wild. We certainly do not want to help the humans!

Then one of the other wolves, the largest of the five, stepped between the two.

There will be no more discussion, this wolf said. *We are here to make contact with this human, and there will be no harm done to him.*

* * *

CLICK

I know I'm losing it now . . . after what I saw . . . or *think* I saw!

What time is it? Let's see. Okay. A little after two o'clock and still dark, so it must be two in the morning. That makes it—what? Saturday? Saturday or Sunday? I don't know for sure. Jesus, I can't think straight anymore!

I couldn't sleep at all last night. My stomach's in a knot of pain, and it's so cold . . . so fucking cold! I doubt that I'll ever be warm again!

Okay. Okay. Focus. Concentrate. This is what happened.

I don't know how I knew they were out there, all right? But something, some primitive sense or something deep inside made me look outside . . . I guess I wanted to make sure nothing was—you know, out there getting after the bodies of my friends.

I had really stoked up the fire earlier, and it was still blazing high when I peeked out around the edge of the plane's door and saw them.

At first I wasn't sure how many there were.

Five, maybe six.

They kept shifting in and out of the shadows, their eyes

glowing bright green in the firelight. It took me long enough to believe there was anything there, that I wasn't imagining the whole thing. I didn't even believe they were real until I saw one of them start toward me.

It was a beautiful animal.

Not large, really. Not as large as I'd ever thought a wolf should be. It had thick, dark fur that was streaked with lighter markings. Some of them—I know this sounds crazy, but some of the markings looked like lightning bolts!

That's when I was pretty sure I was imagining or dreaming the whole thing.

As it approached me, this wolf kept staring at me, not even blinking. I felt like I was under—I don't know, some kind of mind control or spell or something. It wasn't until it was more than halfway to me that I realized it really was a wolf.

There was a whole fucking wolf pack out there in the woods!

And I knew what they wanted.

They wanted *me*.

They wanted to *kill* me and *eat* me.

I knew I had to do something to defend myself, but I was too scared to move. It was like the eyes of this one animal had a hold on me . . . it had hypnotized me and wouldn't let go. I just stood there, staring like a damned fool at this . . . this thing until it began to . . . to, I don't know—it began to, like, shimmer and glow in the firelight.

And then—and I know this is gonna sound completely insane—but while I was watching it, another one of the wolves walked up next to it. This wolf had something in its mouth. It took me a second or two to realize that it was a rabbit.

Anyway, this one wolf drops the rabbit down in front of the other wolf. In an instant, before the rabbit could get its bearings and hop away, the other wolf snapped it up into its mouth and bit it almost in half. Blood squirted like ink all over the snow. The rabbit kicked for a second or two, and then lay still.

And then—oh, boy! Now I don't even believe this myself, but then something *really* weird happened.

I was still watching this whole thing from inside the doorway of the plane when this one wolf started to . . . to *change*.

The first thing I thought was that my eyesight was going bad, or that I was hallucinating, going crazy from being so cold and hungry and lonely. Maybe the whole fucking thing was a dream I was having before I died. But after a while, the—this wolf shape sort of transformed into a woman.

I couldn't believe what I was seeing!

One minute there's this a wolf, standing there, glaring at me like it wants to fucking eat me, and then the next minute there's this gorgeous, naked woman standing in front of me. If she'd just disappeared then, I'd have chalked it all up to a dream or hallucination, but then she smiled at me. Looking me straight in the eyes, she raised both arms to me and said, "We want to help you. We want you to join us."

It was real!

I swear to Christ, she was real!

She was standing there . . . naked . . . unbelievably gorgeous, and not even shivering while snow blew and swirled all around her.

And her *voice!*

Her voice!

It's still echoing in my memory like it's become a part of me or something.

We want to help you. We want you to join us.

She just stood there, extending her arms out to me, and then she started to come closer.

I tried to say something but couldn't.

I knew her for what she was.

She was *Death!*

She was *hunger!*

She was *cold!*

She was the *Winter Queen*, and her embrace and her kiss would mean death to me.

I dropped down onto my hands and knees and felt around until I found what I was looking for.

The flare gun.

I cocked it, making sure it was loaded, and then wheeled around quickly and shot.

The night exploded into red. The light from the flare dazzled my eyes, making it impossible for me to see anything except for the brilliant zig-zags of blue afterimages. I think I heard a loud howl of pain, but I'm really not sure. It might have been me, screaming. I was so overcome that I must have collapsed right there in the doorway. I didn't wake up until much later. I was shivering my ass off because the fire had burned down to nothing.

I know this all sounds absolutely crazy, but in the morning, once it's daylight, I'm going to check around in the snow for footprints . . . and blood. There must have been blood, at least from the rabbit that wolf/woman killed, right?

I really can't talk about it anymore.

I need to rest . . . and some food. I need some god-damned food!

CLICK

*   *   *

"This is Spotter Four calling Sky Chief One. Spotter Four to Sky Chief One. Do you read me? Over."

"Roger that, Spotter Four. I read you loud and clear. What've you got? Over."

"I just saw something that might have been a flare off my left wing. It was pretty far away, and awfully low to the ground, but I'd swear it was an emergency flare. Over."

"I didn't see anything over this way. Make sure you mark your heading and report back to headquarters. Over."

"Roger. I'm going to take a quick fly-by, first. Over."

"If I was you, Spotter Four, I'd hustle my hinder back

to the airport. This storm that's coming in is supposed to be a real whopper. Worse than the last one. Over."

"Roger that, Sky Chief One. Over and out. Spotter Four to base. This is Spotter Four calling base. Do you read me? Over."

*   *   *

CLICK

Eight-oh-five. A.M. I'm pretty sure it's Sunday, so that makes it the twenty-first.

It's starting again. Another storm is on its way. I thought I could feel something coming. All night, there was this . . . this feeling in the air.

I thought maybe it was just me—you know, that I was imagining things again . . . especially after what happened last night. And then finding Jodie.

She died last night.

Probably a blessing, really.

She wasn't going to make it, anyway.

Then again, neither am I.

Not if this is a real blizzard coming. It'll bury me and Jodi and the plane and everything. Maybe this summer or a couple of years from now, some hikers are gonna find the wreck, but by then, my bones will have been picked clean by those crows. . . .

Or the *wolves!*

Sometime around six o'clock this morning, the wind started picking up, and it started to snow. I thought about going out and trying to get enough firewood to last me through the day, but I sure as hell am not going out into those woods in the dark—not with those hungry wolves around. Maybe I scared them off for a while, but if they're hungry enough, which I'll bet they are, then they didn't go very far.

They'll be back.

I didn't go out and check the snow for footprints or

blood like I'd planned. What I saw last night seemed absolutely unreal, but I know I wasn't imagining it. Besides, any tracks would be covered up already by the new snow. I'll probably never know what really happened out there last night.

Maybe it's just as well.

I can hear the wind and snow banging against the side of the plane. It sounds like it's almost ice, rattling like we're being sprayed by thousands of rock pellets or something.

Wait a second. Why'd I say we?

There's no *we* anymore.

There's just me and my dead girlfriend, and four other dead friends I've got stacked up outside the plane like fucking firewood. I want to stay focused, stay positive, but I don't see how I'm going to make it more than another day or two. I'm so hungry my stomach's a constant knot of pain. I haven't even dared take Jodie outside yet. I'm not sure I can bring myself to touch her.

The others—sure it was hard, but I hadn't slept with them—or made love to them. Huh! Except for my manager, Denny. I guess you could say he fucked me over plenty of times over the last few years.

That's not funny!

But with Jodie, though . . . I can't stop wondering if I'd be able to stop myself if I was going to—

To. . . .

Jesus, no! I can't think about it. I'm not going to—I *couldn't* cut her up and eat her, even if it means that I have to die out here!

Oh, yeah—sure, right now I'm so hungry it hurts, but I'm not insane.

Not yet, anyway.

But what if I'm snowed in here for a day or two before I can even dig my way out?

What if I'm too weak to dig myself out this time?

What then?

I won't be able to keep the fire going. And how hungry will I have to get before I finally lose it?

Hungry enough maybe to *want* to do something about it?

Maybe that's why I haven't taken her outside yet. Maybe I want her in here with me in case I *need* her.

How hard could it be to eat human flesh, anyway?

I'd just have to take one of the steak knives from the kitchenette and cut into her, right?

What part, I wonder.

Probably the leg.

Yeah, the upper leg. That'd be the meatiest part.

So what would be the problem?

I'd treat it like any other piece of meat, wouldn't I? Just like a steak. I'm no fucking vegetarian, so what's the big fucking deal?

I can almost kid myself that it's what Jodie would say she wanted me to do, if she could talk. She'd say—*"Come on, Alex. Do it! Let me give you the ultimate gift . . . the gift of life."* I can't help but laugh, imagining her saying, *"Eat me, baby. Eat me!"*

Christ, I've done that plenty of times before . . . in a manner of speaking.

So how big a step could it really be?

A couple of slices, stick a slab of juicy, red meat into the flames, and let it cook.

God knows, even if I'm not hungry enough to do it right now, I'm gonna be soon enough, so maybe I damned well better start getting ready for it.

If I'm gonna survive this, I'm gonna have to do *something* desperate . . .

And soon!

CLICK

* * *

"So tell us what's up with the weather, Dave."

"Well, it sure looks like we're in for another big one, Kimberly. That low pressure area that's been sweeping up the coast is getting into position for another classic

Nor'easter just like the one we had last week. We could see as much as a foot of snow along the coast and, of course, much higher accumulations farther inland. Maybe even two to three feet. I'll have all the details for you when Six Alive continues its morning report."

*　　*　　*

The Tribe was sleeping in the Den. Three of them, besides the she-wolf, had made a kill during the night and, thus, had resumed their human form. But even as the storm raged outside the mouth of the Den, Lyssa, for that was her name, couldn't stop thinking about the man at the plane wreck. She had spoken to him, had invited him to join them, had offered him life—a *real* life of running with the Pack, not living in the sterile, choking confines of civilization.

And what had he done?

He had shot a bolt of red flame at her.

For several seconds after the flare had whisked past her head, Lyssa had stood there, dazed and frozen in her tracks. From the time when she was young and had lived closer to humans, she had known about fire and had learned to fear it. Her ancestors, when she spoke to them in her ancestral memory, told her that control of fire by humans was what had first begun the corruption of Gaia. But she had lost her instinctive reaction of fleeing from fire and had stood there in the snow, transfixed . . . amazed.

Then, as though through a mist, she had become aware of what the rest of the Pack was doing. Realizing that the human may be reloading his gun, she quickly turned and ran off into the forest. Naked and shivering, it was only by traveling between the furry bodies of her friends that she arrived back at the Den alive.

But now, she couldn't stop thinking about the man and how much she wanted to save him. She had reached out to him, had touched his mind, and had felt that he was close to her in spirit.

She and the other members of her small Tribe were different from the rest of their werewolf kind. They were considered outcasts by most werewolves, and had been for centuries. But long ago, back when the Europeans had first arrived in their land, these few members of their Tribe had chosen to live in the Wild, which they cherished and hoped to defend. A few of them—most importantly one of Lyssa's ancestors—had been sickened by the memory of the slaughter of both the natives and the newly arrived Europeans. More than two hundred years ago, they had adopted the Decree, which forbade them from ever taking human life.

Or of eating human flesh.

Over the course of time, this decision—and their dedication to it—had caused inexplicable changes in their essential nature. They found that, once again, as in Ancient Times, they were subject to the Curse of the Full Moon and were unable to control their Change as others of their kind could. Whenever the moon was full, against their will, they would change into their wolf form, and they discovered that, in order to resume their human form, they had to kill . . . they had to drink hot, living blood and taste raw flesh in order to transform back to their preferred human form.

This curse alone would have been easy enough for the Tribe to accept. It was a small price to pay for the freedom they sought and found, living away from society both human and werewolf; but there was one other development for which they couldn't account. While in their wolf form, they discovered that they aged faster than they did in their human form. They soon learned that, while in wolf form, they aged as does a wolf or dog—seven years for every one human year.

So with the Change that came with the Full Moon, their need and motivation to kill became stronger than ever, but they clung to the Decree and refused to kill humans, as was the custom with most of the rest of their kind.

Lyssa arose and hurriedly dressed, putting on her warmest fur cloak, and left the Den. The sentinel at the mouth of the Den asked her where she was going, but she told him nothing as she strode out into the storm.

* * *

CLICK

"... and you don't mind that I'm recording what you said?"

"Oh, no. Not at all."

"I mean—tomorrow morning ... or sometime later, I'm going to have to listen to this all over again."

"It will help you understand it all on a deeper level."

"Shit, I'll need to hear it just to help me convince myself that I'm not—you know, that I haven't completely lost my mind."

"You haven't lost your mind ... far from it, but you *are* in danger of losing your life. That's why I've come here. To save you."

"What do you mean, save me? Are you—You're, like, a—an angel or something, is that it?"

"No ... I'm probably the furthest thing from an angel."

"Who are you, then?"

"I told you. My name is Lyssa."

"Lyssa who?"

"I have no need of a last name."

"So what are you? The Queen of Snow? The Winter Queen? Is that it?"

"No, I'm not those things, either. Look, we don't have much time."

"What the—? Oh, my God! What the hell are you doing?"

"This will save your life."

"But you just—oh, Jesus! You just cut your arm wide open. Look. It's bleeding!"

"Here. Take this."

"Are you crazy? Now I *know* I'm insane! This can't be happening! There's no way I'm going to eat that!"

"But you have to. It will give you strength."

"No . . . I . . . that's a—that's a piece of the flesh from your arm, for Christ's sake! . . . I can't just . . . just. . . ."

"I'm doing this willingly, Alex, to save your life."

"But I can't eat . . . that . . . that's human flesh."

"It will make you become as I am."

"But what if I don't *want* to become what you are? What if I'd just as soon die here rather than . . . than eat someone's flesh?"

"It's the first and only time you'll ever have to do it, Alex. After today, the Decree will forbid you to eat human flesh. But right now, you must."

". . . no . . . I can't. . . ."

"Please. Take it. Take it and eat. Eat it and live."

CLICK

*   *   *

He ran, and the deep snow tugged at his legs, tripping him as he went.

He ran until he thought his chest would burst, until his lungs felt like they were on fire.

He ran, and the sour, coppery taste of blood, the rank taste of human flesh filled his mouth, gagging him. When he clamped his teeth together, they met a rubbery, fatty resistance, and the thought of what was still in his mouth made him want to spit it out.

But he didn't spit it out.

He swallowed it, straining to force the lump of cold flesh down his gullet. Hot vomit churned deep inside his gut.

And still, he ran.

He ran until he fell.

The impact wasn't hard in the soft snow. Cold and cushiony, it reached up to embrace him, and he enjoyed its comfort, if for only a few seconds.

Then something started to happen.

He felt his bones begin to shift and crackle, crumpling like tissue paper inside his body. Nerves and blood vessels roared with pain and new life as the Change came over him for the first time.

He was terrified.

His face was compressed. Then it began to extend outward. His spine curled up and around like it was forming the shape of a question mark. Some of his bones lengthened while others shortened. All of them crackled like a fire raging beneath his skin. Muscles and tendons twanged like taut elastics connecting new and unusual angles of bone. Something tugged back at his face, and he felt his ears slide up to the top of his head and flatten. His eyes shifted to the sides of his head, and when they did, his vision gradually sharpened. He began to see the world in a unique way.

Sights became sounds.

Sounds became tastes.

And all around him, the world exploded with new, deep, and vibrant scents and sensations he had never even imagined were possible.

He wanted to cry out in his misery and joy, but the pain of the transformation began to blend into something else . . . it gradually shifted into a fierce strength and a dizzying, almost terrifying feeling of *power*.

He tilted his head back, filled his lungs with cold air, and let loose a rising, keening howl that echoed throughout the snow-laden forest.

And then he ran, but now he ran on four feet and with a new sense of strength and purpose.

He ran with the Pack!

*　　*　　*

"You're looking at the scene earlier this morning when a National Forest Services ground rescue team finally arrived at the crash site of the private jet which had been carrying Alex VanLowe and some of his entourage to a concert in Portland, Maine, when it disappeared last week.

Bedbugs

"For four days, now, the search for the missing rock star had expanded until last Saturday night, when a Civil Air Patrol pilot reported seeing an emergency flare here in the National Forest northwest of Mount Washington. Because of the blizzard conditions that swept through the area, rescuers weren't able to get to the downed plane until early this morning, just after dawn, but the plane has been positively identified as that of the missing rock star. How it came to be so far off course is still a matter of speculation, but authorities report that the pilot of the jet, Michael DeSalvo, had reported navigational problems. Obviously, they were considerably off course.

"And when the rescue team parachuted down this morning, what a grim sight they found!

"The bodies of four dead passengers, identified as the pilot, Michael DeSalvo, Mr. VanLowe's manager, Dennis Cody, and two members of the road crew, Jeff Connors and Johnny Martinez, were found buried beneath a mound of snow. A fifth body, that of Jodie McDaniels, Alex VanLowe's girlfriend, was found inside the plane. As of right now, the rescue team has not found any trace of Mr. VanLowe.

"Fans around the world are hoping and praying that the rock star will be found alive, but rescuers are holding out little hope. Tracks which the rescue team thinks may have been made by Mr. VanLowe were found leading off into the woods. After following them for nearly a mile, the team lost them in the dense woods and decided to return to the crash site until a larger search party can be formed.

"We'll keep you updated as these events unfold, but for now, things look rather doubtful that Alex VanLowe will be found alive.

"In other news today, the trial in Augusta of the man arrested for shooting his neighbor's cat continued. . . ."

—for Markku Jalava

Late Summer Shadows

Questions is how the whole thing began.

Questions.

Most problems in life start that way . . . with questions. Now that it's long since over, 'n I'm an old man, I 'spoze there's only a few—maybe just one big question that'll end it once and for all. But I sure hope to hell I don't meet George so's I can ask him.

"D'you know why they put gravestones on graves?" George had asked me that August day, so long ago. We was both 'bout ten years old that summer, 'n we were thicker 'n thieves in them days. That afternoon, we was sitting in the shade, on cool, moss-covered stones in the backyard.

My mother and me was visiting George and his family at their summer camp on Little Sebago. They had a place down on Campbell Shore Road, and we generally spent a week or two there with 'em every summer, usually in August. My father had died six years before, in France, fightin' the Kaiser's army. I was only four at the time he died, so my memory of him ain't so good. I 'spect I have no real memory of him at'all—it's just that I've heard so much about him 'n seen old photographs of him that I think I remember him.

Anyways, I was saying—when George asked me that question, I just sat there, starin' at him for a moment or two, suspectin' it was some kinda joke or somethin' 'n he had some silly-arsed answer. George usually did things like that. 'Least ways, that's how I remember him.

The sun was gettin' low in the sky, glintin' white off the water. Late afternoon shadows stretched across the lawn, lookin' thick—almost furry. It was still too warm to do anythin' as active as play croquet or badminton, so we was just settin' 'n talkin'.

"Don't be stupid," I said. "It's just to mark where the grave is—or who's buried down there." I remember thinkin' at the time that my voice sounded like I was on a vibratin' machine or somethin', but I didn't want George to know that his question had spooked me any. It didn't pay to let George know you was scared of anythin'.

You know, though, now that I think about it, George always had a kinda unique talent. He could scowl 'n laugh at the same time. Try it. It ain't so easy as you think. Years later, I used to think George would've made a great school teacher 'cause he could tell you your idea was wrong as rain without really hurtin' your feelings.

"Follow me," he said, suddenly jumpin' to his feet and lightin' out towards the woods behind his folks' camp. "Come on. I wanna show you something."

He ran swiftly along a narrow path, through scrub pine, high bush blueberries, maple saplings, 'n finally into the deeper pine woods where the air was thick with resin. I followed as fast as I could, but George could always run faster than me. I had a tough enough time just keepin' up with him.

He dodged through the woods, duckin' his head under branches or hangin' onto 'em 'n then lettin' 'em snap back with a *whoosh*. I was glad I wasn't followin' too close, 'cause I would've been whooped in the head or somethin'.

I could tell by his general direction which way he was headed—toward the brook that ran between his family property and old man Kimball's. Whenever we played guns or whatever out there in the woods—which wasn't much lately 'cause we was gettin' older—we rarely came over the brook. After a heavy rain, the ground was all soggy 'n such. Our parents warned us 'bout there bein' quicksand out there, too. 'Course, I realize now they just told us that to keep us away from the brook.

At last, George slowed his pace, but he was still a good fifty feet ahead of me when he stopped at the edge of the brook. Callin' it a *brook* really is an insult to them open-runnin', babblin' streams that can make a walk in the woods so pleasant. Kimball's Brook, which was what we called it, was really more of a quagmire—thick, black mud and dense stands of cattails and black flag marked most of its course.

George stood there by the water, waitin' for me to catch up. My breath felt like a fire in my chest, but I tried not to pant too hard.

Pointing in the direction of Kimball's house, George said, "It's up this a'way." His voice had a hushed, respectful tone—almost like he was speakin' in church or somethin'. The discomfort I had felt when he first mentioned grave-stones now got worse. I looked back along the trail where we'd come and saw that the woods was darkenin'. I imagined I saw shapes thickenin' and movin' in the late summer shadows. The sky overhead was deep blue, almost purple, and I knew even then that we shouldn't have come so far from the camp this close to dark.

"It'll be gettin' on time for supper," I said, forcin' my voice not to betray how nervous I was feelin'. "Don't you think we oughta head on back now?"

"You have to see this first," George said. His voice was tinged with wonder and—'least ways as I recall it now—a bit of dread. We pushed and fought our way through the brambles and cattails. Both of us got scratches on our bare arms and legs. I remember looking down at my muddy Keds sneakers and thinkin' 'bout how much hell there'd be to pay when my mother saw 'em. I wouldn't be able to fool her 'bout where we'd been, either—I knew that much. She had a way of knowin'.

" 'S not far now," George said over his shoulder. Even he was beginnin' to sound a bit tired. But there was this determined set to his jaw that I could see, even in the fadin' light, 'n it made me realize we should've considered all of this a bit more before leaving his yard.

"What is it, anyway?" I asked. This time I knew he'd hear the fear in my voice, but I didn't care.

"You wait 'n see," he said, smiling thinly. "You just wait 'n see."

He ducked under a low-hanging branch and then stopped still, frozen like a deer caught in the headlights of an oncomin' car.

"There," was all he said.

When I got up to him, he stood to one side so's I could see. My gaze followed his pointin' finger. At first I couldn't make out anything, it was so dark under that old pine tree where he was pointin'. Then—faintly—I thought I could make somethin' out . . . it looked like the outline of . . . somethin'.

"Go on," George said. "Get closer. You'll see."

I took a coupla steps closer, 'n as I did, the thick, black object resolved in front of me out of the gloom. I stumbled backwards, gasping for a breath, but the air was humid and thick, like takin' a lungful of water.

"Jeeze!" I said. "It looks like a . . . gravestone!"

George was smilin' and noddin' his head up 'n down like some silly puppet. There was a look of pride on his face that made me feel . . . well, somehow worse, like he was just askin' for trouble.

"Not just a gravestone, either," he said, walking up to it

and placin' a hand on the aged, pitted stone marker. "Look."

Bracin' his feet against a rotten log, he leaned forward and, with a belly-deep groan, pushed against the stone with everything he had.

"Cripes!" I shouted when I saw the gravestone teeter back 'n forth. At least I thought it did; it was kinda hard to tell there in the gatherin' shadows.

The effort was too much for George alone, though, and with a loud exhale, he stopped pushin' 'n let the stone come to rest where it'd been. I had this sudden image that the gravestone was like a giant loose tooth, 'n it looked ready to come out if someone gave it a hard enough push.

"Come on. Help me with it," George said. "I think between the two of us we can get it."

"What, are you crazy?" I shouted, takin' a step backwards. My foot hit soggy ground, 'n I went up to my ankle in warm water. "No-sir-ee," I said, shakin' my head back and forth. "I ain't gonna touch that!"

"Aww, come on," George pleaded. He walked over to me and grabbed me by both arms. His hands were covered with a fine, mossy grit. Just the thought of him smearing my arms black made me want to upchuck. My stomach did a quick little flip-flop, somethin' it hadn't done in a long time—not since my last ride on the rolla' coasta' out to Old Orchard Beach.

"I found it last summer, right after you and your mom left," George said. "I've been waitin' all year for you to help me move it!"

"I don't think we should be messin' around with something like this," I replied weakly.

"How come? You ain't chicken-shit, are you?"

I shook my head, unable to speak. It felt like somethin' had a'hold of my throat.

"Maybe what you're thinking is, a tombstone ain't just to mark where someone's buried. Huh? Is that it?" George said, rubbin' his blackened hands together. "Maybe . . . just maybe that stone's put there to weight the dead person down. You know—something they put on their chest to keep 'em from gettin' up and walkin' around."

"Come on . . . Cut it out," I said, looking fearfully over my shoulder at the way we had come. The sky was now a deep purple, and rafts of clouds, underlit by the settin' sun, stuck out like dead, white fingers. "We—uh, gotta get back for supper. Our moms are gonna be *wicked* mad at us."

"Just help me push it over," George pleaded. "I can't do it myself. After that, you can go back to the camp if you want to. I want to check this out."

"We shouldn't be messin' around with stuff like this," I said. "What if old man Kimball sees us out here?"

"He ain't gonna see us. 'N even if he does, what can he do about it?"

We both fell silent as we cast our glances toward the gravestone. It was much darker, now, under the trees. From where I stood, I could hardly make out the stone, but the growin' shadows made it look a lot bigger than before.

Finally, realizin' that George wouldn't take no for an answer, I walked over to him 'n we both approached the stone. Reachin' out, I placed my hands on the gritty surface. I felt this chill go clear up my arms, all the way to the back of my head. My teeth wanted to chatter, but I wasn't 'bout to let George know how scared I was.

"Dig your feet in real good," George said. "When I give the word, we both push with everything we got, okay?" He crouched into position, his foot back by a rotten log, and started countin', "One . . . two . . . three—*heave!*"

I pressed my shoulder to the stone 'n puffed out my cheeks as I pushed as hard as I could. It was kinda scary when the stone started to move, but then it stuck at one point and wouldn't budge any more.

We was facin' each other, 'n I remember thinkin' it was kinda funny the way George's face got all red from the pushin'. We rocked the tombstone back and forth, but every time it would get to that one point and then stick, like it was gonna stay there forever. Gritty black soot covered our faces 'n hands. I could feel sweat tricklin' down my back between my shoulder blades. I was a lot skinnier back then, you understand.

"We'll . . . get . . . it . . . this . . . time," George said, keepin' the stone rockin' back and forth. Then, on his signal, we both grunted 'n pushed hard, givin' it everything we had.

The stone reached its stickin' point again, paused there for maybe one heartbeat, though it seemed like forever, 'n then it slowly toppled over. I thought of how a large tree falls kinda in slow motion as I watched the gravestone keel over with deep-rooted resistance. It hit the soggy ground with a sickenin' squishy sound.

I stepped back quickly from our work, wipin' my hands on my shirt. It was already a mess, so a little more wasn't gonna hurt. We was already in the dog house, anyway.

"Jeeze," I said, barely above a whisper. I looked at George 'n added, "You know our moms are gonna kill us!"

George wasn't listenin' to me. He was down on his hands 'n knees on the ground, lookin' into the hole where the stone had been.

"Cripes! Look at this!" he said, his voice tinged with wonder.

I shook my head 'n started backin' away. "Uh-uh! No way! We've gotta get back to camp before it's all the way dark."

I didn't notice that I was backin' up toward the fallen stone, but when my foot tripped up on somethin', maybe the edge of the stone, I fell backwards onto the surface of that cold stone. I grunted softly as I twisted around 'n managed to bang my knees on the edge of the gravestone. It took off a coupla layers of skin from my knees, but that ain't why I let fly a scream. Hell no, I was scared . . . scared right outta my mind!

I rolled off the stone 'n onto the soggy ground, tuckin'

my head down 'n pullin' my legs up tight to my chest, as if that was gonna protect me or somethin'. George's laughin' at me stung my ears. When I finally dared to look up, though, I noticed somethin' on the stone—some writin' or somethin' we hadn't noticed before. Maybe our pushin' had removed enough of the crud coverin' it, or else I just had the right angle to see it. I crawled toward the stone on my hands 'n knees, tryin' to make out what I saw written there.

"Look at this!" I said. My hand shook like a branch in the wind as I pointed at the stone.

The years had almost totally erased the letterin', but by tracin' each letter with my finger, I was able to spell out the name—"*S-T-E-P-H-E-N-L-O-G-A-N* . . . *Stephen Logan!*" My voice threatened to break into a scream. "That says *Stephen Logan!*"

George looked at me, 'n I could tell by the expression on his face that he was 'bout ready to pass out. He looked white as a sheet.

"Wha—?" he said, but then his voice cut off like he was chokin' or somethin'. He started toward me. His throat all the while was makin' this weird clickin' sound.

"That's what's carved on the stone here," I said, surprising myself by the sound of my voice. I stood up stiffly and rubbed my hands on my shirt again. "Is this someone . . . someone from your family that's buried here?"

For the first time in my life I saw surprise and, I think it'd be fair to say, genuine fear on George's face.

"That's my . . . my grandfather's name!" George said softly. One of his hands was coverin' his face, so the words was muffled. "I was . . . named after him—George *Stephen* Logan!"

"What the heck's he doin' buried out here?" I asked. I was hopin' a sensible question might calm him down, but I gotta admit, I was scared shitless, too. Damned questions! You see? That's how trouble always starts!

George shrugged frantically. "I dunno," he said. "I

mean, all my mother's ever told me 'bout him was I was named after him. He died a long time before I was born."

"But why's he buried out here?" I asked. My voice was shooting up the scale like one of them thermometers in those cartoons.

My cut knee was startin' to sting. My legs were soaked up to the knees. My arms 'n shoulders were wicked sore from pushing against the tombstone. All I wanted to do was get back to camp 'n clean myself up before supper. I knew we was gonna catch a lickin' for bein' out so late, but I could face that prospect a heck of a lot easier than I could the idea that George's grandfather was buried out here in the woods . . . that he was right down there where we'd moved the stone from.

George was about to say somethin' when I saw—I swear to God I saw somethin' movin' behind him. He had his back to the gravestone, 'n I swear to Christ one of them darker shadows under the trees seemed to, like, shift and start movin' toward us. All I could do was whimper and point weakly at the hole in the ground behind George when I realized that the shadow was comin' up out of the hole.

George saw where I was pointin' to 'n just as he started turning around to look, we both heard somethin'—a deep, hollow sound . . . like someone . . . sighin'.

I know we both heard it 'cause George looked at me wide-eyed. I couldn't take my eyes away from the spot above the grave where I could see this shadow gettin' thicker 'n blacker. It looked to me as though it was takin' on a shape. I saw it move, and it seemed like this long, black arm was reaching out toward us. With a loud scream, I turned and started to run.

I wasn't aware of anythin' as I ran. I didn't feel the water I splashed through or the branches that slapped against my face. I didn't even hear George runnin' along behind me. 'N I certainly wasn't about to turn around 'n look! All I could think was that black shape was comin' after us, bearin' down on us from behind. That drove my feet with a speed they ain't seen since, I'll tell you that much.

It must've been luck more 'n anythin' else that kept me on the right path. I sure as hell had no idea where I was runnin'. It was so dark by then, I couldn't even see my own feet as they went *slap-slap* on the soggy ground. I remember thinkin' it was kinda strange how George hadn't caught up with me. He'd always been a better runner than me. I figured maybe he'd gone up through Kimball's field, but I just kept runnin'. I knew, sure as shit, that shadow was closing in behind me.

Finally, up ahead through the trees, I saw the camp lights. The back porch light was on, 'n I could see two people—it had to be my mom and George's mother—sittin' out on the steps, probably just talkin'. I made that light my goal as I pumped my arms like they was pistons 'n gave it a final burst of energy.

I broke out of the woods near them moss-covered stones where George 'n me'd been sittin' earlier that afternoon. Racin' frantically across the lawn, I tried to call out for help, but nothin' would come out. I was halfway to the camp when my foot got snagged on a tree root or somethin', 'n I went down face-first in the grass.

Panic still had me in its grip as I rolled over onto my back and started scramblin' backwards, crab-like, as I stared at the woods behind me. Everything was pitch dark, but I collapsed on the ground 'n cried out shrilly when I saw that one of them shadows under the trees was movin' straight toward me. It came on silently, with a swiftness and a purpose that riveted me to the ground. I tried to get back up and run but couldn't.

The shadow rushed at me out of the woods like a black freight train or somethin'. I knew it was gonna flatten me right there where I was. I tightened up into a ball 'n waited, and then with a loud *whoosh*, it was on me, touchin' me with cold, clammy hands. The shadow wrapped around me so tight I couldn't breathe. The left side of my face felt like it was on fire, 'n then it rushed past me, shooting up into the air and dissolving into the night sky, leavin' behind this wicked nauseatin' stench of swamp water and rot. It must've been then that I fainted.

Hours later—warm 'n dry 'n tucked into my bed with clean sheets—I woke up. I could feel this thick pad of bandage on the left side of my face. I started babblin', tellin' my mom 'bout what had happened. I kept askin' if George was back yet—if he was all right, but my mom just tucked the blanket up under my chin 'n told me to get some rest. She left the room, but I wouldn't let her turn out the light.

'T'wasn't until the next day, round 'bout noon, that they finally told me what had happened to George.

After my mom heard me 'n found me sprawled on the lawn, she and George's mom carried me inside. I started talkin' real crazy, they said, like I was out of my head, but once they pieced together what we'd done, George's father called the Windham police 'n then headed out to the grave alone. It wasn't until later, once I thought about it, that I realized he went straight out there like he'd known all along where that grave was. I was told he found George not twenty feet from the opened grave. He was lyin' face-down in the muck, dead as could be.

Years later, before she died, my mom told me the doctor said George had died of cardiac arrest. A heart attack!

I'm an old man now. I've had to live with this fair to middlin' sized scar on the left side of my face my whole life. Now, I've had a bit of heart trouble my whole life, too, so I know what it's like to have a bad ticker. But one of the questions I have after all these years is—how in the hell can a ten-year-old boy die of a heart attack? Sure, I know all about them congenital diseases 'n such, but still . . . I wonder if maybe George didn't die of pure fright.

'N that's somethin' I've been wonderin' about all my life. What in the blazes did George see that could do that to him? What was down under that stone, what was down in that hole we'd made by pushin' over that gravestone?

Rick Hautala

The nurses here think it's kinda funny, 'specially now that it's August again, how every day 'round six o'clock, after supper, I won't let 'em take me outside. No matter how much they try to convince me what a beautiful day it is and that I need some fresh air, I won't go out there on the lawn as evenin' approaches. I just don't wanna see them late summer shadows, inchin' their way across the lawn. No way! 'Cause you know—and this is my last question: who the hell knows what those shadows are as they slip out silently from the woods behind the rest home?

Like I said, I sure hope to hell I never meet George again so's I can ask him!

—for Glenn Chadbourne

Hitman

Fifteen minutes after Angelo Martelli shot his boss, Tony Vincenza, Angelo's rented car broke down. It didn't cough or sputter or stall even once; it just seized up and died. Angelo gripped the steering wheel tightly as he jerked it hard to the right, and the car coasted to a dead stop on the gravel shoulder of the road. Clenching his fists in controlled frustration, he pressed his hands against his forehead, sucked in a deep breath, and glared out at the snow-covered road ahead.

"You *lou-sy moth*-er *fuck*-er!" he whispered harshly.

Each syllable came out a tiny puff of steam. Then, with a tight, controlled grunt, he brought one fist down hard against the dashboard.

That was it.

His only demonstration of anger.

Now that this new situation had presented itself, he had to clear his mind so he could think things through.

319

Closing his eyes for a moment, he leaned back against the car seat and mentally ran through everything he had done so far to cover his tracks. He was a hitman, and in his line of work it didn't pay to be sloppy or leave any loose ends. Angelo was one of the best in the business. He made up operating procedures Tony had always teased him were overly cautious. In fact, Tony and a few of his close associates had nicknamed Angelo "Overkill," but that pleased rather than bothered Angelo.

Besides, he didn't have to concern himself with Tony anymore.

But Angelo prided himself on his caution. He wasn't the kind of man who left anything to chance. He never traveled with a weapon, always making arrangements through a third party to have what he needed at his destination. He had enough phony I.D.s to fill ten wallets, and he could come up with iron-clad alibis that would convince a Supreme Court justice . . . but *this!*

He couldn't have accounted for a goddamned breakdown!

Right now, fifteen minutes after a hit, a broken-down car was a loose end Angelo couldn't afford or tolerate. He reassured himself that, of course, he hadn't rented the car under his own name. That was standard procedure, but he had taken the extra precaution of wearing thick horn-rim glasses and a blond wig when he picked up the car; so even if someone had photographed him, no one was going to connect him with anything. The major consideration right now was, should he stay with the car or abandon it?

The smart thing might just be to find some other way to get the hell out of this boondock state. He knew the police had equipment that could identify a tire print almost as accurately as a fingerprint. If they matched the tires of this car with evidence they'd eventually find at Tony's isolated cottage on Echo Lake—whenever Tony's body was discovered—then maybe it'd be wisest to leave the car and get the hell out of Maine as fast as he could.

Then again, if there wasn't anything seriously wrong with the car and he could get it repaired quickly, it might be smart to return it to the rental agency as if nothing had happened. With what Phil Belario had fronted him for this most recent job, he could easily pay for repairs and return the car rather than cause any kind of fuss that might draw undue attention to him. Hell, he could buy six or seven of these babies with what would be in his bank account as of nine o'clock tomorrow morning. Right now, the important thing was just to get his ass back to Philly.

"Lousy mother fucker," he said again, glancing up and down the lonely stretch of country back road. The sky was the color of soot, and snow-draped pines leaned heavily over the road, their branches groaning and snapping in the cold. With evening no more than an hour away, everything looked lonely and cold. Angelo had no idea how far it was to the nearest phone booth, and he sure as hell wasn't going to risk using his cell phone. He thought he remembered passing a gas station a few miles back, but for all he knew there might be something closer up ahead. Maybe doing the hit out here in the boondocks hadn't been such a great idea. If only he had been on the Maine Turnpike, maybe across the New Hampshire border, before the rental car shit the bed.

"Okay, okay," Angelo reassured himself. "No need to panic. Nothing to worry about. Everything's covered."

Pulling his leather gloves tightly up to his wrists, he snapped open the car door and stepped out into the frigid January afternoon. The first breath he took nearly froze his lungs and made him cough so hard he almost choked. He was doubled over by the driver's door, coughing, when a battered pickup truck loaded high with bales of hay roared past him. Flecks of yellow hay chaff and a tornado of black exhaust swirled in its wake as Angelo straightened up and—too late—waved his arms to signal for the driver to stop.

"Fuckin' hick!"

He shook his gloved fist high in the air.

"I hope to fuck I see you broken down on the side of the road next!"

He was watching the receding truck so intently he didn't notice the mud-splattered Subaru that had glided to a stop behind his stalled rental until the driver's door opened and slammed shut.

4:07 p.m.

"So, Frank, what did you say you do for work?"

Momentarily distracted as he stared at the road ahead, Angelo shook his head and, glancing at the driver, offered a standard line.

"Oh, I sell insurance—life insurance out of an office in Boston."

The driver, a young man in his late twenties or early thirties, had introduced himself as Mark St. Pierre, a history teacher at a local high school. He seemed like a nice enough fellow, but right now Angelo had enough on his mind. He was in no mood for making friends on the road.

"So, were you up this way for business or pleasure?"

Angelo chuckled. "I can't for the life of me imagine why anyone would come up to Maine in January for pleasure."

"Not unless they're going skiing, I suppose," Mark said. "Then again—No offense, Frank, but you don't exactly strike me as the skiing type."

"No, no—I'm not," Angelo replied. "I was seeing a client in Augusta."

His gaze shifted to the road ahead. His hands clenched in his lap when he saw the overloaded hay truck up ahead. It was moving slower now, spouting thick, black exhaust as it struggled to make the steep grade of the hill. Angelo smiled and, shaking his head, said, "That's the lousy son-of-a-bitch who almost clipped me when I got out of my car."

"Yeah, I saw that," Mark replied. "I thought it looked

322

like he came pretty close. Well, don't worry. I think there's a long stretch of open road after the top of this hill. We'll leave him in the dust."

He pressed down on the accelerator, and the car leaped forward, rapidly closing the distance between them. Angelo stared with cold-eyed hostility at the tall, swaying stack of hay bales on the truck bed, earnestly praying that the precariously balanced load would spill out onto the road as soon as they were past. As Mark came up close behind the truck, he eased out toward the center line and clicked on the turn signal, indicating his intention to pass.

Suddenly he shouted, "Jesus Christ!" and his foot came up off the accelerator. The car slowed down, dropping back rapidly.

"You gonna pass the mother fucker or what?" Angelo asked, narrowing his gaze as he turned to look at the driver.

"Jesus Christ," Mark repeated, softer now as he held the steering wheel tightly with one hand and, staring gape-mouthed, pointed at the truck just as it crested the hill.

"What the—? Did you see that?"

"Yeah, so what? The asshole's got his truck overloaded," Angelo said. "Looks to me like he's gonna spill the whole fuckin' load all over the road. I'd either hurry up and pass him or hang way the hell back if I was you."

The truck rapidly pulled away from them as Mark slowed down. He was gnawing on his lower lip as he looked back and forth between his passenger and the road ahead.

"No! No! It wasn't that at all!" he said. His voice was twisted up high and tight, and his eyes were round and bulging with surprise. "No, it was—I thought I saw . . . something."

Rather than say more, Mark stepped down hard on the accelerator again and sped up to catch up with the truck, which was now gaining speed on the down slope. When they were less than fifty feet behind it, Mark pointed and said softly, "Look! There! Between those hay bales on the left side."

Angelo squinted as he leaned forward; then he almost shouted aloud when he saw a hand—a naked, pale, motionless human hand sticking out from between two of the hay bales.

"Jesus Christ. Well what d'yah know?" Angelo said. His voice was faint and flat; he hoped it registered at least a bit of surprise.

"For Christ's sake! What the fuck are we gonna do?" Mark asked. He kept flicking his eyes over at Angelo, worry and concern etched all over his face.

"What do you mean, what are we gonna do?" Angelo said. This was far from the first time he had seen a dead person—or a dead person's hand. "We ain't gonna do a goddamned thing about it."

"But there's—"

"Could be just one of the hayseed's gloves stuck between the bales. That's probably what it is."

"No. That sure as hell looks like a real hand to me," Mark replied, not taking his eyes off the swaying load in the back of the truck.

"Well, I'll tell you this," Angelo said in a pleasant but forceful drawl. "We're gonna head to the nearest gas station so I can get a wrecker back out to my car before dark. I have—" He cleared his throat noisily. "I have an important meeting back at the home office tomorrow morning, and I ain't about to piss my time away on bullshit like this."

"But that person—What if that's a *dead* person in the back of that truck? What if they—I don't know. What if they had a passenger back there, and they don't even know something's happened?"

"Who the fuck would be stupid enough to ride in the back of a truck in weather like this?"

"Then what if—what if those guys have killed someone. What if they're taking the body someplace to get rid of it? We can't just—just ignore it! What if—"

"What if *nothing!*" Angelo said, squeezing his gloved hands into tight fists that made his leather gloves creak.

For once in his life, he wished he carried a gun so he could threaten this man to do what he wanted him to do. But that would be foolish. He had to get—and maintain—control of this situation.

"I don't have either the time or the inclination to get involved in anything like this. I think it looks like a glove, but even if there is some dead guy in the back of that truck, big fucking deal! It don't concern me or you!"

"But what if—"

"Stop it with the *what ifs!* For all you know, these might be guys you don't want to be messin' with," Angelo said, adding just a touch of menace to his voice.

Mark glanced at his passenger, obviously trying to gauge just how dangerous he might be. Then, when he saw the truck up ahead slowing down for a left-hand turn, he pulled to a stop on the side of the road. Gritting his teeth, he took a deep, controlled breath, then let it out slowly and said, "Look, Frank, I have to follow that truck—at least to see where they're going. I think there's a gas station a mile or two up the road from here. You can walk or hitchhike to it if you want."

The sun was low on the horizon, and the sky was deepening to a rich purple. It was going to be dark soon. Angelo considered how ball-busting cold it was outside; then he grunted. "Too fucking bad you don't have a cell phone," he said. He settled back in the car seat, thinking—*Okay let this do-gooder find out what's going on; then I'll be rid of him.*

"I swear to God," Mark said, gripping the steering wheel with both hands, tracking the overloaded truck as it moved down the long stretch of country road. "This isn't a main road or anything, so they can't be going far. Just let me follow them to see where they're going. Then—I swear to God—I'll drive you to the gas station. You can get a wrecker to pick up your car, and I can call the cops from there. I can't ignore something like this. I at least have to find out where they're going."

Angelo smiled grimly and said, "Okay, then. Better step on it, though. You don't want to lose them, do you?"

With a loud squealing of tires, Mark cut across the main road and sped after the pickup truck. Fighting back a hot surge of anger, Angelo settled back in the car seat, wishing to hell someone else—anyone else—had stopped to help him. Then again, what could he expect out here in the boondocks like this?

4:29 p.m.

"End of the line, Markie-boy," Angelo said when he saw the pickup truck slow for a turn into a driveway. "Now turn around and let's get the fuck out of here."

Both he and Mark stared down the one-lane dirt drive lined with snow-covered pines and high, dirt-streaked snowplow ridges.

Mark braced his hands on the steering wheel as he pulled a quick U-turn across the road and then stopped the car opposite the driveway entrance. His face was pinched tight with concentration as he looked down the darkening, tree-lined alley.

"You don't think we should check it out first?" he asked. "Just to make sure?"

Angelo shook his head tightly and said, "No, I don't. I think you should get your and my asses out of here." He looked thoughtfully down the driveway and added, "You have no idea what you might be getting yourself into."

Mark gnawed on his lower lip while he considered. Then, after glancing up and down the road, he sucked in a deep breath and turned off the ignition. Pocketing the keys, he snapped open the car door and put one foot out onto the road.

"Then you can sit here and wait while I check it out," he said. "I can't just ignore something like this." He stared a moment at the screen of pine trees that blocked his view of whatever was down that road; then he glanced at his wristwatch. "I won't be more than fifteen minutes."

"The fuck you will!"

Angelo checked himself from lunging across the seat and grabbing Mark by the collar to force him back behind the steering wheel. With the heater turned off and the door open, cold air invaded the car, probing like icy fingers under Angelo's coat collar and down his back. He couldn't repress the shiver that wracked his body.

"Look, man," Mark said in a trembling voice. "I don't know where the fuck you're coming from, but *something* . . . something *really* weird is going on here, and I have to check it out." Again, he glanced down the driveway. "You can either sit here and freeze your ass off, or you can come with me."

Angelo tempered his response and, smiling thinly, said, "Or you could leave the car running so I can have some heat."

Mark smiled thinly and shook his head. "Look, Frank, I'm not exactly saying that I don't trust you, but what's to stop you from driving off once I'm gone?"

Angelo's thin smile widened. "Nothing at all—except my word."

"Why don't you just come with me," Mark said. "Look, we don't have to go straight down the driveway. We can cut across that field there and stay in the woods the whole time. No one's gonna see us if we keep to the woods."

"You got a description of the truck and where it is. Why not just give that to the cops and forget about it?"

" 'Cause I have to see what the hell they're up to," Mark answered.

"You're full of shit, you know that?" Angelo said, shivering wildly inside his coat.

He wondered which would be colder, sitting here in an unheated car or traipsing through the woods with this asshole do-gooder. After a moment, he decided that, at least if he was walking he might work up enough of a sweat to stay warm. Looking warily up at the darkening sky, he nodded slowly.

"Okay," he said as he clicked open his door. "I'll take a little pleasure walk with you." He got out and slammed the car door shut. Glaring at Mark across the car roof, he jabbed a gloved forefinger at him and said, "But we're talking fifteen minutes, tops. I ain't about to get myself lost in the fucking woods, not with night coming on."

Mark nodded agreement, and the two of them dashed across the road. They walked no more than fifty feet up the driveway before darting into the snow-filled woods. As soon as they were out of sight in the woods, Angelo wished for the dozenth time this afternoon that he was packing a gun so he could waste this jerk. He could take the asshole's car, get back in Philly, and ditch the car at some chop shop long before anyone would miss the sorry bastard.

But he didn't have a gun; so instead, he trudged through ankle-deep snow, all the while silently cursing himself for being a fool. If he was going to be walking in the cold, he should be heading to the nearest gas station. At least there wasn't much snow under the trees; it was sheltered and did feel a bit warmer than it probably would have been in the car.

"I think I see a building over there," Mark said, crouching behind a tree and pointing off to his right. Angelo looked in the direction Mark was pointing and shrugged when he saw the dark bulk of a barn and an unoccupied farmhouse. A single bare lightbulb glowed inside the barn. The overloaded pickup truck was backed up and parked in front of the barn door.

"Great," Angelo said. "You've seen where they were going. Now let's get the fuck out of here."

"Just a minute. I want to see what they're doing in there."

"You know," Angelo said, "did it even occur to you that it might not have been what you thought it was?"

Mark turned and regarded him with one raised eyebrow.

"I mean, now that I think about it, I ain't so sure I saw any hand. For Christ's sake! For all I know, it could have been a piece of rope or a feed bag or something."

"All the more reason to check it out, then, don't you think?" Mark said. "I'd feel kind of foolish, getting the police involved if that really *wasn't* a hand." He straightened up and began moving carefully between the trees, angling his way over toward the barn. "You coming or not?"

Angelo glanced back the way they had come, then followed a pace or two behind Mark as they moved in a direction that would take them out behind the barn. When they were halfway there, they heard the sound of grinding gears and the irregular sputter of the truck's engine. Mark pointed to the overloaded truck as it started backing up into the wide-open barn doors.

"I'll bet there's a window or an opening out back where we can see what's going on inside," Mark said.

Angelo scowled and considered leaving the jerk behind and heading back to the car to wait; but he sucked in a deep breath and followed, mentally cursing both himself and Mark for fools.

They crouched in the fringe of pine trees that backed the barn and spent a minute or two studying the battered, ship-gray structure. It was old and weathered, the shingles looking like slabs of slate. It looked as though the next strong gust of wind would knock the damned thing over. In the gathering gloom, the barn had a hulking, dark presence that bothered Angelo. For some unaccountable reason, he imagined that indeed the barn was barely supported, and it could come crashing down on top of both him and Mark at any moment.

"So, Frank"—Mark whispered—"what do you think?"

From inside the barn, they could hear the chugging of the pickup truck, muffled voices of men talking, and heavy thumping sounds as the men tossed the hay bales to the ground. The surrounding woods were perfectly silent except for the faint hiss of wind in the pines high overhead. Angelo shivered, thinking how he could have been comfortably seated at The North Pier in Boston by now, eating a seafood dinner if that goddamned rental car hadn't quit on him.

"You want to take a peak through that window there?" Mark asked, indicating a small, dark rectangle on the backside of the barn. Most of the panes had been painted out, but on the lower left side was a hole about the size of a golf ball, through which filtered the mellow yellow glow of light.

"I could just about give two shits what they're doing in there," Angelo said, his voice barely above a whisper. "And if you had half an ounce of brains, you'd—"

"Keep it down, will you?" Mark said. "I'm just gonna take a look. I mean, what if they're, like, burying the body in there or something?"

"It ain't none of my concern," Angelo said with a derisive snort. He stood back in the snowy darkness of the trees, slapping his arms to stay warm now that they had stopped moving.

After casting a cautious glance along either side of the barn, Mark skittered out across the open ground and flattened himself against the side of the barn to one side of the window. He edged around like he must have seen on television cop shows and, crouching low, peered in through the small opening. Angelo tried to deny his own slight stirrings of curiosity as he watched the light-trimmed edge of Mark's face. His curiosity rose sharply when Mark's eyes rounded in shock and his mouth opened into a wide *O* when he suddenly jerked away from the window.

"Jesus Christ!" he whispered, staggering backwards and grabbing Angelo's arm for support. His voice was a raw, ragged gasp. "They've got a—Oh, my sweet Jesus! There's a dead . . . a *dead* man in there! For real!"

Angelo smirked, only half-believing Mark as the young

man gripped his wrist and tugged him in the direction of the barn.

"You've gotta see it!" he whispered. "I want you to verify what it is so when we go to the police, they'll believe me."

"We ain't going to no police," Angelo said firmly, but he allowed himself to be led over to the barn window. From inside the barn, they could hear the sounds of the men, moving about.

"Go on. Look," Mark whispered. His voice assumed a deep tone of command. "See for yourself!"

Squinting one eye as though looking through a telescope, Angelo bent down and peered through the opening. The strong, musty smell of rotten hay and old manure assailed his nostrils and almost made him sneeze, but he checked himself. His heart did a cold, hard flip in his chest when he saw—and recognized—the dead man lying on the barn floor.

It was his boss, Tony Vincenza—the man he had killed less than an hour ago.

"Mother of Christ!" Angelo muttered.

His legs went rubbery on him. He turned and collapsed back against the side of the barn, gasping for breath.

"Yeah, I know," Mark said softly. "I haven't seen many dead people, either." He shook his head as though mystified. "I can't imagine that I'll ever get used to seeing a stiff."

Angelo opened his mouth to say something, but nothing would come out. All he could think was, *how in the hell had this happened?* Tony had hired him to kill Phil Belario because Phil was muscling in on some of Tony's business concerns, but Angelo had cut a better deal with Phil and had taken out Tony, instead.

So what the hell was Tony's body doing out here?

How had these men found it so fast, and what the fuck were they doing with it here?

"I can't—No!—I don't—" but that was all Angelo managed to say before dropping to his knees in the snow and

331

throwing up. He leaned forward, his face almost buried in the puke-stained snow as wave after violent wave squeezed his body. A thin sheen of sweat broke out across his forehead.

Mark knelt down beside him and gently placed a hand on Angelo's shoulder.

"Hey, man. Take it easy there," he said. "I know that seeing something like that's gotta be pretty upsetting, but you have to keep quiet." He hooked his thumb toward the barn and looked around cautiously. "I mean, if those guys in there hear us, we're in deep shit."

Angelo's vision blurred. Strings of vomit dribbled down his chin as he looked up at Mark and stammered, "We've got to—to get the hell—out—out of here. Now!" He ran his forearm across his mouth, smearing the vomit across his cheek and coat sleeve as he struggled to stand up. "These guys—I don't know how they—I'm not sure what the hell's going on here, but we gotta get moving!"

"Come on, then," Mark said calmly as he eased his arm around Angelo's shoulder and directed him back into the woods. "Let's get back to my car. We have to find someplace to call the cops—"

"*No!*" Angelo snarled. He was trembling as they walked into the deepening shadows under the pines. "No cops! Not while I'm around!"

"Why? What's the problem?"

"Nothing. I just don't want to—"

He cut himself short when a wash of yellow headlights swept down the driveway. Both men dropped and flattened themselves to the ground as a tow truck pulled into the dooryard. Angelo's stomach went cold and watery when he saw his broken-down rental car attached to the back of the tow truck.

"Oh, sweet Jesus! Oh, shit!" he whispered, squinting as he watched the tow truck pull to a stop in front of the barn door. Two men got out. They were nothing more than black shadows in the gloom as they walked around to the back of the truck and lowered Angelo's car to the ground.

"Say," Mark said close to Angelo's ear. "Isn't that your car?"

His breath washed over Angelo's face like warm water, but Angelo could barely nod agreement as he looked in amazement from his car to the dark farmhouse.

"Wait just a fucking second," he said, easing himself up into a crouch and brushing snow from his coat. "Just what the fuck is going on here?"

"Nothing much, Angelo," a cold voice from behind them said suddenly.

Angelo let out a startled cry as both he and Mark spun around to see who had spoken. Silent figures resolved out of the darkness as they came around the back of the barn. Angelo couldn't tell for sure, but it looked like four or five men. As soon as he realized that one of them was Phil Belario, he knew there must be at least half a dozen more staying behind cover with guns trained on him and Mark. Snow crunched underfoot as the group of men moved slowly toward them.

"Sorry 'bout this, kid," Angelo said to Mark, "but I tried to warn you. I think you got yourself into something you ain't gonna like."

"What?" Mark asked, his voice high, constricted. "How do you know these men? And why'd he call you Angelo? I thought you said your name was—"

"Shut the fuck up and let me do the talking," Angelo said. "Maybe I can convince them to let you go." Taking a bold step forward with his arms upraised, he called out, "Hey! Jesus Christ, Phil!" He laughed a high, dry laugh and shook his head as though dazed. "Goddamn, I got to hand it to you. You really had me going there." He looked around casually. "So what the fuck is all this about, anyway?"

"Why Angelo, I'm surprised at you," Phil said in a soft, grating tone of voice. "One of the best in the business, and you haven't figured it out yet?"

333

"Whaddayah mean? Figured what out?"

"This is a hit, Angelo," Phil said. "I'm taking you out."

"What the fuck?"

Angelo took a few steps backward, but he knew damned well that there were several armed men behind him, ready to shoot him on the spot if he turned and ran.

"What the fuck you talking about?"

"You're a loose end, Angelo," Phil said. "You worked for Tony—how many years? Ten? Twelve?"

"Yeah—'bout twelve, I guess," Angelo said, fighting back the tight trembling in his voice.

"And when he put a contract out on me, how long did it take you to cut a deal with me, huh? Not even one full day! You betrayed your boss like that!" He snapped his fingers. The sound sounded like a gunshot in the cold air.

"Well, now, wait—wait just a second there, Phil," Angelo stammered. "You and me—we've known each other a long time." His chattering teeth diced every word as he spoke. "I've known you almost as long as I've known Tony, and—to tell you the truth—I couldn't see what he was getting all bent out of shape about. I told him I didn't want the contract, but he insisted on using me, so I figured—you know—that I'd tip you off."

"It didn't take you very long to decide to double-cross your boss, now, did it?"

Finally at a loss for words, Angelo merely shrugged.

"So you must understand why I can't trust you, Angelo," Phil continued. "I'm taking over *all* of Tony's interests, and I have to have people around me that I know are gonna be there for me, one hundred percent."

"But I was there for you, Phil! I didn't clip you even though there was a hundred large in it for me."

"But I have to be sure no one's gonna double-cross me at the first opportunity," Phil said mildly. "You can appreciate my problem, can't you? I have to make an example of you."

Angelo was silent a moment; then he frowned deeply

and said, "So what the fuck—? How'd you set this up."

Phil snickered and smiled broadly. "A little dash of sugar in your gas tank took care of the engine," he said. Before Angelo could say anything more, Phil reached into his coat and withdrew a pistol equipped with a silencer.

"Recognize this?" he said, holding the weapon up so Angelo could see it against the darkening sky.

"Yeah—I think so," Angelo replied.

"It's the gun you used to clip Tony," Phil said with mock earnestness as he sadly shook his head. "And I'm afraid I'm going to have to use it to silence you. You must have heard of Larry Fiero."

Angelo nodded and took one more step backwards. "Yeah, sure. One of the best. Operates out of Chicago."

"That he does, but just this afternoon you've been out for a little joy-ride with him. Here yah go, Larry." Phil held the gun out and Mark stepped forward to take it. "Angelo—I'd like to introduce you to Larry Fiero. Larry—this here's Angelo Martelli."

"End of the line, Frankie-boy," Mark said as a thin, mean-looking grin spread across his face. "Or should I say *Overkill?*"

"Fiero! What the—?"

Angelo was stopped cold when Mark raised the pistol and aimed it squarely at his forehead.

"That's right," Phil said with a snorting laugh. "And you must know that, like you, Larry's one of the best in the business. Matter of fact—" He sniffed with laughter. "After tonight, he'll be the *best*."

"You lousy mother fucker!" Angelo glared at Mark, who was bracing his right arm with his left hand and taking careful, steady aim at him.

"And that's the last time I'll have to hear you use *that* expression," Mark said.

"Wait just a fucking minute!" Angelo said. "This is god-damned ridiculous. How'd you—why'd you go to all this trouble to get me out here like this? It don't make sense."

Unable to believe that any of this was really happening, Angelo stared earnestly back and forth between Mark and Phil. Mark coolly squinted at him over the circled opening of the gun. Phil had the self-satisfied expression of someone who just hit the lottery.

"Christ!" Angelo said, helplessly raising his hands. "You could have whacked me any time after I left the state. Why'd you set me up like this?"

"Yeah, you lousy mother fucker, I could have," Mark said with a cold steeliness in his voice as he started to apply pressure to the trigger. "But don't you think it's been a lot more fun doing it my way?"

—for Marty Greenberg
and Ed Gorman

Perfect Witness

". . . see, see! dead Henry's wounds
Open their congealed mouths and bleed afresh."
—*Richard III*, I. ii. 55–56.

I'm confused, really confused.

I can see bright lights all around me.

Too bright.

I know there are people nearby, too. Sometimes it sounds as though there's a whole crowd, milling around somewhere in the outer darkness behind the blinding lights. A faceless, nameless mass of people, like an audience, unseen, but their presence is sensed behind the glare of stage lights.

At other times, or maybe at the same time, I can tell there are a few of them—maybe three or four—standing close to me.

I think they're doing things to me.

I don't know where I am or what's happening to me.
Can anyone tell me?

I try to move my arms and head, but my whole body feels
like it's a wet lump of senseless clay. There's no sensation
in my legs. Absolutely none at all. Not even the sensation
of pain.
  Nothing.
  It's almost like my body doesn't even exist.
  What the hell's happening to me?
  I don't remember a thing, not since. . . .
  When was it?
  Earlier tonight?

Yes, I remember. . . . I was walking back from the Wild
Horse Theater to my apartment on Irving Street, in Cam-
bridge, when a man—hell, no! He wasn't a man. He was
just a kid, for Christ's sake, stopped me and demanded that
I give him my wallet.
  At first I started to reach for it, but then in an instant I
decided not to hand it over so easily. I think I might have
tried to fight him, to get away from him.
  Was that what happened?

*"We have to administer the rest of the drug very slowly. I have
no idea if he will experience any pain, but I don't want to risk
losing him again."*

Hey, who said that? Who's there?
  It sounds like a woman's voice, but no one answers me.
  Did I speak out loud?
  Probably not.
  I strain to open my eyes but I have this weird sort of
dull sensation that they're already wide open. I keep trying
to see better, but the light gets steadily brighter, almost
stinging. My eyes don't seem to be able to adjust to it, but
at least there's a slight tingle of pain.

Thank God!

If there wasn't any pain, then I might think I was paralyzed or . . . or dead.

At least I know I'm alive.

Just barely.

I think it's almost funny how those gray shapes keep drifting around in front of me like . . . floating by like there's a group of people, milling around me.

I wish I knew who they are.

I wish I knew where I am.

I wish I knew what's happening, but my body still feels totally numb.

"Mr. Thurmond, I hope you keep that video cam running. If this works at all, I don't want to miss a single second of it."

Miss any of *what*?

Who said that?

Where the hell are you?

In the distance, I can hear other voices, buzzing around me like the droning hum of a beehive. I can't make out anything anyone is saying. It still reminds me of the indistinct chatter of a crowd, talking softly in the dark in expectation of a show that is about to begin.

Come on!

Somebody!

Please!

Talk to me!

Why won't anyone tell me what the hell's going on?

Why can't I see you?

I can't feel anything, but I am positive, now, that they are doing something to me.

What the fuck are you doing to me?

Rick Hautala

Oh, shit!

Wait a second.

I think I know what's happening. I remember, now. I did try to fight with that kid, and I think he might have— Shit, *yes!* That's it! He had a gun!

I've been shot!

I must be dying!

Oh, God, I'm afraid that might be what's happening!

I remember clearly, now; that he was holding a gun, aiming it straight at me. He was standing too close, and I made a grab for his wrist, hoping to push the gun away, but there was an explosion of light.

Funny, but I don't remember hearing anything. There was no loud blast. No pain. Just a burst of intense white light, and a dull feeling, like someone punched me lightly in the stomach, and then . . . then. . . .

. . . nothing . . .

So that's it.

I've been shot!

I must still be lying on the sidewalk where I fell.

Am I bleeding to death?

Why can't I feel anything? Even that faint whisper of pain is gone now. These people must be paramedics from the rescue unit or something . . . and the others must be the crowd that's gathered around to watch.

To watch me die!

Shit, that's it!

I'm dying on the street.

They're trying to save my life, but I'm dying anyway!

Oh, Jesus! Oh, shit!

I'm scared!

"You have to remember, your honor, that this is the first time we've attempted to do something like this. The medical technology is new. We have to proceed with extreme caution."

That was a woman's voice again, but why did she say, "your honor"?

What the hell is she talking about? Is she a doctor or something? And who's she calling "your honor"?

Hey, wait a second. . . .

I think she's the one doing something to me. For a moment, there, I could almost feel my body again . . . at least a little bit. There's something hard underneath me. Is it concrete? Am I still lying on the sidewalk? It sort of feels that way, but it also feels as though my knees might be bent.

Aww, shit! This must be the way I hit the ground after I got shot.

"Given these rather unusual circumstances, do you gentlemen agree that we can dispense with the usual formality of swearing in the witness."

Swearing in?

What the hell are they talking about?

Jesus Christ, stop talking nonsense and do something to save my fucking life!

Even as I think this, I can feel a warm current of sensation returning to my body. The heavy, lumpish feeling in my chest is starting to loosen up, and I think—yes! I can feel the dull throb of pins and needles as it spreads slowly into my arms and legs. The center of my chest feels like it's on fire.

I can't tell if I'm turning my head or merely shifting my eyes back and forth, but when I look around, the light becomes more diffused. The figures leaning over me—I think I can count three of them now—are still indistinct. They're surrounded by these weird halos of light that ripple with deep blues and purples like colors I've never seen before!

It's beautiful, but I'm still scared.

Oh, Jesus, I'm *really* scared!

"I object, your honor. I think this entire experiment is nothing more than a . . . a charade . . . a mockery of justice. Considering that we are videotaping this, I respectfully ask that we sequester the jury so they won't have to observe this . . . this macabre spectacle."

I wish I knew what the hell this person is talking about, but I'm so swept up by the gushing, almost burning sensation of feeling as it rushes through my body that I can't concentrate very well on anything anyone is saying. I imagine my body is an ice-bound river, and warm spring winds and the steady tug of strong, flowing water underneath the ice are finally breaking apart the hammer-lock grip of the frozen surface.

I'm dizzy with a heady rush of euphoria as my vision clears even more. I can see that I am not lying in the street, bleeding to death.

No, I'm in a room.

And I'm sitting up in a chair.

My hands are clamped to the chair arms in a viselike grip. I know, even if I wanted to, I wouldn't be able to move them. Across my chest, I can feel the tight pull of a restraint that makes it difficult—no, impossible to breathe. I know that the strap holding me, not my own strength, is what's keeping me sitting erect in the chair.

When I try to open my mouth and run my tongue over my lips, there is almost no feeling whatsoever, as though my whole face has been shot full of Novocain.

"Objection overruled, Mr. Applegate. While I grant that this is a most unique situation, I'll reserve judgment as to whether or not the evidence we receive is or is not admissible."

Bedbugs

As my vision continues to resolve more clearly, I try to look around. Off to one side, I see the source of light—a high bank of windows through which bars of iridescent blue light are streaming. The light shimmers in slow, sinuous waves that maddeningly flicker through the colors of the spectrum. Everything appears to be watery and insubstantial. Halos of rainbow light surround everything.

Arrayed against this wall, below the windows, are numerous dark shapes. . . . People, I realize. They seem frozen in place, as immobile as mannequins.

I try to blink my eyes, and it seems to take forever for the rough, sandpaper feeling to scrape across my eyeballs. I am startled when I rotate my head slowly to my left and see the dim silhouette of someone standing close beside me. The nimbus of light surrounding him—at least now I can tell that this looks like a man—masks his features as he leans close to me. I get a faint whiff of something stale, almost rotten, and that makes my stomach growl.

"Can you hear me, Mr. Sinclair?"

I want to answer him, but when I try to clear my throat and take a deep breath, I have no sensation whatsoever of breathing. My chest feels like it's encased in iron bands. I lean forward, and the restraint presses into my chest, but, surprisingly, there is no pain. The indistinct features of the man's face loom closer to me, resolving like a slowly developing photograph out of the shimmering haze. I see a terrifying, cartoon face, with a wide, smiling mouth frozen in the center of a round, white balloon, and two dark, dimensionless balls that must be his eyes.

When he speaks to me again, repeating his question, his lips move in flabby, rubbery twitches that seem to be not at all in synch with his words.

"Do you understand what I'm saying to you, Mr. Sinclair?"

Again, I try to take a breath and speak, but the best I can manage is a slight nod of my head. I'm not really sure if I've moved at all. There is no pain, but I have the sense that the bones in my neck are dry and splintering, and if I move even the least little bit too fast, my spine will snap in two like a piece of rotten wood.

I try to focus on this man's face and am surprised to notice that I feel no need to blink my eyes. I can't even move them. The lids are frozen wide open as though I am permanently terrified. I stare blankly forward, hoping that my vision will resolve so I can turn my head and see who this is talking to me.

"Can you see my hand?"

Something that looks like a huge, black crow flying across a stormy sky flashes in front of my face. It goes by so fast I can't possibly turn my head fast enough to track it.

"I would ask, Mr. Charles, that you not push him quite so hard."

This is the woman's voice again, speaking from somewhere off to my right. She's trying to make it sound like she's in control, but I detect a near frantic edge of worry in her voice. When I try to turn my head to look at her, the total lack of sensation makes it feel as though my eyeballs are detached and rolling around inside my head, completely out of control.

"I understand, Dr. Murphy, but you indicated that we might not have very much time when he is even semi-conscious. I repeat, Mr. Sinclair, can you see how many fingers I'm holding up in front of you?"

Again, the black crow flaps across my vision.

This time I see two blurry lines, like fence posts, pointing straight up.

Two, I think, but there is no way I can even begin to say the word. As much as I strain to speak, I can't feel the vocal cords in my throat. They might as well be cut. I feel like I'm a disembodied entity, floating in a hazy, gray soup of vague lights, shadows, and sounds.

"I could administer a small amount more, your honor, but in my opinion, we've already pushed this to a dangerous level."

"I respectfully submit that this is a complete waste of the court's valuable time, your honor. My client and I request that you strike all references to this shameful . . . incident from the record, and that we proceed in a customary manner."

"Again, Mr. Applegate, your objection is noted and overruled. Please proceed with your line of questioning, Mr. Charles."

While this exchange is going on, I am only half listening to it because I am trying so hard to make my throat work, but it's like trying to flex the muscles of an arm that has been amputated.

There's nothing there—not even the lack of sensation.

. . . nothing . . .

After a few moments of struggle, I feel another, stronger gush of warmth that's centered in my chest. The heat radiates outward, like a faintly glowing coal being fanned by a gentle breath. My throat tenses. The tendons and muscles are as stiff as bars of rusty iron. I can feel a faint thrumming that brings with it an agonizing jolt of pain.

". . . two . . ."

In a sudden, nauseating rush, my vision resolves more clearly, and I see where I am.

To my right is a tall, oak-paneled desk, behind which, high above me, sits a man dressed in a dark robe. The few wisps of gray hair he has are combed straight back from

345

his wide forehead. His face looks pale and is crisscrossed by thin, red lines of exploded capillaries, particularly on his nose. "Drinker's tattoos," I always called them.

Beside me, to my left, is a man wearing a fancy three-piece suit of dark blue. His necktie is a design of squares with dark circles in the center. It looks amazingly three-dimensional against the blinding white glare of his shirt. He is leaning forward with both hands on the arms of the chair in which I sit.

In front of me, a little to my right, stands a rather attractive, dark-haired woman. She is wearing what looks like a white laboratory smock. It swells out due to her ample breasts. She has a syringe in one hand, and I can see that a needle and the plastic tube of an IV feed have been taped to my exposed left forearm, which is strapped to the other arm of the chair.

Perhaps the most shocking thing I notice is the color of my own skin. It is pasty white, almost gray, and looks exactly like the senseless, immobile clay I imagine it is.

"Very good, Mr. Sinclair. That is correct," the man in the three-piece suit says, smiling broadly as he leans closer to me. "I'm holding up two fingers."

His features don't look quite so cartoonish, but they are still horrifyingly animated as the smile spreads across his wide face. His teeth look big and flat, and for an instant I am consumed by the fear that he is going to dart forward and bite me.

"I know it must be difficult for you to speak, Mr. Sinclair," he says, "but if you please, can you indicate with either a sound or a motion of your hand that you understand what I'm saying?" He glances over his shoulder. "Is this acceptable to you, your honor?"

As I stare at him, the halo of light that surrounds his head gradually blends from vibrant blues and purples to deep, fiery reds and oranges that shift across his features like flickering flames.

Unaccountably, I feel the cold, hollow stirrings of hunger.

Yes . . . hunger!

"My name is Raymond Charles, Mr. Sinclair. I'm a lawyer. I'm representing you in this case."

I want to ask him exactly what case that might be, but I'm fairly certain that it has something to do with the night I was mugged and tried to fight back. I realize that I must have been wounded, and I wonder if I have been in a coma all this time and am just now coming out of it.

"You may remember that, on the seventeenth of December, you were accosted on your way home from work by a young man. Do you recall that incident?"

". . . yes . . ."

It takes every bit of effort I can muster to say that single word, which reverberates like the heavy clang of metal in my ears.

"Mr. Sinclair, I am informed that we don't have much time, so I must get directly to the point. I have to ask you, do you think you would recognize your assailant if he were to be presented to you?"

I turn away from Mr. Charles, sensing that the painful stirrings of hunger inside me are only intensified whenever I look at the glowing curtains of red light that surround his face. The fleshy folds of his skin fairly vibrate with energy and life. I try to concentrate on remembering exactly what happened that night—when?

How long ago?

It could have been days or weeks, or it could have been several months or years.

I have no way of knowing.

The image of my attacker's face swirls into my memory like a face looking up at you from underwater. Dark hair, shifting in heavy, oily curls, swirls around his face. Eyes, dark and liquid, slide nervously back and forth. Thin, tight, almost bloodless lips are pursed, and the pale skin above his upper lip is marked by the faint wisp of a mustache. His skin is greasy-looking and pimply, but it is what I see *inside* those eyes that I remember most clearly.

Fear. . . .

Fear and silent desperation.

". . . yes . . ."

Even as I say the word, I see this boy's face materialize like a mirage in front of me. It, too, is surrounded by a sparkling sheet of red light, and the gnawing hunger that is churning inside me intensifies until it becomes excruciatingly painful.

This hunger is now the only pain I know.

The woman, apparently a doctor or nurse, says something to the man who has identified himself as my lawyer, but her words are lost to me as I stare again into that boy's dark, desperate eyes.

"Is this the man who attacked you, Mr. Sinclair?"

I hear the words, but they mean almost nothing to me. The gnawing hunger that is growling like a disease inside my gut is more demanding. I am distantly aware that my mouth has dropped open, and my teeth are grinding back and forth as I strain forward, but the strap across my chest holds me back. I try to raise my arms, but they, too, are firmly held in place by my restraints.

* * *

" . . . yes . . . "

"I object, your honor!" a voice suddenly yells, sounding in my ears like a sudden clap of thunder.

"Overruled."

"I ask you again, Mr. Sinclair, and if you can, I would like you to speak a bit louder for the sake of the jury. Is the man standing in front of you the same man who accosted you on Irving Street on the night of December seventeenth and, at gun point, demanded that you give him your wallet?"

" . . . yes . . . "

"If it please the court, I would like it noted for the record that Mr. Sinclair has identified the defendant, Mr. Leroy Peterson."

"So noted."

"Objection, we haven't established the credibility of this witness."

"Overruled. Who better to identify his assailant, Mr. Applegate, than the murder victim himself?"

"Your honor, I think we're losing him again."

When the woman speaks this time, even through the boiling pain of my overwhelming hunger, I recognize the edge of panic in her voice.

All around me, there are explosions of shadow and light, blending and swirling in an insane riot of color and sound. I am dazzled, confused, and the only clear thought I carry through this confusion is that I am hungry. . . .

Hungry!

"Your honor, I realize that this is a rather unusual request, but I would beg the court's indulgence to allow me to ask if Mr. Peterson would please step forward and touch Mr. Sinclair on the hand."

"I object! This has gone on long enough. It's well past the point of morbid curiosity."

"May the court ask, Mr. Charles, exactly why you are making such an unusual request?"

"I beg your indulgence, your honor, but it is an ancient tradition that, if a corpse is touched by the murderer, the wounds which were inflicted by that individual will begin to bleed again, thereby identifying the murderer."

A corpse!
What the hell is he talking about?
I'm not a corpse!

Voices explode around me, but I am so consumed by hunger and the numbing fear that embraces me that I don't understand a single word. Stark terror squeezes me with a mounting pressure that soon becomes intolerable.

"I object! This is patently absurd! Why, this is a . . . this is medieval superstition we're talking about, not modern jurisprudence. Your Honor, I would like to request that these entire proceedings be declared a mistrial, and that the—"

"Please calm yourself, Mr. Applegate. In light of this rather unusual situation, which is certainly something *I've* never experienced before, please instruct your client to do as Mr. Charles has requested."

"I will not!"

"You will, or I'll find you in contempt of court."

Every fiber of my being is charged with tingling jolts of electricity. The raging urge to eat . . . to kill . . . to rip into the throbbing, living flesh so close to me is absolutely overpowering, filling me with a spiraling insanity. I feel myself thrashing wildly against the restraints. My head begins to reverberate with a loud, crashing sound that I soon realize is my teeth, gnashing together. Hot, sour saliva floods my mouth and the back of my throat, and then—through it all—I feel something else.

I feel a touch . . . like a pin prick . . .

On the back of my hand.

It sizzles and crackles, but for only an instant; then dark, rolling clouds churning with thick clots of ropy gray and black descend across my vision. All colors fade, and once again I am clutched by the sensation of being frozen into immobility. My muscles go rigid. My bones feel like iron spikes.

I can feel the touch on the back of my hand for less than a second, and then the dull leadenness seeps like poison throughout my body.

"Oh, my God! *Look!*" a voice suddenly cries out. "He . . . he's bleeding!"

I am so lost in my own internal agony that I can't distinguish whose voice it is.

I no longer care.

It sounds so impossibly far away I would cry . . . if I could.

"It's true! The stomach wound is bleeding again!"

"But that's impossible," I hear someone say. It might be the judge or it might be the man who claims to be my lawyer.

"A corpse can't bleed!"

I am past caring as darkening waves descend and engulf me, pulling me under with powerful, irresistible surges. All of my senses are dimming. The last thing I hear before everything resolves into pitch black again is a faint, echoing voice.

"That will be all for now. Thank you, Dr. Murphy. You may return Mr. Sinclair's body to the morgue now."

—for Ed Kramer

Piss Eyes

Transcript of a conversation with Ajut, a member of the Inuit tribe.

Part One:

I am an old man now, but when I was a child, I recall fondly how my mother would tell us children stories at bedtime. These stories were told to entertain us and, at times, to frighten us into good behavior; but no tale she ever told us scared me half as much as something that happened during my eleventh year. This tale was told to me by Ootek, my father's brother, and it was all the more frightening because he insisted that it was true.

Now, I never believed him, of course, at least not until a year later when he took me out onto the ice and showed me the fire-blackened hull of the big wooden sailing ship from the south. Then, in my twelve-year-old wisdom, I allowed as how some of his tale *might* have an element of truth in it . . . but not much. I was young and didn't know much, I admit.

I understand now that I no doubt didn't want to believe what I heard, but I will tell you the tale as it was told to me, more than sixty winters ago, and you can judge for yourself. In fact, we are within a two-day journey of the old ship, so if you would like, I could take you there to see it.

I remember food was scarce that year, as it often is for the People. Kaila the Provider had not supplied our men with nearly enough seals and whales during the annual summer hunt. For long periods of time, the sky remained dark and cloudy even during the summer, when the sun never sets. When winter came, and snow and darkness filled the sky and covered the ground, and the wind howled like a woman in pain outside our igloos, we remained inside our igloos many days at a time. Only a fool would dare to go outside when Paija the Evil One was prowling about, looking for anyone foolish enough to brave the long winter darkness alone.

Ootek, my father's brother, lived alone. His wife, Howmik, had died the spring before when the ice upon which she was walking split open beneath her weight, and the *inua angkuni*, those great ghosts who live below the ice, caught her by the feet and dragged her under to dwell with them. No one can gaze long upon the faces of the *inua angkuni* and keep his thoughts straight afterwards. Howmik was alone at the time, so no one saw any of this happen, but what happened proves that the *inua angkuni* are always looking for someone foolish enough to be out on the ice alone. Howmik's footprints were found on the edge of ice near the open water, and everyone in our village could read the story those tracks told.

Throughout that winter, Ootek kept very much to himself, rarely coming to visit even when we offered to share with him the meager supplies of our food. During the long, dark winter, he made a habit of going out for long walks in the night. Even when the wind howled like Amow the wolf, and the snow drifted like thick smoke across the ice, he would go outside, telling no one where he was going or what his intentions were. My father suggested to my mother that Ootek's wife had returned to Ootek in the form of an *ino*, and that he was spending his time sporting with her in the frigid darkness. Of course, I believed him because I know many truths about the spirit world. Just because I am now a Christian, it does not mean that the spirits and demons of my people have all disappeared.

After supper one night, my sister and I had been put to bed, but I was unable to sleep. I remember that I felt a sharp tingling in the air, like on those days in the summer when lines of fire reach down from the sky and touch the earth, and the booming sounds like that of shifting ice fill the air. There was a different smell in the igloo, too, like the stinging in the air after it rains. I grew fearful and was unable to sleep, but I dared not disturb my mother and father, who I could hear talking in hushed tones near the whale oil fire on the other side of the igloo. My father was sharpening the point of his harpoon. As I lay there, huddled under my caribou blankets, my childish imagination carried me away. And then, beneath the howling of the wind, I began to hear something else—a low, distant moaning sound, coming from outside. Just then, our dogs began to bark loudly.

Of course, my first thought was that the *inua angkuni* were about, moving invisibly from igloo to igloo, looking in on everyone and trying to decide who—if anyone—they would take with them next. Naked and shivering, I huddled beneath my warm caribou blankets, knowing that if the *inua angkuni* looked in on me and I saw them, I might never again be right in my mind.

Suddenly, a scream loud enough to be heard above the roaring wind and barking of the dogs filled the night. I sat up in bed and looked at my father, feeling only a small measure of relief when I saw that his eyes were wide with fear, too. I knew that he had heard the sound as well as I.

"Ootek," he said simply, staring at my mother.

I remember how his wide, dark eyes glistened in the reflected light of our small fire. He laid his harpoon aside and made a move to put on his outside clothes, but my mother held him back by both arms and begged him not to go outside.

I remember the twisted torment I saw on my father's face as he considered what he should do. If in fact his brother was outside and in danger, he of course must try to help him; but if the *inua angkuni* were nearby, to go outside meant that he, too, risked death . . . or worse.

After what seemed like a very long time, my father twisted out of my mother's grasp, pulled on his thick snow pants, coat, boots, and mittens, and went outside. The wind had died down to a whisper, and the dogs stopped their barking the instant he went outside. After that, I could hear nothing else, not even the heavy tread of his boots in the snow. He was gone for what seemed like a very long time to me, and I began to cry softly to myself, thinking that maybe my father had joined his brother on the journey to the land of the dead. But some time later he returned. I will never forget the look I saw on his face when he told my mother what he had found.

"Yes, it was Ootek," he said, shifting his gaze away from my mother as though he were afraid to look her in the eyes. "He has seen Paija, the Evil One."

Well, my friend, it is time for our meal. I will tell you more of this after we have eaten.

Rev. Robert Crocker's journal entry, July 14, 1964:

I've been travelling with Ajut and his family for a little over three months, now, as they journey across the ice toward their summer hunting grounds. There is a stark beauty to the Arctic, but after days of unending daylight, when the nights are marked by nothing more than the sun's grazing swing close to the western horizon, a mind-numbing monotony begins to set in. Here in these vast, endless stretches of ice, it amazes me that Ajut and his hunters seem to know at all times exactly where they are and where they are going. They seem to have an uncanny, some might say almost supernatural ability to navigate by an internal compass; either that, or else they see a remarkable diversity in this landscape which, to my civilized eyes, seems to be nothing but vast stretches of windblown snow and ice, and then more snow and ice.

We travel much of the day, and in the evenings, after talking with Ajut and other members of his tribe, I am busy transcribing the stories he tells me. I am particularly interested in the one he began to relate to me earlier today. When I expressed some skepticism, he repeated his promise to take me out across the ice and show me the remains of the burned wooden ship. As if that would prove his tale. I don't see the connection, but he insists that the ship is no more than a two-day trip from where we are now. He has promised in the morning, that is when the red ball of the sun rebounds off the flat, western horizon, that we will go there, and I will see for myself the proof of his tale.

I wonder, though, if there really is a sailing ship nearby. What could it possibly be?

Could there be a sailing ship, perhaps a whaler from more than a century ago that got ice bound? How could it have not been destroyed in all this time? Ajut is nearly seventy years old, and if, as he says, the ship was old back when he was eleven, it would have to be at least a century old. Why hasn't it been crushed by the shifting ice or buried by snow, or destroyed long ago? It is a mystery to me, but much about these people, the land they live in, and their sense of the spiritual is mysterious. Perhaps I'll know more when—and if—I get to see that ship the day after tomorrow.

*   *   *

Rick Hautala

Transcript of a conversation with Ajut, a member of the Inuit tribe.

Part Two:

In fact, my father's brother, Ootek, had not seen Paija, the Evil One, but he had seen an *ino*, one of the "great ghosts," as our people call them. From that night on, his mind was never right. He didn't become shaman, as often happens when men of our tribe encounter one of the gods or spirits of the ice. Instead, he became only a little bit crazy, like a man of the People who has had too much too drink of the white man's alcohol.

Sometime shortly after that night, Ootek told me about what he had seen that night on the ice. His wanderings had taken him far and wide on his solitary journeys. A great distance to the north of our summer village, he had discovered the place where a ghost lived within the hull of the ship from the south that had been cast up onto the ice. Ootek told me he once caught a glimpse of the *ino* there, lurking in the darkness inside the ruined ship, but he was fearful for his life and left as fast as he could. But the *ino*, being a spirit, could travel much faster across the ice than he could, and when Ootek arrived back at his igloo, which was near to ours, the *ino* was there, waiting for him.

He told me that the ghost stood at least eight feet tall, and had long, flowing black hair and wrinkled, gray skin. He described to me the *ino*'s skin, which he said was shriveled and cracked like that of a corpse that had been buried for a long time in the ice. But the worst thing about him, he said, what had let him know that this was truly a demon, were his eyes.

His eyes!

Huge and bulging, he said they were, and stained with a milky yellow glaze, like the yolk of a rotten egg. I joked with him, and said that his *ino*'s eyes must have looked like the snow where one has relieved himself, but when I asked if his *ino's* name was "Piss Eyes," Ootek didn't laugh. He told me in a stern voice that I should show respect for the spirit world. He then told me that he had screamed because he had seen the demon moving in silence among the igloos of our people, looking for his next victim to claim. In my mind ever since that day, though, I have always thought of Ootek's *ino* as "Piss Eyes." He warned me that if I didn't show more respect to the *inua angkuni*, they would come to claim me during the long, cold winter night. Perhaps, he said, the *ino* was looking for me that night! For a long time I was fearful of that happening, but—well, as you can see, I have lived a long time, now, and I have never in my life encountered "Piss Eyes."

My friend, if we are going to make the journey to the old ship, we will be gone for five or six days. Let us pack our provisions and begin now that we are well rested.

Rev. Robert Crocker's journal entry, July 17, 1964:

After traveling across the ice for two days, now, I am absolutely exhausted; but before I rest, while Ajut builds a small, temporary igloo for the night, I must write down what we have found.

At least some element of Ajut's and Ootek's story is true. There is, in fact, an old sailing ship out here in the middle of nowhere on the ice. I am amazed that Ajut could find it so easily. It was as if he had followed a clearly marked trail directly to it. The ship looks like it had at one time been a grand, three-masted sailing ship. It might possibly have been a whaling ship, but, as Ajut told me, it has been nearly destroyed by fire except for a large portion of the hull, which is heeled over onto the frozen ground. Drifting snow and ice have all but covered the blackened hull, which stands out against the blinding whiteness of the land like a beached whale carcass.

Amazed as I was to see something like this, where the flat, snow-covered ground stretches to the horizon in all directions, I asked Ajut how far we were away from open water. He told me that it is still more than a two-day journey to the open sea, so I have no way of knowing how this ship got here. Perhaps we shall never know.

Exhausted as I was from our traveling, I set out to explore the derelict. Inside the fire-blackened hull, sheltered from the elements like the interior of a small cave, I found evidence that someone had indeed been living within this ruin some time in the past. After staring at the bright glare of sunlight on the snow for so long, it took a while for my eyesight to adjust to the darkness; but as I wandered about inside the ship, I found to my horror what were obviously human remains scattered about. Many of the bones had been stripped clean of flesh and broken lengthwise, apparently to remove the marrow. It was obvious, even to me, that this was not done by any scavenger. My first impression, as horrifying as it might be, was that the survivors of this shipwreck from some long-ago forgotten time had been trapped here and, in a vain attempt to survive, had resorted to the un-Godly practice of cannibalism.

The thought nauseates me even now as I write it.

I hurried out of the ship's hull, back into the white glare of the snow, but I have vowed, tomorrow, after I have rested, that I will go back into the ship and try to discover the identity of those poor souls who were reduced to such a horrifying end, and tonight I will say a prayer for them.

Transcript of a conversation with Ajut, a member of the Inuit tribe.

Part Three:

As I told you yesterday, I have never seen "Piss Eyes" myself, but besides Ootek, who died more than twenty winters ago, there are several members of my tribe and other tribes who have reported seeing him, at least at a distance. Of course, the People believe that there are many spirits who wander out here on the ice, especially during the long winter night. It is only a fool who would want to get close enough to identify any of them.

There is a man named Kakumee in our tribe. He died many winters ago, too, but he told me one time that he had seen and actually spoken to "Piss Eyes." I know this could not be true because if he had in fact seen and spoken to an *inua angkuni*, if he hadn't died right there on the spot, he would have never again been in his right mind. No one can speak to one of them and live. But Kakumee used to tell us how, many years ago, when he had been traveling across the ice to a fishing hole, he had seen the dark figure of a man off in the distance. Because the *inua angkuni* seldom appear in broad daylight, Kakumee had guessed that this must indeed be a man, although he said the being stood at least eight feet tall. The man or spirit saw him, and as he approached, Kakumee saw beneath the being's ice-fringed hood a face that was gray and wrinkled like that of a dead person. He also said that the spirit's eyes—because as soon as he was up close and got a good look at him, he saw that he was no human being or even a white man—were glazed a bright, milky yellow.

As yellow as the eyes of "Piss Eyes"!

By gestures, Kakumee said the creature made it clear to him that he was hungry and would allow Kakumee to live if he shared his meager food with him. When a spirit demands anything of you, it is wise to give it to him. "Piss Eyes" appeared to be very thankful for the food, but then, Kakumee said, again by way of gestures because the language the spirit spoke was like nothing Kakumee had ever heard before, the spirit made him understand that he would kill Kakumee if he didn't provide him with his sled and dogs.

Now, as you can no doubt guess, to be left out on the ice far from camp without any means of transportation is almost certain death, but Kakumee had no choice but to give "Piss Eyes" his sled and dogs. He almost died during the long trek back to the tribe, but he lived to tell his story many times around the lodge fire. Of course, maybe members of the tribe never believed him, and they thought that he had made up this story to hide the fact that he had lost an entire team and sled, nearly the entire measure of a man's wealth out here on the ice.

Rev. Robert Crocker's journal entry, July 18, 1964:

As tired as I was, I slept poorly last night. The wind howled around our makeshift igloo, whistling with a shrill whine that rose and fell in plaintive, hollow notes. I couldn't help but think that it sounded like Ajut's *inua angkuni* wailing in the icy desolation.

In the morning, after a breakfast of dried caribou meat and tea, I dressed warmly and went out to the ship's hull to begin exploring. After walking around the perimeter of the ship several times, making hurried sketches of the ruins from several angles, I took a small oil lamp, lit it, and entered the split side of the hull where the day before I had seen the human remains. This time, I was better prepared for what lay within, and although the thought of the horror that had occurred here some time in the past made my stomach turn again, I moved past the human bones and proceeded deeper into the hollow belly of the ship.

It seemed obvious to me that the sailors, whether they were whalers or explorers, had indeed tried to survive here for some time before succumbing to the hunger and cold. The obvious remains of cannibalism made it clear to me that, as each man died, the survivors partook of the dead man's flesh. Why they never tried to leave the wreck and travel south seemed obvious. They must have known that none of them would ever make it back to civilization. Why then, I wondered, as I looked around the insides of the scorched ship, why would they prolong the inevitable by engaging in such an unholy act as eating their own kind?

But I already knew the answer.

They, like all of God's creatures, had clung desperately to life, no matter how futile or foolish the attempt to save it may seen. Perhaps, I speculated, the last survivor, crazed with loneliness and hunger, had tried to burn the ship to stay warm, or perhaps he had tried to burn it with himself inside. This seemed a likely scenario except for one significant fact: the broken bones inside the charred hull had shown absolutely no evidence of having been burned. It was obvious that whomever had eaten the human flesh and dug out the bone marrow had done so *after* the ship had burned.

No matter how long and hard I pondered this desperate situation, I knew that it was and would remain a mystery for all eternity. In the grand scheme of things, it was as if Ajut and I had never discovered this antique ship and never pondered the fate of the wretched individuals who lived and died here.

I made my way slowly through the interior of the ship toward the stern, guided by the flickering flame of my oil lamp. I passed through a warren of wrecked rooms and storage areas where much of the wood making up the inside of the ship had been stripped, no doubt to be used as firewood by the survivors. Deep inside the bowels of the ship, I noticed some things on the floor that did, in fact, look like fire-blackened bones, but I didn't investigate them too closely.

I lost track of the time as I wandered through the wreck, trying to muster up some images, some indications of the fates of the men who had been here so many years ago, but finally I gave up, knowing that the secrets of what had happened here would remain locked in ice and time forever.

Suddenly, I heard Ajut calling my name from outside. After signaling that I had heard him, I started back toward the opening in the ship's side, moving carefully so I wouldn't fall over or bump into anything.

Perhaps it was the hand of God that directed me to place

my hand on a particular cross beam, but whatever it was, I shouted aloud and jumped backwards when something white suddenly fluttered in front of my face. The frantic motion as I fell backwards almost extinguished my lamp, but after a few seconds, it burned brightly again. At first I thought I had merely knocked off an accumulation of snow, but once the initial rush of fright had subsided, I saw that I had knocked down a folded piece of paper that had obviously been secreted up on top of one of the wide cross beams.

Ajut called out my name again, sounding extremely concerned or excited. As I bent down to pick up the paper, I shouted to him, assuring him that I was unhurt. I took a moment to unfold the paper and noted that there was writing on both sides of it. The script was small and cramped together with no margins or paragraph breaks. It was written in French, but fortunately I had studied that language in college, and even with only a cursory glance, I recognized several words and phrases. I was trembling with the excited speculation that this might be a page from one of the survivors' diaries or perhaps from the ship's log. Hopefully by reading this, I could glean some idea as to who these people had been and what had happened to them out here on the ice.

As I stepped out of the darkened ship into the open, a sudden blast of cold wind took my breath away. My eyes instantly began to water from the stinging brightness of the snow that surrounded me. It took me a moment to notice Ajut, who was standing some distance from the ship and waving excitedly to me as he pointed with one hand toward the sun-hazed horizon. I tried to see what he was indicating, but my vision was still no more than a watery blur. He kept yelling excitedly as he pointed out across the rippling expanse of ice.

"There he is, see? Someone is out there on the ice, Father Robert," he called out as I slowly made my way over to him.

In all the time I had known Ajut, I had never seen him this agitated or excited. He was practically jumping up and down as he pointed toward the northern horizon.

"He is gone now, but he was there! Did you see him? I tell you, I saw him go by."

"Who?" I asked, still dazed by the sudden brightness and unable to think clearly. "What are you talking about?"

"Piss Eyes! I'm sure it was Piss Eyes!" Ajut said, practically shouting. "I saw him pass by. He was driving a sled, being pulled by a team of dogs. Do you mean to tell me you didn't see him?"

"No," I replied, shaking my head as though dazed. "I didn't."

Of course, I immediately suspected that Ajut was having a joke at my expense, but after tucking the folded paper into my parka pocket, we walked out in the direction he had indicated. More than a mile out onto the ice, we saw fresh, clear impressions of dog tracks and the runners of a sled.

Ajut knelt down and inspected the tracks carefully. "That sled was carrying a great weight," he said. "And I could see, even at this distance, that the man in the sled was very tall." He stroked his chin thoughtfully. "If it was Piss Eyes . . ." He lowered his voice as he stood up and, squinting, scanned the distant horizon. "If it truly was him, we would be wise to start back to rejoin the tribe as soon as possible."

We went back to our temporary shelter to settle down for the night, but before I went to sleep, I translated the page I had found.

Journal, date, 18—? . . . Unknown:

I have been dwelling in this realm of ice and snow now for I don't know how long—an eternity of misery and suffering. The nights are long and cold, and the days are no better. Measuring time by the sun makes no sense here.

Long, eternal hours are spent in darkness, and when the sun rises, it weaves and bobs along the horizon like a blazing red disk that casts no warmth. Almost all of the time, my stomach, my entire being growls with hunger and suffering. Following the death of my creator, I wandered I know not how long across the ice, intent on killing myself out here in this vast desert of snow and ice. My wanderings eventually brought me to the northernmost point of the globe, and there I sought death, but no matter how loudly I cried to the heavens to let the spark of life inside me expire, I ever clung to life, knowing that it must be the will of all living things to stay alive. At one point, I had been intent on building a funeral pyre and destroying myself, but this far north where trees do not grow, I could not find anything with which to do that. No wood, and no spark to kindle it. From time to time in my wanderings, I have seen pass by those native people who are suited to living here in the frozen North. On occasion, I have encountered one of them and eaten their food in order to sustain my miserable existence. At times, I have been forced to steal their dogs and sleds. In time, I came to think that I must stay alive, that it must be my creator's will that I could never allow death to release me from the agony and torment that I so richly deserve. I have no idea when it was that I found this abandoned sailing ship which I have been using as a home. These ruins had sustained the bare existence of these nameless men for some time, but they were all dead by the time I found them. After rummaging through their supplies, I found in the captain's quarters this single sheet of paper, a quill, and ink, which I thawed over the fire I made by using the iron and flint I also found in their supplies. After writing this short account of my miserable existence, I lit the ship on fire, intending to thrown myself into the flames to destroy once and for all the abomination that I am, but as flames licked the dark, frozen sky like hungry tongues, I was again unable to destroy myself. I must live, I realized, even if it is to consign myself to this frozen wasteland for all eternity where I will dwell in the solitary agony of what I am. This is my punishment for having destroyed my creator.

Transcript of a conversation with Ajut, a member of the Inuit tribe.

Part Four:

We were lucky to have seen what we have seen and still be alive to tell about it. Even now, as the wind howls around our shelter, I can feel the presence of unseen spirits, moving about on the ice. I know what we have seen must have been "Piss Eyes" because I remember what he looks like as clearly as if there was a picture inside my head from the way my father's brother described him to me.

Yes, we are very lucky to be alive and still in our right minds. Tomorrow morning, we will leave this place to rejoin the tribe. I have already shown you more than I promised. Once we are back with the tribe, I will tell you more stories.

Rev. Robert Crocker's journal entry, July 22, 1964:

I doubt that mere words will in any way convey the true depth of horror, of pure terror which Ajut and I experienced following our evening meal after I had explored the burned ship's hull and translated the paper which I found there. Totally exhausted, we settled down to sleep. The igloo was illuminated by the single, teardrop-shaped flame of a whale oil lamp. Sleep came fast, as it always does to Ajut, who dropped into a heavy slumber almost the instant he lay his head down. I, on the other hand, lay there shivering as I listened to the steady hiss of wind and snow blowing outside. Usually, I find only beauty, not terror, in this stark, desolate environment; but on this night I was unaccountably filled with agitation and nervous speculation.

Could that truly have been "Piss Eyes" that Ajut had seen out on the ice. I had seen nothing except the evidence of sled runner tracks in the snow, but I knew my companion well enough to know that he would not make light of the situation. True, at times he and other members of his tribe have shown a remarkable sense of humor, but Ajut's entire demeanor seemed not to be that of someone who was attempting to perpetrate a practical joke. He was obviously nervous and on his guard. Before settling down to sleep, he told me that we might have made a mistake, making our shelter so close to what had been—and obviously still was—the dwelling place of a spirit. Perhaps our presence will anger "Piss Eyes." I showed Ajut the piece of paper I had found inside the ship, and I explained to him how it indicated that white men from the south, people like me, had been living here, but he would hear nothing of it. He insisted that we should leave this area immediately upon waking so as not to anger the spirits. I can tell by Ajut's reaction to all of this that my mission here to bring him and his people to Christianity will take a great deal of time, perhaps longer than my lifetime.

Sometime after I had drifted off into a thin and disturbed sleep, I awoke to hear our dogs barking wildly. The instant I opened my eyes, I saw that Ajut, with rifle in hand, was already up and crouching in front of the igloo opening, looking outside in an attempt to see what was disturbing the dogs. My first thought was that it might be a polar bear, wandering nearby. When I asked Ajut what was the matter, he silenced me with a quick hand motion.

We sat for long minutes, waiting for the dogs to stop barking, but they were yelping and leaping about, frantically pulling at their leashes as though they either wanted to attack whatever was in the vicinity . . . or run away from it.

Gripping his rifle tightly, Ajut was preparing to go outside when the side of the igloo behind me suddenly exploded inward. After that, everything happened so fast, it is still nothing but a blur to me. Through the shower of ice and snow, I remember seeing a huge, dark figure lunge at me. In a shattering instant, I was startled by the sudden report of Ajut's rifle, sounding close to my ear. The sudden brightness inside the igloo stung my eyes, and I had no idea whether or not Ajut's bullet hit its target. The whole world spun crazily around me. As I fell backwards, I saw Ajut bolt his rifle and try to fire again, but no sound followed. I guessed the chamber had jammed.

My mind went blank with panic.

One of the few clear thoughts I had was that it must be a polar bear, crazed with hunger, that was attacking us. I saw thick, long arms reaching out for me, but in a single, shattering instant, I realized that they were not paws, but large, human hands. A powerful grip took me by the shoulders, picked me up, and shook me roughly as a voice roared in my ears.

At the time, I thought Ajut was shouting to me, but then I realized that the sounds, unintelligible as they were, were coming from the creature. Wide-eyed with terror, I looked up to see a terrifying countenance glaring down at me. My first, fleeting impression was that it was the twisted, ugly face of a dead man. I was repulsed by the creature's hideous features, its flared nostrils, its snarling mouth; but what drew and held my attention was the creature's eyes. They stared at me with a violent gleam of bright, burning yellow, like a hideous sulfur fire.

I sensed more than saw Ajut as he charged toward the creature. Still clamped in the monster's violent embrace, I saw Ajut swing the butt of the rifle over his head, but as it came down in a whistling arc, the creature casually swept the blow aside. The impact sent Ajut staggering to one side where he hit his head hard against the side of the igloo and fell down.

"Ou est le papier?"

The words exploded in my ears, and I thought for a dizzying instant again that it was Ajut who had spoken, but he was lying facedown on the hard-packed snow floor, and I could see a bright red splash of blood on the snow. I looked into the creature's face again and was nauseated by the sour, rotten stench of its breath. All strength drained from my body when I saw the snarling anger in the creature's yellow eyes.

"Ou est le papier?" the beast bellowed.

It took several moments for my terror-stricken mind to register that this . . . this creature was actually speaking French. Stunned into silence, all I could do was nod my head to signal that I understood he wanted to know where the paper was. I had absolutely no doubt what paper he meant, and I was simply hoping that he wouldn't kill me before I could give it to him. I couldn't recall the French words for, *It's in my pocket,* so I shouted in a hoarse voice, *"Oui! Oui! Le papier!"*

Grunting softly, the creature eased its grip on me and lowered me to the ground. My first impulse was to go to Ajut and see if he was still alive, but the instant I started to turn away, the creature grabbed me and dug its fingertips painfully into my shoulder hard enough to make me cry out.

"Vite!" the creature roared. *"Le papier! Vitement!"*

Trembling with fear, I reached into my parka pocket and extracted the folded piece of paper. My legs almost gave out beneath me, and I almost lost consciousness as I handed the paper to the creature, who grunted as he snatched it out of my hand.

"Merci," the creature said; and then, without another word, it shouldered through the gaping hole it had made in the side of our igloo and disappeared.

I stood there for a moment, absolutely stunned, watching numbly as the creature dashed across the ice at a speed that was much greater than any normal human being could run. Within seconds, it seemed, it was nothing more than a black speck on the sun-glazed horizon. A low groan from Ajut drew my attention, and I turned to aid my fallen companion.

Rev. Robert Crocker's journal entry, July 26, 1964:

It's been four days since the monster attacked us. Fortunately, Ajut's injuries were minor, and he was able to guide us back to the tribe. Aside from a sharp headache and a purple bruise the size of a baseball on his forehead, he seems fine.

Last night, I went to him and asked if he would tell me more tales of his people and their beliefs, but he flatly refused. When I pressed him, he finally spoke to me in a low, even-toned voice. Not once did he take his gaze away from the small, flickering flame of the whale oil lamp.

Transcript of a conversation with Ajut, a member of the Inuit tribe.

Final Entry:

You say, Father Robert, that you came here to teach us your religion, to bring us the truth of Christianity. During our time at the old sailing ship from the south, I have seen you embraced by an *inua angkuni*. You looked the spirit straight in the face—you spoke to it in a language that I have never heard before, and you did not lose your mind when you looked into the spirit's yellow eyes. You not only lived through this experience, but as far as I can tell, you are still in your right mind. This makes me think one of two things: either your religion is very strong and it protected you from the spirit, or else you never were in your right mind in the first place. A third thought occurs to me, that you perhaps are also an *inua angkuni*.

I have much to think about.

The demon may not have harmed you, but he left some

of his evil inside my head when he touched me. I can feel his evil spirit, shifting about inside this painful swelling on top of my head.

Please leave me for now. I have much to think about.

Rev. Robert Crocker's journal entry, August 3, 1964:

Apparently Ajut's injuries were worse than they appeared, or maybe he was simply too old to survive them and it was simply his time to go. The Lord alone knows, and He moves in ways that we mere mortals cannot always understand. Regardless, Ajut died shortly after I spoke with him. I can't help but feel responsible for the death of this man. I hadn't known him for very long, but in the short time we spent together, I recognized a strong and loyal individual, and I would like to consider him my friend. I grieve his loss as does his entire tribe.

But many of the things he said to me have made me question exactly how strong I believe my faith is . . . and it makes me wonder.

Ever since I began my conversations with Ajut, and after seeing what I have seen, the events that occurred out at the ruined sailing ship have become confused in my mind. They are making me begin to question the very foundations of my faith. In spite of the confusion that day, I think I know *exactly* what I saw. It was an extremely tall, ugly, gray-skinned man with yellow eyes who spoke and, apparently, wrote in flawless French.

But how can that possibly make sense?

How can anyone or, if he truly is not human, any*thing* exist alone out in this frozen wilderness?

How in God's name does it survive?

How does it stay warm?

What does it eat?

Since the events of that day, especially following Ajut's death, I have begun to see that life here in the North— even life in the spiritual world—is very different from life in our so-called "civilized" world. Ever since then, my sleep has been plagued by terrifying dreams that awaken me several times during the night. I sit in the frozen darkness, sweating and panting heavily as a wrinkled and scarred face with glowing yellow eyes—"Piss Eyes"—drifts in the darkness in front of my vision. Sometimes I watch as the features on this horribly ugly face gradually melt into the smiling face of my dead friend Ajut.

After considering things for several days, I believe I finally know exactly what I saw out there on the ice. I did, indeed, see and was touched by an *inua angkuni*, one of the evil spirits the Eskimos believe inhabit this icy realm. And I have decided that, with or without the help of anyone from Ajut's tribe, I must go back out onto the ice and search for this creature, whatever he may be, whether man or spirit or demon. I will search for it until I find it.

—for M. S. and Steve Bissette

Served Cold

"Revenge is a dish best served cold," isn't that what they say?

I can hear the tremor in my voice as I say this.

I'm leaning forward with both fists on the kitchen table as I stare straight ahead at the man sitting in the chair across from me.

His name is Roy Curry.

Almost thirty years ago, we served together in Vietnam. We saw plenty of action in Binh Dinh province. A lot of friends died there.

And a few people who should have died there didn't.

But that was years ago.

Maybe a couple of lifetimes ago.

Today, I should be happy. I'm having a dinner party.

A dinner party for two.

But right now, Roy doesn't look so happy. He looks like he doesn't want to be here. In fact, I've had to strap his arms and legs to the chair to keep him here. I sure as hell don't want him moving while my back is turned. It's hard enough, slaving over a hot stove in such stifling August heat.

I don't need any more trouble, that's for sure.

I'm cooking a dish I've always loved. I call it Chinese gingered tuna, although I suspect there's some other, fancier name for it. It's my absolute favorite meal, but I haven't had it in years.

Not since Ma died.

Given the choice, though, I think Roy would just as soon not be here today.

I'm glad he doesn't have a choice.

Too bad for him.

You see, I owe him one.

A big one!

Our time—at least my time—in Vietnam was pure hell.

I'd been drafted in 1965, right after graduating from high school. The Army sucked, especially for a country boy from Hilton, a little doo-hickey town in western Maine.

The whole fuckin' war sucked.

I was surprised and happy as hell when my tour of duty was up, and I got out of that fuckin' hellhole with only one wound.

One physical wound, anyway.

A small piece of metal, a fragment from a grenade, had shattered my left kneecap and torn through my leg. The scar that runs up the inside of my knee, halfway to my balls, looks like a narrow, twisting mountain range.

Ever since I got discharged, for almost thirty years, now, I've been walking with a limp. In the winter, I have to use a cane because the knee joint stiffens up so bad in the cold.

And it's all Roy's fault!

Like I said, I owe him a big one!

"Jesus Christ, Roy! Stop staring at me like that, will you? I swear to Christ, I'm gonna. . . ."

I know my voice doesn't sound as strong as it should, but—Shit! I can't stand the way he just sits there, staring at me.

And that fucking smirk of his!

"Yeah, just keep smilin', asshole! You just keep it up!"

Roy doesn't say a word.

But he doesn't stop glaring at me, either. It's like there's a secret fire of hatred, still burning deep inside his eyes.

But he doesn't scare me.

Not anymore.

I think I've finally gotten over all that. Probably because of what I decided to do.

I have to be careful that I don't get too mad and start yelling. It might get my neighbors upset. The walls in this fucking building are paper thin. I wouldn't want anyone calling the cops or anything.

I might have to stop my dinner party if they did.

I try to calm myself down by controlling my breathing as I turn my back to Roy—Shit, he ain't going *nowhere!*— and continue to prepare the meal. I work for a while without turning around to look at him, but I talk to him over my shoulder, describing every step of the recipe.

"Besides the ginger, which *has* to be fresh, the next most important ingredient is the pineapple. It has to be sweet, but not too ripe. Canned is okay, but fresh gives the dish its distinctive taste. You can also use canned tuna. Fresh is better, too, of course, but it doesn't really matter."

As I'm chopping the fresh pineapple slices into tiny cubes and stirring them into the sauce that's simmering with the vegetables in the wok, the knife catches the tip of my index finger.

It only stings for a moment.

I watch as the cut beads up with a little scarlet drop of blood. Squeezing the tip of my finger, I shake the blood into the mixture and stir it in.

Why not?

Blood for blood.

"Isn't than another famous old expression, Roy? Blood for blood?" I ask.

Roy doesn't answer. I can tell by his expression that he doesn't know or care.

As I work, though, I start to feel increasingly uncomfortable.

I know what Roy's doing behind my back.

There's no way he can get away from me, but I can feel him, staring at me.

And I can feel the nearly thirty years of hatred he's focusing on me.

As well he should.

The aroma of cooking food fills my apartment like a dense summer fog. The snap of ginger burns my nasal passages. The sizzle of everything in the wok sounds like a long string of firecrackers going off.

Or something else.

The sound sort of reminds me of distant gunfire.

Nighttime firefights.

The flashbacks haven't been very bad for the last ten years or more, but I think seeing Roy after all this time is bringing it all back. Images and memories seem sharper than they've been in a long time!

I shake my head and focus on my cooking.

I've always hated cooking, mostly because I've never seen the point of taking so much time and making a big mess for just one person.

I live alone. Never got married or anything.

But when it's a dinner party, even for just two people, it's probably worth the extra effort.

It certainly is worth it for Roy.

Like I said, I owe him a big one.

"It's about ready," I say.

I lean close to the wok and inhale deeply.

Then, for the first time in almost fifteen minutes, I turn around and look at Roy.

He's right where he was, sitting there in the chair, ramrod straight. Eyes straight ahead.

Fucking officer! Always has to look so goddamned good!

Bedbugs

Using two cooking mitts, I pick up the steaming wok by the handles and carry it over to the counter. I fetch two plates from the cupboard, put a pile of dried Chinese noodles onto each plate, and then scoop about half the mixture onto each plate.

The smell is intoxicating. I haven't had this dish in years, not since Ma died, back in '79.

I go over to the table and slide one plate in front of Roy, and put one where I'll be sitting. Then I get two beers from the refrigerator.

Sam Adams I.P.A.

I've spared no expense for this dinner party.

I open both bottles of beer and place one at each setting. Then I put a fork on top of a napkin beside each plate. Before I sit down, I open another cupboard door and take down a small bottle I have hidden way in back. The bottle is filled with a fine white powder.

"This is the finishing touch," I say.

I can tell that Roy isn't impressed by my smile.

After unscrewing the cap, I sprinkle a generous amount of the white powder onto one of the plates. It looks like snow on the mountains. Then I sit down, take a long slug of beer, and pick up my fork.

"Should we wait . . . until it's cold?" I ask.

My voice is shaking terribly now, but this is the moment I've been waiting for.

For nearly thirty years.

Although he may not know it, it's the moment Roy's been waiting for, too. I'll bet for him it must have felt like an eternity.

Using my fork, I mix the white powder into the gingered tuna until it dissolves. The additional ingredient doesn't change the smell. The ginger's too strong. But as I scoop up a forkful and hold it, steaming, under my nose, I know it will change the taste, ever so slightly.

No matter.

It's just not gonna be the way Ma used to make it, no matter what.

"I've owed you for a long time, buddy," I say, nodding at Roy and holding my forkful of food out like I'm toasting him. "A very long time."

The gingered tuna is still steaming as I open my mouth and slide it onto my tongue.

I was right.

There's a sharp, almost bitter taste that cuts like a razor through the delicious sweet-and-sour flavor of the gingered tuna. I crunch a sliver of water chestnut between my teeth, and wash everything down with another long guzzle of beer.

"Come on, Roy!" I say, still smiling. "Why are you just sitting there? You should try this. I'll bet it's the best damned meal you've had in . . . probably in thirty years."

I almost laugh out loud, but Roy doesn't move, doesn't even bat an eye as I scoop up another forkful of the food. I can see a large, whitish lump of the rat poison I've mixed into it, but I open my mouth and eat it anyway, swallowing the food quickly in spite of its heat.

Another swallow of beer washes it all down.

By now I can feel a prickly sheen of sweat breaking out on my forehead, but I ignore it as I continue to eat.

Roy still sits there, doing and saying nothing.

I notice for the first time that his mouth is hanging open. He looks like he's hungry and wants to eat, but then— Stupid me!—I realize why he isn't eating.

His hands are still tied to the arms of the chair; and even if they weren't, even if he could load up his fork and get the gingered tuna up to his mouth, I'll bet he wouldn't be able to swallow because of the belt I have looped around his throat and tied to the back of the chair to keep his head up.

I stare straight into his eyes and try to ignore the sudden, sharp twisting of pain I feel deep in my gut. Without looking, I fork more food into my mouth and swallow it without even chewing. A little bit dribbles onto my chin, but I wipe it away with the back of my hand.

"You know how sorry I am," I say in a low whisper, "for everything that happened."

Roy doesn't even blink. His sunken, staring eyes seem to glow with hatred.

Hatred for me!

"I know I should have warned you when I found out a couple of the guys in the company were plannin' to frag you."

By now my voice sounds thick and draggy to my ears, and I have trouble focusing on the crazy swirl of thoughts inside my head.

I have no idea what I'm thinking and what I'm saying out loud.

The heavy humidity and the sharp smell of cooked food fill the room. For all I know, it could be thirty years ago, and Roy and I are sitting in our hooch in the sweltering heat of Vietnam.

"That night, though," I say, "when we were sitting there, stoned on our asses, and I saw that live grenade roll in through the door . . . I probably shouldn't have done what I did, huh?"

I stop speaking only to take another bite of the gingered tuna and swallow.

Roy's blank eyes never shift away from me. I can feel them, peeling back the layers of my soul, staring back at what happened that night, nearly thirty years ago.

"But you see, Roy, I *knew* that grenade was meant for you, not me. I'd been with some of the guys when they were talking about doing it. I know, as your friend, I should have warned you about it, but I still had almost nine months to serve in that fucking country. Those guys were gonna be covering my ass, just like I was gonna be covering their asses. I couldn't betray them.

"I couldn't do anything to stop them!

"You have to believe me, Roy!

"Jesus, stop looking at me like that!"

Tears are filling my eyes, making it almost impossible for me to see, but I take another forkful of food and, leaning forward across the table, slide it into Roy's mouth. I push it far back on his tongue, but almost immediately, it slides back out and drops into his lap.

Roy doesn't react.

How could he?

"But all I could think about that night, was saving my own ass," I say. "So when I saw that grenade, all I wanted to do was get out of that fucking hooch before it went off. I know I shouldn't have pushed you out of my way, and I sure as hell didn't mean for you to fall down right next to it; but I paid for it, anyway. When that fucker went off, a nice hot, jagged little piece caught me in the leg. I felt bad that it blew you apart, but—shit! Like I said. I knew that grenade was meant for you, not me!"

The sharp pain in my gut is getting stronger. There's a stinging, metallic taste in my mouth that even the beer can't wash away.

I see flashes of trailing white lights across my vision, like shooting stars.

With a sudden, violent squeeze, my stomach convulses and tries to get rid of the poison I've eaten, but I clamp my jaws tightly shut. When I vomit into my mouth, I swallow it back down. Hot chunks of vomit burn in my nasal passages.

"I only moved to this godforsaken town in Georgia so I could be near you, near to where you were buried."

The pain in my stomach is almost intolerable now. It sure as hell feels much worse than when that grenade fragment ripped into my leg.

I try to stand but lurch forward and bump into the kitchen table, hard. The edge of the table hits Roy's chair arm, and I watch in silent horror as his body tilts to one side. His head catches on the belt looped through the back of the chair, and I hear a loud crack that might be his spine, or maybe his death-dried tendons snapping.

"I waited a long time until I had the courage to go out there to the cemetery and dig you up, Roy," I say in what sounds like my last, gasping breath. "And believe me, it wasn't easy, digging up your coffin or getting you up here into the apartment building.

"It was a bitch, even at night.

"I'm sorry you had to spend all those days out there in the trunk of my car. Especially in a heat wave like this. But you ought to be happy now. You finally did it, Roy."

Vibrating walls of darkness are squeezing in on me with almost intolerable pressure from all sides. The pain spreads through my body like a raging fire. My vision swirls with trailing sparks and shadowy, shifting smears that move in and out of focus.

"It's been almost thirty years since you died," I say, "but you did it . . . you finally . . . got . . . your . . . revenge.

"Come on, Roy. . . . Hurry up and eat . . . before it . . . gets . . . too . . . cold."

Author's Note

Just a quick word or two. . . .

I considered writing a brief introduction to each story, to explain where I got the initial idea, what—if any—autobiographical elements are involved, or why I like or, in some cases, don't like the accompanying story. I decided against doing this, figuring that ultimately each story (just like all of us in our lives) must stand or fall on its own merits.

That being said, I should point out that each story has been revised—to a greater or lesser degree—from the way it originally appeared in print. One time on a panel at NECON, we were discussing revisions and when—if ever—a short story is truly finished. F. Paul Wilson made the comment that revision is like sex . . . "You know when you're done." To which Chet Williamson added: "Or you can't do it anymore."

Well, these stories are done. This is their final form. Never again will I go back to any of them and tinker.

Which version is the author's "preferred text"?

385

Rick Hautala

If you actually take the time and bother to compare them, I'd have to say whichever one you like better.

Before I go, though, I would like to thank Rich Chizmar for publishing this collection. You are a true friend, Rich. I also want to thank my *compadres*, Matt Costello, and Jim Connolly for their contributions to this collection and for their abiding friendship over the years. And I especially want to thank my good friend Glenn Chadbourne for doing an *incredible* job with the illustrations in the front of this book. I couldn't be happier with our collaboration.

Thank you, Rich, Matt, Jim, and Glenn.

And so for now . . . for all of you. . . . "Good night. Sleep tight. Don't let the . . ."

Afterword

Matthew J. Costello

I know . . . this is the place where I should give some heart-felt closing words about Rick Hautala, the writer of all the stories in this book. And I will. In a few moments.

But first, some other *words* of some relevance.

When I decided to stop reading comic books and start reading books I . . .

No, I better stop right there. That's a lie. No decision was involved. It was a *discovery*. Paul on the way to wherever and a thunderbolt knocks him off his DC Comics book horse.

The above, as a side note, is a fragment. Not a complete thought, as the nuns used to opine. As was the sentence just before the one you're currently reading. Interesting. Become a writer and you can violate rules of grammar.

And you can even start a sentence with "and."

Not that I would ever do that.

But I digress. My apologies. The point I was on my way

to making was this: when I jumped from *Challengers of the Unknown* to *Seven Days in May* not only did I discover the sweet wonder of the world of books, I discovered that there were people behind those books.

More importantly, I discovered that each imagined world, the events, the people, all those words came from someone who walked out to the front yard to get his paper, or was raising kids, or writing lots of other things because we all know how hard it is to be just a novelist. So hard now, to be sure—but yes, even back then.

For example, I love the now-lost adult fiction of John Christopher, books that, for reasons I should really save for a really big digressive essay, were seminal to a lot of what happened in 70s genre.

But those books are all gone. Amazing works. My copies of books like *The White Voyage* and *Not a Blade of Grass* were all destroyed in the Floyd flood and—what the hell is a hurricane doing coming to suburban NYC anyway and washing away my entire library? Jeeez!

John Christopher eventually made a name for himself with his tripod series of YA books, classic SF and fantasy that was as good as it gets in the YA world. Harry Potter should hide himself in shame.

And (see, I did it again!) when I went to find John Christopher, to track him down, to enlist him as a guest for the Horror Writers Association conference, I discovered that his name was really Sam Youd, and that he lived on the island of Jersey, that he still was writing. . . .

Key words there, my friends . . .

Still was writing . . .

Because you see that is what it's all about. It's not about hitting those best-seller charts, though, god, we'd all love to be there. (At least those of us who write. I guess readers would feel a bit confused if somehow they landed on the *New York Times* list.) We want the big movie, the success, the people on the beach all oiled up and writhing as we scare and suspense them while they turn nut brown.

We want that.

But what this writing life is really about is . . . doing it.

Writing books. Creating characters, trying different things, changing, letting that river of words flow and—most importantly—getting it out to the real world to read.

It's what people like old Sam in Jersey did. Forgotten. But not by me.

And it's what Rick Hautala has done for nearly two decades. I've seen Rick when he was tasting some of that good stuff I talked about before—you know, money, success, and I've seen him when he's been on a break from that particular feast. . . .

The one constant through it all has been his work. He's always looking for the next book, his imagination is always filled with characters that won't go away. It's a writer's legacy, a body of work accumulates, a library of books that represent what real writers do. Write, probe, grow, challenge, wonder . . .

And this collection?

Very special indeed. I've always told Rick that I felt he brought special freedom to his short fiction . . . as though the short stories didn't have to fit into a certain niche of Rick Hautala books, and he could just wail. Some of these you've read in magazines, some have never appeared before—but any long-time reader of Rick's who comes to this book will emerge with a different view of him as a writer.

It's kind of like that moment in *The Godfather* when Lee Strasberg is taking Michael to task for whining about the organized crime life. "It's the business we chose," Strasberg almost spits out at his former student Pacino.

Rick knows that I'm sure. Though he might say the choice was the other way around. Some were born to dance, some to write . . . (and some to hype, but don't even get me started on that one, honey).

Rick Hautala

So I'm really glad this *Bedbugs* volume appeared, collecting so many great stories written over so many years. It's Rick playing at his craft, and art—and for an artist, play is the real work. And boy does Rick love to play.